THE LEAG
AGAINST CHRISTMAS

M… …rtin is the author of four previous comic
novels … … Self-Made Man, The Replay, The Plastic
T… …ter and The Cove Shivering Club, published
by Four …state. He lives in Limerick.

3 0012 00071549 9

D1635355

WITHDRAWN

THE LEAGUE AGAINST CHRISTMAS

MICHAEL CURTIN

FOURTH ESTATE • *London*

First published in Great Britain in 1989 by
André Deutsch Ltd

This edition published in 1997 by
Fourth Estate Limited
6 Salem Road
London W2 4BU

1 3 5 7 9 10 8 6 4 2

A catalogue record for this book is available from
the British Library.

ISBN 1–85702–740–X

Typeset in Sabon by
Avon Dataset Ltd, Bidford on Avon B50 4JH

Printed and bound in Great Britain by
Clays Ltd, St Ives plc, Bungay, Suffolk

For John Frawley

PART ONE

BATEMAN

THOUGH BATEMAN WAS prepared from experience to suffer the rigmarole and the chastisement necessary to land another job, he still needed to suck courage from a Player's Medium before he could enter the Margaret Mead Bureau. He was aware that it was no longer a beggar's market: they did not offer you tea in the agencies any more. But he had confidence in Margaret Mead. Her face was her logo and it shone from every magazine, newspaper and underground station in London. She listened like the good confessor he had expected while he rattled off his history: six months in a bar, a year as a wages clerk, eight months a data processor, two years a betting office settler, three years a factory hand, two summers in the building trade, a bingo-hall attendant, bus conductor . . .

'We certainly like to move around, Mr Bateman.'

There was an answer to that but it did not apply during a recession. 'Not yet ready to settle down' was not acceptable from the over-forties in Tory England. Bateman tried to smile. Margaret Mead looked like a woman in her sixties who only looked like a woman in her fifties. Her maternal pearls rose and fell in accompaniment with her bosom as she prosecuted on:

'Do you have anything particular in mind?'

'Do you have anything unusual?' Bateman bluffed. Margaret Mead had heard that before. It meant: Have you anything at all? She managed to ask a question simply by raising her chin and forced Bateman to continue: 'Scene shifter in a theatre, undertaker's assistant – just so I can live on the wages.' Bateman had been reciting it for twenty-four years – lucky, in that he had never been offered a position as scene shifter or undertaker's assistant. And Margaret Mead had been listening for more than forty years. She was experienced and kind. Twenty years earlier – possibly. In the boom sixties when they flitted all over London *tasting* jobs. But not now. She extracted a card from a file and held it up for Bateman to read:

Man Friday, non-fuddy duddy,
to brew cuppa and cheer, run Derby
sweep and be a dear and get two
buttered scones round the corner, ta.
Suit retired, active person. LV's.

Bateman nodded. He stood up and said: 'Thank you.' Margaret Mead continued to hold the card between her thumb and forefinger as he walked out of her agency. She had always loved her clients. It was her policy. It shone from her logo. But there was so little one could do now.

Bateman missed a smoking carriage at Oxford Circus but when he changed at Notting Hill Gate from the Central to the Circle Line he was able to take out his fags. They were not as much comfort to him as he anticipated: nowadays the smoking carriages were invaded by nonsmokers. One's rights were all but gone. And one's prospects. He was only forty-four, too young to run the

Derby sweep. At least tomorrow night was solo school night. Foster was due back even though Diana Hayhurst was still away. She was an atrocious player but he missed her. It was not the same with just himself, Foster, Ellis and Gosling. He got out at Gloucester Road and walked to his bedsitter in Evelyn Gardens. He had it for twenty-five pounds a week now which was cheap, unlike when he first rented it for two pounds two and six when it was dear. He had almost seven thousand pounds saved in a deposit account over twenty years. It was a lot of saving but not a lot of money. He would cry soon. It was not possible for most people in the world to win. But it was not his diminishing prospects or middle age that caused him to sit so often in his bedsitter over a pool of ash crying like a child. The ache was more uncommon and more painful.

He was distracted from his despair when he opened the hall door and saw a telegram in his pigeonhole. He brought it upstairs to his room on the top floor and tried to invest this landmark in a dull life with good news. But the message was predictable:

YOUR FATHER ILL.

F. TIMMONS.

Bateman crumpled the telegram and rammed it between his teeth.

FOSTER

'I WONDER WHERE he could have got to then,' Gosling speculated, causing Foster to flinch. Gosling was not his type. The school would be better off without Gosling. Gosling was no more than an aged glorified potman. All right, you would travel far to encounter a species as odd as Bateman but at least the Irishman had a smattering of erudition and could keep up with one. And Ellis, who insisted now in dealing four imaginary hands, had been the London Area Manager of NatWest Finance though one would not think it to look at him now in cords and braces, workman's shirt and that cigarette on his ear.

'I'd have had a spread,' Ellis pointed out. 'Ernie you had a certain bundle but I'd have outcalled you.'

'Let me see.' Gosling examined the cards.

'Don't you think this is a bit idle, Ellis?' Foster spoke primly.

'What's that, Foster?'

That was a habit of Ellis's, taking everything in his stride now that he imagined he had cut loose from the cares of the world, when in truth he was as daft as Bateman. During an evening when they had taken a break from the cards to get to know each other, Ellis had told them his life story. And Bateman had followed on. Foster had even contributed himself. But he was damned if he had given them more than he felt they should know. So, they all knew each other now. Or thought they did: they didn't know *him*. They knew he was Kenneth Foster of Foster and Son Company Limited, Chartered Accountants and Public Auditors of Nottingham and London. A branch office in London, that was the way to treat the capital. He had worked in London in the sixties but he woke up and went back to Nottingham to establish a practice in civilised country. Now, in the King's Arms in Shepherd's Bush where they lacked the quorum for the solo school because Diana Hayhurst was on holiday and Bateman had simply not turned up, Foster sat impatiently in his grey suit and silver tie and polished dark brown shoes. He had not let himself go, like Ellis. His hair matched his tie, short and combed back neat as a ledger entry. The gleam of his spectacles distracted attention from his face yet he managed to convey a type encrusted with the limited confidence of one who has done his lawn-mowing and liked to mix in the company of those who had done theirs. London had mocked him in the sixties. He was then at the stage when he had worked, studied, married, given birth to a son and was about to set himself up while all around him were dressed like second-hand hussars or in beads and curtains, drugged up to the eyeballs and spending all their time making what they called free love. He had never been out of a suit except to play golf.

It was intolerable to Foster to think that London should have his son Robin in its clutches. But there could be no other explanation for Robin's decision to live with a woman for the rest of his life without any intention of marrying her. Gladys and he had assumed that Robin had fallen for a tart. But not a bit of it. Deborah was Personal

7

Assistant to the Managing Director of a large travel agency that was audited by Foster & Son. She was as respectable as Robin himself. For a time Foster senior was pleased that they did not rush things but after eighteen months he heard himself saying: 'You'll be thinking of settling down one of these days.' He had put it as lightly as that. And the response – in his own study when they came on a visit to Nottingham – was:

'Dad.'

'Yes, Robin?'

'Would you try not to keep on about our getting married in front of Deborah? I think it makes her uneasy.'

'I don't understand.'

'We *are* settled down. We've been together eighteen months. But we're not getting married. That just isn't on any more.'

From Robin, not one of your drug addicts or media persons. He had been careful not to exacerbate the situation by having recourse to anger or emotion – that was not his style. He had spoken to Gladys. And what had Gladys said? 'Kenneth, you do go on.'

Gladys did not know about the solo school in the King's Arms. She would mock him if she did. She mocked him whether she realised it or not. Her tolerance of Robin's carry-on mocked him. And she had to go and mention their private business in front of Nick and the others when they were out together on Saturday night. Nick had his hand on her thigh when he delivered his judgement: 'Youth must have its fling, Gladys, as the bloke said when he threw the cat out the window.' She had shrieked at that.

Twenty past nine. Bateman would not come now. They would not have a game. He bought a second glass of beer. Single fellows like Bateman, drinkers, they had their lives reduced to a stamp, they could be depended upon to fulfil fixtures. Maybe Bateman had put his head in the oven after all. The Irish were not a sound people.

If Saturdays at home only ended the way they began. He would have the deep-fat fryer half-full with oil – he never filled it more than half-full in case the fat frothed up over the sides. He liked to watch Gladys in the garden while he prepared their Saturday evening meal. He would drop a cube of bread into it – he was above using a fat thermometer – and when the cube turned brown in fifty or sixty seconds the oil was ready to use. Gladys wore a pair of his old trousers in the garden and that practical touch and her rubber gloves prompted him to bite his lip. He liked to open the window and admonish outdoors if he thought she was stooping too long without straightening: 'Be careful, Gladys, mind your back.' He would have one pound of potatoes already peeled and cut into chips, dried and in the basket. He would lower the basket gradually into the oil. He always shook the basket occasionally to prevent the chips sticking together. They were done when they were cooked to the centre but still pale in colour. He would drain the chips and leave them on one side. Gladys always straightened up slowly, so slowly that he always, as he drained the chips and put them to one side, worried: 'All right, Gladys?' Having removed the fins and large bones he coated the whiting fillets in seasoned flour and dipped each fillet into a beaten egg, draining off any excess egg and then dusted with toasted breadcrumbs. He loved when Gladys came in for her long warm bath. He liked to see the steam at the top of the landing and his trousers that she had been in folded across the bannisters. He had suggested it once but she had only laughed: 'We wouldn't fit, Kenneth.' She probably thought he was joking. He did not believe in being slapdash: the oil was reheated and tested and then the fillets were placed in the basket one or two at a time. He would twist the tail with a fork to curl it while cooking. He did not want to do anything with her in the bath, just be with her in the bath, maybe lean towards her and squeeze the sponge on to her breasts and she might have got her own back by needling his penis with her toe, gently, the way a grandmother might fondle a baby's nose with her finger. He would let the fillets cook for five to eight minutes, she would usually be finished with her bath by then. He was always very curious about her method of cleaning herself in the bath, about how thoroughly was it necessary to penetrate between her legs and did she penetrate as far as she should? And when the moment came to lay back and luxuriate did she relax with one leg up on the edge of the bath or did she plop her breasts together. Did she sigh? He removed the basket from the deep-fryer and carefully took out the fillets with a fish slice. He put them on kitchen paper to drain off any extra fat. He reheated and tested the oil again and again placed the chips in the basket and cooked them in the oil until they were golden-brown. During that three minutes she would dry herself. How vigorously did she rub her body between and how far in her legs? How methodically into the rear crevasse, staining the towel? Her panties having the benefit? There were so many things like that that he did not know and would have liked to know, not because he was one of your perverts but so they might be more pally. But she always skitted and said: 'Get on with you.' The steam coming from the bathroom always dried his throat. He could hear her padding into the bedroom. He had used to watch for the exact moment and be at the foot of the stairs, accidentally, looking up. But she had been stern: 'Kenneth, if you don't mind.' He drained the chips in the basket. They were now piping hot and ready to serve with the fish. He sliced two uncooked tomatoes.

'Ready, Gladys.'

'Coming.'

She wore only her bathrobe and slippers to the meal. It was his ex-bathrobe that he had persuaded her she could have when her own had grown too small, and he liked that. They had a glass of milk each with the fillet, chips and tomatoes. It was a meal that was soon eaten and Gladys always insisted on clearing up straight away as otherwise she could not enjoy watching television. She would not let him help with the washing-up as she had her own way of doing it. He could do it all or she could do it all but she said they got in each other's way sharing. That was a disappointment. He liked sharing: his thigh might bump against her leg inside the bathrobe. Sitting beside each other on the sofa, she leant back and the bathrobe fell away from her white crossed legs and he could see two floppy breasts inside the bathrobe. Without her brassiere or her roll-on, she was comfortable and without her make-up he saw her flesh in the raw but it did not deter him for even early in the evening and even on BBC there was now the likelihood of a scene apt to put a thought in his head but when he put his hand on the white knee she lifted it off: 'Stop, Kenneth, later.' And a little later he would have his own bath and dress and come down to find she had dozed off and her mouth was a little open and her nostrils in piston harmony. He would shake her. 'I must have dozed off. That time. I'd better move then, shan't take long.' It was impossible to think of a pretext to invade the room while she dressed. Did she put the panties on first or the bra? Did she make up in the nude?

'Kenneth.'

'Yes, dear?'

She had left her tights downstairs in their seethrough wrapping. He had a memory of a stocking being unfurled over the heel and up along her leg and over the knee and

11

up the thigh to meet her suspenders but it was all tights now. He would have liked to see them go on too, they went all the way up over the bum, but all she would allow was that he throw them up to the landing. When she was done up she was nothing like the relaxed body in the bathrobe – a double string of pearls around her neck, her best blouse and navy suit, belly in and chest out and daring earrings. He had put them on once. On himself. He had gone up to the room like a burglar while she was out and opened her drawers intending to feel about with her underclothes, but he was checked by the fear that he might drop dead and be found clutching a fistful of silk. All he had done was put the earrings on, holding a hand close to each of them, ready to pluck them and fling them at the slightest sign of a pain in the chest.

They drove to a country inn Saturday nights to meet Nick and Olive Bentley & Company. Nick was an extrovert: 'You got here then.' Nick always kissed Gladys on the cheek. They drank in rounds: gin and it, gin and tonic, vodka and white, Teachers and a drop of red. The lounge had a circular corner where the men flanked the women who sat side by side, but Nick usually sat by Gladys and when the conversation was general Nick often gripped her knee as he listened to her, or more often, while she listened to him. He never trusted ladies' men, no matter that Nick lived down the road. And Nick was an insurance broker. 'Youth must have its fling.' Where was the humour in that? But Gladys 'Nick, you are a one.' At the end of the night when the women had had their quota and there was talk of whether the men would have one more, Gladys would shake her head: 'Kenneth, you know another won't agree with you.' He would not take that in front of Nick. Because she said that and not because he wanted another he did have another and it did not agree with him and back at the house after the silent car if he swayed ever so noticeably while plugging in the kettle anger came through the make-up: 'You don't listen, do you?' He often suspected she was tipsy herself when halfway up the stairs she remembered to shout down: 'Don't forget to lock the back.' Nick might have had his friendly hand on her clothed thigh all night but after he had that one that did not agree with him Gladys would not put her hand back in bed and touch his knee as was her way when she was in the humour.

He had been proud of his control all his life, his stiff-lipped recognition of Gladys's right to privacy as she took her bath or unfurled her tights, needing the permission never granted for the drink he did not want but always had. And all she could say about Robin shacked up like a drug addict, was: 'Kenneth, you do go on.' Different if she had been in the habit of calling out from the bathroom: 'Want to grab a feel, Ken, now's your chance;' if she had been the type to invade his ablutions and kneel beside the bath and cocksuck him – yes, he knew the expression, those drug addicts thought they had invented everything – if she had been that type he would not have looked out the window and worried lest she might do damage straightening up. And the chips would either have been soggy or burnt. When Robin and Deborah came on a visit Robin did not pace up and down the living-room looking at the clock while Deborah titivated herself upstairs. Robin was up there with her.

He could see what he needed himself. It was not much. It made sense that he lacked little as his was a well-laid-out life. He needed only to be allowed look up at her when she came out of the bathroom or poke his head in through the steam an odd time while the fillets were doing or – he knew she would not stand for him watching her dress – at least be guaranteed that he would not die from a heart attack while he played with her clothes when she was out of the house. He thought of putting it to her: that it was not against any statute, that he simply wanted to go into her room while she was out and put on her earrings and a daub of lipstick and dress up in her underclothes, and if anything happened know that on her return she would tidy up before calling the doctor and the undertaker. But he did not put it to her. He knew her response. She would divorce him. And she would air her grievance in the circular corner of the lounge with Nick edging close in sympathy exerting finger pressure on her knee. And Nick would say to his own wife in his own home: 'Olive, you think I should drop in on Gladys this evening, see she's okay?' And Nick would drop in and fuck Gladys up and down the stairs, in and out of the bath and dance around with her panties on his head and she would blubber: 'Oh, Nick, you are a one.'

Ellis and Gosling were talking about Christmas. In September. 'Hope Dian's gettin' better weather,' Gosling said. 'I mean it's like bleedin' Christmas. I didn' take an 'oliday yet, you wouldn't be encouraged, my missus Linda said what's the point an' Betty she don't fancy sittin' in a pub in Brighton lookin' out the window.'

Ellis put away the cards. 'Ernie, if you don't mind, it's one word I don't like to hear mentioned.'

'An 'oliday? You're what they call a workaholic then.'

'Christmas. Just don't mention Christmas.'

'I don't like it neither meself. Guess what they do to me Christmas. Linda and Betty, we all got to go round to Linda's Uncle Albert's house cos Albert's Betty's brother an' all she's got. Uncle Albert makes his own beer even though 'course I always bring a bottle Albert insists everyone drink his home-made beer an' it's not even piss. But I wouldn't mind that so much. I could get over that, tank up before I go an' after a while if it was piss you don't know no better. But he makes me wear this paper hat. The minute you go in Albert's door he says: All right, everybody got their hats. I say it every year to Linda, I'm not going if I have to wear that stupid hat but all Linda says is Ernie, why would you want to upset Uncle Albert at Christmas? An' I say back, Fine, what does he want upsettin' me for? But Linda says an' Betty backs her up, she says Uncle Albert can't know he upsets you an' I say it makes no odds I'm not wearin' that hat, but what happens? Every year I go and every year Albert says, right, got your hats everybody now give us your glass. I suppose you think I'm silly. You think I'm silly Mr Foster?'

Foster shook his head slowly in agreement. He had suggested to Gladys that now with Deborah and Robin they spend Christmas night at home, like a family. Watch some telly and have a quiet night but Gladys said: 'And miss all the fun at Nick's?' Nick did not brew his own beer, he did not stint on the liquor and after a time Nick took off his paper hat and threw it anywhere over his head and declared: 'Sod this daft hat! Put on some records, Gladys, let's show them how to tango.'

'I don't think you're silly, Gosling. In fact Christmas should be abolished.'

'I second that, Foster.' Ellis was morose. He could see Nick stretching out his long leg Valentino-fashion and bending low over arched Gladys and holding the pose dramatically under the mistletoe while everybody else stood back, glasses in hands, and cheered them on until Nick looked up, surprise, surprise and saw the mistletoe and took rather more advantage of the occasion than the occasion allowed, pretending to give Gladys a smouldering Valentino kiss when what he was at if you were not a fool was a big Nick slobberer with his magic fingers stuck in her back.

'You don't care for Christmas, Ellis?'

'Foster, if Christmas was a person I would go out into a foggy night and cut its throat and then I'd hand myself over and happily spend the rest of my life watching videos in prison.'

Foster thought that observation warm even though he considered Ellis a fanatic, bringing a rectangle of linoleum along to the solo school every week to place under his feet.

'Percy can't stand Christmas neither. Wonder where he's got to tonight, he never misses out. You reckon he might 'a' done it at last like he talks about, done hisself in?'

THE SAVILE ROW SUIT

WHEN PERCY BATEMAN was twelve years of age the Young Thomond Rugby Club, Mellick, Ireland, organised a monster raffle as part of its ruby anniversary celebrations. The prizes were the usual for the time: a ton of coal, a gramophone record of Count John McCormack, a thousand cigarettes, a Clubman shirt with two spare collars. The first prize was a Savile Row suit. With the suit there was an all-expenses-paid trip to London for a fitting. Percy's father Johnny Bateman won the first prize and that was no turn-up for the books as Bateman senior was famous for winning raffles. He won turkeys and hams at Christmas. If he invested a penny at a carnival he won a doll. During the coral anniversary of Young Thomond he drew a horse in the Grand National. He sold the ticket to a bookmaker for four hundred pounds and used the money to buy his house from the Corporation. The horse slipped up crossing the Melling Road. People used to say to Johnny Bateman: You should enter for that.

At the time Johnny Bateman won the Savile Row suit he had a brother working in Toronto as a plastic injection moulder and this rich uncle of Percy's had promised to send fifteen dollars to buy Percy's first long pants suit for his thirteenth birthday. Young Percy heard about the Savile Row suit at breakfast. He had no idea then what Savile Row connoted but he was proud for his father's sake. The fact that it was as big an event for his father to get a new suit as it was for himself made the boy feel grown up. At dinner the talk was still all about the Savile Row suit and the all-expenses-paid trip to London for the fitting. The young Bateman joked to his father: 'And I'm only going around the corner to Bernard Green.' The dollars arrived that afternoon.

At tea time there was no more talk about the Savile Row suit though when Percy came in from playing on the street he caught his father saying to his mother: 'What do you think?'

And he heard his mother answer: 'We'll see, we won't talk about it now, Johnny.'

For years afterwards whenever he thought back on it Bateman acknowledged that the exchange proved that thought, discussion had gone into their decision. Yet however profound or lengthy their deliberations the manner of their conclusion being broken to Bateman lacked subtlety. The next morning, between mouthfuls of bread and margarine, his father shot it out at him.

'Percy, you might have to wait till Christmas for your suit.'

Johnny Bateman had already given his son the top of his egg but that was not as a sweetener. He always gave Percy the top of the egg. Again later, when he looked back, Bateman realised that his father topped the egg lightly and the top rarely had as much as a stain of yolk. His father did not like the white and often gave Percy the bottom of the egg as well.

'Why, Dad?'

'You're not short of clothes anyway, Percy, thank God

and your mother. You see, Percy, when I go to London I won't be just representing myself you know. I'll be standing in for Young Thomond, for the family, for Mellick. You could say I'll be representing Ireland if you like. I'll be representing you, Percy, do you understand that?'

The boy nodded. 'But what has that got to do with my suit, Dad?'

'I can't go to London looking like I'm in *need* of a suit. I'm not going to wear my railway duds, am I?'

The boy laughed. 'You'll wear your best, Dad.'

'Now you see it, son. The question is: is my best good enough?'

His mother joined in. She pointed out that his father would have to get a new suit and shirts and socks and underclothes and shoes and pyjamas and a new case, they weren't going to let anyone think they were in need of anything, he would have to take off his clothes for the fitting over there. It was a question of what people might think. And that was where the Canadian dollars would come in handy.

The boy was too young to understand. The horror of another day in short pants gripped him. He was the only boy in his class in short pants. He wept.

'Now don't start crying like a baby,' Johnny Bateman said. 'Nobody is taking anything off you, we're only postponing your suit until Christmas when we get the diddly club.' Johnny Bateman walked up and down the kitchen running his hands through his hair, trying to find the words to show how reasonable it all was, trying to stop his son 'whinging'. 'I was only saying to Mammy last night when we went into everything, if I never had to go to London representing Young Thomond, look at the way you're growing. Frankie Timmons even says you're big enough to put into the three-quarters on the under-fifteens but I told Frankie I'm not going to rush you.

Percy, in three months you could be grown out of the suit you'd buy today.'

Because he was brought up in a rugby-mad house in a rugby-mad neighbourhood in a rugby-mad city in a rugby-mad province the idea that he might be good enough for the under-fifteens obfuscated the outlandishness of the allegation that he would grow out of a suit in three months. For when he did get his suit at Christmas at Bernard Green's out of the diddly club there was enough slack in the measurements to be let down or out for a long time. Two years later he was wearing the suit to school.

It was hard on a child but it did not stop there with Bateman. He was a tough young fellow then. Not a bully but able to look after himself. Frankie Timmons had suggested that he was good enough to shove into the three-quarters on the under-fifteens and Frankie Timmons was not a mentor easily pleased. Percy Bateman at thirteen was tough and hard but the Savile Row suit was the seed of change in him. He began to study his father. He saw that his father held an elitist position in the house. The pillow covers on his own bed and sometimes the sheets, the shorts he wore playing for Young Thomond were all made by his mother on her sewing machine out of Rank's flour bags. When his shoes wore out he had to sit in while his father repaired them with leather bought in a hardware shop. Someone in the road had an anvil that was used by so many families that it was communal so there was nothing unusual in his having to sit in watching the tacks between his father's teeth. But Percy Bateman began to compare everything that happened to him not with what happened to other children but with his father's privileges. His father's shoes were mended at the shoemaker's. His father did not wear anything made out of a flour bag. His father's bad teeth were pulled immediately by a dentist while he had to wait three weeks for an appointment at the clinic, the throbbing palliated by a concoction called Mrs Cullen's Powders.

Percy Bateman began to hate his father.

He could hardly look at his father, the man he had so loved, the man who had stood him on the kitchen table and taught him to sing:

> Beautiful, beautiful, Thomond,
> Star of my life fade away.
> I sigh when I think of Young Thomond,
> For whom I played many a day.

When Johnny Bateman was dressed to go to London for the fitting the neighbours came into the kitchen and walked around him and were satisfied that he would not let anybody down. And the club sent Frankie Timmons along to mind him. Frankie Timmons was famous. He had played for the Province against the All Blacks and lost the use of his left ear after going down on the ball.

For five years after the Savile Row suit Percy Bateman was buried in books as was everybody else his age who was not pulled out to be a messenger boy or join the Army. It was the only way up at that time – there was not an electronics industry to absorb those who kept their heads empty. Bateman flew through school and won a scholarship to University College, Cork and as an undergraduate he thought that the way Bateman senior was the centre of his own life was something that he could now outgrow. But it caught up with him again when he was twenty.

During the Easter recess Percy Bateman was chosen as full-back for Young Thomond against Garryowen in the under-twenties cup. Young Thomond men were made in the under-twenties cup, especially against Garryowen;

21

they went on to the full Young Thomond team like Johnny Bateman had and all Percy's uncles. But young Percy had begun to change at thirteen when he was done out of his suit. He did get the suit at Christmas out of the diddly club but that meant that it was a poor Christmas all round. His father gave him a florin to hansel the suit and ruined the gesture by reminding his son how he had kept his promise. Percy started to hate not alone his father, but everything with which his father was associated particularly Young Thomond and, more seriously, the Young Thomond ethos. He managed to avoid the youth team by affecting to have to study hard to get the Leaving Certificate Honours that would render him eligible for a college scholarship. His father understood. Johnny Bateman put it to Frankie Timmons that a good job was important too and Percy would not go stale, he would be fresh coming back to the game and it was about time that they all came into their own, Percy would be the first Young Thomond man with a degree.

At UCC Percy had to play for the college but despite the skull and crossbones on the jersey it was college rugby, a different style to Young Thomond rugby, a club whose motto was: *Non Manus Vincere Sed Pes*. But that Easter he could not avoid togging off with Young Thomond particularly that year when it was Johnny Bateman's turn to have charge of the goat. The goat dated back to the occupation when Young Thomond won a famous match against the garrison of Welsh Fusiliers and captured the soldiers' goat, their mascot, and which ever after was Young Thomond's mascot. The goat was togged out in the red and white colours – the blood and bandage of Young Thomond. And Johnny Bateman wore his Savile Row suit even though the day was a Saturday.

As befitted a college boy Bateman had an excellent positional sense. With twenty minutes play remaining and the sides scoreless Young Thomond were attacking on the Garryowen twenty-five. The Young Thomond three-quarters were stretched diagonally across the field in classic attacking formation – a superfluous echelon since Young Thomond, true to its motto, had never run the ball in its history in a cup game. The heel from the scrum was ragged. Garryowen wheeled, won the ball and initiated a foot rush. Bateman immediately retreated towards his own goal, supposedly to cover, actually to avoid the foot rush. But when he turned he saw that he was the last man between Garryowen and a certain score. He ran out to the ball and fly-kicked. The ball sliced off his boot and up in the air. The Garryowen pack arrived. His jaw was dislocated, he was knocked unconscious and a try was scored under the posts.

His father refused to visit him in hospital. On the way home from the game Johnny Bateman threw the goat over Sarsfield Bridge into the Shannon where the unfortunate animal perished in the spring tide. Percy's mother tried to console him in the hospital by saying that it could happen to anyone, that he was to try and forget it, his father would get over it in time, and he would yet prove himself. On the day of his discharge Percy Bateman waited stubbornly at the tea table until his father came home from work. Johnny Bateman hung up his coat and washed his hands and sat down and asked.

'How is that face?'

'It's all right.'

Johnny Bateman did not speak again until on his third cup, which he poured for the purpose: 'I've been thinking all day at work.' He did not look at anyone, only straight ahead. 'They say charity begins at home so it may as well do it here. Everyone, including Percy, is entitled to one wrong turning so what we'll do is we'll never mention what happened again in this house.'

Percy's mother nodded: 'Good, Johnny.'

Between Easter and summer Percy did not go home at weekends. He survived at college by building on his disdain for his father's opinions, those of Frankie Timmons, the neighbourhood, Young Thomond. And he showed just how far removed from them he was in no small way.

At tea his father noticed that he had had a haircut. 'About time. Frankie any news?'

'I don't know.'

'What does that mean: you don't know. What sort of an answer is that?'

'I didn't see him.'

Educated though he was, removed from their tiny ways, he could not stop himself looking guilty. Johnny Bateman tried to camouflage his own rising colour with soft logic.

'You must have seen him if you had a haircut mustn't you? He doesn't put blindfolds on people.'

'I went to Hackett's.'

In the pantry his mother dropped a cup in the enamel basin. Johnny Bateman put down his fork. He did not speak because he could not speak. Percy did not have the maturity for confrontation. He rushed on: 'Frankie can't do a proper crew cut, he's out of date.'

'Jesus, Mary and Joseph,' Johnny Bateman whispered, and then roared: 'You'd do this to me now? When I'm trying to get over the disgrace, you'd renege on Frankie Timmons? ON FRANKIE TIMMONS?'

Johnny Bateman left the table and placed his forehead against the mantelpiece. Framed in the pantry doorway Percy's mother gripped the dishcloth. 'Johnny, don't do anything.'

'For God's sake, Mam, don't encourage him.'

Johnny Bateman turned, the white imprint of the mantelpiece on his forehead dissolving like water from the shell of one of his boiled eggs. He held out his hands as though hungry for someone to choke: 'Have you lost – *all* – respect?'

'Please. Please don't start. I don't think I can take it.'

'START? You cowardly little bastard you, how could you do it? Frankie lost his ear for the club, the man is your godfather, what sort of a treacherous nancy boy have I under my roof?'

'You have no idea how ridiculous you sound.'

Johnny Bateman lunged at his son but Percy managed to keep the table between them.

'Johnny, don't . . .'

'I've had you,' Percy hissed. 'You robbed my suit money when I was thirteen, you wouldn't visit me in hospital, you murdered a goat instead, and Frankie Timmons is a thick, a THICK, and Young Thomond are a pack of animals and you are a savage, a THICK, IGNORANT savage and FUCK YOU, FUCK YOU AND EVERYTHING ABOUT YOU.'

Johnny Bateman rammed the kitchen table against his son and grabbed him by the short hair. Percy's mother screamed: 'Johnny, don't, his jaw, mind his jaw!' Johnny Bateman's open palm stopped just short. He pulled the table back towards himself He breathed: 'Get out of this house. Go now. While the grace of God is minding you, *run!*'

Percy had done the examination for the town hall so that he would be on a panel if he did not qualify for college. He was called and accepted. Another uncle, on his mother's side, had taken him in, a bachelor uncle, fond of drink who only spruced himself up on Saturday to go from pub to pub with the wrapped liver for his tea in his pocket, a tea he never made. Out of his first pay packet Percy rented a room away from the neighbourhood, out in the Garryowen direction. He stayed eight months in the town hall inching himself away from his background into the society of those who sincerely believed Young Thomond belonged to the dark age, and he did not once go back to the house. But alone in his rented room he was visited by fits of misery when he saw that he would never be anything but a coward and a traitor in the eyes of a man of no sensibility save a love of his own comfort. But the man was his father and Percy could remember before his father won the Savile Row suit standing on the kitchen table singing 'Beautiful, beautiful, Thomond'. The fits of misery grew longer and more intense and he sat in his room smoking and crying over a pool of ash until eventually he fled.

'I had a pint with him the night before in the club,' Frankie Timmons explained. It was four p.m. the Friday after the telegram and there was not a single customer in the barbershop. Frankie Timmons was waiting for the fashions to change when people would once again want their hair cut properly by a man, a barber. 'He called in here the next morning as usual to read the paper and have the chat. The kettle was just boiled. He had his cup out and I was filling it, and without as much as a warning he gave a shudder and toppled straight out. His head would have hit the floor if I hadn't dropped the teapot to catch him.'

'Had he been complaining?' Bateman's question fell on the deaf ear, crudely sewn back on the day the province was beaten three-nil by the All Blacks. Bateman repeated into the good ear: 'Had he been complaining?'

'Your father? No. But that wouldn't mean there wasn't something up. Your father would have kept it to himself.'

Bateman looked down at his father and saw a querulous old man in a hospital bed who had never kept a headache to himself. Tufts of white hair were all that remained on the stubborn head, like cotton wool haphazardly aping snow on a crib. At eighty the man was all bone and his six-foot frame appeared to have shrunk.

'A week ago they wouldn't let you in to see me, they thought I wouldn't come out of it. Look at me now.'

'You were in intensive care. You'll need rest.'

'You've no job. That's great news, isn't it? We only see you when there's a death. You were at Mammy's funeral I know that. How do I know it? I was told it. I didn't see you. You were seen at the gate of the graveyard, you weren't at the church, you weren't standing beside me when people shook hands with me. And you didn't come at all for Frankie's wife. Your own godmother. Frankie can hold his head up, the shop mightn't be going too well but he has the pension and Young Thomond won't see him short. Frankie can hold his head up. And I can't. He went down on the ball against the All Blacks. And you didn't – against Garryowen!'

Bateman would not let the abuse penetrate his flash point now. It was so long ago. The man in the bed was eighty and ignorant and sick.

'Don't get worked up, you need rest.'

'I wouldn't have minded so much, you were young, you could have made up for it. But did you?' Bateman did not blink. Never was a question more rhetorical. 'No. You turned your back on us. On your own. It was brought into Frankie's shop by the man himself you had the bet with. The year before the golden anniversary year. You had ten pounds on Garryowen to beat us in the senior cup. I was there when the man told us. Ten pounds was more than your week's wages then.'

'Garryowen had four current internationals and nine interprovincials. If I hadn't taken his ten pounds off him someone else would. The game was over before half-time.'

'Don't tell me the results. It was thirty-four-nil. I know. I keep the records. You don't even understand now what you did. You moved out of our house, you rented a room.'

'You threw me out. You didn't visit me in hospital.'

'I didn't go outside my own door for three days. People used to ask me about you. "I don't see Percy around much." I never knew what to say. I couldn't tell them that you couldn't live with us, that you told me to my face that I was ignorant that you used language to me that I never used in my life, language I never needed to use and I never met the man I was afraid of. Where did you rent the room? Where did you go? Out to the Garryowen area. You drank in the Garryowen pavilion. You were a Judas.' The old man's face had grown redder and redder as he spat out the accusations and Bateman's jaw rippled and rippled. There was no answer to the charges. They were all true.

'You shouldn't bring all that up now to upset yourself. You should be resting, the doctor said you need all the rest you can get. It's ancient history anyway.'

'Is it? Is it ancient history that you're in your forties drawing the dole and no wife or child to come after you? When people ask me about you now I say you have a big job in London.'

'Can't we stop arguing? It's twenty-four years since I let you down, can't you forget it? If it happened today no one would notice.'

'This is now and that was then. I can't forget it when I remember it. It was the thanks I got for keeping you at school. You left us. You stopped thinking like us. You were like a Garryowen person, smart. Solicitors and doctors. Do you think they'd have working men?'

'Because someone isn't a Young Thomond man that shouldn't make him an enemy.'

'If he's up for Garryowen it does . . .' But Johnny

Bateman's lips quivered with doubt. Young Thomond and Garryowen intermarried now. 'I gave my life to the club, it's in my blood, your uncles . . .' Percy shook his head to signify that he was not heeding the threnody any further but he was surprised when the old man obediently shut up. His father's teeth were in a glass on the bedside locker. The old man kneaded his gums and wet his lips with his tongue.

'Will you send me out my Savile Row suit? I want to wear that, no point in sparing it now.'

Percy nodded and made to leave the ward. It was a private ward, not a Rank's-flour-bag ward. He stopped with his hand on the door and looked back at his father. The old man turned his head away on the pillow. Bateman addressed his own hand on the doorknob so his father would not see that he was crying.

'Do you know that I can't have a glass of wine over you?'

'What are you talking about now?'

'Nothing,' Percy sobbed and left.

He bought a pint of milk and a banana and went to his father's house. There was tea and bread and butter to go with the banana and milk and after supper he sat smoking until he had a pool of ash at his feet. It would have taken too long to explain about the wine and his father would only have said: What do you want to drink wine for? In truth he did not and never had wanted to drink wine but the fact was that he did not know how to drink wine. He did not know how to behave with a woman or how to walk with confidence or to know happiness. If his father had not won the Savile Row suit he himself might have come up through the ranks of Young Thomond in the normal way, qualified as a Bachelor of Arts in UCC, gone on to the Young Thomond senior cup team and won

Munster cup medals, found a good job in his home town teaching, married, become a father, learned how to dine out and drink wine, have had friends and attended gatherings. Over the mantelpiece hung the Young Thomond scroll bearing the motto *Non Manus Vincere Sed Pes*. How often had he shouted as a boy: Feet, Thomond, feet. Kick ahead, Thomond. Garryowen had tried to cheapen it: Kick a head – any head. The house was a museum with *Non Manus Vincere Sed Pes* the exhibit of honour. Photographs of teams through the years clogged the kitchen and parlour walls. Pennants of Cardiff, Newport, Llanelli, New Zealand, South Africa and Australia were thumbtacked to attention. Frank Timmons' bloodstained jersey was in a glass case.

Bateman went upstairs to his father's bedroom. He opened the trunk. It was full of programmes, cuttings, the ball from the same game as Frankie Timmons' bloodstained jersey, the washboard his mother had used to clean the gear in the old days, scarves, rosettes, dolls. Over the bed there were photographs of Johnny Bateman in his Savile Row suit taken in Trafalgar Square.

He brought the ball downstairs to the parlour. He slipped out of his jacket and took the jersey from the case and put it on. He placed the ball five yards in front of him on the floor. Clumsily, aware of the hard floor, he threw himself on the ball. He lay there with the ball under his stomach and brought his hands up to protect his head: Good lad, Percy Bateman. Jasus, he's his father's son. Good on you. Thomond, Thomond. Fair play to you, Bateman. He's a great bit of stuff. But the parlour was silent. There was no pack on top of him. He was too far gone for daydreams. He released the clenched fingers from around his head and sat up.

He put the jersey back carefully and took the ball upstairs to the trunk. He sat on his father's bed. The old man in the hospital was once a strong man lying on his own bed, capable of holding his son up in the air and twirling him around like an aeroplane. Bateman remembered that and remembered when his favourite colours were red and white, when he was in short pants and life was uncomplicated because his father was God; when he was under twelve and Frankie Timmons was coach and life was rooted in absolutes.

Bateman was experienced at drinking anonymous pints. He went to a pub outside the neighbourhood called the Shakespeare and had his drink at the counter staring at the chrome and brass fittings and the ducks swimming in the mirror ponds. The proprietor was a pleasant fellow who had served his drink with just the right amount of comment on the weather. 'Some summer is right, we've even got the card up already for Christmas, I put it up as a joke to kid the lads, no one had a decent holiday. Want to try your luck, be the first? Fifty pence.'

Was there a god there at all? This otherwise inoffensive publican was holding a Christmas raffle card in front of Percy Bateman in September. A raffle card. Christmas. How could anyone know except a bird of a feather what loneliness is inflicted on the lonely by occasions of celebration. It was hard to suffer Christmas at Christmas but to have to observe the countdown fangless from the malcontent's eyrie was to be put in the stocks before on the rack. But he did not protest. As though it was a spoonful of cod-liver oil he accepted the publican's Biro and wrote the first fictitious name and address that surfaced: Arthur Ellis, The Lino Shop, Shepherd's Bush, London.

ARTHUR ELLIS

WHEN HE WAS the London Area Manager of NatWest Finance Arthur Ellis pined for a Britain with unemployment quadrupled, the welfare state abolished and children going to school with holes in their shoes. He recognised that this was an odd longing in a man of his position but he could come to his own defence. There were smart people who called the good old days the bad old good old days. They cited no bathrooms, no showers. They recalled outside loos. On that particular point Arthur Ellis maintained it was more civilised to do it outdoors, you didn't have to run around after yourself with air freshener. He had put the case to Tammer. Tammer was a jogger. He had drawn the riposte from Tammer: 'Arthur, I'm afraid you're not exactly filling me with nostalgia.' There was no depth to Tammer.

Arthur Ellis was a deep man and when his thirst for frugality emerged in middle age he did not run off to slake it immediately but faced the curiosity honestly. What was the difference between an Arthur Ellis who cleaned himself in a shower and an Arthur Ellis who washed his feet in a basin? All other things being equal there was no difference. So why did he long for one over the other? Because he could remember, dammit, that he was happy then with the loo in the backyard and his feet in a basin in front of the kitchen fire. Warmed by his own candour Arthur Ellis discovered that he liked cold but could no longer have it since he'd moved south to the capital and become a success. As well as seven bedrooms and three reception, there were three centrally heated bathrooms in his centrally heated house in the stockbroker/professional soccer player belt. And two televisions and a video and a music centre. And he may as well have been dead. From the porch to the attic the whole place was insulated. Aluminium windows. And he had flu all year round. As a lad in Leeds he used to get into bed at night with a pennyworth of toffees and an Agatha Christie and wait until his body warmed the bed and the bed warmed his body and read his book until he fell asleep. And in the morning when he was called for his breakfast he put his feet down on cold lino. And when he came home from school he ran straight out back to the toilet and while sitting there carved the map of Britain on the whitewash with the nail of his thumb.

There had to be more to his discontent than a simple lack of frugality otherwise all he had to do was strip himself and sink into a cold bath every frosty morning before sitting down to tea and dripping. For instance, the spending power of teenagers depressed him and as a consequence he fell out of love with his paunch. There had always been plenty of room in clothes when no one under forty had a bob but now every garment was designed for an athlete. Most of his colleagues, like Tammer, paid tribute to the invention of self-supporting trousers by running ten miles to work in the pursuit of hips. They were dapper where he could not tie his shoelace without having to stuff his shirt back into the waistband when he straightened up. He felt isolated when he golfed with Tammer to sit in the locker room and observe the complete absence of flesh handlebars around Tammer's waist. Tammer's slacks snugged into him. His own made as vain an effort not to sag as might a worn shilling try not to slide down a wall of jelly.

Ellis was inspired to take his first historic step into the past: he bought braces and trousers a size bigger and was reconciled to his paunch. Fuck hips and all who designed for them. With braces Ellis was able to keep his trousers up but his spirits continued to sag because he knew he would never again carve the map of Britain on the white-wash of an outside toilet or read Agatha Christie or warm a bed with his body – he did not expect his wife to sacrifice her electric blanket. But there was one thing he could do and did, and that was to step out on to a strip of linoleum every morning. When his father died in Leeds he flogged the house and contents except for a strip of lino that he salvaged as a keepsake. His wife at first was understanding about the strip of lino – it was on his side of the bed. But rather than bring him comfort the lino tugged him back every day to the contentment of his boyhood that could not be relived.

He was telling his story to the solo school in the King's Arms in Shepherd's Bush and paused now to gauge his audience. Bateman was attentive but that was not surprising given Bateman's own saga. Ernie Gosling as ever rolled a cigarette. And Diana Hayhurst was smiling with the correct degree of courteous interest. But he could see that Foster was sceptical, not that he cared. Diana Hayhurst was a fine-looking woman. He blinked her out of his thoughts and continued:

'Lawdidaw. That was their word for the South and all its ways. Before he died I hadn't seen either of them for eleven months – the Christmas visit. I remember when I was a mere thug in the repossessing department I went home on holiday. We went to the pub. I had a vodka. He said: Ale isn't good enough for you then, gone lawdidaw, you want to watch that, Arthur. Do you know that for twenty years I tried to get them to instal a bathroom? – I gave up trying to get them to move house. But no. They weren't lawdidaw. Lawdidaw. My wife wasn't either before I met her. She was a typist in Delinquent Accounts. But still when I brought her to Leeds that first time to see them one of the concessions they had to make to lawdidaw was toilet paper. I made them. He always said the *Mirror* did its job. He didn't approve of the HP either, thought you should wait. When we next went I noticed that they had toilet paper in. He was used to it now. And he'd recarpeted the parlour, cut rectangles out of the old carpet and put one in each bedroom over the lino. I looked forward to having them in London, to showing them what I had achieved, the house and the grounds, but it was a waste. They were only impressed on my behalf. It was not for them. He just couldn't see beyond corner shops, pigeons and short-sleeved Fair Isle jumpers.

'It didn't affect me careerwise – in finance nobody looks beyond the glint in your eye, parentage doesn't count. My mother took ill first. He told me in a way I didn't grasp: "Your mother is poorly, Arthur." And it was too late when I realised I hadn't seen as much of them as I should have done. After the funeral I discovered the bedroom carpet square had spread wall to wall. He'd replaced the lino. I felt so let down for him.

'He wouldn't come and live with us. He was gone in six months, she used to do everything for him. I put the house on the market. I got twelve and a half thousand with the furniture, I sold the furniture to a dealer, the people who bought the house didn't want it. I found my strip of lino under the stairs and brought it back to London. They were good parents. I was happy as a lad.

But I wanted to rise in the world. And I wanted to repay them the love they gave me only I didn't realise they didn't want a return, not that kind. It hit me when they died. I was alone for the first time, I had to look at myself. I didn't like what I saw. I saw a man less sure of himself than his father had been. I missed him. I wanted him back. I knew he wasn't coming back so I tried to recapture the nearest thing to him – frugality. I think, Bateman, you might understand that.'

'I might. But I don't share your longing for hardship. My position is that I'm a coward. Full stop.'

Foster cut in severely: 'Look, Bateman, ashamed of not having your head kicked in, that is rather Irish you know. As for you, Ellis—'

''Ere, Ellis, 'ave you considered what would happen if the kids today were back to outside loos, you think they'd sit there and carve maps in the whitewash with their thumbnails? They'd do it on some OAP's face with a razor. I mean they do that anyway even with bathrooms inside the 'ouse.'

Ellis was patient with them.

'My wife liked to entertain and be entertained. Our next dinner party at home I brought the rectangle of lino into the dining-room and placed it under my chair. Of course it caused comment. I explained myself like I did to you lot just now. There was much banter. My wife was mortified. When the guests left she burst into tears: I had given her no warning, did I not realise Tammer was there with his wife? I was unmoved. When I went upstairs that night I found the bedroom door locked. I could come in but I was to leave that filthy tarpaulin outside. I corrected her. I said it was linoleum. I slept in one of the guest rooms. But next morning she apologised for locking me out. She ceded my right to a talisman if it meant so much to me but from then on it must be our secret, she insisted.

But I had already decided on my plan. I hoped to bring her with me, to see it my way. But it was not to be. A week later we were expected to dinner. As we left the house I gathered up my talisman and tucked it under my arm. My wife stopped. She looked at me. I didn't flinch. I told her people would have to accept me as I was. I said: You'll have to accept me as I am. She turned hysterical, she had accepted me as I was, she shouted, but now I wasn't what I was. How could I expect to bring a piece of lino to our host's house and put it on his carpet and not have people thinking I was barmy? She tore open the hall door and drove off in her car.

'My plan was a simple one. I had realised I was in a position to strike a direct blow for lino. I telephoned Tammer and instructed him that from now on I would be dealing with house furnishing. That I would present myself in person. Tammer was arch with me. I had always felt that he doubted my financial nose. I didn't jog. As it turned out he had a pair of applicants for that afternoon. A Mr and Mrs Tuart. Tammer showed them in.'

The Tuarts were an efficient couple: he was a teacher in a comprehensive and she was a nurse, their only frivolity the borrowing habit. And in that they were no different from any other couple in England. Nobody saved any more. Maybe it was that an entire generation were fearful lest the Bomb drop without their owing something. Or maybe it was the powerful advertising campaigns of the lending institutions. Or a bit of both. Ellis saw from their file that they had already put the bite on for three thousand pounds to purchase portables – beds, three-pieces, cooker, washer, perhaps even a dishwasher. Who knew? Certainly not the NatWest. So long as they could feed the loan, it did not matter whether or not they wanted the money to benefit a cats' asylum. Now they felt they had lived on the varnished floorboards of genteel poverty for long enough. They were here for the two thousand five hundred to buy carpets.

'Do you know, I'm not sure you're wise,' Ellis filibustered.

'Pardon?'

'Not carpets in every room surely? Certainly not the bathroom?'

'We did think to,' Mrs Tuart said, rushing in, as a woman will do.

'I know you don't have the patter of little feet yet but the most careful of us adults, we are inclined to shake a little pee about, aren't we? We may not notice it ourselves but guests do, it hits them, the accumulation of all the misdirected drops. I once knew a case of missed promotion in that regard. But you just think, with lino the tiniest puddle is visible and soon mopped up and you don't have the insidious absorbency that you would have with carpet.'

Not bothering to disguise her body language, Mrs Tuart intimated with wide eyes to her husband that they were closeted with a nut. But Mr Tuart knew that Ellis was the top man as that Tammer had said: Mr Ellis himself will look after you.

'Do you mean vinyl, Mr Ellis?'

'We call it lino here. Linoleum. I have always thought them the four most beautiful syllables in the English language. Think about the hall. I have yet to see a carpeted hall that did not have a protective plastic covering. Unless of course the occupants had no regard for anything and we don't deal with that type here. You take our climate: no matter how careful one is we drag rain in after us ten months of the year. In a good year. And snow. All that money invested then not in carpet but protective plastic covering. With lino a wipe, a wax and you're yourself whereas – I can say this to a married couple –

the act just isn't the same wearing a sheath.'

Mrs Tuart's body language was free of all rein now. But Mr Tuart began to feel the stir of what he had probably been born with but had long since subjugated to the pursuit of conformity – a sense of humour. He smiled cagily at Ellis.

'You put it most unusually, Mr Ellis.'

Ellis nodded a smile back. 'Take the living-room, reception, dining-room, whatever name they go by now, there I would almost insist carpet. We don't want to live in the past. But common sense should make us see the bathroom and hall in a different light. Now the bedroom, the bedroom is *tricky*. Again you're a married couple, more to the point a young married couple. I know what hot blood is. How often does one fail to hold off until the bed? Honestly now? That's one up for carpet, I admit,' Ellis raised a numerative finger, 'though there is the probability of spillage. But at least the guests don't penetrate so far . . .'

Mrs Tuart was looking at her husband as though this was the first time she had witnessed his indecisive side. Tuart studied Ellis for evidence of fanaticism but he could only discern the light of ratiocination, mildly oiled by Ellis's authority on his subject.

' . . . dust. I know, I know, we set a time aside for doing the vacuuming, the best of us, but who reaches every particle? All those hours we lie asleep think of the dust, in through the mouth or up the nose, affecting our lungs or sinuses according to one's style. Whereas lino hides nothing. Not a speck. Two: the smell of wax. Think of what it must do for one legally and subconsciously compared to the lot you read about today with heads stuck in bags sniffing glue and ask yourself was there any of that in pre-carpet times. Three: . . .'

Ellis saw that Mr Tuart was beginning to shake his

head slowly and that Mrs Tuart was hypnotically trying to get her husband to turn to her so that she could communicate her agreement that they were in the presence of the deranged. Quickly Ellis changed tack.

'But let's get down to business. Two thousand five hundred you feel you need. Suppose we settle on a ratio. The bathroom and the hall lino. Elsewhere downstairs carpet. The bedrooms as yet a matter of opinion, say one lino, one carpet and one fallow for the time being depending on which side you come down finally.'

Ellis saw that Tuart was thinking. He pretended not to notice, busied himself running his Biro down the acceptance form. Ellis knew what Tuart was thinking: What to do? Old boy's round the twist but don't let on, get the money and save the story for the local.

'All right?' said Ellis.

'But we're not thinking of – of *any* lino.' At last Mrs Tuart.

Ellis ignored her. He offered the Biro to Tuart who accepted.

'But . . .'

'It's all right, dear.'

'Now what I suggest is go ahead and order – and don't worry if you have underbudgeted, we'll pay the suppliers direct and that will save fuss and temptation and provide us with an inventory in the unlikely circumstance of there being a necessity for repossession.'

Tuart's journey with the poised Biro toward the bottom of the acceptance form halted abruptly. He raised his head.

'Can you not just let us have the cheque?'

'No need.'

'When we borrowed for the furniture the other chap – Mr Tammer – Mr Tammer issued a cheque, we didn't even discuss what furniture we intended buying.'

'Did you buy furniture?'

'Of course.'

'But you might not have done? Not yourself, but a different type of client might not have done. And I don't doubt for a moment that you will buy carpet and lino as agreed. But try and see this from our point of view here. I have to organise my branch for the general run. It's a tightening up, the past ten years have seen a cavalier attitude to borrowing and lending. I tell you I wouldn't be surprised if some of our clients didn't take the stuff from us to back the Derby favourite. It just had to stop. But it will be no inconvenience to the genuine customer I'm sure you'll agree, it's simply a safeguard against your spiv.'

At last Mr Tuart looked at his wife. She half rose but so did Tuart's hand to check her.

'Mr Ellis, apart from the carpets there were one or two knickknacks we hoped to buy. We know where there is a bargain in a chandelier and . . .'

'Now, now, I'm not going to be pedantic. Of course. Just bring in a *proforma* invoice for it along with those for the lino and carpet and anything else in that line that you fancy. A chandelier is a nice touch, you're a couple of taste. Thirty-six months, was that what you had in mind? Or do you feel you could cope with a shorter term?'

'Three years is fine please. Look, it's – we're honestly not that keen on lino in our hall . . .'

'Or in the bathroom.'

Ellis could see now by the way she hid her teeth that Mrs Tuart was not at all tractable in the cause of linoleum. He conceded the hall and tried to save the bathroom.

'Fear of neighbours? Not many are without it today. Very well then, carpet the hall. Lino for the bathroom and one bedroom, I'll settle for that.'

'You don't understand, we don't want lino any place, tell him.'

Ellis ignored her and offered his friendly face to Mr Tuart.

'Tell him.'

At last Mr Tuart was decisive. He stood up. 'Come on dear.'

Ellis saw them out of his office with the air of one who had been treated with contumacy. His 'Good day to you both' was cold but not as cool as their lack of response. He looked out of his window and saw them fighting in the street below. It was his impression from the way they gesticulated – Mr Tuart was holding up his thumb and forefinger – that there was the difference of a piece of lino on a bathroom floor between them.

They would probably continue arguing through five tube stations. But eventually they would discover that they had a common enemy in Ellis and maybe celebrate with a performance on the varnished floorboards and afterwards giddily pretend to search for anything that might have spilled. They would go to the pub later – people had recourse to drink to commemorate lesser watersheds – and there regale the idle. And when the guffawing died down some ombudsman in their midst would emerge with: I shouldn't take this lying down you know. And all the best brains in the comprehensive common room the next morning would be roped in to compose an epistle. Or they might phone, the coward's method of communication, phone Tammer.

Ellis had to face the real world. He might count on small pockets of support for his lino crusade, cranks and fanatics would come to his side. But no one knew better than the London Manager of NatWest Finance how easily cranks and fanatics were defeated and outnumbered.

They came with the most pathetic of supplications periodically inspired by the easing of lending restrictions. There was that bearded chap who called himself a poet and who was older than Ellis was at the time. One hundred pounds the poet proposed to borrow. Jobless. Without even a rich mother. The poet needed the money as working capital. Ellis was not a Philistine and thought to offer the poor man the price of a ream of foolscap out of his own pocket on condition that the provenance be deemed anonymous. But the poet wrote on toilet paper – before the invention of Babysoft. He needed the working capital to spend on drink. As a trainee Ellis was taught how to anticipate and deal with every denomination of liar but at no point was he warned against the applicant who told the truth. The poet proposed to 'drop in from time to time' with repayments ranging from two shillings to a guinea, or to clear the debt at one shot in the event of his work becoming commercially recognised. It was sad that any man – even a poet – could suffer the delusion that the NatWest welcomed a settlement of one fell stroke. Ellis thought he was gentle in inviting the poet back at such time as the poet should have become a rate-payer. But now he regretted not having given the fellow the till.

For the moment those Tuarts were a pair of corpses in his cement garden that someone's careless pneumatic drill would stray upon. Tomorrow or the next day or the next. There was no point in trying to anticipate the postman or intercepting telephone calls. No. It was destined to land in Tammer's lap and Tammer would do his duty.

'This Tammer went over your head then did 'e?'

'Of course. I didn't do badly out of it, nobody wants a scandal in finance. A rescue package was put together that saw me off the premises handsomely. My wife got nine-tenths of it but I had enough to set up.'

Kenneth Foster studied Ellis, trying to be fair. They were rum times. Unlike a different age, say thirty years ago, one was grateful now not to be attacked on the streets. One had no choice but to build on that. Today, today Foster did not know. Ellis seemed in every way as reasonable a companion as one could have expected to draw in the lottery of a solo school if it were not for that business of carting around a segment of lino. He liked to step on something cold in the morning. Some people did like a touch of cold, the Prime Minister herself attributed her capacity for hard work and long hours in part to the aid of a lack of warmth in staying alert. But with Ellis could one be sure it stopped at that? Were there not people – otherwise respectable people – who paid others to whip them? Maybe there was no more to Ellis than met the eye. But if every damn fool ran out into the street following an impulse where would they all be? Without Foster and his generation's recognition of marriage, form, etiquette, topiary and what not there would not have existed the stability on which rested democracy. Had Ellis thought of that? And look at the way Ellis was dressed. Foster always thought that that class of a shirt was only suitable for those Canadians who felled trees. Cord trousers held up by a vulgar pair of braces that Ellis made no effort to hide under a pullover or jacket. A workman's peaked cap and he had grown a red beard. Without the cap or with a different style of hat he would have looked a hillbilly. And dammit if the fellow wasn't sitting there happy as Larry. Operating out of a falling-down warehouse that he rented for a song around the corner from the King's Arms, actually living in a species of loft inside the warehouse and according to himself making a packet. Those decent-sounding people, the Tuarts – instead of the Tuarts and their type as customers, look at the dregs Ellis was happy to consort with in his new-found trade,

44

blacks and Irishmen. He had heard stories of how those people lived, there was no smoke without a fire, the wonder of it was that there was room for lino in the houses with the numbers sharing if half of what he heard was true and a lot of what he heard was from Ellis himself.

'I haven't a passageway in the warehouse now with the stocks. At first, though, business trickled in. It was all landlords then and that suited me. There was no nonsense about matching colours it was a case of how much a yard. There was one chap, he's been back to me since – one of your own, Bateman, he's from Kerry I think he called the place – he had six houses up in Kilburn rented exclusively to building workers. We made it up on the back of a cigarette box, me and Mr O'Halloran. There was an average of ten bedrooms a house. He bought all the same colour because as he pointed out it was no business of the bunch in one room what colour lino was in the other fifty-nine, and anyway they were all usually so drunk getting into bed that he could have had crocodiles on the floors and it wouldn't matter. He was a businessman, I could deal with him. And I got business from him by referral. And then you had the black landlords. I get along fine with them too although I have to admit I used to be a racist. But not any more. I see a man now and I say: There's a lino man. And I'm at home. I might have made a living out of the landlords but they weren't what I was waiting for. What made it for me was the ordinary people, even young couples, jobless, taking their time over the purchase, going into shade and durability and price. I suppose I have Maggie Thatcher to thank for that, bless her.'

If she had only happened on one of them she would have found treasure but to stumble on four gems: an Irishman, why had she not thought of an Irishman before? Poor Foster upset that his son was shacked up and Ellis positively barmy. And dear old Ernie.

UNIPOLITAN WOMAN

OVER HER DEAD body, Diana Hayhurst professed, would the man's viewpoint get into *Unipolitan*. She did listen to Malcolm Canning but Malcolm was too close to her and Malcolm was not a man. His hairpiece was black, goatee ginger and shirts pink. He wore a green three-piece tweed suit and a floral handkerchief flopped out of his breast pocket. Every year he went to San Francisco on a three-week holiday. At a gathering in Malcolm's house she had studied his bookshelves: Maugham, *A Passage to India*, Gore Vidal, *Giovanni's Room*, Coward, Isherwood, *All for Hecuba*, Auden, all the lads were there.

> . . . the super-absorbent tampons blocked
> the vagina, causing possibly toxic blood
> to seep back into the Fallopian tubes, the
> peritoneum . . .

'Fine, Diana, that's fine.'
  'It's no good.'
  'I really think it is.'
  'I mean it's no good trying to continue like this. I need somebody instead of Fyncham.'

'Get married again.'

'Fuck off, Malcolm.'

Diana Hayhurst launched *Unipolitan* from a small office in the Pentonville Road when she was twenty-eight. Fifteen years later she discovered a touch of grey in her hair and immediately dyed the lot silver. She used Flex Instant Conditioner to protect her hair from the hot heat of hair dryers, heated rollers and too much sun as Flex had a unique balsam and protein formula which gave her hair body, bounce and shine.

Inside the jacket of her favourite burgundy suit she wore a plain silk blouse through which her burgundy uplift bra could be seen and was meant to be seen. Her single halter of pearls dangled provocatively any time she bent over Malcolm Canning's drawing board and his lack of reaction confirmed that he was not heterosexual. She made do with Crystal sheer glossy 15 denier Pretty Polly tights that cost only ninety-nine pence because she liked a man who liked to take them off and in the circumstances Diana Hayhurst did not expect to be stripped as though she were wearing vestments. Her shoes were Roland Cartier burgundy kid and always with a strap around the ankle. She wore matching panties.

To combat her dry skin she relied on Helena Rubinstein's moisture-retaining formula which was based on natural milk protein that held moisture at the surface of her skin and kept it soft and smooth and gave her a fresher, more vital look. She did nothing about the lines on her forehead because, together with the dimples at the corners of her mouth, they sang of sex. She spent a fiver a week for a twenty-minute medically approved electrolysis treatment for the removal of unwanted hair at the Tao Clinic in the Brompton road.

Unipolitan now had offices in New York, Paris and the head office in Regent Street where she conferred with

Malcolm Canning. International editions were published in Australia, Italy, France, Germany, Brazil and Greece.

'Why not, Diana? You're still beautiful.'

'I'm not beautiful, Malcolm. I never was. But I'm dynamite.'

'Then get married. Make someone pay for it, why give it away free?'

'You're a man in that attitude. When a man fucks me nobody accuses him of giving it away and when I fuck a man I'm in the same boat. I'm a *Unipolitan* woman. When I think of the fart I did marry.'

Hooper was a publisher then almost fifty to her twenty-eight. He had an American feminist best seller on his list and telephoned *Unipolitan* to arrange an interview with the writer. The three of them had a lunch from which the writer was abducted by her agent for a television programme, and Diana Hayhurst was alone with Hooper and thrilled to be with a real-live famous publisher.

'I feel we've arrived now that you've contacted us,' Diana Hayhurst told him.

'You've arrived as much as that fucking eyesore who's just left us.'

'Her book's wonderful.'

'I wouldn't know. I haven't read it.'

'Come.'

'I'd be delighted to.'

Diana Hayhurst blushed then for the last time. Hooper took her hand. 'Don't pay any attention to me, it's just the way I am. I think I'm taking a fancy to you.'

Diana Hayhurst fingered her hand free. 'What do you think of my magazine, Mr Hooper?'

'Fuck the mister. Leonard.'

'Look, could you cut that out? Please?'

'What?'

'That language. Of all people I wouldn't have thought you'd have to use it.'

'Poor girl. I'm one of the few people entitled to use it. *Unipolitan is* a proper rag. It can't miss. Take my advice: get after the agencies that handle the sanitary towel people. Get them and the rest will follow. Because if there's one thing I can't stand it's being reminded that women menstruate. And I've noticed people fall over themselves to buy what I dislike.'

'I'm sorry, Mr Hooper.'

'Leonard. Sorry? Sorry for what?'

'I'm sorry we menstruate. If we knew it upset you we wouldn't.'

'You're fucking gas, I like that. We'll have dinner tonight and afterwards I'll fuck you and teach you how to swear.' Hooper laughed at his own outrageousness. 'I'm terrible, you should know me.'

'Goodbye, Mr Hooper.'

At the age of twenty-three Diana Hayhurst left Toronto and her lovely parents to discover swinging London. She had a degree in commercial art that allowed her to sneak into a job on *Woman's Own*. She worked in the art department under Malcolm Canning who at that time in that staid establishment did not dare to risk a floral handkerchief flopping out of his breast pocket. Her parents never doubted that she would become an independent success – they were both general practitioners – and the loving care they'd invested in her childhood was amply rewarded when she flew home every single year to be with them at Christmas. *Woman's Own* at that time as at all times was undecided whether to go backward or forward so remained inert. Diana Hayhurst discovered an uneasy longing to soar from the art department and become a contributor. This was a slow process in any house and particularly so in *Woman's Own*. But after four years Diana Hayhurst became First Assistant to the agony aunt, Lady Simone Menzies-Hogg, an old lady dressed in crochet whose real name was Betty Barnes.

Her experience at *Woman's Own* would have driven anyone to launch *Unipolitan*. Though she tried to tone them down her ideas were considered too strident. *Woman's Own* was aimed at a pseudonymous Mrs Herne Bay who was never without her secateurs in hand and who had the ingenuity during sudden rainstorms to simply rush out and hold a large umbrella over her rotary clothesline. Mrs Herne Bay gratuitously donated this presence of mind to the letters page. Mrs Herne Bay's mother lived within a home-made jar of marmalade's throw of her and preserved gas masks from the Wars. Diana Hayhurst knew what she was about in stepping clear of Mrs Herne Bay's world but Leonard Hooper was too far from it for her comfort.

His flowers arrived in the afternoon. The card read: Don't fuck about, Diana. I'll pick you up at seven. She did not take the flowers out of the box so absorbed was she with the words on the card. She recognised sophistication. When Hooper picked her up he said: 'Fuck the dinner, let's go for a drink.' In the pub he explained.

'Right, I can't take it from the small vocabularies, granted, but coming from the likes of myself it is acceptable. And would be from you too. It's actually necessary. I strike my thumb with a hammer: Fuck. Delight. Who has time to look around for the proper words? Fucking marvellous. Otherwise the moment will have passed. Now you try it. Go on, have a go.'

'Here?'

'Yes. Say something about me if you like.'

'You're a fucking pain, Mr Hooper.'

Hooper smiled. Diana Hayhurst fell back against the

upholstery and shrieked: 'Yippee.' Her skirt ran up her legs, followed by Hooper's eyes. She looked around. Nobody had taken any notice of her. She stood up and roared: 'And fuck Mrs Herne Bay.' She was not even a moderate distraction to the other customers. This was swinging London.

'Who is Mrs Herne Bay?'

They were married a week later and had fun for ten months. They started work early, finished late, fucked and swore. Hooper got her a sanitary towel account and all the other sanitary towel accounts followed plus the designer jeans and body fresheners and deodorants for every orifice and occasion. Diana Hayhurst reacted to Hooper's opinion on everything by commissioning articles in favour of all that he loathed. *Unipolitan* grew. She had had a few affairs before she met Hooper but in retrospect they were lifeless. She and Hooper were magnificent when they made love thanks to his insistence that they both scream. He maintained it was unnatural to perform as though they were dummies. They might have been the happiest couple in England, but his age caught up with Hooper. He fell in love with his wife. He told her so on the telephone without one expletive. 'Diana, I've an idea. Let's have a baby, I think I'd like to be a father.' It was eleven in the morning. For the rest of the day she struggled to harness her feelings. There was no point in talking to Malcolm and Fyncham was as dry as his figures. She could not confide in the female staff whom she had hired for the bits of fluff they were.

When she met Leonard for dinner that evening he stood up and held her chair back, a gesture foreign to him. He was smiling as though he already were a father.

'What do you think, Diana, do you see me as a daddy?'

'I don't see me as a mammy, Leonard.'

'Of course you do. I can just see you . . .'

'You can't, Leonard. Forget it.'

'Diana!'

'Leonard, what's got into you? You don't want a baby?'

'I want to be a father. There comes a time when a man should be a father.'

'I don't want to be a mother. I have *Unipol*.'

'You do, Diana, you don't realise it but of course you do.'

'I don't, Leonard. Are you fucking deaf?'

'Easy.'

'What?'

'I don't want to have to divorce you.'

She moved out of Hooper's Knightsbridge flat that very night, passing Alec Guinness who raised his hat to her on the way to her taxi. She slept in the Pentonville Road office, a sleepless night that led her to establish living quarters in Regent's Street when *Unipolitan* took off.

At first she thought Leonard was joking, that it was all bluff. But she also had to accept that he might have found someone else to teach how to swear. Someone younger. Still Leonard Hooper rang her and wrote to her regularly: all she had to do was give him one child.

Leonard behaved like a gentleman, the bastard. It took him three months to get some woman pregnant. He told Diana she now had grounds for divorce. But she was damned if she was having that. She had a fucking reputation to look after. She told him: 'Out of sentiment, I'd like it to be in that pub where I fucked Mrs Herne Bay.'

He was a young barman from Mayo who worked off and on at the buildings and the bars under assumed tax-dodging names and he could not have agreed more quickly with her suggestion that he go into the ladies' with her at closing time if her name had been Elizabeth

Taylor. Leonard Hooper did not have the character to be a witness himself but, as arranged, her own divorce surveillance officer did the job and attested to what he had seen.

She forgot about Hooper except to remember, in relation to every article she considered for *Unipolitan,* what would Leonard think? If she thought he would hate it in it went. Had it the whimsy that used to appeal to him? Out. That lasted until she heard of his costly divorce which lost him the custody of his two-year-old daughter as well as a lot of money. She felt obliged to ring him with sympathy.

'You didn't look for custody of the child.'

'Not on your fucking life. Are you free tonight?'

'Goodbye, Leonard.'

Unipolitan was by now so successful that there were very few men around of the old style, that is, pigs. In the evolution of the species *Unipolitan Man* had arrived. Off whom would she bounce her features to keep *Unipol* on a straight course?

Fyncham was in his fifties when she employed him to run the office. He was already an office manager by profession: the Black Death of the computer had not yet gobbled up office management. *The Unipolitan* vacancy and high salary was brought to Fyncham's notice by his daughters who thought *Unipolitan* the best magazine in the world. He had seen the rag lying about the house but an office was an office and more money was more money. He kept his contempt to himself. He had the office organised and running itself within a year, and was doodling in his sleep one afternoon when Diana Hayhurst burst in on him without knocking as was her ignorant habit.

'Sorry.'

Fyncham's hand shot out to cover his scribbling pad

but Diana Hayhurst was a nimble lady. 'May I?' Leaning over him, her pearls tickling his nose and her breasts shamelessly visible, a woman divorced from a respectable publisher for fornicating in a public-house toilet with a navvy.

> You are at a party. Do you:
> (a) Grab a drink and seek out the plainest person in the room
> (b) Consider yourself the plainest person in the room
> (c) Avoid the plainest person in the room

Diana Hayhurst recognised it as part of the party test in the current issue of the magazine. But at the bottom of the pad Fyncham had added:

> (z) Get as much drink inside you as fast as you can so that everything becomes a blur.

Diana Hayhurst walked around Fyncham's desk studying him frontal, profile and pole.

'Mr Fyncham?'

'I was just seeing how the magazine could be improved.'

'Yes? Do tell me.'

'I did this month's party test and I came out pretty poorly. According to the test if I scored seventy or more I would be the type who has ladies clutching at his trouser legs. Fifty or more and I am part of a reliable corps who constitute the backbone of England. My tally is less than eighteen. It lists three counselling centres here to any of which I am urged to have recourse.'

'Poor Mr Fyncham.'

'I can take it. But think of the harm it might do

someone who can't. The test is unfair and restrictive. There should be an optional factor, a 'z' factor as I've indicated.'

'You really think so, Mr Fyncham?'

'Yes, it's obvious. The lack of options in the party test is the product of a circumscribed mind.'

Diana Hayhurst ran a nail along an eyebrow. 'How would you like to set a party test yourself, Mr Fyncham? For a fee of course.'

'Do you mean that?'

'Yes, I do, Mr Fyncham.'

But when Fyncham set about composing a test from scratch his imagination failed him. The fact was that he was not a party man, when his daughters did have people in he was banished to the local in his cardigan to drink brown ales. Fyncham asked Malcolm Canning for assistance.

'May I ask you, Mr Canning, do you go to parties?'

'Parties? One fits in with the general civilised pattern of behaviour.'

'Could you tell me something about them, what they're like?'

'That depends now, doesn't it, Mr Fyncham? There are parties and – what have you in mind, Mr Fyncham?'

'A party where the general civilised pattern of behaviour is observed.'

'Never been to one.'

Fyncham explained what he was about and Malcolm Canning assured him that a typical party could be concocted from the back numbers of the party tests.

'Just stand there with drinks in their hands. Would you not have someone singing?'

'Not unless some drunken Irishman gatecrashed.'

Samples from Fyncham's first draft ran:

You are at a party. A drunken Irishman gatecrashes and starts to sing. Do you:

(a) Continue your conversation and pretend he is not present
(b) Catch your partner's eye and indicate that you wish to leave
(c) Seek out your hostess and comfort her
(z) Listen to the song.

You are at a party. The conversation has turned to orgasms.
Do you:

(a) Yawn
(b) Freely contribute your own experience
(c) Say nothing but afterwards titter at what you call the pathetic boasts of the others
(z) Point out that it is not a fit subject for discussion.

When Fyncham completed his full party test he answered it himself, conscientiously choosing the 'z' option in every instance. He received top marks and was adjudged intelligent, humane and sophisticated. Diana Hayhurst could not believe her luck.

'Excellent, Mr Fyncham. I'll print it.'

Diana Hayhurst was back in Fyncham's office next morning. Would Mr Fyncham give his opinion on the entire issue? He tackled the problem page where Diana Hayhurst herself doled out the advice under the name Penny Corsini. It was the usual nonsense: My 14-year-old boyfriend wants to go all the way and I'm afraid I'll lose his love if I won't. But my mother says I should wait until I'm 17. Fyncham made short work of that. I have found love again at 54. He's a grandfather and assures me that I can't conceive. But even though I have not menstruated in years I once read in a *Reader's Digest* that a woman in the Himalayas conceived at 96. Am I being overcautious? Penny Corsini's advice to the lady of fifty-four was that she was right to be concerned, that some women maintained the properties of youth into advanced age and that to be on the safe side she should consult a gynaecologist. Fyncham approved the response as kindly. No point in expecting the silly woman to see sense. Let those gynaecologist-fellows earn their living for once.

When the first issue blessed with his imprimatur came out Fyncham closed the door of his office and treated himself to a perusal. His party test was included as he had written it – except that the 'z' option was omitted. This made a mockery of his creation. The wrong people would get top marks. He turned to Penny Corsini's advice. The fifty-four-year-old woman was told she should see not a gynaecologist but a psychiatrist; that it was not uncommon for the wrinkled to entertain delusions of fertility as a prophylactic against the onset of old age.

Every other article that Fyncham had deemed objectionable was printed and what he had rated as abominable was set in upper case and italicised. Perhaps there was some bungling in communications with the printers. He went to see Diana Hayhurst.

'Ah, Mr Fyncham.'

'I don't understand. I'm not in here at all.' Fyncham tapped the magazine. 'This test is a mockery. And where I agreed with Penny Corsini's advice I see it's now been rejected. It's a case of throwing away the wheat and printing the chaff. Nowhere – absolutely nowhere is the man's view represented.'

'Are you sure, Mr Fyncham?'

'Of course I'm sure.'

'Bingo!' Diana Hayhurst clapped her hands. 'We did it.' She prodded Fyncham into a chair. 'Sit down, Mr Fyncham. The fucking man's view goes into my magazine over my dead body. A fifty-four-year-old woman thinking of sex? She should read *Woman's Own*. My readers have firm busts, bodies that can pour into Gloria Vanderbilt jeans. Everything happens for them. You must see that, Mr Fyncham?'

'You used me as a guinea pig.'

'No. A filter. You were wonderful.'

'You made a fool of me. I told my daughters I was helping out with the creative side.'

'Mr Fyncham, could you run the office if there was no money coming in? Tell me! Tell me you can and I'll let you write the entire magazine. It can't be for men and it can't be for women who don't menstruate. In this edition, look, we have full pages for five different sanitary towels: extra-absorbent; double grip-strip; leak-proof lining . . .'

'I can't work without Fyncham, Malcolm. All these years he kept me on course. He's sixty-five, he's already had two bangs to the heart. Even though he wants to stay on I'm going to retire him, I owe his wife and children that much.'

'As I said, get married again.'

ERNIE GOSLING

ERNIE GOSLING WAS tall and now gaunt in his sixties and liked to dress up on his night off because he felt he owed the solo school his best. They did not take unkindly to him, a potman. He got the same respect they showed each other and that included insulting him just as they sometimes insulted themselves. There was none of this walking on eggs, they used their big words when it suited them. On solo school night he liked to wear his navy slacks and brass-buttoned red blazer and his yellow silk cravat that Betty had given him at Christmas and he pulled the collar of his blue check shirt up to cradle his ears. He always eyed his appearance in the mirror before leaving the house and when satisfied patted his strands of dark, oiled hair and brought his trim moustache in fleeting contact with his nostrils. He rolled a gasper to smoke as he strolled down the road in his beige crepe-soled shoes. He did his pools every Wednesday night same as anyone else but then he walked by the post office and plopped his entry into the nearest litter bin. Linda would do her nut if she knew.

Couldn't leave him be as it was, pools night. She might be sat there watching telly with her mum, but that never stopped her keeping an eye out.

'Now Ernie, QPR aren't goin' to draw with Liverpool in Anfield, now are they?'

'I got an 'unch, Linda.'

'My eye. You're soft 'cos they're your team. Go down Loftus Road and wave your scarf Saturdays I understand that. But doin' the pools is doin' the pools. It's different, Ernie. You let your heart rule your head, no wonder you 'aven't won nothing.'

Ernie would occupy his tongue with a cigarette paper, asking between licks: 'Who's fillin' in the coupon then?'

'The day comes we do click an' we're goin' straight out on the town – you too, Betty – and 'ave ourselves a time.'

'No we ain't. That's just what did for all the others. We ever do click, Linda, I'll have a kipper for me tea same as usual. Play it cool and take it handy like.'

'Sod that. Down to Cook's and find out the next cruise more like.'

'There you go, that's more of it. You start that lark, you've only got to pick up the *News of the World* every other week an' there it is, on the town, round the world, fur coats and the next thing it's marriage bust and 'fore you know where you are end up drinkin' meths and 'avin' to sell your story to the papers for a few bob.'

''ear 'im, Betty. You don' 'alf take on, Ernie. I s'pose you think I should keep me job on too an' next you'll tell us you'd stay potman down the King's Arms.'

'What's wrong with bein' potman, then? You sayin' I should be 'shamed of it?'

'Course I'm not sayin' any such thing, Ernie. Just there won't be no need is all. Same as I wouldn' 'ave to be up seven every morning to clean no bloody offices.'

'Don't swear, Linda.'

'I'm not swearin', Betty. I'd see a bit of the world, I

would, what'd be so wrong with that?'

'Not for me, Linda. I seen my share an' it's enough.'

'You could stay home then couldn't you, me an' Betty, we could go by ourselves.'

He carried an image around with him of Linda and Betty in North Africa bein' felt up by Arabs. Worse, they'd make him go with them. They always got their way, like gettin' him to Albert's at Christmas and havin' to put on that silly paper hat.

'Anyway, we 'aven't won nothing, 'ave we? Soon enough to think about all that when we 'ave.'

Now that he was in the solo school Ernie Gosling could rightfully say that he was loved for himself and not, for instance, for the money he might have if he did win the pools. This was why he could no longer risk posting the coupon. Even before the solo school Ernie was happy doing his potman's job, collecting leftovers and topping up the drinks of blokes down on their luck. You got to meet people being a potman, real people with real problems, unlike if he was a guv'nor – people wouldn't talk to him as free, he'd be cut off, like he would if he clicked. But it hadn't bothered him so much before, he posted his entry in the post office never really thinking he'd win. But now he just wouldn't take the chance. Linda wouldn't let him be a potman any more, she wouldn't hold with it and he couldn't blame her, could he? She couldn't buy things. Suppose she set her heart on a fur coat, how could a potman's wife go round in a fur coat? If she came in the King's Arms with a fur coat on Saturday nights when she liked to treat Betty, he could just imagine what the customers would think. There wouldn't be any more tips for Ernie and nobody calling: Have one yourself, Ernie.

A big win was not something you could keep mum about either. True, people sent off their entries and ticked the box NO PUBLICITY but they were hopping their heads off a stone wall. The pools people went out of their way to find something wrong with winners who wouldn't have publicity, maintained the coupon didn't arrive in time or an X wasn't where it should have been and they covered themselves where it said their decision was final. No, if he did win he'd have to go to the Savoy like everyone else where they'd put a bird with big boobs on his lap to tart up the photo.

Linda often said: 'If we did click, Ernie, just think, Christmas every bleedin' day.' He did think: first thing Albert would invite them all round for a party to celebrate, not that Albert would be trying to get his hands on some of the money – at least not any more than could be expected from a man with a nephew-in-law that had clicked. Albert was just a bloke who liked to celebrate and break out the paper hats. And Albert was the type who would single him out and call: Quiet everyone, order. Speech. Come on Ernie, give us a speech.

But before the solo school started up he had ideas on what he might do if he did click, serious ideas, not going on the town or up North Africa on a cruise. He thought that if he won the pools, whether or not he hung on to his potman's job, he'd still have time on his hands and there was so much stuff he hadn't learned as a youngster. Linda had said: 'You talkin' about night school, Ernie?'

'I don't think I like the way you say that, Linda.'

'I didn't say nothing, Ernie, did I Betty?'

'Look, history's something I could be interested in. All those telly programmes that run for weeks, Henry the Eight and all that crowd, I sometimes don't even know the years those blokes were there. You hear of these Tudors an' Plantagenets an' Windsors an' Mary Queen of Scots an' all, they're all mixed up in me 'ead, I don't know one from the other. Aren't we always sittin' round

63

the telly askin' each other when did this happen then? I mean it's our history, it's a thing we should know an' then for another frinstance, there's the Irish Question, none of us can't follow that.'

'They chuck bombs about. That's all I need to know, Ernie, they get drunk and chuck bombs about. Sod 'em.'

Another night Linda said, and she shouldn't have said it in front of Betty, it wasn't fitting even if she was pulling his leg: 'How do I know somethin' isn't goin' on down the King's Arms, you're that fond of playin' potman.' Course she didn't mean it but she shouldn't have said it, specially not in front of Betty. It was true, there was a lot of how's your father around these days, you saw them pawing each other on the tubes and on the buses, but he never did go in for it himself, not as a married man, never had done. He didn't know how many nights down the pub, going from table to table, he'd had his chances with the cheeky lot that was going. But he never paid no attention, just to say: the glasses please, luv, and pass on. 'Now, Linda, I won't hear that talk in front of Betty, an' I won't hear it behind her back neither. These,' Ernie held up his gasper, 'a jar, a few cross doubles an' trebles, see QPR of a Saturday, that's enough to keep me 'appy. An' you know it too, Linda, so don't pretend otherwise.'

'I don't know why you do the pools at all then, I don't. You'd be just as well off Wednesday nights, 'stead of posting your coupon you chucked it in the nearest litter bin.'

They had moved in with Betty short-term after the War and somehow had never moved out to a place of their own. He had no regrets there. He liked Betty. She had never made him feel that he was not the man of the house, except that when he got the urge to move the furniture about Betty moved it back again. That, and having to go to Albert's Christmas party because Albert was her brother and she didn't have no one else. He knew, too, that Betty approved of him – because he had always mucked in and coped, never a day idle. In the early days he had turned to this and that until he got in at the motor-factor factory and worked in Stores where he was happy for twenty years. Happy, that is, till Maggie Thatcher came along with her idea that we'd all be better off if everyone else was out of work skint. Only he was one of them as had lost out. Even then he didn't give up the ghost. He hunted till he got the potman's job.

THE SOLO SCHOOL (I)

THE IRISH AND non-European quotient patronising the King's Arms was low for an area such as Shepherd's Bush. This statistic was a compliment to the Guv'nor who simply would not tolerate riffraff. The Guv'nor, his wife and his wife's brother and his wife's brother's wife were all the full-time staff. Then there was the potman, and the part-time barmen and cooking and cleaning ladies – all of them Londoners. The Guv'nor had once received a telephone call from the Emerald Staff Agency: The Emerald had on its books a number of experienced barmen and barmaids who were willing to sleep in. 'Sleep in where exactly?' the Guv'nor had enquired. 'Over the pub, I see. What did you say your name was? Mr O'Donovan. Actually, Mr O'Donovan, that's where I sleep myself. My wife and family. Are you saying you have people who want to move in with us?'

'No, no, of course not. Please don't misunderstand me, most pubs nowadays have staff accommodation, it pays you know, but I understand your position. We also have qualified barmen and barmaids who are happy to sleep out but obviously they would have to be paid more and you don't have them where you might want them after counting the till at closing time.'

'I don't have any vacancies at the moment, Mr O'Donovan, but I'll certainly keep you in mind, all right? Thank you very much. Don't mention it. 'Bye.'

The Guv'nor had been a barman himself and his wife had been a barmaid, and it was his experienced opinion that bar staff were low types as he himself had been and that they fiddled as he had fiddled his own way to the top. The last thing you wanted was to give them the run of the house, on their feet all day in such cheap shoes the bedrooms ponged. And all they did with what little they earned after keep was donate it to the bookies, except for those who like himself aimed at the top and you could not keep an eye on them, they were artists.

The King's Arms was divided into a lounge, a games room, a dining area and public bar all serviced by one circular counter so that the pub was easy enough to run with the help of his wife, in-laws, part-time staff and the eyes in the back of his own head. Unlike the full-time, qualified barmen recommended by the Emerald Staff Agency whose stock-in-trade it was to 'sleep in' – as though that tendency were a qualification to put after your name – the Guv'nor's choice of part-time help reflected his own blunt way of doing things. He hired those who had good full-time jobs by day but who needed a supplementary income for a purpose: getting married, a foreign holiday, a new carpet or extension. A few hours a couple of times a week and all hands on deck Sunday mornings. And he told his new recruits: Okay, we're all English, right? So we know what we're about. I don't know how any of you feel about coloureds or Irish or what not, if you've got prejudices keep them to your-selves. You have problems with people like that in your own jobs, I don't want to hear it. But the coloureds are here and the Paddies are here and there's no hiding it. All

I expect from these people is that they behave English. No more. No less. They behave like us, they're welcome. They don't, they're not. You get someone chucking abuse at you, you ask yourself would I take this from an Englishman. If you wouldn't, then you don't take it from anyone else neither. That's it. Except you work hard, I pay you well. You fiddle, I'll knock your fucking head off. Now jump to it.

Of course the Guv'nor did not arrive at a streamlined model of a pub overnight. He had to go through the lot: the sleep-in crowd who owned one shiny pair of trousers apiece; those who enlisted to become writers; those who thought it would be a bit of gas. He did not want any of those on either side of his counter. After ten years as Guv'nor he was happy with his ship, his crew, his captaincy and his passengers. And then one night Ernie Gosling asked him for a job.

The Guv'nor had always thought Ernie Gosling as good a model as any for the non-English. A solid worker by all accounts, there was never any shiftless or anti-management talk out of him. He was one of the half-nine to ten o'clock regulars who drank a few light and bitters and behaved quietly chatting about football or racing or cricket in season, the garden and that. In the games room Ernie was often seen to volunteer to take chalks at darts, and organised raffles with cloakroom tickets for modest prizes in aid of expenses when the dart club played away. Weekends Ernie brought his wife and mother-in-law in with him and swapped the games room for the public bar on their behalf. On occasion all three of them contributed to a pleasant singsong, the mother-in-law obliging with a quavering 'Two Little Girls in Blue'. It wasn't always that easy to enjoy a singalong when there were too many coloureds in the public bar. They were inclined to want to jazz things up, click their fingers and writhe in their tight trousers with big white smiles. Which was not the English way at all. The Guv'nor was happy that he had his own way with the coloureds; he had settled for less but not much less than their behaving English. When they sneezed snot after a loud laugh and wiped themselves with florid hankies the Guv'nor approached: Would you like to laugh that bit quieter, boys, we are indoors. But they laughed all the louder and said: Man, you's somethin' else. And the Guv'nor thought: That I am. The Paddies had been a problem with all those anti-English songs. The odd Saturday night he'd had to come out from behind the counter and put it to them: 'You being kept here against your free will then are you?' In the long run they shut themselves up having read in the morning papers where some of their brothers had left their calling cards in department stores. He'd had little out of them since then.

When the motor factors went to the wall the Guv'nor had called for his part-time staff and addressed them through Alan, the longest serving: 'Now Alan, I want you all to look at it this way. They've been good customers of mine for a while now, you couldn't have better. They've all got their bein'-kicked-out money but you mark my words the day'll come when one or other or more of them is going to look for a drink on the nod. If you've any regard for them you'll come down heavy and say sorry. All right?' There was no need to spell things out to Alan or the lads, they knew his way. Some of the men from the motor factors now took to dropping in for the odd one in the morning or early evening before tea. But the Guv'nor had noticed that Ernie Gosling stuck to his ways. He dropped in as usual between half-nine and ten of an evening and supped just as steady till closing. He still brought his wife and ma-in-law Saturday nights and sang along with them nice as you like. Which was why the Guv'nor was so took aback the night Ernie spoke.

'Guv'nor, d'you mind, could I have a word?'

'Of course.' He would say no. He could not have a man in his sixties turn tapper at that age. And God, the poor blighter was blushing. 'What is it, Ernie?'

'I was wonderin', you need any extra help these times by any chance?'

'Look around, Ernie.'

'I don't mean Wednesdays. I was thinkin' maybe busy nights.'

'You see yourself everyone's on busy nights, we can cope.' Christ, Ernie was sweating.

'No I don't mean in there, I'd hardly be capable, got to admit that, but d'you ever think you could use a potman like, keep things movin' that bit, it was just a thought come in my head when I see you 'avin' to come out collectin' glasses when things is hectic.'

Ernie was not barman material, that the Guv'nor knew. But that Ernie recognised his limitations and faced up to them impressed the Guv'nor. Ernie, even wearing shamrock and carrying a bomb, would not find his way on to the books of the Emerald Staff Agency regardless of whether he was willing to sleep in or out. The Guv'nor said: 'I don't know, Ernie. How are you coping, you finding things tight?'

'It's not that, Guv'nor, but same as everyone I can always do with a bit extra – things keep croppin' up that you don't bargain for, don't they? No. It's all the things I used to do about the 'ouse: I do 'em daytime now, see? An' I thought if I 'ad somethin' to keep me occupied I'd be better off all round.'

'Tell you what, Ernie, I'll talk to herself. I'm not promising anything so don't go raising your hopes. But I'll talk to herself and we'll see.'

'I'm obliged, Guv'nor.'

There is a way of hiring people – and firing them when necessary – and the Guv'nor had that way. He let the weekend come and go without mentioning the subject to Ernie Gosling and Ernie showed the Guv'nor that he knew the form by not mentioning the subject either. But come next Wednesday the Guv'nor called Ernie over.

'I been thinking of what you suggested the other night, Ernie. Maybe I could do with more help. If you're still interested.'

'I am, Guv'nor. I mentioned it to Linda, she said it was a good idea. She laughed, she said I'm in here all the time anyway.'

The Guv'nor did not laugh. 'I wouldn't need you Wednesdays, I hardly need myself. Let's say Friday, Saturday, Sunday nights. The Sunday morning session. Sunday morning's murder, you know that yourself. I'd pay you for that same as nights. Seven quid a session, that's what I'm offering. It's as high as I could go, that's if I *can* go that high. We'd have to try it out, see does it work.'

'All right by me, Guv'nor.'

'There might be other nights when there's somethin' on, like when we're at home to a darts team. I'd expect you to be on call if I needed you, you go along with that?'

'More nights the merrier where I'm concerned, Guv'nor. I don't do nothing else with my time nights, do I?'

'Right. You'll have to get yourself a jacket, show you're staff. You know your own fit, so you buy it I'll pay.'

'Blue, same as the part-timers?'

'No. Get a different colour. Get a red one. There's just one thing, Ernie: the job's more than gathering glasses, you have to do your bit. You'll be my eyes and ears out there. You spot customers you feel aren't behaving the

English way I expect you to tip me the wink. You know how I run things, you'll run your end same as I do mine.'

'I think I have the idea, Guv'nor. When would you like me to start?'

'Tomorrow's Thursday. Start tomorrow, break yourself in, you mightn't get every Thursday but I'll pay you for tomorrow. No point trying to find your way about Friday night when none of us don't know if we're coming or going.'

The Guv'nor could say to himself after only a few weeks that he was pleased with Ernie Gosling. Saturday nights when he liked to do his VAT and deductions before joining his friends for a drink in the lounge, he would often lift his head and see from the office that Alan and the lads were under pressure and that meant leaving the books till the panic eased. But now Ernie Gosling was as alert to the needs of Alan and the lads as Alan and the lads were to the needs of the customers. At the end of one Saturday night after the clean-up when the Guv'nor was having his usual couple with the part-timers, Alan had said: 'Not a bad bloke, Ernie, is he? Not afraid of work.' Ernie had already left. And that was a special mark in Ernie's favour, that he didn't as a potman have to be told he didn't qualify for a drink with the Guv'nor and the part-timers. And Ernie knew how to deal with the customers. He might have gone to a school for potmen. At first they got it up for Ernie, his old mates from the motor factors.

'You still talkin' to us, Ernie, now you got your red jacket?'

'You're not objectin' to me doin' me job I hope, Fred.'

There was a delicacy about the way Ernie did his job but no more than his job. Old Mrs Dixon with arthritis who sat at a table and called on the regulars to bring her drink down from the counter, her money up and change back, Ernie took her over officially, passing her by regularly: 'You all right, love, you ready yet?'

And when the coloureds got smart in the beginning and said: 'Hey boss man, bring us down five pints', Ernie, if he was idle, licked his cigarette paper and answered:

'Didn't know you was knocked up, boys, you looks 'ealthy to me.'

Soon the Guv'nor could not remember how he managed without a potman. And soon the regulars, including the mates from the motor factors, came to the counter and ordered their drinks and added: 'And a light ale for Ernie.' Even the Paddies included him every so often. In time the coloureds accepted him and shouted: 'And a drink for the boss man.' To show that Ernie had the master's touch, on Wednesday nights when he was off duty and the bar run by the Guv'nor himself or herself or the in-laws Ernic would lean his back to the public-bar counter and notice who was slow going down his glass. And Ernie would put money on the counter and order: 'Fill a Scotch for Harry on me.'

During his first six months as potman in the King's Arms there was only the one occasion when Ernie Gosling and the Guv'nor did not understand each other. Or rather when the Guv'nor did not understand Ernie. Ernie saw the Guv'nor's side of it. Too bloody clearly. Boxing night. 'Can't come Boxing night, Ernie? How's that?'

'It's Linda's Uncle Albert, we got to go to a party there.'

'I see. A party. Wish I could go to a party myself. Christmas night I put the feet up. Well, have a good time, Ernie.'

'Hold on, don't misunderstand me, Guv'nor, I don't want to go, much prefer be on duty, but I 'ave to. They make me.'

He had tried. But Linda had said: 'Ernie, you doin' that job or's that job doin' you? I can just see tellin' Uncle Albert you can't come cos you have to do potman in the King's Arms.'

'They make you go, Ernie?'

'Straight up.'

'Wish someone would make me go to a party.'

It was Wednesday night and the Guv'nor waited for his eyes and ears to report on the bloke sitting in the corner furthest from the public-bar counter. The chap had a flat cap and a red beard, braces and a check shirt, and he was entertaining himself with a deck of cards and not in the games room. The Guv'nor had noticed Ernie speak to him a half-dozen times at least, he'd even taken his order and brought it to the counter – to the Guv'nor himself. Maybe the bloke had an affliction like Mrs Dixon's arthritis. Still that was Ernie's business: if he wanted to rise beyond the call of duty for a customer, all well and good. But it was Ernie's night off. He wasn't wearing his red jacket.

'Ernie.'

'Yes, Guv?'

'Who's our friend?'

'Oh, that's Mr Ellis. You know, the new lino shop in part of what was the motor factors.'

'What lino shop?'

'Didn' you notice? He's taken over part of the old warehouse. Funny, I called in there Saturday for a bit of carpet for Betty's room and guess what, he don't sell nothing but lino. I mean I know he calls it The Lino Shop but you'd still expect to get a bit of carpet, wouldn't you?'

'What's he doin' in here?'

'He's 'avin his drink, Gov. 'Appened to ask me where's

the best pub round here so naturally what else would I say?'

'He Irish?'

'Mr Ellis? No. No, he's not Irish. From Leeds, he said.'

'He talk like he's from Leeds?'

'I wouldn't say that. He talks London if you ask me, 'e's been 'ere years. Used to be boss of NatWest, 'e told me.'

'You believe him?'

'I din't see why not.'

The Guv'nor lifted the flap and swept Ernie before him into the office.

'Ernie, I'm surprised at you. Here's a chap you never seen before in your life. Now I'm telling it back to you like you told it to me so correct me if I'm wrong. You never see this bloke in your life. He has a lino shop that sells nothing but lino. No carpet. He's a red beard. Coloured shirt, cap. Where's a good pub, he asks you and the King's Arms across the road. He comes in and sits there with his cards playing by himself when there's a games room – how come you didn't tell him move into the games room, Ernie?'

'I did. I said he'd have company. He doesn't want none. Only game he plays is solo, you want four for that. I couldn't think of anyone in the games room plays solo, I play it myself I told him. But he said 'e was 'appy where 'e was an' I 'adn't the 'eart to move him out seein' as how he was playin' by himself.'

'Okay. He tells you he's from Leeds but he doesn't speak like he's from Leeds. He tells you he was the boss of NatWest. Now here's a question, Ernie. S'pose you're the boss of NatWest, would you leave it and come down the Bush and open a lino shop selling nothing but lino? Would you do that, Ernie?'

Ernie's moustache moistened.

'Here's what I want you to do, Ernie. Play up to him. Be pleasant, don't make it obvious. You got friendly with him so don't go back on it. But whatever he says, you tell me. Maybe he is on the level. Maybe my name's Napoleon. And you watch, any time he ever comes in here carrying anything, even what looks like a lunch box, and tries leaving it behind, you follow? Meantime, I'll get on to the police, tell 'em the situation.'

THE SOLO SCHOOL (II)

SUPPOSE HE NEVER did get another job, Percy Bateman considered as he embarked on the distraction of a tube journey, an expensive tube journey in search of a cheap haircut. Who would credit his reason for chucking the settler's job in the King's Cross betting shop? It was a small place, London, if you were tube-minded which of course everybody was. A bedsitter in Evelyn Gardens, a job in King's Cross and now a haircut in Shepherd's Bush. People said: The money's good and it's only three minutes' walk from the tube. Or: The bus drops me five minutes' walk from my own house. It didn't matter if the tube or bus journey took ten hours it seemed, as long as the walk to or from the tube or bus was measurable in minutes. He had his father to thank for spending the best part of his life underground instead of walking a walker's distance daily, as was presumably intended for a species with legs. Actually, he had left the settler's job because of the dirty pictures. Otherwise he had loved it. In winter when the last horse jumped the last fence early in the afternoon and only the fanatics who backed dogs kept them settling sporadically, Bateman and the settlers played solo to kill the last hour. One of his colleagues had a brother a radio officer at sea. The radio officer brought home photographs and the radio officer's brother brought them in to his fellow settlers. 'Get a load a that then, Pat.' Huge tit and cock, twosomes, threesomes and foursomes, close-ups of white, viscid secretion. Bateman feigned longsightedness and held the pictures at arm's length and said: 'You'd give your right arm.' But you could only put up with it for so long. And in all decency he could hardly tell his fellow settler that he didn't want to look at the pictures, pictures that the radio officer had gone to a good deal of trouble to bring home from far-off lands. That would be churlish. Instead he stayed home and wrote for his cards.

It had been that colleague had given him the location of a barber near Shepherd's Bush. Before he'd gone to one of those places where you're handed an album of androgynous styles and asked if Sir sees anything there that takes his eye and charged four pounds for the privilege. 'Sod that, I go to a bloke in Acton, eighty pence and what's wrong with it, go on, Pat, what's wrong with that hair now, go on, tell me.' Bent barbers with adopted French christian names! Suppose he never did get another job? His last pay packet was a month ago and since then he had cut his budget savagely, going so far as to stay in one night a week which was a considerable sacrifice for a lonely man accustomed to the anonymity of crowded pubs. He never did have an exciting encounter in a pub or anywhere else. The spoils went to the action men. How many times had he walked in and ordered a whiskey and sat looking intelligent, and *not* been approached by a lady pushing a silver lamé purse in front of her on the counter, long gloves up over her elbows? He could go home and live in the house – his ignorant bastard of a father would take him in – and draw whatever kind of dole they were giving there these days and retreat into himself, if there was any further to go along that line. Or he could stay in Evelyn Gardens, doing all the things he had not had the time for as a worker: walking round the city inspecting statues and façades, get a ticket to the BBC and watch a show being recorded, visit the Old Bailey, look into St Paul's, the British Museum, see the rhododendrons in Kew Gardens, visit Charles Dickens' house, try Covent Garden. But he had no appreciation of architecture, did not know a rhododendron from a daisy, had no love of opera, never learned how to drink wine. It was all part of being stunted, fringe drawbacks to not diving on the ball. He could go again to a strip club and join those with their hands dug deep in their pockets, minds full of sexual violence. He could sit in his bedsitter crying over a pool of ash. Although it was near six o'clock by the time Bateman reached the barbershop he found a queue of seven before him. They sat on chairs arranged in an L-shape and moved along them. Bateman read the prominent handwritten sign: HAIRCUTS– 80p. HAIRCUT & SHAVE – £1.40. No wash and blow-dry, no tints, no styles. The barber himself as befitted a barber was bald. The only question Bateman heard him ask was: 'Shall I take much off, Sir?' And the answer in all cases was: 'Don't take too much off the top.' Bateman settled down with a six-year-old *Reader's Digest*. But when the moment came to move up a chair he noticed the oddest thing. His immediate neighbour took a mat of lino with him. Also, while everyone else was occupied with a *Digest*, a motor magazine or coverless Sunday supplement, his neighbour was dealing out four hands of cards on to his knees – a chap wearing a flat cap, with a red beard, check shirt, braces and corduroy trousers. I'll go a bundle, the man said after consulting the first hand. Pass. Pass. And after studying the fourth announced: I'll spread them. The barber, obviously unacquainted with the client of the moment, called out:

'How's the lino business then, Arthur? Still exclusive, are we?' And laughed.

'It's doing all right, thank you, Alf. Nearly as good as you're doing yourself.'

Alf held a rectangular mirror to the back of the customer's head. The customer looked into the large mirror in front of him, turned left and right then bent his head and evidently satisfied with what he saw said 'Fine.' They moved up the chairs, Bateman's red-bearded neighbour gathering up his cards and his lino mat which he again placed under his feet on the tiled floor. The barber knew his next customer and their talk was of Piggott's imminent retirement. 'Often cursed the bugger,' the new customer said, 'but when you come to think of it, there was no one like him, was there?'

'Good old Lester,' the barber agreed.

The Arthur chap dealt out four more hands of cards on to his knees. He arranged the cards in the first hand into suits. Ace, king, queen, jack, ten, nine, eight, seven of hearts; a lone ten of spades; the jack and three small clubs. 'Galling,' the Arthur chap said. Bateman could agree with that. Eight sure tricks bar an unlucky rough. A possible hope of a trick out of the clubs but it would constitute a reckless bid.

Bateman abandoned his *Digest* and risked the opinion: 'Hard to pass a hand like that.'

'You know the game, Sir?'

'I've played a bit.'

Arthur did not need to sort the suits in the next hand. He simply said: 'Pass.' But the third hand had four low spades, five low clubs and three low diamonds, all including the deuce. And a lone six of hearts. Arthur studied the hand and then slowly shook his head. 'No. Definitely no.'

'I would have thought it an impregnable spread.'

'You would, would you? You don't see anything vulnerable about a lone six of hearts? I thought you said you knew the game?'

'You have eight hearts there.' Bateman tapped the first hand, 'ace to the seven. There is no possibility of discards there.'

'And how is a chap to know the distribution of the cards?'

'Well of course . . .'

'Yes, well of course. You didn't think of that did you?'

'Sorry. I didn't realise you were operating on that basis.'

'There isn't any other basis.'

'I'd still chance it. The odds are against the four low hearts being evenly divided. And depending on the lead a higher heart could come into you.'

'It so happens I was dealing for the hand that passed. It would be my lead.'

A real oddball. Bateman smiled. 'Even so, I'd lead the six and take my chances.'

Arthur Ellis smiled back. 'So would I. My play reflects my character.'

'Next, please.'

'Let's move along. You play often, do you?'

'Not recently. I used to work in a betting shop. We used to play after work during the hunt season.'

'Post Office sorter's best for that. They play all night. Or in car assembly. Tell me, did you ever play with a suit out?'

'It's not the same.'

'Of course. But it's a damn sight better than playing by myself. The reason I ask, there's a pub across the road. There's a chap there can play, the potman. This is his evening off but he'll be there anyway after nine o'clock sometime, if you're interested.'

The Guv'nor could not have asked for more courteous treatment from the police. He was never a police basher anyway. No, he would leave that to the immigrants, disrespect for the London bobby. Inspector Blake had invited him into his office and instructed Constable Taylor to provide an extra cup of tea and biscuit. Then Inspector Blake said: 'Guv'nor, first of all let me thank you for coming to see us. I often say to Constable Taylor here that the day the public stop calling in is the day that will bother me. If all the public were alert, not paranoid of course, simply kept their eyes open and their wits about them, our job would be so much easier. We've checked out your Mr Ellis and he is everything he says he is. He's from Leeds originally, worked with NatWest most of his life and he was London Area Manager when he simply chucked it to open his lino shop. So it looks as if you have nothing to worry about as long as he keeps paying for his drink.'

'I thought it odd that he should appear out of the blue, Inspector.'

'You were dead right, Guv'nor. As I say, we're grateful you came to us. I'm not saying I'm ruling him out – of anything. He's everything he says he is but maybe he's more. We don't know, do we? And I'd be obliged if you continued to keep your eyes open. Constable Taylor, myself, the Force, we can't be everywhere. When I ask you to be vigilant, Guv'nor, I know you'll be discreet. Mr Ellis has his rights. If he's clean we don't want to infringe on those rights in the slightest way no more than we would on your good self. Can we count on you, Guv'nor?'

Later, Inspector Blake had said: 'Well, Taylor, what do you think?'

'With respect, Sir, I wouldn't encourage him too much.'

'Too much, no, Taylor. But the chap was disappointed, you saw it in his face. And we don't want to dash his hopes completely, do we? As it is, he'd only have felt really useful if we had surrounded the pub and hauled Ellis out. Human nature.'

'You said, Sir, that Ellis had his rights too.'

'Yes, Taylor, I did. But the King's Arms doesn't catch us napping twice. You've heard the story, you know how it was. George Blake and Bourke, and my predecessor, all supping their pint within feet of each other – George Blake newly sprung from the Scrubs, by Bourke just twenty minutes earlier. The one a double agent serving forty-two years. The other in for postal bombs, what else. And the next we hear from Blake is from Moscow and Bourke's all over the Irish television telling the world how they had their first pint. So you see, Taylor, you could say the King's Arms got me this job. I don't want the King's Arms to lose me the job.'

'We did check Ellis out thoroughly, Sir.'

'And what did we find? You heard that chap, what's his name, Tammer. Without any encouragement from us, all we did was mention the name Ellis and what did Tammer say? The looney. Right? Wouldn't lend people money to buy carpets. It had to be lino. Not indictable of course, Taylor, but worth watching all the same. Worth watching, Taylor?'

'Yes, Sir.'

The Guv'nor looked at his watch. They were playing that damned game the best part of an hour now, Ernie, the lino man and the newcomer and Ernie hadn't said yet who the third man was. The Guv'nor had gone out sniffing, collecting an empty glass at their table and Ernie, the dummy, said: 'All right, Guv, I'll look after it.' Didn't Ernie understand it wasn't the bloody glass he was after?

He was entitled, as Guv'nor, to hover and say: Drink all right, Gentlemen? They had thanked him most politely and commended the drink. What sort of a daft game was it anyway? They took all the spades out of the deck and played with the other three suits. He'd heard Ernie say, 'I'll chance a bundle' and the new man say in the next deal, 'I'll go a miz.' They stayed at it until closing time, when Ernie had seen them off like old friends: 'See you next week then, Percy. See you, Arthur.'

What with no part-timers Wednesdays and Ernie on his night off the Guv'nor was not necessarily allowing Ernie to get uppity when he told Ernie lock up and join him at the counter for a nightcap.

'Ernie.'

'Yes, Guv?'

'That was a stranger there tonight. We haven't seen him before.'

'Oh, you mean Percy. Percy Bateman 'e said 'e was. He come in wiv Arthur. They were both 'avin' haircuts over at Alf's. They got talkin' an' it turned out Percy was a player. So Arthur invited him along.'

'Just like that. He Irish, Ernie, by any chance?'

'Dunno, Guv. I doubt it. He don't speak Irish, he speaks cultured if you ask me. Percy's okay, I reckon. Reckon I can tell by now.'

'You don't think it a bit odd, Ernie, do you? I mean you have Ellis first appears out of nowhere with his deck of cards and now over at the barber's he picks up a player just like that – I mean, Ernie, I'm sitting at the barber's, a perfect stranger invites me into a pub for a game, I'd feel I was going to be rolled. Specially if I had a cultured accent.'

'Not if you was a solo player, Guv'nor.'

'What's that to do with it?'

'Solo players, how do I describe it? I suppose it'd be

like me if I won the pools and went off up North Africa on an 'oliday an' bumped into a bloke say from Newcastle. Turns out he's a potman, it's likely we'd fall in together 'avin' things in common. Same with solo players only more so.'

'I heard you saying you'd see him next week. He's coming again then?'

'Yeah, we agreed tonight we'd 'ave a game every night I'm off. Percy lives some place off the Gloucester Road so it's not as though he could come every night.'

'Why Alf's then?'

'He told us: said some bloke 'e worked wiv put him on to Alf's for the eighty-pee job. Seems any time 'e went for an 'aircut round the Gloucester Road they giv 'im the works – perm an' 'ighlights near enough, an' charged accordin'.'

'He used to work as a settler. What's he do now then?'

'He's in a factory up in 'Arlesden. He likes to move around, he said.'

'With his cultured accent, Ernie. It seems he does get about a bit. Maggie Thatcher's work aint done yet, is it, Ernie? Jobs all over the place for blokes like your friend. How come you found out so much about him, you playing cards or gabbing?'

'It's the game, Guv. It's solo. It's not like poker. See, in solo you 'ave to know who you're dealin' with. So you'll know what you can expect. Frinstance, you're playin' with a bloke you know minds himself, never has a drink too many, still has his sixth-birthday money, you know he's not goin' to buck no mad spread.'

'You what, Ernie? I don't understand that damn game.'

'Sorry, Guv. It's you go no trick an' spread your cards on the table after the first lead. Less it's cast-iron there's no one cautious-like will chance it. You get to know each other, see, an' someone says he'll chance a bundle – that's you gotta make nine tricks – say he's cautious, you know bloomin' well he's got a certain nine tricks, maybe ten.'

'I don't know, Ernie. First the lino man and now a bloke from all over the place, breakfast in Paris, haircut in New York. Didn't I hear you say once it takes four to play this solo?'

'That's right but you can manage with three after takin' a suit out. Four's ideal, three's messy but it's better than no game. Definitely better than 'avin Arthur play by himself imaginin' the whole thing.'

'Ernie, I'm going to have a little bet with you. I'm going to bet you a bottle of light you'll get your fourth down the barber's or out of the sky or whatever, and I bet he'll sound barmier than the other two put together.'

'We are always on the lookout, Guv, you must 'ave heard Arthur or me askin' anyone play solo.'

'A bottle of light, Ernie. And mind you keep your ears open an' your eyes peeled.'

Inspector Blake had asked him to be vigilant, was counting on him. Yet he was nervous about calling round the station again: he had nothing to go on. Or had he? Three weeks passed, the third man – Bateman – turning up every Wednesday as promised, and the three of them settled in to their daft game. The Guv'nor did not even ask Ernie for developments beyond: 'Enjoy your game tonight, Ernie?'

'You can say I did, Guv. I got thirteen tricks tonight, didn' I. Course it's easy with three. Different if we 'ad four.'

Thirteen tricks. Nine tricks. No tricks. Cobblers. Three weeks passed. There was no sign of a fourth man. And then, tidying up: 'Funny, remember you asked if my friend Percy was Irish an' I said I didn't think so, he speaks cultured '– turns out he did come from Ireland after all.'

'He *is* Irish, Ernie?'

'Well he come from there. Been here nearly twenty-five years, reckons he's a Londoner now. But funny you should've asked, I mean he don't even look Irish. Got to admit Arthur does at times an' he's from Leeds an' Percy from Ireland doesn't look it. Comic that is.'

The Guv'nor was assailed by the mad suspicion that Ernie himself might be in it – whatever it was – with them. But no. If Ernie wasn't a hundred per cent then the Guv'nor didn't know the Duke of Norfolk from a darkie. The Guv'nor went to the police station. No tea and biscuits this time and no invite to a chair. But Inspector Blake was friendly all the same.

'How are you, Guv'nor? Everything all right I hope?'

The Guv'nor told his story with an apologetic preface: he didn't want to be taking up the Inspector's time, his imagination was probably running away with him. But the Inspector had put him at his ease: 'That's what we're here for, Guv'nor.' Again they thanked him – at least the Inspector did. That young constable had seemed a bit stiff, but then that was probably discipline: presence of a superior officer and all that. His own part-timers were expected to look sharpish when he was around himself. They would certainly look into it and be in touch.

'What do you think now, Taylor? Forget rank and give it to me man to man.'

'You see for yourself, Sir, the chap's clean.'

'I can see that. He was clean. He is. But will he always?'

'We have no reason to suspect otherwise, Sir.'

'Haven't we? Mellick. He's from Mellick, Taylor. That ring a bell?'

'I don't think so, Sir. Should it?'

'Bourke. That's where Bourke came from. Bourke that had his cheeky pint with George Blake in the King's Arms nearly twenty years ago. What do you say to that, Taylor?'

'I suppose that is a coincidence, Sir. But it's the third largest city in the country, Sir. You couldn't go into a bar in Kilburn without finding half a dozen from Mellick. As a matter of fact, Sir, I've an idea that Richard Harris is from Mellick.'

'Who's that, Taylor?'

'The film star.'

'It must be twenty years since I've been to the pictures. But I seem to have heard of the name. Where is this Richard Harris now, Taylor?'

'I've no idea, Sir.'

'My guess is he's in the Bahamas counting his money, not some place writing to the revenue commissioners inviting them to call and collect. What are you smirking at, Taylor, I'm right, am I not?'

'Most likely, Sir.'

'I mean he's not for instance in the King's Arms playing solo. And all those people from Mellick up in Kilburn, *they're* not in the King's Arms playing solo.'

'In the twenty-five years he's been here, Sir, we haven't had him up for as much as staggering after the pubs closed.'

'All right, Taylor. You're probably seeing this clearer than I am. You'll have to watch me, Taylor. Never thought about that damn pub until the Guv'nor dropped in. Now I'm obsessive about the place. And yet, Taylor, the Guv'nor, he doesn't sound like a crank, does he? It's not as though he has a history of being in here reporting every damn-silly thing, is it?'

'He's entitled to an *idée fixe* once in a while same as everyone, Sir.'

'The same as me, you mean.'

'I didn't say that, Sir.'

'You mightn't have been far off the mark if you had,

Taylor. Best put it out of our heads. Come on. Let's do some work.'

Foster supposed that he could say it was Nick Bentley who indirectly led him to the solo school. It was one of those weekdays when he dropped into his local without Gladys. He was content alone with his thoughts but Nick was in the bar – that was Nick, liked to mingle with the crowd in the public bar. Nick had joined him in the lounge, had his drink sent through.

'Alone tonight, Ken?'

'Gladys didn't feel up to it.'

'Well, we can't have the women along all the time, can we? How are things with you, Ken, still bothered about young Robin?'

'Yes, I am bothered as a matter of fact. I should think I have reason to be.'

'You know I often think, Ken, you don't ever let rip, do anything wild, do you?'

'I don't think I understand you.'

'Relaxation. You don't relax enough.'

'We're a busy firm, anything up to twenty articled clerks at a time, five senior partners. What do you expect me to do? After dinner and a shower I call in here for a glass or two. I watch an odd programme on BBC 2. I read books. We have to attend functions. I have a round of golf on Saturday when the weather obliges. We go out with you Saturday nights. Maybe not very exciting by your standards, Nick. But it serves me.'

'I'm thinking of Robin, Ken. Maybe I see something you don't. You're too close.'

'And what's that?'

'You garden?'

'Gladys has the green fingers in our neck of the woods. I do the mowing, the leaves.'

'Tinker with the car on Sunday?'

'Aren't we getting away from the point, if there is a point? No. I never touch the damn thing. If it stops I get out and walk. No idea what's under the bonnet.'

'It's as I said, Ken, you don't give yourself a break.'

'Such as?'

'Gambling. Other women.'

Was it possible that he was trying to steal Gladys from under his nose? Was Nick now going to ease himself into a suggestion of wife swapping? He heard of that happening in the most unlikely of places among people you'd least suspect. 'I suppose I should be flattered. But I always considered myself fortunate to have landed Gladys. And I don't approve of gambling. If that makes me a dry stick – but whatever are you on about?'

'Robin, Ken. I'm trying to help you see it his way. You tell me, would you consider yourself a liberal?'

This was it. If that word didn't lead to wife swapping nothing did. 'As a matter of fact, Nick, I do consider myself a liberal. Though not a libertine, I'm afraid.'

'I'd say you're a moderate.'

'Thank you.'

'But that's just it, Ken. Put yourself in Robin's place. Robin's right enough, we both know that. But Ken, everybody rebels against something. Every one of us at some stage of our lives. But in proportion, Ken. Always in proportion. If you'd been a parson stuffing the good book into Robin all his life, chances are he'd be a right little swinger by now. Or if you'd been a gay dog, been irresponsible, he'd 've reacted against that. But what did you leave him? Moderate liberalism. Not much there for an adolescent to kick against. Still it had to come, it's the nature of the animal, Ken. Okay, he's mature, you're moderate. So in his case we're talking minor gestures, right?'

Nick was an insurance broker. He could talk. To anyone. Yet Foster had to give him this much: he might be on to something here.

'Is that what you call Robin's behaviour, a minor gesture?'

'That's all it is today, Ken. Cohabitation wouldn't get you a headline in a church newsletter now. I move around in my business – more than you do. I see it. Finish your drink.'

Nick was a more knowledgeable man than he was obliged to let on in his business and his business flowed into his private life. As it happened, Foster was not as concerned about Robin now that he had allowed to surface his own ambition to wear Gladys's things. But institutions were not to be mocked. When Nick brought the drink, Foster took a cogitative sip. 'Interesting so far, Nick. You've obviously thought on this. For which I suppose I should thank you. But go on.'

'That's it, Ken. Hope you don't mind my mentioning it.'

'You're saying that if my character had been different Robin might have embraced matrimony without a second thought?'

'That's how I see it.'

'And because I am what I am there's nothing to be done about the situation? Just sit back and admire Robin shacked up?'

'So change. Give it a whirl!'

'Meaning what?'

'Go wild once in a while. Back a horse. Take a lover.'

Unluckily, Foster had raised his glass. The beer went down the wrong way, up his nose and on to his shirt. And Nick didn't laugh. The damn fool probably meant well. Foster went to work with his handkerchief.

'So you propose I should shake off the cobwebs. By

way of encouraging my son to marry I should haunt betting shops, crawl round red-light districts, catch a disease.'

'Look, it's your problem that Robin doesn't want to marry. He's not bothered, is he? If he *saw* you weren't bothered – I don't know, I just put it to you as a theory.'

'Staying theoretical, you say take a lover. It's not like going into a shop and picking out a can of beans. In short – and I am being theoretical – who would have me?'

'Why not?'

Foster tried a guffaw but he coloured. 'I'm not God's gift to women.'

'You have an office in London. There's Bayswater, Paddington, Shepherd's Bush – Don't ask me to spell it out. I'm trying to be helpful. If it's not your fancy, remember that. Just trying to be helpful.'

Foster was pleased to see that Nick was now uncomfortable, probably sorry he had raised the subject at all. As he should be. Unwarranted interference. And then there were certain things one knew about oneself from an early age: one knew one wouldn't ever vote Labour, wear a hairpiece, let one's property run down, take drugs, consort with tarts. And one knew one's son wouldn't shack up. Nick had given him an idea, but no reason Nick should know that. A dry run was what he needed. He saw himself in a part of London where there was no likelihood of bumping into anyone he knew. He would pay the lady in advance, explain his requirements and show her out, first having satisfied himself that her wardrobe was suitable. There would be no point in having to make do with wriggling into a black leather miniskirt. She would have to be a mature lady of the night. Knickers were a must. It would be preferable if she were outsize, on the lines of Gladys herself. Slips, roll-ons, the lot. The irony was that they probably charged you more for what they regarded as the unorthodox. Well, he would pay. And it would be in their own interests to take the garments off him if he did peg out. And put him in a dustbin, as he would request.

'I'll do you the honour of keeping your theory in mind.'

'Yes, do that. Think about it. I wasn't saying you should run out of here with your flies open.'

That was Nick all right. Cheap.

Foster parked the car and strolled around the Bush. He had picked his night. He reasoned that on Wednesdays, in any trade, people were grateful for business. Already he felt jauntier, looser, a spring in his step, devil-may-care, his contentment less index-linked. He was a long way now from having first considered Nick's proposal, as he might have a souped-up balance sheet presented as collateral. And yet his antimacassar life style had not fitted him for nosing ambiguous postcards in shop windows without looking over his shoulder. He reminded himself that nobody took a blind bit of notice in London.

Escort Service: Ring 749 72024

Home Typing. Ask for Angela 322 74965

Lost: Yorkshire terrier, answers to the name Brutus. Ring Mr Hudson 446 27389. Reward

Riding lessons day or night. Enquire within. Box No. 39

Qualified masseuse. Discretion guaranteed. Call Mrs Murphy 202 51348

Foster went to the telephone booth and dialled 749

72024. As he listened to the ringing tone he kneaded his forehead: he was sweating.

'Hallo.' It was a man's voice. Deep. Not an Englishman's voice, not a white voice.

'I'm enquiring, I'm enquiring about your escort service.'

'Yeah man.'

'Can you tell me what the procedure is, please.'

'What you want man? Where you want it? Don't beat about.'

'I'd simply like to know your range.'

'Go fuck.'

Foster stood outside, leaning against the booth. People passed by. He looked at them to see if they looked at him. When they saw him looking at them, they looked at him and quickly looked away. He should have been cleverer with Nick, asked Nick: And suppose – and I'm being theoretical – suppose I did go to one of those Bayswater districts, do I simply pick up a phone and say I'd like one woman please?

He forced himself back into the booth and rang Mrs Murphy. A cracked voice coughed into the phone: 'Yes?'

'I'm enquiring about your service, please.'

'Where are you ringing from, dearie?'

'From a coin box opposite the market in Shepherd's Bush.'

'Here's what you'll do then, dearie. You walk a mile or so down the road from the market, you'll see a pub the King's Arms. Go on till you come to The Lino Shop other side of the road. Turn left and stand under the first lamppost for five minutes. Okay dearie?'

Foster was in a crazed condition going down the road from the market. He was excited at how far he had gone, and yet he was depressed knowing he would go no further. He should maybe have had a drink or two.

In the King's Arms, having bought a glass of beer from

the cold man behind the bar, Foster sat near some low types playing cards. Not knowing the layout and not having thought about his approach, he had happened upon the public bar. He watched the card game without seeing it, listened to the bids without hearing them, taken up as he was with how near he was to wrapping female garments around him and yet for want of recklessness how far.

'You don't 'appen to play by any chance, Sir?'

Foster was jolted by this invitation from an ageing spiv. He reasserted his persona: 'Sorry, I don't gamble.'

'Wasn't suggestin' you blow your lot at Monte Carlo.'

You could get a knife in the ribs for giving a polite answer. That idiot Nick. But he was the bigger fool to have listened to him in the first place. Heavy with disappointment, he sat on and eavesdropped. Odd game whatever it was. I'llgoabundle. I'llgoamiz. I'llgomadandspreadthem.

'How're things at the plant then, Percy? Still don't know what you make there?'

It was true: Bateman worked at carting boxes on pallets from one part of the factory to another under the supervision of a young chap armed with the authority of a docket in triplicate. He could not, to save his life, name the end product.

'I've given notice.'

'I expected it, Bateman. Hard to cure itchy feet.'

Foster was surprised at a pertinent remark like that from a fellow dressed like a mechanic.

'I had forgotten how coarse a group of men can be, gathered together in the name of cheap labour.'

An odd trio.

'You what, Percy?'

'From morning till evening I hear people telling me what stupid cunts and proper charlies they are. Every decipherable hieroglyphic in the toilets is a lewd limerick incorporating a paean to the penis. Men's minds are full of filth and I have my father to thank for my lifelong sojourn among them. Ernie – you didn't return my heart, Ernie.'

'Oh. Sorry. You're puttin' me off you are, talkin' about pains in your privates. You wouldn't want to let it get you down, Percy. All those troubles of yours was long ago.'

'Ernie's right. The thing is to shake off the past. You see me. I did it.'

'Yeah, Arthur, you did an' all. Oh, oh, here's old Murph, must be 'ard to turn a trick Wednesdays, gettin' past it if you ask me. Goodnight, my love.'

'Goodnight, dearie.'

Foster inched closer to the solo school, convinced she would recognise him from his voice on the telephone as he now recognised her cackle. But Christ, he could thank his stars. That scarf. The flyblown overcoat without buttons that hung on her, inside which she wore nothing more glamorous than a potpourri of cardigans and safety pins. She dragged her feet after her in slippers. Suppose they were part of her or she of their set and she called out: Let down tonight I was, dears. There was only one way to duck for cover.

'I say, excuse me, are you actually short a player?'

'Oh, you do play then? We could do with another an' that's no mistake, couldn't we. Couldn't we, lads?'

The three of them were immediately friendly, introducing themselves and shaking his hand.

'Foster. Kenneth Foster. The fact is I don't seem to have come across the game. Perhaps you could run through the rules and explain it to me.'

Apparently he made their night if not that of Mrs Murphy. He spoke quietly in case his voice travelled to where she sat at a table near the counter but he would have been safe had he shouted, as his three companions fell about with laughter. 'Just like that. Explain it to me,' the spiv chuckled. Ernie Gosling he said his name was, and he looked it.

'I happen to be an accountant.'

'Sod it. I've just put the spades back in the deck.'

'Leave them in it, Ernie.' That was the fellow with the red beard. 'We'll give it a try. Not because you're an accountant Foster. As far as that goes, we'd much prefer that you were a messenger boy. Not that you see a messenger boy nowadays. See if you can follow this: we deal out the cards, thirteen each. Highest card triumphs in all suits. You have a choice of bids. You may go nine tricks specifying a suit as trumps. You may be outcalled by someone going the lot, thirteen. You may go a misère – that is, your objective is to score no trick but that bid may be outcalled by someone going a bundle – that is, nine tricks. The bundle may be outcalled by a spread misère: no trick but you expose your cards to the rest of us after the first lead. All right? Clear as mud?'

'What is a trick?'

'See Arthur? Wastin' your time.'

'You play a card, Foster. I play a card. Bateman plays a card, Ernie plays a card. Whichever one of us has played the best card wins. That's a trick.'

'I understand.'

'If you bid and your bid is defeated you pay the rest of us. Five pence a miz, ten pence a bundle, fifty pence thirteen and thirty pence a spread. Shall we begin?'

'What if my bid is successful?'

'If such a miracle occurs, Foster, then of course we shall pay you.'

Ernie Gosling dealt. Foster studied his hand. He had a distribution of suits and sorted them accordingly: five hearts, four spades, two clubs, two diamonds. 'What do I do if I can't make a bid?'

'You pass.'

'I pass.'

'I've nothing . . .'

' . . . rubbish.'

'Nor me.'

Arthur Ellis put his hand out for Foster's cards. He spread them on the table. The three of them analysed them. They nodded to each other. Ellis said: 'Your own deal, Foster.'

'Must get meself a drink.' With the arrival of a third, and the founding of the solo school proper, it had been decided they would buy their own.

'Am I to stand you a bottle of light, Ernie?'

'How's that, Guv'nor?'

'You have a fourth man.'

'Oh. No, I doubt it, Guv. He don't know how to play.'

'I thought—'

'We're teachin' 'im. S'posed to be.'

'Who is he, Ernie? Where'd he come from?'

'Search me. He's an accountant, Mr Foster's his name, he just blew in.'

'Well, keep your ears open.' It was three months since the lino man brought in the Irishman. They boxed clever. Later, he would double that bet of a bottle of light that they had their fourth. He would bet that this new bloke would be here every Wednesday night. This 'accountant'.

Foster dealt the cards. Ellis passed. Bateman bid a spread, drawing from Ellis the supposition: 'Genuine, of course, wouldn't take advantage of the L-plate in our midst, would we?' Ernie Gosling passed. Foster too passed. Ellis led the three of clubs through Bateman. Bateman played the deuce, Gosling the knave and Foster,

not quite sure why, won the trick with the ace of clubs.
Bateman then spread his cards:

CLUBS   lone 7

DIAMONDS   2,4,6 and 9

HEARTS   3,4,5,8,9 and 10

SPADES   lone 2

'A rum spread, Bateman, if ever I saw one.'
'No talk please, Ellis.'
'You are 'avin' a go, eh, Percy?'
'I said no talk.'
Foster studied Bateman's cards. Without any experience
he could see that the spades and diamonds were safe.
The lone seven of clubs and the hearts were vulnerable.
He looked at his own hand:

CLUBS   4,8,9 and 10

DIAMONDS   3,7 and 5

HEARTS   2,7, king and ace

SPADES   lone 5

Foster thought to lead his four of clubs in the hope that
with the deuce and three already played, Ellis and Gosling
might have the five and six between them forcing
Bateman to take the trick with his lone seven. But what if
the five and six were both in Ellis's or Gosling's hand?
Foster thought again. He studied the heart situation.
Bateman had six hearts. He himself had four hearts

99

including the deuce. There remained three hearts between Ellis and Gosling and he could identify these as the queen, knave and six. Foster reasoned that all he had to do was lead hearts three times. Ellis and/or Gosling would then be out of hearts. He would then play his deuce and Bateman would be obliged to beat it. Game over.

Foster led the ace of hearts, Ellis played a spade. Bateman the ten of hearts and Gosling the knave of hearts. Foster led his king of hearts. Ellis played another spade, Bateman the nine of hearts and Gosling the six of hearts. Gosling's play puzzled Foster. The only heart remaining apart from Bateman's and his own was the queen, and it had to be in Gosling's hand since Ellis had been unable to follow the two heart leads. Foster had two hearts left, the deuce and seven. If he led the seven Gosling would have to play the queen and so win the trick. From Foster's viewpoint Gosling should have discarded the queen and knave on the leads of the ace and king, instead of discarding the knave and six and holding on to the queen. But maybe the game was more abstruse than it appeared. Yet he could count. It was his profession.

'Take your time, Mr Foster. We have all night. At least until closing time. And then we can always finish under a streetlight.'

'Don't pay no attention, Mr Foster. Percy's just tryin' to put you off. You leave 'im be now, Percy, he's only learnin'. You're doin' fine, Mr Foster – oh dear. Oh dear, oh dear. I've made a booboo.'

'No talk, please!'

'Bateman's right. Shut up Ernie and let Foster get on with it.'

Because Gosling had not played according to convention as Foster saw it, Foster was now in rough country. But as he tried to reason out the next lead,

Bateman began to drum his fingers on the table: 'I think we should order sandwiches.' Foster ignored him. He could (a) lead his seven of hearts, in which case Gosling would take the trick with the queen and then Gosling would be in the driving seat; (b) lead the four of clubs as he had originally been tempted to do, hoping for a distribution of the five and six of clubs; (c) lead a low diamond and let whichever of the two of them who wanted take command. As an accountant Foster liked to do things by the book. There was no more justification for leading the four of clubs than there had been first day – less so, as Ellis by discarding spades showed that he was safe in clubs and of course had no hearts. Gosling had not had a chance to indicate his position, whatever Gosling was up to hanging on to the queen of hearts. The idea of leading a low diamond to let Ellis or Gosling take command was anathema to Foster – one did not wash one's hands of affairs. So, despite Gosling's erratic performance, Foster played by the book. He led the seven of hearts. Ellis discarded the eight of spades, Bateman played the five of hearts and Ernie Gosling won the trick with the queen of hearts.

Ellis, assuming the deuce of hearts was in Gosling's hand, turned to Bateman: 'Pay up and look happy.'

'No talk.'

Ernie Gosling bit his nails as he studied his hand:

CLUBS	queen and king
DIAMONDS	queen
SPADES	3,4,7,10, queen and ace

He could not lead his king or queen of clubs and allow Bateman to get rid of the seven. The queen of diamonds was too high a card to use in an effort to let Foster back in. Although he had six spades himself and Ellis had been discarding spades at least Bateman had one spade, the safe deuce. There was a chance of putting Foster back in with a spade. Ernie led the three of spades. As it happened, Foster had only one spade, the five and Ellis – having no spade under the five – played the king, Bateman the deuce. Ellis, now in command, studied his remaining cards:

CLUBS	5 and 6
DIAMONDS	8, 10, jack, king and ace
SPADES	knave

Ellis ruled out leading back the knave of spades – Foster had only been able to muster the five on Ernie's lead of spades. Maybe Ernie wanted a spade back so as he could discard a high club. But if that was the case the spades must be in Foster's hand. Where the hell was the deuce of hearts? What were the two of them up to? Was the deuce of hearts missing from the deck? It was too early to put the five or six of clubs through Bateman's seven, as the only club under the seven yet unplayed was the four and one or other of his partners would have to be out of clubs for that to succeed. There was only one thing for it. Play a low diamond and let one of those two bloody fools back in. He led the eight of diamonds. Bateman followed suit with the six. Ernie Gosling played his last diamond, the queen. Foster, who had the three, five and seven of diamonds, played the three.

'Oh dear,' Ernie Gosling said.

'No talk.'

'There will be when this game is over,' Ellis threatened.

Ernie's remaining cards read:

CLUBS   queen and king

SPADES   4,7,10, queen and ace

To lead the king or queen of clubs would make Percy's seven safe. A better idea would be to lead a low spade: admittedly it would give Bateman a discard, but it would put Ellis in and he could come back a diamond and put Foster in and then Foster could play his deuce of hearts and catch Percy. Yeah, that was it, that was the way.

Ernie led the four of spades. Foster discarded the five of diamonds. Ellis played his knave of spades. Bateman had to make a decision. The deuce of hearts was out there some place and he had three hearts left himself. Here was a chance to discard one of them. Or he could get rid of his seven of clubs. The seven of clubs might or might not be safe whereas the heart was definitely at risk. Yet a club would have to be led soon – only four out so far – whereas whoever had the heart might not get back in. He discarded the seven of clubs. They were down to six cards each. Ellis could see Bateman's spread out on the table:

DIAMONDS   2,4 and 9

HEARTS   3,4 and 8

His own hand read: 10, knave, king and ace of diamonds. One of those two fools had the deuce of hearts. Bateman's bid should have been defeated long ago. There bloody well would be enquiries. He could not put either of them in by leading a diamond, as he calculated there was only one diamond out between them and that was lower than the diamonds in his own hand: he could recall Ernie playing the queen. There was no choice but to lead the five of clubs. Bateman discarded the eight of hearts. Gosling played the queen of clubs. Foster followed suit with the ten.

Ernie Gosling looked at his remaining five cards, and began to roll a cigarette. His king of clubs was unbeatable, Mr Foster had played the ace in the very first trick. And he had failed earlier to put Mr Foster in with the lead of the three of spades. And when he, Ernie, had been put in again and come back with the four of spades Mr Foster had been off. The fact of the bleeding matter was that there wasn't another spade out except his own. He tipped over his cards.

'That's it. I'm in an' I can't get out.'

The Guv'nor tore the band off a cigar. Wednesday night was bad for business, but it was odd – he always did like Wednesday nights. Gave you a chance to take stock of your situation, relax and think where you were going, how far you'd come since you were a fiddler yourself. Herself was out in the lounge chatting to the few who liked a quiet drink – although you couldn't get much quieter than the public bar at the moment. There were no more than half a dozen in the games room and they had just been served. He had a chance to light up. Old Murphy over there, must have been Irish once – poor sod, a bloke'd want to be hard up. Still, she managed a bit weekends, blokes steamed, older blokes with maybe a once-a-year itch. She sat there so quietly, eating a cigarette and pulling that old coat together around her to keep out the chill. The poor old thing probably had memories, been good-looking once, romantic. On Wednesday nights you got a chance to see how well off you were in comparison to some poor sods. He uncapped a bottle of light to bring out to Mrs Murphy, give her a treat. Maybe he should stand to the solo school. That was an idea. He might pick up something in a manoeuvre like that that Ernie mightn't spot in a month.

'How's Mrs Murphy tonight then?'

'Keepin' the best side out, Guv'nor.'

'Have this one on me then.'

'That's decent of you, Guv'nor. Cheers.'

'You didn't see it? YOU STUPID DAFT BUGGER, ERNIE! Say come cards come. Say COME CARDS COME, Ernie!'

The Guv'nor had begun to pour the light into Mrs Murphy's glass. He knocked the drink on to her lap and let the bottle slip out of his hands. He was at the card table just as the lino man was on his feet battering the cards at Ernie who was holding his hands above his head to ward them off. The Irishman was leaning back in his chair, laughing. That was their form, used to it.

'What the hell's going on here?' The Guv'nor caught hold of the lino freak's hand.

'It's all right, Guv'nor, only a joke,' Ernie said. Ernie was grinning.

'A joke? You call a rumble a joke, Ernie?'

'Not a rumble, Guv, all part of the game.'

He had run over to protect Ernie, and here was Ernie and the lino man and Paddy all laughing at him. The fourth man, boxing clever, sat there stony-faced, his lips prim.

'What's it all about then, Ernie? What's all the shouting and chucking the cards about, eh?'

'Reckon I deserved it, Guv. See, I never spotted the queen of hearts in me hand, hidden behind a spade it was, an' cos a that Percy made his spread. It was just one of those things.'

Only for Inspector Blake he'd've bounced the lot of them. At least here they were where they could be watched. Come closing time the Guv'nor stood Ernie a nightcap.

'Thank you, Guv. Looks like you were right, Mr Foster says he can be here Wednesdays. He stays overnight in London once a week. So I owe you a bottle of light, Guv.'

'Save it. How'd he happen in here tonight, Ernie?'

'Mr Foster? Doin' some business this area so he said. Some company's books, he didn't say which – seems he fancies a stroll after all his office work an' just dropped in.'

'Out of the blue—'

'Yeah, you could say that. But know what, Guv? I can't hardly believe it meself: he never played before, never once. I mean never played no game like it neither an' he sat down an' picked it up jus' like that. Mother's milk to him, it was. We were all watchin' an' he didn't play one wrong card.'

'Stays overnight in London, does he? Where's he from then?'

'Nottingham. He 'as this accountancy business that has a branch in London. I reckon that's how he picked up the game so fast, bein' an accountant an' all. That and card sense – that's what Percy said, 'e said it had nothing to do with Mr Foster's profession, that you either 'ave it or you don't.'

'A branch in London? OK if it was the other way round— Foster. Hang on, get a Biro. What's his first name, Ernie?'

'Kenneth. You suspicious of him or what, Guv'nor?'

'I'll put it this way, Ernie. Are you suspicious of him?'

'I wouldn't think so. I mean he could be checked up on, couldn't 'e?'

'You're damn right he could.'

'Well, Taylor?'

'He has a busy practice in Nottingham, Sir. He does

have a branch in London. He does come down once a week, stays at the Regent's Palace.'

'We accept all that, Taylor. But why, Taylor, after ten years, does he suddenly pop up in the King's Arms and make up a fourth for their solo game when he's never played cards before in his life? Explain that to me, Taylor.'

'I accept that is a coincidence, Sir.'

'No, Taylor. We'll leave the coincidences to Agatha Christie. Although I'm damned if I can make head or tail of it. We've no connection whatever between any of them. But it's a rum world today – all this ideology, you've no idea who'll suddenly emerge as a terrorist. From the best of families. Breeding, education. That Bourke, you know, the bloke who sprung Blake, over in Ireland his education didn't get beyond reform school. Yet what was Bourke doing in the Scrubs? He edited the prison magazine. You know me by now Taylor, I'm not a hard man. But you wonder sometimes is it a good idea to turn prisons into universities. I had just about accepted Ellis and Bateman. You could understand a lino nut getting together with a drifter, all those jobs Bateman had, hardly stopping long enough in any one place – except to set up something that we don't know of yet?'

'They do that, Sir. The Irish. They move around. I think it might be something to do with the fact that they're immigrants, Sir. They find it difficult to settle down even though they're well received here. It could be that they're so near yet so far away from home.'

'There is that, Taylor. This Gosling, he doesn't disturb me. A gregarious bunch, potmen. I should imagine they have to be. But dammit, Foster doesn't fit. Accepting all coincidences, Taylor, forgetting we're policemen, leaving aside all suspicions: let Foster wander in off the street and have a night's cards with strangers – ignore it that he never played before and takes to it like a duck to water – what would make a chap as respectable as we know Foster is, what would draw him back to mix with a potman, a lino man and a Paddy?'

In the country inn on Saturday night Kenneth Foster looked back with contentment on the six months since he had happened upon the solo school in the King's Arms. It was Saturday nights Nick said, in his snide way: 'Golf this morning, Ken?' That was the life the dull lived, golf on Saturday mornings. And Nick knew that on Saturday afternoons Gladys did her gardening while he prepared the evening meal. But neither Nick nor Gladys knew that that very afternoon, only six months since he joined the solo school, after coating the whiting fillets in seasoned flour he had stolen away to her bedroom. He had opened her underwear drawer and put his head in and sniffed. And he had rushed immediately back downstairs.

Nick had his hand on her knee to accompany his trifling conversation. But what would they say if they knew he played cards? What, you Kenneth? Play cards with a potman? Go on, you're pulling our legs. Yes, a potman. And a madman. Listen to him! Yes, a madman: divorced by his wife, linoleum cited as correspondent. Go on, Ken, somebody interfere with your drink? And a shiftless Paddy can't hold a job down for more than five minutes? He *is* comical tonight, a potman, a madman and an Irishman – I know, he's up to something in London once a week and that's his cover-up. You'll have to do better than that.

That he was good at solo, that he was in fact the best player in the school, proved to Foster that he was adaptable. He was not just a good accountant, he would have been good at whatever he had taken up. And he took the madman's observation as a compliment: 'You know, Foster, for an accountant you play with flair.' That was how Ellis saw it. And Gosling had an absurd theory that those who were orderly in their affairs played solo with reticence. Not the way Gosling put it of course. What they did not understand was that he was prepared to take a chance now that he was gambling – not that that was how he saw his adventurous bids. No, it was the decision to turn up again and again every Wednesday constituted the audacity, how he played merely an extension. He considered Bateman an in and out player, erratic, no doubt a boost for Gosling's theory. But Bateman's private life was a model of consistency. Founded on the notion that the mark of Cain was on him because he was reluctant to have his head kicked in as a youngster Bateman was obdurate in his nomadic pursuit of the means to keep himself in misery. They were overburdened with imagination. The problem was historical, it was down to not having had to govern. Still, the fellow knew his place and when he did offer his tuppence worth it was not abrasive. And Gosling, in defiance of his own creed, was a conservative with the cards in his hand. He did not take chances. And when Gosling did succeed when he manifestly should have failed, Foster's conduct of the postmortem usually established that either Bateman or Ellis was at fault.

If Foster himself had flair, Bateman was erratic and Gosling conservative, it was difficult to categorise Ellis, the founder of the solo school. They all knew something of each other by now, knew Foster's concern for his son Robin, Bateman's cross, the little irritations in Gosling's life. And of course they had been subjected to the lino crusade. Foster tried to put himself in Ellis's place and failed. There was Ellis in his forties, as he himself and Bateman were, cut off from all intercourse with his rightful social grouping. He lived in a loft over the lino shop. Foster would concede that Ellis might be fulfilled peddling lino to his rough customers but when he closed shop in the evening, fried his egg or whatever, how did he cope with his own company before putting his talisman under his arm and shuffling over the road to the King's Arms? For the sake of argument accepting Gosling's theory, Foster tried to construct Ellis from his play. But Ellis was simply and purely mechanical. There was no life to either his mistakes or his triumphs. Complimented or chastised his attitude was that of indifference. It was as though the game was as much a staple of his existence as bread and butter and there was no etiquette governing the consumption of such menial fodder, and if there was it did not apply when one dined out in rags on a desert island. Ellis's play was indeed lifeless and – a tick in the box here for Gosling – this was because Ellis was dead. By the way, Gladys, Nick, one of our players is dead. Ellis had said on that first night to Bateman: 'The thing is to shake off the past. You see me. I did it.' Ellis tried hard of course. He wrapped his lino round him, clutched his cards, grew his beard, pulled on his cords but like the dust that escaped the vacuum in his hated carpets particles of the past ducked through.

One week the solo school philosophers nibbled at the shacking-up problem, the next the loneliness of the linoleum lover, the properties of paper-hat fetishists or – and here they were obliged to be delicate, they didn't want to have to play with three – the desirability of Bateman keeping his head out of the oven.

'Know what I think, Percy? I think you done the right thing not 'avin your 'ead kicked in an' as it was you got your jaw busted, didn' you. An' that other bloke, what d'you say 'is name was?'

'Frankie Timmons.'

'Yeah, that bloke, chap you said lost his ear, that was plain daft if you ask me.'

'Frankie Timmons will be remembered for ever with affection for his gallantry. If I had children they would inherit my shame.'

Ellis saw a contradiction. 'Bateman, you just told us nobody goes to him for a haircut.'

'The older brigade do. Those with the memories.'

'They can't have much hair. They must be dying out.'

'You don't understand. None of you.'

'I don't,' Foster said severely. 'What about discretion being the better part of valour? Or would you have it that that is indigenous to Britain?'

'It's a question of honour.'

'To be kicked in the head?'

'It was honour then. When I saw the Garryowen pack I didn't fly-kick from any motive other than cowardice.'

'If it comes to that, cowardice isn't a crime, you know.'

'It used to be. There were no psychiatrists then. Pre-carpet days, as Ellis might think of them.'

Bateman had a bitter sense of humour. Probably the saving of him. Though he would never put his head in an oven. Too un-Irish that – too prosaic you might say, for their mad imaginations. Ironic, Foster could thank Nick there with his hand on Gladys's knee for having led him to the solo school and awakened the philosopher in him. And he could stand back and see himself as well as the others. They were all escaping reality in the solo school. For some, himself, the change was as good as a rest. He had discovered as well that he could mix outside his own circles, give as good as he got. He rather fancied now that he might even have survived the Army and he could imagine what a low lot were to be found there. As for Gosling, it surely made his day to be in the company of younger men above his station. But the other pair, Ellis and Bateman: Foster was doubtful. Ellis rejected life, there was no other way to look at that. Ellis would probably become deranged – or eccentric, as a tolerant society liked to put it – end up kicking a dog out of his way on the footpath, that sort of thing. Muttering to himself, hoarding his money behind loose bricks. Bateman just might soldier on to the end: they had low expectations, booze, a roof over their head, the occasional sirloin.

And yet, dammit, during the six days of the week that Foster was not playing cards in the King's Arms in Shepherd's Bush, he actually missed them. Looked forward to the solo school. Looked back with satisfaction. So much so that he discovered Gladys was kicking his leg: 'Kenneth. Kenneth, you nodding off? Olive's talking to you.' And Olive: 'A penny for them, Kenneth.' Nick, of course, winked at him.

THE FIFTH

'AS I SAID, get married again.'

Quaint, that, coming from Malcolm. Gay men were so tolerant of the institution, wishing it on everyone except themselves. *Unipolitan* was directed at single chins, rock-like busts, bellies-in and taut bums: the not so young and those who wished to remain not so young. It was a vade-mecum that demonstrated in simple language and simpler pictures how to trickle a spoor from eyes across a crowded room all the way to the nearest registry office. *Unipolitan* was successful. So much so that it devoured its own market. In marriage chins doubled, busts drooped, bellies sagged and bums took to sloth and the tenants of the run-down assets defected to knitwear, recipes and *Woman's Own*. But sales were not irretrievably lost since marriages ended in divorce except among the poor and the spiritual, who could not afford divorce, *Unipolitan* or its advertised products. If marriage was not for *Unipolitan* then Diana Hayhurst was not for marriage.

She was now wearing pleated gaberdine culottes, a brown leather belt, a striped silk blouse with padded shoulders and front overpanel, a paisley-patterned wool/

mohair-mix cardigan and gloves; she carried an umbrella and briefcase, and altogether that lot had cost her £872.35.

'Diana, why do you need a sounding board? Remember at *Woman's Own* you looked into your own heart and found *Unipolitan*. You were on your way before you met Hooper or Fyncham.'

'I used to think that too, Malcolm, but there were pigs everyplace then. Now they're all cured, you can't find one. There isn't a pig of a real man left or if there is I don't run into them. It frightens me that I have deballed the Commonwealth. Apart from Fyncham I don't know an old-fashioned man and yet they must be someplace – wherever it is, like elephants, they go to die.'

'They're all over the place, Diana.'

'Where? Tell me where?'

'In the public bars, I expect. In the clubs. You can't find them because they don't congregate in female society.'

'Malcolm, take me to a public bar.'

'I do not frequent public bars.'

Afterwards the Guv'nor claimed that he had said to himself Ay, ay, as soon as they walked into the public bar. But this was just a figure of speech. It was not the Guv'nor's habit to talk to himself. The woman would have made his lounge look shabby let alone the public bar. Bold as brass, she was, crossing her legs on the bar stool so that the Guv'nor had to draw his own knees together, something he did not have to do very often nowadays in the public bar or anywhere else, what with being so busy and on the go all the time and what with herself usually on duty with him.

'I'll have a gin and tonic, Malcolm, please.'

You didn't get Malcolms in public bars either. Freds, Alfs, Ernies. But never Malcolms. This Malcolm was edgy: 'Gin and tonic. I'll have a lager and lime.'

He didn't look a ladies' man but you never knew, probably had money. Ugly as pigs some of the richest men in the world were, and you saw them photographed in the papers with racing glasses round their necks and stunning women linking them.

'Happy now, Diana?'

They had their backs to the counter. The Guv'nor thought that rude. He would have been happy to pass the time in polite conversation had they shown a willingness. It was not as if there was anything else to entertain them in the bar Wednesday night. Only Ernie and his gang of pontoon players, or whatever the daft game was again. She slinked off her stool and the Guv'nor's knees hugged each other as he watched her high-heel it towards the solo school. The Malcolm chap shook his head and turned round. 'Quiet tonight, Guv'nor?'

'Yes. But it would be Wednesday night. Not many places doin' much Wednesday nights.'

It must be a treat for Ernie and the boys having such an audience. She just stood there with her arms folded watching them and the gormless lot trying to act casual as though they were used to that class of society. And then:

'Would you gentlemen consider playing dealer out?'

The Guv'nor could hear what she said because she was obviously a woman of authority who liked herself to be heard. But Ernie and his bunch of morons were a gang of whisperers, except when they were at each other's throats, having one of what they called their post-mortems. He watched their heads move consulting each other and dammit if the next thing wasn't her ladyship pulling a chair up to the table and ordering back: 'Malcolm, may I have my drink, please.'

What sort of a game was 'deal her out'? Did she blow

in from the same place they all did, the blue, with a brand-new game they all just happened to know how to play – if he could be allowed to believe his own eyes and ears? And here was our friend Malcolm making off with the gin and tonic and his own lager and lime, leaving the Guv'nor deserted and not knowing what the bloody hell was going on. This Malcolm taking up a position as spectator and nodding away at Ernie and the mob as though it was the most natural thing in the world. Greek peasants weren't that friendly to tourists for Christ sake and this was London. The Guv'nor leaked with curiosity. It was his own bar. He was entitled to go out and collect glasses.

'All right, Ernie?' The Guv'nor enquired. Ernie was sitting there rolling one of his gaspers, and here was the thing: Ernie didn't have cards. Ernie wasn't playing.

'Goodnight Guv.' Ernie winked.

'Ernie, would you like to have a look at the draught-lager barrel for a sec? I seem to be having trouble with it.' The Guv'nor winked back.

'Sure, Guv'nor. Excuse me folks, won't be a tick.'

It was a criminal waste, was what it was. Given *half* his chances, less even, and the Guv'nor would have out of them what Ernie couldn't suss in a month of Sundays. He was a trier right enough, it was just that he was never meant for a plant – not devious enough. No, what the job cried out for was an ex-fiddler: the kind of dab hand with the books that the Guv himself had been in his young day.

'You can search me, Guv'nor. We dunno who she is yet. I didn't take much notice of her as she come in, I had a sure nine tricks: ace, king, queen of hearts seven times and the ace, king, queen of—'

'Sod what you had. I heard her. She walked up and asked you to change your game. She had a new game and you all knew how to play it, just like that.'

'No, no, Guv. You 'ave it wrong there. We didn't change our game, Guv. We just agreed to play dealer out.'

'Isn't that what I said, am I talking to myself, Ernie? And when I come down for the glasses I see you're not playing. What's going on, Ernie?'

'We're playin' dealer out, Guv. It's my deal so I don't play that hand. Percy's deal, 'e don't play that hand and so on. You can only play with four, you must know that by now, Guv, from 'earin' me talk.'

'From 'earin' you talk, Ernie, what I must be is round the twist. Are you tellin' me it's a game for four, you have four and suddenly someone comes along wants to play and you say right one of us will fall out every hand to let that someone play? You telling me that, Ernie?'

'Yeah, now you have it, Guv. You seen her. She asked, we just looked at each other and none of us said no. You seen her.'

'So she's a looker. Ernie, in your time in the motor factors, suppose some stranger calls in, even a looker, right? Calls in out the blue and says Ernie how would you like to piss off for a few hours and let me do some of your job and collect some of your wages cos that's what it sounds like to me, Ernie, job sharing like you hear nutty professors on the telly saying we should be doing to get down unemployment. Would you like that, Ernie?'

'Course I wouldn't, Guv, but this is different, this is often done where you've got five want to play, I did it in the Army.'

'She knows how to play?'

'Yeah, but she's not great. She just let Mr Foster get away with a spread, he had four diamonds without the deuce an'—'

'Stop! Don't talk like that. It hurts me. Ernie, get back up there and keep your ears open. Ask questions. At closing time I want to know what she has for breakfast. You understand?'

At closing time the Guv'nor was unlucky in that he was bending down slotting empties into a crate when he heard the scream. He hit his head off a shelf. With his hand soothing his pole he looked out and saw the woman clutch the Irishman by the cheeks and kiss him on the forehead. It was then the Guv'nor realised that it hadn't been a scream, more a cry of delight: 'Yippee,' she had shouted, and if he was not mistaken she had also roared 'Fucking marvellous!' He pressed a two-pee piece to the lump on his head but it was not as apt for the job as an old half-crown might have been. She'd toddled off with her Malcolm shouting 'Toodle-oo' back at them.

The Guv'nor had not the patience to let Ernie empty the ashtrays. 'Give us your glass. Now. What you got, Ernie? Didn't I just hear your new friend swearing? Did I see her kissing Paddy? Eh, Ernie? Did I? Or am I dreaming, Ernie?'

'No, you're not dreamin', Guv'nor.'

'Well then.'

''Member I was tellin' you she let Mr Foster get away with 'is spread when he 'ad four diamonds without the deuce—'

'Ernie!!'

'Sorry, Guv. Only it was just then after she copped on she'd blown it – after Percy an' Arthur pointed it out, that is, she said Fuck. But I'm getting ahead of myself. Like you told me I acted crafty after a couple of hands an' I said "By the way my name's Gosling, Ernie Gosling," an' I went around the table an' introduced Arthur, Percy and Mr Foster. So then she hadn't much choice but to say who she was. An' you'll never guess who she turned out to be.'

'Who?'

'Her name's Diana Hayhurst but that didn't mean nothin' to me. But she started askin' what line we were all in so I said I was more or less retired which is the truth apart from my job here an' Arthur didn't need much proddin' to tell the story of *his* life over again, about the lino an' all. She had to drag it out of Mr Foster that he was an accountant – an' Percy, well, you know the score there, Guv'nor, he don't like to talk much about 'is job, he hates it. He said he was – an' I'm sayin' it like 'e did – 'e said 'e was an itinerant unhandyman, somethin' like that. Then naturally I said what line of business was she in herself, if she was in business tho' I'd been thinkin' the bloke wiv her watchin' us was loaded an' she was 'is wife. But it turns out she owns a magazine an' the funny thing about it is Linda reads that magazine even Betty sometimes flicks through it, *Unipolitan,* I seen it lyin' around the 'ouse—'

'*Unipolitan?* She *owns Unipolitan,* Ernie?'

'She said she did.'

'I see, Ernie. She owns *Unipolitan* so the natural thing for her to do would be to drop in here on Wednesday night for a game of solo, wouldn't it, Ernie? I mean it would follow, wouldn't it?'

'I think you're bein' sarcastic, Guv'nor.'

'Me, Ernie? I wouldn't. But you carry on, Ernie. Don't mind me.'

'She's originally from Toronto in Canada an' she goes back home every Christmas for an 'oliday without fail, she told us an' her parents are two doctors – they used to always play solo with two other doctor friends once a week just like our school, but just a couple of years back one of their doctor friends dies an' they hadn't four. Just before a Christmas it happened and when she turns up the doctor whose wife died or the wife whose husband died, I forget which, they was all there in the 'ouse for drinks an' moanin' that their solo game was bust up an' she said she'd give it a go.'

'You believe that, Ernie?'

'I do, Guv'nor, cos it figures. The way she played tonight you could tell she was rusty. You take meself, it was years since I played when Arthur come along an' I had to be reminded of the game meself. But the bit I find amazin', Guv'nor, is the language comin' from someone of 'er class. You can't shock me, Guv'nor, over twenty years in the motor factors let alone the Army. I see the bints in the motor factors changin' from the days when they'd crack the odd blue joke an' blush to where they'd fuck you to your face, if you'll excuse me bein' so blunt. But you don't expect it from the better-educated, do you, Guv?'

'I don't know about that. You'd hardly call them thicks in the BBC, Ernie, *they* wouldn't think of themselves that way, I bet, an' they're the teachers at it, aren't they? You'd have to put your kids and granny to bed when the BBC puts on a play. Realism, they call it. But she has a mouth on her, has she?'

'She has an' all, Guv'nor. As I said, when she let Mr Foster get away with 'is wonky spread she said Fuck an' I thought it was a one-off but then she made another mistake, which was understandable cos she was rusty, but when she does she says: I've made a balls of that, Gentlemen, sorry. An' it went on like that, Guv'nor. You never heard such language but no one wanted to be the first to mention it, least I didn't, I felt somehow it wasn't my place bein' a potman an' her bein' who she was—'

'Hold on, Ernie, I don't like to hear you talk like that. If the prime minister came in here with a mouth like that you'd have as much right as anyone to say put a stop to it. I won't have you run yourself down, you hear?'

'It was Percy done it in the end. I thought if it was to

come from anyone it'd be Mr Foster but it was Percy. We were just sayin' we'd time for one last hand when she started askin' how often we played an' when we told her it was once a week Wednesdays she invites herself along, she says Wednesdays is perfect for her an' we'd see a better player next week. Well, we weren't goin' to tell her we had enough by ourselves an' that we didn't need her because that's not the way solo players do things, it's like if I was a fifth meself I'd appreciate people playin' dealer out to let me in. An' so would Arthur and Percy. But up pipes Percy an' I had to laugh the way he put it, he says "Excuse me but if you do intend to join us I'm very much afraid you'll have to conform" – that was the word – "conform to our standards." We was all lookin' at 'im, Arthur, Mr Foster an' me, not knowin' what the bloody 'ell he was on about an' her ladyship likewise. She says "And how do I do that exactly, Mr Bateman?" Percy says "You'll have to buy a bar of soap." Arthur, Mr Foster an' me, we still don't know what Percy's on about no more than she does, raisin' 'er eyebrows. An' Percy says "To wash your mouth out" cos Percy says he's not goin' to be here next week to listen to her cheap vocabulary an' what does she do but roar out "Yippee!" an' grab him an' plonk a smacker on his forehead an' go on about Percy bein' fuckin' marvellous.'

'And then she went off saying toodle-oo. What does that mean, Ernie?'

'You what, Guv'nor?'

'Ernie, there's toodle-oo and toodle-oo. Did she mean Toodle-oo goodbye nice to have met you but you won't see me again, or did she mean Toodle-oo see you next week, and the week after and for ever until a sixth comes along out of you know where?'

'It's hard to say, Guv. But you can rest easy about anyone else showin' up wantin' to play. Dealer out's as far as we go, school's full. Anyone else shows up wants a game can start their own school.'

'You sure, Ernie? I don't need to draw up plans for an extension then?'

'Go on, Guv, you are comic tonight.'

'Well, Taylor?'

'Sir?'

'This Hayhurst person, rum, eh?'

'Like all the others, Inspector, she turned out to be exactly who the Guv said she was.'

'That's not the issue, Taylor. You've seen her on chat shows, you tell me. How would you describe her, Taylor, how would you classify her? Would you describe her as a balanced type?'

'She's a very successful businesswoman in a tough market. I'd have to say she strikes me as very balanced indeed. As you see from the report there was once a suggestion that she might feature in the honours list but her personal life told against her at the time. She might yet make it.'

'That does not impress me in the slightest, Taylor. The Beatles, not to mention owners of strip clubs, have found their way in. You know I often think, Taylor, when I think of England, I often think to myself who is England? And do you know Taylor, I sometimes think of myself. I see a retired chap who's put it in from day one all along the line. Regardless of schooling. Everyone does not have the same advantages. But I see someone who has gone straight and kept his head down, and at the end of his days on pension out in the garden in some place comfortably distant from the big cities – especially this city. And I think to myself. That's England. Every time I see something on television or in the papers, say, Dunkirk, the Battle of Britain, Remembrance Day, I think: For what? For Whom? And I see a figure tending his roses or his runner beans. I don't see the Beatles, Taylor, or strip-club peers and I can tell you I don't see this damn woman either. Are you with me, Taylor?'

'Yes, Inspector. Though you must agree that the Beatles did make a positive contribution to the balance of payments.'

'Taylor, we are not really a nation of shopkeepers, as some have found out to their cost.'

'Yes, Inspector.'

'Look at this, Taylor: she was married – Hooper the publisher, not that I'm suggesting he would have been an angel no more than anyone else in his business, although you do have the house of Macmillan. But they weren't getting along. Did she go about the business in a civilised way? They could have cited mutual incompatibility or the very reason that they did want to split up, which was that Hooper wanted an heir and she wasn't having any. No. This candidate for the honours list as you see her, hauled an Irish navvy into the lavatory of a public house and had him service her with a divorce witness present to record the event for posterity. Why? To protect her honour. You can just imagine the circles she moved in. Of course you may well be right, Taylor: Her Majesty may decide to step down, Prince Charles might fall off his polo pony, we could be in for a King Andrew. And since even with her Majesty there safe and sound we've already had a chap nicknamed Sleazy Weazy being told to arise Sir Stanley I wouldn't be one damn bit surprised if this Hayhurst didn't become a dame of the British Empire.'

'I thought the honours list was drawn up by the government of the day, Inspector.'

'Don't split hairs, Taylor. Now, consider this. Let's get serious and stick to the point. Take that very incident with the navvy in the lavatory. I don't know if you're familiar with Ireland? I must say I'm not as much as I should be. But this navvy was from a place called County Mayo on the western seaboard. They're big mountainy men in that part of the country. They should be dying out because I gather every damn one of them emigrates as soon as he has his legs under him. They have big shoulders, hands like shovels, you have a share of them in the Irish police, you have them in the building trade here. In America, they're the same: in the cops or on the roads. Everything about them is big. Very big. Everything about them. Are you getting my drift, Taylor?'

'I'm not so sure that I am, Inspector.'

'I'm saying these Mayo chaps are big men. Big in every way. Big, shall we say, Taylor, big in endowment. Don't ask me to spell it out, Taylor: BIG. Every place. You with me now, Taylor?'

'I think so, Inspector.'

'We both know of ladies just as, shall we say, respectable as this Hayhurst but once they've had a taste of ethnic sex – to be blunt about it, your ordinary Tommy 'Atkins won't satisfy them any more. Now just supposing, Taylor, Hayhurst was more than satisfied in the lavatory with the Mayo navvy while she was seeing to her honour? Nobody ever said that's a lovely bar of chocolate and not gone on to buy a second bar, have they? I'll be fair to this Hayhurst, everything I say applies the other way round. To men. Sex is sex. Judgement flies out the window. Every terrorist group we've ever heard of at home or abroad, they're having it off amongst themselves. It's the juiciest ideological carrot there is because it strikes the mind out first shot. Smile all you like, Taylor, but now shoot me down. Go on, drive through my theory!'

'With respect, Sir, you've driven through it yourself.'

'Educate me, Taylor.'

'If Diana Hayhurst is as experienced as you suggest, and we do know she is, then some poor labourer won't turn her head toward subversion, no matter how good he is.'

'I'll grant you that. But I wasn't leaping from A to Z. As a matter of fact she probably never saw that particular Paddy again. Use your imagination. She might be at a party. You can imagine the parties in publishing circles. The League of Nations isn't in it: writers, playwrights, the lot. They cross national barriers. She turns left and meets a famous underground Chilean poet, right the latest defecting Russian – and *they're* all poets, aren't they? She moves among the guests, mingles, suddenly she's talking to the new Brendan Behan. She thinks: Irish, interesting. She remembers Paddy from Mayo. You must remember she's ever on the lookout for something a bit different. It's natural, she's bored with too much of the same old ding-dong. So she progresses from the Mayo mountain man to Paddy the poet and so on, until the day she meets Paddy the freedom fighter. Taylor, your left eyebrow is operating independently of the rest of you. But this type of thing has happened before, Taylor, people are ensnared to fall in love with a cause. Agreed?'

'I was thinking, Inspector—'

'Yes, Taylor?'

'The stereotype of the Irishman doesn't depict him as an accomplished lover, Inspector. When you take into account all the drink.'

'It doesn't interfere with their fertility, Taylor. You could give them the red rosette in the breeding stakes.'

'That's true, Inspector, but in the case of Diana Hayhurst from what we know of her it's the quality of the knock on the door that counts not how many pictures are hanging in the hall.'

'Quaint, Taylor. You haven't Irish blood in you by any chance? But let's stay with it: I think you take me too literally, Taylor. We have to consider the possibility that this Hayhurst some place along the line might have allowed her sympathies to be enlisted on the side of the nationalists. It's not that far-fetched. These people in many respects do have a case, they have sympathisers in the House of Commons in all parties and my imagination is not running away with me there. She could have known Bateman before the solo school set up shop. Remember her first night there she kissed him on the forehead and said he was fucking marvellous. I know. I know the way Ernie explained it to the Guv'nor and the Guv'nor passed it on to us but we'll leave the police work to ourselves. Lovers have itchy fingers trying to touch each other, it might have been Hayhurst's way of making physical contact. It would explain a lot, Taylor, if Hayhurst and Bateman were old friends, wouldn't you think?'

'Certainly, Inspector, if we could establish a link between them. But we've investigated both of them thoroughly. Their worlds are miles apart. Outside of work Bateman has no friends. And certainly no lady friends. He's been in the same bedsitter for over twenty years. All he does outside of the solo school is the Gloucester Road pub-crawl weekdays, the geegees on a Saturday, and books. He borrows from the library, mostly quality fiction. Compare all that with the *Unipolitan* life style. Diana Hayhurst is liable to take the Concorde to New York for a conference lasting an hour. As a matter of fact, Inspector, far from being involved with Diana Hayhurst, I'd almost bet that Bateman is a virgin.'

'She could have had scouts out to find the only virgin left in the British Isles, Taylor. All right. What you say is sound, Taylor. I could reason on those lines myself and I would if you could explain this solo school to me. You accept they all came together as it's come to us through the Guv'nor?'

'I'm afraid, Inspector, that I actually do accept it, odd as it is.'

'All I'll say is this, Taylor: lightning isn't going to strike this station twice.'

PART TWO

YOUNG THOMOND

JOHNNY BATEMAN AND Frankie Timmons prepared the lodgement behind the closed door of the barbershop on Friday at lunch time.

'I'm not wanted anymore,' Frankie Timmons said. He did not speak to Johnny Bateman who was counting the money a second time. He spoke to himself in his barbershop mirror as though the revelation could not be trusted to anyone else. Johnny Bateman, knowing Frankie Timmons spoke the truth – his own son had caught the disease over twenty years earlier and still had it – protested angrily.

'You're making me lose count. What are you talking about? Of course you're wanted.'

The meeting to appoint the Young Thomond senior team coach was divisive. Frankie Timmons' name was put forward by Johnny Bateman himself. But the nomination was opposed. A younger man was put forward by the younger crowd. In the end Frankie was appointed by a majority of one vote. The Young Thomond team was a young team now. More than half of them attended a university or institute of higher education. Their play was sophisticated. *Non Manus Vincere, Sed Pes*, they considered an antediluvian tactic. They did not carry out instructions in training. Frankie Timmons roared at them: 'Ye're not listening to me. On the ground!' To have been opposed as coach, worse, that the opposition was not laughed out of the pavilion, and to have been installed by a miserly single vote. And that only after a historical speech by Johnny who had to remind them of the great sacrifice against the All Blacks.

'I can't get over Sean Reilly. Did you try and talk him out of it?'

'What can he do, Johnny? The redundancy's gone.'

'You're down to twenty-seven now.'

Twenty-seven. Out of all the people in the neighbourhood and all the members of the club. It seemed like only yesterday that over a hundred and forty were in the Christmas club. Sean Reilly was saving a fiver a week. Thirty weeks gone, less the fiver he would not pay this week, that would be a hundred and forty-five pounds they would have to hold back from the lodgement to pay him all that he was due. And he'd spend it before he knew where he was and then have nothing to come at Christmas.

'They're no good anyway,' Frankie Timmons said.

Johnny did not argue. He had gone to see them training and it was a miracle that they had not driven him back to his hospital bed.

'At least you're getting them fit, Frankie.'

'What good is fit?'

'They're only playing Old Crescent first round.'

'We're long-haired college boys ourselves now. Out of twenty-three I had in training last night not one of 'em ever came in here for a haircut. I wouldn't mind – if they only went somewhere for a haircut. My own father used to shave my head before a match, nobody could get a grip on us. They bring hair dryers with them. After a shower they dry their hair with hair dryers. The only shower we ever had was if it rained on the way home.'

'You'll get them right, Frankie.'

'I don't know, Johnny. They flash the ball about. They don't listen. They have ears but they don't listen . . .'

'A hundred and forty-five pounds for Sean Reilly, that doesn't leave much left to lodge. Are you watchin'? Here's my own two pound that I'm puttin' in.'

'There's my pound.'

When Frankie started out saving a pound really was a pound. Back in the old days when there were queues in his shop up to seven o'clock Saturday nights. But a pound now wasn't so much as the price of a pint of Guinness. He was not doing much better himself with his two pounds. The total savings every week averaged between a hundred and forty and a hundred and sixty pounds, and the money was lodged in the Trustee Savings Bank. The two of them shared the interest at the end of the year and all those who paid into the club dropped them a hansel on pay-out night. That used to be a great night. Collecting the money from the bank, bringing it home and counting it again, and recounting it, putting it into brown envelopes and writing amount and name on the outside. The pay-out took place in the pub with all the women allowed in for that night only, and did not have to stay in the snug which would anyway not have been big enough for the crowd. Everybody sang that night. Now with only twenty-eight – twenty-seven with Sean Reilly pulling out – it was a poor night they could look forward to. People did not save any more as they used to and those who did saved on their own, keeping their own interest. Everybody had a chequebook now, you could see them cashing cheques in pubs to pay for their rounds. Cashing a cheque to buy drink. People now were ashamed of thrift, of old rugby, of showing respect. There was Dan Reddan saving ten pounds a week in the club, five hundred to come at Christmas. Fair play to him. Dan had started with a broken-down car parked outside his door next to his own. From early morning till dark of night he was underneath that wreck of a car till he cured it and sold it and bought another that was at death's door. Hillmans and Morris Minors. Now Dan Reddan had the biggest motor works in Munster and fourteen garages in the city. No one could imagine what kind of money Dan dealt in. And yet he saved ten pounds a week in the Christmas club and didn't mourn the interest going to Frankie Timmons and Johnny Bateman unlike some of the miserable Johnny-jump-ups who advised their mothers to cop themselves on. When they were building the club house with volunteer labour Dan Reddan drove to the field in his Mercedes, got out in old clothes and mixed cement.

Mrs Quinn was saving this year to have a sink put in to the kitchen to save her going out to the tap in the yard. Thirty bob a week, however she managed it. On her own, she was, with only the pension. A bag of coal was over eight pounds, and free coal November to March only. Mrs Quinn often said she'd love to meet the minister who had no fire on in April. And no matter how they protested she made the two of them accept thirty bob each out of her envelope because that was the way it always was. Last year Johnny had brought Mrs Quinn's envelope to her house in case she lost it on her way home from the barbershop. He'd backed out the passage sharpish and pulled the gate to after him. But next day she arrived in the shop and handed them thirty bob each, and would not leave the shop until they allowed her out without the two thirty bobs.

'I don't know how we'll manage it, but we won't let Mrs Quinn stand to us this year.'

'We've tried everything.'

'We'll try something else.'

There were the two Miss Houlihans who never married and lived second-next door to him. He saw them shopping. Like himself they bought small cuts. And mince. He had known their father, Tough Houlihan, a great line-out man and quick around the field. They both worked for a kiosk-owner, selling sweets and cigarettes. One Miss Houlihan opened the kiosk at eight in the morning and worked until four, when the other Miss Houlihan relieved her and continued until eight at night. The man who owned the kiosk did Saturdays and Sunday the kiosk was closed. They saved three pounds a week each in the club and at Christmas they bought clothes and cosmetics because even in their fifties, being single, they looked after themselves.

There was Peg Morrissey – he remembered her grandfather – with six young children. She saved five pounds a week, however she managed it and however she hung on to any of it at Christmas, married to a man who not alone did not follow Young Thomond but who wasn't a Garryowen man either, who beat her and drank what he could. Soccer he supported, what could you expect? In memory of her grandfather he had knocked at her door when he could bear the screams no longer and been told by the soccer supporter to fuck off. Fuck off. Words out of a neighbour's mouth. But when you thought his own son had said as much . . . Over in England idle. He had grabbed the soccer supporter with one hand by the throat until the face turned purple. And was told when the boyo recovered his breath: 'Only for you're an old man I'd do you.'

And then there was . . .

Johnny Bateman and Frankie Timmons minded each other on the way with the lodgement to the Trustee

Savings Bank as they had done years before in London to lay claim to the Savile Row suit.

THE LEAGUE AGAINST CHRISTMAS (I)

THE SOLO SCHOOL was fifteen months in session when Bateman's father had the stroke causing Bateman to miss out on two Wednesday nights. The only other occasion Bateman had not had a game was the previous Christmas when there had not been a game. Diana Hayhurst had gone to her parents in Toronto; Foster's accountancy empire had closed down for a fortnight and he had no excuse to travel to London; Ernie Gosling had to go to Uncle Albert's Boxing night party; Arthur Ellis went back to his boyhood Leeds, put up at a hotel (bringing his strip of lino for his feet) and strolled among his memories for a few days. On Christmas Day itself Bateman succeeded, as he had on twenty-odd previous Christmas Days, in not committing suicide. But it was a close decision this time and for that he had the solo school to blame – or thank.

What was Christmas anyway? He was something of an authority on it now. Was it for the poor? No. The rich? They followed the sun at that time of year and celebrated in short sleeves under a parasol with long cool drinks on the table and tanned drops of swimming-pool water sparkling on the crossed legs of their blonde companions. The lonely? O Sweet Jesus, Christmas was the tap of a mallet on the stake in the heart of the lonely. The sensitive? The world was a cramped place now and there was little room for sensitivity at Christmas or at any other time of the year. Who then? The smug. By rights, it ought to be: 'Smuggy Christmas and a Complacent New Year!' It was for them all right, but they were too disingenuous to admit it. Instead they proclaimed: Can't stand Christmas, one bleedin' time of the year that gets me down. Different when I was a lad, looked forward to it then. Though it was the oxygen that kept them going for the rest of the year they denied Christmas all the more, and the more they denied it the more they made damn sure that Christmas would not catch them out. Everything they wore at Christmas was in mint condition from Dickens & Jones, a snip in the January sales after the previous Christmas. Carefully, last year's decorations, bulbs, tinsel tree and paper hats were passed down from attics so that the skim of the deposit account might be minimal.

The smug were a breed that Bateman could not avoid; they were not in an isolation ward that he could skirt, they were everywhere in small, lethal doses. And Christmas was the global convocation of the smug: they hauled up their drawbridges oblivious to Bateman outside staring at his own sorry reflection in the moat. They were smug and snug and insulated against the shiftless, miserable and lonely whose spiritual resources were no match for a dull day let alone the intimidating hours, minutes and seconds of the day of all days. They closed their doors against their very own, against that unreliable uncle or brother-in-law of the wife's who had taken his talents out of the ground to act the spark and ended up a scrounger. They passed the paper hats and pulled the crackers and kipped during the Queen's speech, and when the unreliable uncle or brother-in-law was mentioned they said: He never faced up to his responsibilities. Christmas, they said, was family-time, all gathered together indoors: I never set foot outside the door Christmas Day. Suppose all families behaved like that – and they did – the streets would be empty, the shops, pubs and picture houses closed. And they were. Loneliness and emptiness. On Christmas Day unreliable uncles and brothers-in-law and Bateman, locked out of the empty streets, shops, pubs and picture houses, gathered themselves to themselves in their hermits' cells and did not set foot outside the door either. Over twenty-odd years Bateman sat imprisoned in the bedsit plugged into a book, a bottle of whiskey and hatred of the maniac in the Savile Row suit who murdered Christmas when Bateman was only thirteen.

Here was Bateman in September with the signs of another Christmas beginning to manifest themselves. Only the other day in the Shakespeare bar in Mellick he'd had a raffle card put up to him on which he signed the name Arthur Ellis and forked out his fifty pee. Every moment now until the confinement itself he would be assailed from all directions by harbingers of the hateful approach. Where are you Baby Jesus? You didn't close any picture houses, you opened up stables. Remind them. Send them out into the streets where everyone can join in and be equal.

Missing two solo school nights because of the trip home to see his stricken father Bateman began to realise just how besieged he was. His father might not amount to much, his father might have been a backward savage who destroyed his son's life. But if the whole world gathered together to point the finger at Percy Bateman standing in the middle of the street and asked: Who are you anyway?, Bateman could point back to his aged father and reply: I'm connected there. But the day was not far off when he would not have that answer in his locker. His then-next of kin would be the solo school – which, come Christmas when most he needed it, would shut down on him too.

He had sent a card from Mellick to Ernie explaining his absence. He had never sent a card to anyone before in his life. Buying a stamp in the post office he noticed a sign on which was printed the last date for posting to Australia and New Zealand before Christmas. This uncalled-for information, on top of that raffle card, was another reminder that the Christmas bastards began their operations early and finished late, leaving him but few months of peace – a peace he could not enjoy confronted then by the bastards' summer metamorphosis into fathers and mothers and grandads and grandmas and children and buckets and spades *en famille* en route to the seasides. Where he had no doubt he too would have been welcome – to sit by himself, that is, with the legs of his trousers rolled up, his braces dangling and a handkerchief knotted on his head.

It was intolerable now, at the beginning of October, as he set out on the tube at Gloucester Road for the solo school, to have the terror of Christmas enter his thoughts. Worse, he knew the terror would stay with him until Boxing Day, blighting the solace of the King's Arms. As a group they had their place in the bar: they attracted spectators. Alf the barber had altered his routine to be there on the periphery of the game every Wednesday night. Mrs Murphy no longer sat in isolation. She had her drink at a table near them and they heard from Ernie that the Guv'nor had instructed her under threat of banishment to keep her business cards to herself where the gentlemen in the solo school were concerned. The arthritic lady, old Mrs Dixon, had also moved to their corner but not to the same table as Mrs Murphy to whom nevertheless Mrs Dixon was polite with a 'Goodnight, dear'. Bateman often brought Mrs Dixon's glass up and drink down when her needs coincided with his own. And she always said: 'Ta, Mr Bateman, you're very good.' The dart-and-backgammon boys from the games room idled on their way in and gave him the nod, one pro to another. The Guv'nor gave him his full title and not the ubiquitous 'All right, mate?' The Guv'nor's wife discovered excuses to come out and gather glasses and clean ashtrays but her motive was see-through: she wanted to get a load of Diana Hayhurst. Ernie's Linda and his mother-in-law Betty embarrassed poor Ernie by turning up to have a gawk and though Ernie reported that he'd given them a bollockin' for their brazenness, they continued to come and eventually Ernie acknowledged their presence by buying them drinks. Bateman guessed that they were proud of Ernie in such good company, especially that of Diana Hayhurst – proud and a little jealous. And why wouldn't they be? He himself was proud of the company, especially Diana Hayhurst's. He had listened to swear-words in his time, worked with a settler whose brother the radio officer brought home pictures of unimaginable filth. In his ragbag of occupations he had been obliged to listen to ladies on assembly lines deny their femininity with the coarsest of conversation. He had aired his distaste with the solo school, all of whom were clean-spoken, told them of how he choked on the obscenity in the Harlesden factory. They were crutches for each other and it made no difference that consolation was wrapped in chaff. That was the English way. And so when Diana Hayhurst joined the school Bateman could no more tolerate fuck coming from her than he could turn a blind eye to soot upon a rose. He checked her and, for his pains, was declared fucking marvellous. She was a strange woman, possibly mad. How else to account for her almost falling out of her chair with delight at the most commonplace of his utterances? She invited comment from all of them on a variety of daft topics, from what they thought of politics to parties. None of them had much to offer on the party line, except Ernie who was pressed into action once a year by Uncle Albert. Altogether then they were a contented school, comfortable with each other, and Bateman might have been close to a limited happiness if that bloody Christmas had not been around the corner.

It was Ellis and Gosling mentioning Christmas that put the idea into Foster's head. That was a fortnight ago when Bateman had not turned up and they speculated that he might have put his head in the gas oven. He had heard himself say: 'Christmas should be abolished. It should be sabotaged.' To be in agreement with a fellow like Ellis on a subject like that. On the journey back to Nottingham next day Foster brooded on the vehemence of his own cold anticipation of the feast. Of course it was Nick. What else? To have to suffer Nick doing the tango with Gladys was bad enough on the night but to have it brought to his mind in September was an irritant. If there was some way of getting out of going to Nick's. There was the year Gladys had the flu and he instructed the doctor to confine her to bed. No good. She wouldn't miss Nick's over a few sniffles. And if he had been laid up himself he would have had to command Gladys to go without him otherwise he would wait a long time before Gladys again put her hand on his knee after drink. No, there was no way out of going to Nick's. But what about this scenario: suppose, once at Nick's, they were to discover some essential had been left behind? He could nip back home. No danger of Gladys leaving Nick's. No likelihood of callers, everyone they knew would be at Nick's. He could chance dressing up in her clothes. But if he collapsed? Nick bringing her home. Coming in to see that Ken's all right. Putting his arm around Gladys to soften the sight of Ken dead in her undies. There must be *some* bloody way a man could dress up in his wife's clothes without fear of detection.

Last week for the second Wednesday in succession when they didn't have a game, Christmas came up. Ellis lost ground at Christmas. The poorest of his customers were driven by the fever to go off some place and buy carpet for one room. He knew because they told him. They said – for the millionth time – that he would do better if he also stocked carpet. They needed carpet for reception purposes even if that only amounted to having the post-man in for a whisky or the refuse people collecting their blackmail. Ellis could get over that because famine always followed feast. He did not know what he was doing thinking about Christmas now at the start of October, but now that he was thinking about it there was a nasty stink off its approach. He could not go to Leeds again because they would see him second time round as a character and what was Christmas but the celebration of a prophet unhonoured in his home town?

Last year, without the solo school to detain him in London over Christmas, he had nipped back to Leeds for a couple of days. Wearing his casual clothes he had signed the book in a good hotel giving his address as The Lino Shop and was treated with a certain deference. He informed reception that when the maids cleaned his room they would find a rectangle of lino beside his bed and that he would appreciate if they applied a rub of wax. At night Ellis took the waxed lino under his arm around the pubs and where there was carpet placed it under his bar stool, or under the little table if he was seated on one of those backless leatherette affairs designed for the bottom of a pygmy. He had the occasional unfortunate experience in bars where the floor covering did not offend him so that he stood with the rolled lino under his arm – he was told: 'No Peddling Allowed.' But once he established his credentials there was much understanding. Those old acquaintances from his boyhood too were a comfort, nodding eagerly at his tale of chucking finance for the lino business: 'You're out on your own then, Arthur. Good on you.' Showed they held broader views than government, bankers, financiers and credit companies. The self-employed and sole traders had been made to sweat for their loans at the NatWest, and they wouldn't have been there in the first place if they hadn't got the bum's rush from the banks proper.

But it was sad that people accepted the preacher and not the creed. Lino was good in itself, could his old neighbours not see that? He had taken out his order book and tried to do business not for the profit but as an extension of his ministry. Promised to organise a lorry in London if he had enough takers, and have the consignment in Leeds within a fortnight cash on delivery at a price unbeatable in the British Isles – or in Japan, for that matter. At first they thought he was joking. Apostasy was that deep-rooted. What could one man do on his own? Still, it was better to light a candle than curse the darkness. He told them that all the best people in London were switching back to lino now – the Sloane Rangers, for example – and that did impress them somewhat. But of course for the wrong reason. It was sad that his home town had backslid so far. There was nothing for it but to strike at the heart in London and let the message flow from there to the dominions: convert the king and the subjects would follow.

Funny, the way the Guv'nor was so suspicious for so long but Ernie was satisfied now that the Guv'nor seemed to be over it. Who'd have thought it just a couple of years back in the last days of the motor factors. Who'd have said: Ernie, in two years' time you'll be playing cards every Wednesday night with the owner of *Unipolitan,* an accountant, a man as has his own business and an Irish bloke what can't get a job. Although the Guv'nor didn't admit it outright, really he had to admit they was all above board. Maybe the Guv'nor was jealous of him? That lot in the games room were, he could see that. Some of them were shirty that he made the potman's job for himself before ever the solo school got off the ground, Fred his mate from the motor factors narking him all the time: 'Still talkin' to us, Ernie, eh?' People were jealous of you having a piece of good fortune, there was no doubt about it. He could understand it in a way, only human. Just imagine if he won the pools, if they begrudged him a bit of decent company how would they feel if he won half a million? He could imagine. Even Linda. And Betty. There was the night he clean forgot. Going out the door spruced up and Linda says: 'You forgettin' somethin, Ernie?' He searched his pockets. He had his wallet. His tobacco and cigarette papers. His hankie was in the breast pocket. Shoes polished. He felt with his hand, he was zipped up all right. And then: 'You didn't do your pools, did you?' Did she go on about it though. Said it was her nibs, wasn't it, his mind wasn't on his business no more, not that she blamed him, she was a bit of all right, but there was no need to be late, Linda herself would fill in the coupon. He knew same as if he could see into the future that she'd click if she filled it in. They had a right row. He said 'No thanks I'm not 'aving me luck broken' and she come back 'What bleedin' luck?'

Grabbed the coupon together the two of them, a tug o'war ended up with the coupon torn in half and the two of them saying together 'Now look what you've gone an' done' and Betty shouting at them to behave themselves. He said Fred always had spares, he'd get one and fill it in down the King's Arms. Linda had to go and play the fool coming in that night with Betty, and the two of 'em staying on their own – wouldn't let him buy them a drink, just sat there stiff clutching handbags practically broadcasting that there was something up. It got worse closing: back home he'd said 'Just for that I'm not goin' round Uncle Albert's for Christmas and sod his paper hats.' That drove Betty crying up to bed. Up till one in the morning then to make it up cos they never did carry rows overnight. Ended up laughing at the whole silly carry-on, Linda claiming he owed her for the drink they wouldn't let him buy them. It showed you how things could blow up outa nothing.

'Well, Taylor?'

'Sir?'

'It's taken almost two years for them to show their hand. Just think, Taylor, we'd almost written them off, hadn't we? Where would we be now if we'd sent the Guv'nor packing about his business first day? Eh? I'll tell you, Taylor: my backside would have been out of this desk faster than my predecessor's after he let Bourke and Blake walk out of that pub. As it is, if the Guv'nor hadn't stepped out from behind his counter to collect glasses and get a load of the Hayhurst person we mightn't be any the wiser. Gosling – whom we have to accept isn't in on it – Gosling wouldn't have spotted it. It was the Guv'nor catching the word 'sabotage', that was our stroke of luck. And then what he got out of Gosling who's so innocent he sang for the Guv'nor and still hasn't an idea what he's sitting on. I presume you are on my wave-length, Taylor?'

'I'm sorry, Sir.'

'Dammit, Taylor, you're not accepting last night's performance at face value?'

'I have to, Inspector.'

'But the Guv'nor saw it. I see it. What's the matter with you, Taylor? You're my sharpest man, why can't you see it?'

'Perhaps if you guided me, Inspector.'

'All right. I will. They haven't had a game for two weeks. Why? Number one: Bateman's in Ireland, spins a yarn about his father having a stroke—'

'We can check that out—'

'All right, Taylor, I know we can, and we'll find his father did have a stroke. They're not so dumb as to let themselves be caught on that one. Now don't interrupt, let me finish. Bateman never goes home, not even at Christmas, we have that from Bateman himself through Ernie through the Guv'nor. I think Bateman slipped up there. He hates his father, so would he rush off when the old boy has a stroke?'

'If we were to take the different nationalities as caricatures, Inspector – the Welsh singing, Scots stingy, that business – we ourselves are seen as less emotionally attached to our parents than the Irish are. And you and I, Inspector, would rush to our fathers' bedsides in the same circumstances.'

'It's their mothers they're attached to, Taylor, not their fathers. Look, Bateman's over there for ten days. Hayhurst is in Paris, New York, Amsterdam. Hotbeds of sympathy for every movement.'

'She makes a trip like that a few times a year. I actually heard her on a chat show talking about that, something about keeping her finger on the international pulse.'

'Taylor, she's away, Bateman's away, they come back and all of them decide it would be a wheeze to sabotage Christmas. Just like that, Taylor, sabotage Christmas. I don't see them going to the North Pole to let the air out of Santa's tyres, do you, Taylor?'

'No, Sir.'

'It's no laughing matter. Sabotage. Here, Taylor, look it up. Open my dictionary and tell me what sabotage means. Be careful, the pages are loose. Had it since I was a lad, you won't find any of your psychedelic modern words in there. What's the joke now, Taylor?'

'Psychedelic's old hat today, Sir. Here we are: "wilful damage or destruction of property perpetrated for political or economic reasons".'

'Now, Taylor, the joke is over. Sabotage is a serious matter. Nor is it my imagination that that is what we're up against: it was the Guv'nor brought in the word, he heard it. I've never had to deal before with people who hated Christmas. At least not Christians hating Christmas. You yourself, Taylor, I think I'm safe in saying you don't hate Christmas?'

'As a single man, Inspector, you've had me on duty the last three Christmasses.'

'We could all be on duty this Christmas if what my nose tells me is right. It didn't turn you against Christmas, did it, Taylor?'

'No, Sir. The double time is welcome.'

'Cynic. What if it did, Taylor, what if you turned sour, you wouldn't set out to sabotage Christmas, would you, Taylor? Hurry now, they might have a vacancy.'

'I don't think they meant it, Sir. I think what they have in mind is to cock a snook at Christmas.'

'I'm all ears, Taylor. How do you come to that conclusion?'

'From the way the Guv'nor presented his evidence.'

'We'll go through it then. Ernie, as usual is first in the bar last night. Ellis and Foster arrive more or less together. Next comes Bateman. Ernie asks him "How's your father," intending the words to mean exactly what they do mean for a change, wipe the grin off your face Taylor – Bateman tells them the old boy's recovered. Diana Hayhurst arrives bronzed and fit from her travels and the solo school is back in action with a mob of spectators all trying to get a glimpse of her leg or whatnot. We'll take it in chronological order according to the Guv'nor. He reckons there's an hour gone by the time he gets the urge to go out and join the throng – and get the fill of his eyes and ears although by now, Taylor, the Guv'nor is resigned to accepting them as what they appeared to be, that is, a bunch of odd bods with a game of cards in common. Just as we ourselves had come to accept, though reluctantly on my part you'll agree. So the Guv'nor is not acting in his capacity as our man on the spot. Even so, he runs a tight ship. He's got a handful of glasses, grateful for but bemused by the custom, and he's about to back behind the counter about his business when he hears: I propose sabotage.

'The Guv'nor quickly deposits the glasses on the counter and hurries back to the scene. At first the Guv'nor thinks maybe it's part of the game because he's heard expressions like "I'll go a bundle" or "I'll chance a spread" or "I'll go nine" and he thinks "I propose sabotage" may be a bid. The more so since these lads take their play seriously: they don't speak while the game is in progress. Now although his back was turned the Guv'nor recognised it was Bateman's voice proposing sabotage. Bateman spoke just as the cards were dealt and there was no further chat until the hand was played out. Next item on the agenda Foster says: "What have you in mind, Bateman?" Bateman shrugs and says: "Strike at something symbolic." The Guv'nor is all ears now. To the Guv'nor's astonishment he hears the voice of Ernie Gosling: "I know, if we could find the factory where the paper hats is made and burn it down." This is all throwaway stuff, Taylor. Hayhurst is gathering up the cards for her deal and – watch this for cleverness, Taylor – the Guv'nor hears Hayhurst, and he says she's dead serious when usually she's falling all over the place like a schoolgirl, the Guv'nor hears her say: "Count me out, gentlemen, what a weird lot, it makes me shudder." The next hand is on, Taylor, and no more talk. The Guv'nor says it was a call by Ellis, a spread. A tricky one where Bateman, Foster and Ernie combined to defeat it and after which Ellis claims it was bad play on their part that beat him, they should have defeated him in a different way. Or some such rot. The poor Guv'nor doesn't know whether he's coming or going. Here Ernie goes to the counter for a round for himself and his missus and his mother-in-law and the Guv'nor sees his chance. Ernie tells him: "Oh, Percy and the boys was just wonderin' how we could sabotage Christmas." The Guv'nor nods and says: "Of course." He can be quite dry, the Guv'nor. He can't get much more out of Ernie at this stage but first chance he gets he's out on duty again. And what does he hear? From Ellis this time: "I'd much rather sabotage a carpet factory." Hayhurst, still po-faced, she starts begging them to stop, she can't listen to such sedition. Her word. Foster comes in with the observation that he's not surprised she hasn't the stomach for a man's work. That sets the cat among the pigeons. She's not having that. She says anything they can get up to she can get up better. All a show of course, Taylor. The Guv'nor's wife needs him in the lounge, and when he comes back they're actually talking during the playing of a hand. Ellis is saying Christmas must be done and it must be done this Christmas, agreed?

Bateman and Foster nod and say: "Agreed." And to the Guv'nor's horror, Gosling says: "Count me in and sod Uncle Albert." Hayhurst gives herself away to my mind by keeping the pot boiling. She says: "Well, gentlemen, let's hear your proposals." And one frivolous suggestion follows another until Bateman says "Eureka!" and they all look to him. Bateman says: "The diddly club." And immediately Ellis agrees: "That's it." They look to Foster and he puts on a show of thinking and nods slowly. We now know, Taylor, from the Guv'nor filling us in from what Ernie told him, that they propose to go to Mellick and knock over Bateman's old boy's diddly club, right?'

'Correct, Inspector.'

'This is all out in the open with idlers standing by enjoying the show. Now, Taylor, for the diddly club I ask you to substitute the following: Harrods, House of Commons, the Palace, Mrs Thatcher, etc., etc., etc.'

'Sir, why didn't they congregate privately and hatch their plot in comfort?'

'I'm surprised at you, Taylor. To cover their tracks, that's why not. Is it possible you don't see the seriousness of the situation, Taylor?'

'I see the *possible* seriousness of the situation, Inspector, if the situation turns out as you suggest. I simply can't convince myself that it isn't all a giggle. Not that I think robbing poor folks' Christmas savings is a joke. I doubt if they intend to keep that money if they do pinch it, but just in case I think we should alert the Irish police.'

'No, Taylor. We'll do no such thing. If I was sure it was the diddly club of course I'd be in touch with the Garda Siochana as they're known. Pronounced gar – as in car – da as in your Da or Bateman's. Garda Siochana, that's she-o-kawna. I was given a lesson in the Erse once by a colleague who'd been there on holiday. Took me an hour and a few beers to get it right. Taylor, the Irish police are a sound lot as we have reason to know and be grateful for but suppose this thing is political? I have no doubt that the *gardai* – that's the plural, gar-dee – I have no doubt that if they happened on Bateman and his gang robbing a bank for the Cause, I have absolutely no doubt that they'd round them up and bung them inside. But the situation is complicated. Turning the key in the lock the *garda* might feel obliged to say: I'm sorry about this, sad day one Irishman locking up another all because of the bloody Brits. Now if over in Mellick they got the word that Bateman's real mission was London then I'm very much afraid your Mellick bobby might be inclined to shrug his shoulders and go home to his tea and give his feet a rest. You follow, Taylor?'

GARDA BEN HANLEY

BORN IN WESTPORT, County Mayo in 1952, Ben Hanley finished school after taking an Intermediate Certificate Honours and went about his father's business of fishing for mackerel in Clew Bay during the dark of bitter nights and early mornings. There was no tradition of higher education in the family or in the area, as all that book-learning ever led to was a job in Dublin in the civil service plotting the collection of water rates and taxes.

In winter, without the tourists, the romance of the mackerel industry quickly faded. And when the emigrants returned at Christmas from England and America all dolled up the mackerel men in the pubs were seen to be shabby, playing rings and going slowly down the pints. Big Ben Hanley followed the trail to London where there was no problem getting the start. But after a year in the tunnels Ben's Honours Intermediate Certificate told him there was no profit in risking pneumonia in winter and he signed the books of the Emerald Staff Bureau. Since he was Irish and raw he was obliged to begin at the bottom in the Kilburn pubs where the customers were just as Irish and just as raw. Sleeping in, the wages were low. Tips were meagre, being tapped the more likely occurrence.

Ben Hanley was the right man in the right place at the right time: it was 1968 and the Irish were at the zenith of their popularity among the English, that is they were no longer openly despised thanks to the worldwide sympathy still lingering since the Kennedy assassination. Some of the central city pubs let down their guard so far as to take the occasional recruit from the Emerald Staff Agency. Ben Hanley worked his way up from Kilburn to Acton to Fulham to Chelsea, becoming more polished as he graduated until he could say: Two similars, Sir? as shamelessly as a solicitor talking guineas. Ben thought he was at the top of the tree in Chelsea, till the director of the Emerald Staff Agency himself sent for him.

'This is a big chance for you, young Hanley. I hope you understand that.'

'Yes, Mr O'Donovan.'

'You haven't let me down yet.'

'I won't either, Mr O'Donovan.'

'Now. You'll sleep out of course. And you'll pay for it. You'll need a good address. Find an attic some place fashionable. You'll need clothes to be seen in when you arrive and when you leave. For work you'll be supplied with a dickey bow, white shirt and dark trousers. Get a good pair of shoes. Black. Keep them polished. I'll advance you a week's wages. You should triple what you earn in tips if you know your business. You'll have to begin at the beginning, pubs off Regent Street don't stock draught Guinness. Show me your hands. Dear, dear. Go to a hairdresser's and have that thatch tamed. A hairdresser's, not a barber's. You'll be dealing with top people. From the media. If someone calls Where's that bollix of a barman? You say Yessir! and jump to it. This is an opening for you, young Hanley and for the Emerald. Now: any questions?'

'When do I start, Mr O'Donovan?'

'Good lad.'

Ben Hanley soon discovered that Mr O'Donovan's vision of top people in West End pubs was a caricature. Nobody called him John or Pat and certainly not a bollix of a barman. Perhaps Mr O'Donovan's view from his ethnic bunker might have shown things how they were pre- the swinging sixties but no longer. These were democratic times. Everybody was taken on merit now, and it was an irrelevance that nobody had any. Nobody could act, write, sing or play an instrument and everybody was an actor, writer, singer or instrumentalist. But as with paper money the lack of rigid standards was an irrelevance so long as there was confidence all round. Ben was as good a barman as any of his clientele were proficient at their callings. If anybody noticed that Ben came from the Emerald Staff Agency nobody bothered to bring it up. Ben was pop art.

All the ladies wore miniskirts, including the fully fledged film stars who had not found it necessary ever to have been starlets. A star was born every week: the highest birth rate since the Renaissance. The actors, every one of them a Hamlet, even unto their choice of cigars, were a moody lot, young and aged at twenty-four. They were coolest to Ben and he to them, since they saw themselves but a thin stratum removed from his job and since he noticed they had little money to throw away on tips. Ben was nervous with the miniskirts because they obliged him surreptitiously to finger his penis flat up against his abdomen before he could come out in his tight trousers carrying a tray over his shoulder.

Youth learns quickly. Soon Ben was at ease as he would ever be among his customers. The Pub – that was its name, The Pub, a piece of coyness that stood out even in those trendy days – The Pub also attracted the publishing fraternity and sorority, and they became Ben's favourite customers for, though an abstemious lot themselves, they were all the time entertaining writers who depended for sustenance on drink – and praise. Among publishers, Leonard Hooper was Ben's favourite though he did not entertain writers: 'Buy drink for those fuckers after publishing their shit? No thanks. Keep the change.' That was an attractive expression of Hooper's: 'Keep the change.' Better than: 'Have one yourself, go on, have a light ale.' Hooper liked to sit by himself. He instructed Ben: 'When I look up from my paper and raise my little finger, you start filling and ignore the rest of those half-naked whores and dossers.' Ben was impressed by a man who was so unimpressed by the talented and famous: 'Talented? Do you mean by any chance their complete inability to spell? Act, write, talk, whistle? What's more, we're all fucking in it together: there's a vast uneducated audience out there who must be satisfied by the un-educated hangers-on in here. My good boy, if I blew the gaff I'd go fucking bust. Keep the change.'

Like all barmen, on his night off Ben went for a drink. Outside of his own customers, he did not have any English friends or acquaintances and while he was not so much a recidivist as to return to the sawdust company of Kilburn, neither could he rise above a visit to Ward's, the Irish House in Piccadilly. He was smug in Ward's. His brothers in service there thought themselves crack troops, the elite of the Emerald Staff Agency. Their idea of a top person was an out-of-work actor from Dublin out of work in London who far from giving tips bought a packet of cigarette papers and tapped the barmen for the makings of a smoke. Ward's also hosted the rugby crowd over for the English match every second year, a vulgar mob who put up at the Regent's Palace and clogged the lavatories.

Ben drank incognito in Ward's. He did not want Ward's barmen dropping into The Pub to see him on their night off. Ben's story was that he was a systems analyst on a contract basis. He was safe with that. Then even systems analysts did not know what systems analysts did. A generation earlier one had said one was in costing where one was a clerk.

Ben Hanley accepted Hooper's derision of the dolly birds and in time his tight trousers could cope. Until one evening Hooper came in with a woman. A real woman. Even if Ben had not been able to recognise the real thing Hooper's uncharacteristic attention to the lady would have marked her out. Hooper introduced Ben: 'Diana Hayhurst: She runs a mag, Ben, not the worst. Diana, best fucking barman in London.' Although she looked old – Ben guessed that she must have been pushing thirty – she was more desirable than the miniskirted crowd. Her dress was a couple of inches below the knee, until she sat down when it ran an inch above the knee and that inch to Ben was more alluring than nudity. He noted all this on Hooper's behalf. Hooper had taste. Ten minutes later Ben was professionally prodding the optic with a brandy glass when he heard the shout: 'And fuck Mrs Herne Bay.' He turned his head and saw Diana Hayhurst on her feet, giggling. Ben accepted the outburst calmly. Mr O'Donovan of the Emerald Staff Agency would have been proud of him. The rest of the crowd rigidly affected not to have heard and in this they showed themselves to be fools or phonies. Had they an ounce of breeding every head would have turned and a silence prevailed. They were only a cut above Ward's crowd. Hooper and his lady were way out in front.

Hooper and his lady were in The Pub every evening for the next week. Then they missed three days. Ben missed them those three days. They turned up on the fourth evening and Ben thought Hooper was going off the rails when the publisher began to introduce her again. But Hooper said: 'Ben, meet Diana Hayhurst my wife. Best fucking ride in London. Keep the change.' Ben blushed only a little at the lady with the sex lines on her forehead and the dimples at the corners of her mouth. Ben was the undisputed flagship of the Emerald Staff Agency.

Ben was as pleased as if he had brought them together himself. It put any foolish thoughts he might have had of loving her out of his head. She was just right for Hooper but too old for Ben, Ben reasoned. He was the pal in the pictures happy to bring the male and female leads together. For ten months they were regulars, laughing and swearing. Of course they knew or nodded to most of the other customers but there was a love ray around them that encouraged the other customers to keep a distance. Ben was allowed through the ray. Ben was proud. Suddenly, a whole month passed without Leonard Hooper or Diana Hayhurst coming into the pub. Then Hooper came in on his own. Ben could see he was in the dumps. He sat by himself as he used to in his single days and raised a little finger.

'Diana been in here, Ben?'

'Not for a few weeks, Mr Hooper.'

'If she does come will you give her a message for me?'

'Of course, Mr Hooper.'

'Tell her my offer still holds good. You got that, Ben? My offer still holds good.'

'Your offer still holds good.'

'Yes. Keep the change.'

Another two months passed during which neither Hooper nor his wife appeared. Then near closing time on a Wednesday night when it was quiet Diana Hayhurst turned up drunk. She was with a character who did not have any of Leonard Hooper's style, a chap who did not have anyone's style. Diana Hayhurst did not even mention his name though she did introduce Ben: 'This is the best fucking barman in London.' Ben was disappointed. Diana Hayhurst was to Ben what Ben was to Mr O'Donovan of the Emerald Staff Agency. Ben did not like to see her letting herself down. Come closing though, she seemed to sober up. She came to the counter and whispered to him: 'Ben, I want you to do something for me.' He assumed she wanted him to contact Hooper. She pushed the door that led out to the toilets and jerked her head for him to follow. She opened the ladies and pulled him in after her. Years later Ben could remember the words: 'Now don't panic, Ben, just put your arms around me. No, don't speak. Here, give me your hands. That's it. Now Ben, kiss me. Kiss me slowly, Ben.' Years later, sitting in a cold Garda car on his way to wreck a poteen still, Ben could feel her fingers inside the belt of his black barman's trousers, pulling up his shirt and grabbing his penis. She lifted her dress and folded it as might someone crossing a stream. Then she unrolled her tights down to her ankles and wiggled her panties below her knees. She opened her buttons. Years later he could get an instant erection recalling her orders: 'Suck the tit Ben and shove him up between my legs.' Ben could hear someone at the handle of the door but a bomb might have been over his head and he could not have ducked. He was moaning and ejaculating as the man without style clicked the camera. Diana Hayhurst rearranged her garments, kissed him on the cheek and patted his head: 'Thanks, Ben, you're the best fucking barman in London.'

Ben never saw her or Hooper or the man without style again. He was ecstatic and miserable for a month, with the thrill of the deed and despair at the dwindling prospects of its repetition. He went as far as looking up the number of *Unipolitan* but best fucking barman in London as he was he did not make the call. And then one Wednesday afternoon when he went on duty at half-past five The Pub filled to standing room in minutes, with every dolly bird prodding at the newspaper on her bare knees and hooraying: 'Congratulations, Ben.' He had slept late and only read the back pages of newspapers anyway. Mr O'Donovan should have been there as Ben watched his own name leap out at him from the divorce citation. Ben was able to keep his professional cool, grin modestly at the dolly birds, breathe on the manicured nails of his fingers and rub them off his white shirt. The phone rang. He was to be in Mr O'Donovan's office first thing in the morning. That evening when he left The Pub to hold up his hand for a taxi a two-seater sports car zoomed to a stop, and Ben saw long miniskirted legs in the driving seat and heard his name: 'Get in, Ben.' Years later he could not remember her name. Sandra? Susan? She took him to her South Kensington flat where she did not allow him one minute of sleep. In the morning Ben went to the Emerald Staff Agency where he was kept waiting for twenty minutes, squashed in among prospective sleep-in merchants. Before admitting Ben, Mr O'Donovan interviewed three such applicants even though his flagship was in plain view. When the third left, Ben stood up out of turn and walked into the office.

'Can you see me now, Mr O'Donovan? I have to go and change for work.'

'What's all this about, then? Sit down. What's it all about then, eh? Nice carry-on. I take you from the gutter. Well? Don't just sit there. Explain yourself.'

'How do you mean, Mr O'Donovan?'

'How do I mean? When I came in here yesterday morning that telephone was dancing and who was on the other end? Bishop Casey, patron of the Emerald. He said he saw we were hitting the headlines. I told him I'd investigate. I'm investigating, Hanley.'

'Call me Ben or call me Mr Hanley please, Mr O'Donovan.'

'Oh. I see. It's that way now, is it? You young git. What the hell do you think you're playing at? I'll give you half a minute and your explanation had better stand up, Hanley.'

Ben stood up. 'My private life is my own affair, Mr O'Donovan. Good morning to you.'

Ben felt sorry for the poor sods hoping to sleep in as he paraded out of the Emerald, the best fucking barman in London.

There were other Sandras/Susans. Ben soared away from the Emerald Staff Agency. He ignored the lament of a letter from his mother with his father's stern postscript: a well-wisher had showed them Ben's name in the English paper. But he was too polished now even to think of Mayo though he continued as always to send money home. He rode the wave for five months: plenty of birds, lots of money. And then one morning the papers screamed:

BASTARDS!—   The Sun

ANIMALS!—   The Star

OUTRAGE!—   The Mirror

SEND THEM HOME—   The Express

There was a photograph of the rubble of a Wimpy Bar and a catalogue of the ages, marital status and occupations of the nineteen dead and assorted maimed. The IRA claimed that they had telephoned their warning in time but this was disputed. Nobody said anything to Ben that night in The Pub. Near closing he was alert to hold the look of a Sandra/Susan but no look came. The Pub cleared early, the clientele finished the night elsewhere.

The Pub did not become an out place overnight. There were further outrages and accompanying graphic headlines in the tabloids. Custom dwindled. At closing on a slack Friday night the boss handed Ben an envelope in which were enclosed his holiday money, severance pay and cards. The boss said: 'Sorry, Ben, it's not your doing and it's not my doing but that's the way it is. Sorry.'

Ben brooded on the injustice for a week and then needing to share his grievance he went to the only person he knew who would understand, Mr O'Donovan. He had never let Mr O'Donovan down. His only mutinous act had been to take a stand over his right to a private life and a respectable nomenclature. There were twelve in the waiting room before Ben and Ben waited his turn. Mr O'Donovan was cold.

'Hanley, isn't it?'

'Yes.'

'Well?'

'I've lost my job.'

'I see.'

'I didn't do anything, Mr O'Donovan. I didn't nick or anything. Twas the bombs. The customers stopped coming in. The boss even said he was sorry to lose me but what could he do.'

'Look, Hanley, you serviced one of the customers in the ladies' toilet. Did it occur to you that that might have something to do with your dismissal?'

'That's over a year ago, Mr O'Donovan. The boss said twas on account of the IRA. You can ring him. The other business, the boss congratulated me, he said he never knew I had it in me.'

'I'd suggest, Hanley, that that's a testimonial you should omit from your curriculum vitae. However, what can the Emerald do for you?'

'I was wondering if you have any vacancies at the moment.'

'It's hard to place people today, Hanley. But if you give me your word that you'll mind your business there's a chance of a spot in Kilburn.'

'Have you anything more central, Mr O'Donovan, I've gotten used to the city, if you had a place like where I was in The Pub . . .'

'I'm afraid those days are gone, Hanley. Gone and not coming back for a long time if ever. When I ring up I don't get past whatever bottle-washer answers the phone. They don't want to know.'

'What about Ward's, Mr O'Donovan, the boss said he'd give me a good reference. He suggested Ward's, he seemed to think I wouldn't have a problem getting in there.'

'There's a waiting list for Ward's. A mile long, Hanley. And nobody in Ward's is going to leave his job unless he drops dead. Not these days, Hanley. Now, this Kilburn job, and listen carefully to me, Hanley, are you listening? This is the only vacancy I have on the books. The lot in before you this morning I took all their names and addresses, their false names I shouldn't wonder, but I held on to the job. We're beginning all over again from the bottom up. Despite your proclivities you're probably my best bet. The wages aren't great but you'll be sleeping in and you'll be grubbed.'

Shit for dinner. No soup. Rock hard fried egg and two sausage for tea alternating with rock-hard fried egg and two rashers. Sharing a half-size television with a mob of the unkempt staff. Sleeping three to a room, the few pound notes under the pillow. Factory Paddies tapping.

The building crowd at weekends pulling their brown envelopes out of the arse pocket, getting pissed, calling him Pat or John or that bollix of a barman, shouting up the Republic and bawling out patriotic ballads. The only women in the bar oul wans. Ben lasted three weeks.

Back home in Mayo, Ben acted a combination of the prodigal son and returned Yank until his savings melted. His mother suggested: 'Have you thought of the guards?' as though professions were chocolates in a box with Ben's fingers indecisively poised. Better than shivering in a mackerel boat, though. The usual political influences were beseeched and Ben was sent to Templemore, County Tipperary for training. Qualified, he was posted to Mellick where again he proved the right man in the right place at the right time.

Off duty one morning Ben sat over a pint in the Shakespeare which was just across the road from Henry Street barracks. He wore civvies. He did not shop in uniform, would not wear even the blue shirt off duty. He owed it to himself not to: he was no *garda* by vocation, but he had learned a sense of what was fitting in his London days. Another world. Ben had been irritated to detect his partner's disbelief in the toilet episode in The Pub and the succession of Sandras/Susans. It was a world blown skyhigh by the IRA and nothing left to show for it, no shred of evidence with which to confront the disbelievers. Ben left the Shakespeare and headed towards O'Connell Street where he had a room. As he passed the Bank of Ireland two figures dressed in face masks backed out of the bank, one carrying a sack and the other an Armalite. The armed fellow shoved Ben out of his way with the butt of the rifle. Ben grabbed at the weapon, a voice behind the mask shouted: 'What the fuck – this is the IRA, you prick.' Ben brought his knee up to the IRA testicles, wrested away the gun and clobbered the two

164

masked heads with the butt. From a car parked by the kerb Ben heard 'We're bollixed, put the foot down,' and poked the gun barrel through the window. He marched the four captives the short distance past the Shakespeare and across the road to the Henry Street barracks, escorted at a safe distance by shoppers and all the idle in the vicinity. He was awarded the Scott Medal for Bravery. The four men had no connection with the IRA. They were simply what came to be known as ordinary decent criminals.

The Henry Street superintendent forecast: 'You'll go a long way in the force, Hanley.' Ben accepted the prediction as though it were a sentence. He had no ambition in that direction. He knew neither fear nor, therefore, courage as a policeman. He was simply indifferent to the job that was a substitute for his genuine calling. This attitude gained for him the reputation of a cool cop. When it was decided to promote him to sergeant Ben caused a sensation by declining the honour. He knew that if he accepted he would never be the best fucking barman in London again. The super wanted to kick him out the Henry Street door but he was handicapped by the Scott Medal for Bravery and was obliged to leave Ben in the ranks.

Around this time there was an outbreak of an epidemic identified by the newspapers as 'joy-riding'. This term was meant to be applicable to the practice by the disaffected jobless from housing schemes, of stealing cars and driving them until they crashed into a wall, an old age pensioner or a police car. It elicited such concern that the brains of the best and the brightest were ransacked for a cure. A well-known doctor with socialist leanings proposed on *The Gay Byrne Television Show* that in the major cities municipal tracts of land be converted into racetracks, old cars bought with public funds and those on the live register who so inclined be encouraged to drive off their frustrations without danger to public or private property or person. This suggestion attracted a certain number of adherents in the letters page of the *Irish Times*.

'Christ,' Ben's partner swore when they received a call that a stolen Mercedes was being joy-ridden around the Brian Boru estates by a youth wearing a glue-sniffing bag. In their Fiat they chugged to the estate where they saw the Mercedes being reversed into lampposts, driven forward into stationary cars. When they approached the Mercedes backed into them and then shot off around the estate. They followed but were soon lapped and rammed in the rear. Ben's partner broke his neck. Ben got out of the police car and stood in the middle of the road until the Mercedes came round again. He jumped on the bonnet and grabbed the wipers for support. The Mercedes managed another circuit before it crashed. The estate was on the edge of the city. Ben took the young driver for a walk until they reached a field that provided an ashplant. Ben handcuffed the driver to a tree and lashed him. He carried the driver back over his shoulder and dumped him in the estate. It was the last documented or undocumented incident of joy-riding in Mellick. Although second time round Ben turned down the sergeant's job with less conviction, he also stumbled on the truth that there is a cachet attached to refusing promotion. The Scott Medal had made his name and lashing the joyrider spoke to the very depths of the man in the street, and his colleagues on the beat and the judges on the bench who were handcuffed by the law. But it was staying in the ranks that burnished the legend. And then a sergeant's job could lead to detective and so on unchecked until he became commissioner, locked in an office analysing trends. All right, deep down he knew he would never be the best fucking barman in London again but he was closer as a *garda* than he would be as commissioner. He was in touch with the people as he had been in The Pub, and when the people recognised him through his fame and said 'Hello, Guard', what they were really saying was Keep the change.

Mad Dog O'Dwyer was wanted in the North in connection with thirty-five murders and in the South for the theft of money from banks and trousers from policemen. It was a kink or quirk of Mad Dog's when apprehended by the unarmed *gardai* to point his revolver, steal a uniform, drive off in the patrol car and leave his victims in their vests and underpants. Whatever about the thirty-five murders in the North, the *gardai* in the South thought it no joke to be embarrassed. Mad Dog O'Dwyer was a wanted man.

At three in the morning Ben Hanley and his partner were returning to Mellick after a visit to a poteen merchant in the Clare Hills. They had sampled the contraband and were mellow in the comfort of the *garda* car. They were travelling on byroads, where they were surprised to come upon a parked mini and a lady flagging them down. They got out of the *garda* car and immediately from behind a hedge were commanded: 'Step out of those uniforms like good boys.' Ben's partner said: 'Christ, it's Mad Dog.'

'That's right boys. Now step out of those uniforms. Give Concepta the keys.'

Mad Dog came out from behind the hedge and began to slip out of his trousers though keeping his gun pointed. Ben nodded to his partner who started to unbutton his tunic.

'You too, bogman, hurry.'

Ben walked towards Mad Dog.

'Hold it just there, hold it!'

But Ben kept going till halted by the gun barrel in his

neck. Then Mad Dog whooped: 'Concepta, it's Ben Hanley. Fucking Ben Hanley. Get 'em off you, Ben.'

'Here's what I want you to do, O'Dwyer. Listen to me. Listen carefully. I want you to put the gun to my head and blow my brains out, you follow? That's the only way you'll get Ben Hanley's trousers.'

'They're probably too big for me, your mate's will do. Now hop to it.'

Slowly, Ben put his hand on Mad Dog's wrist, tightened his grip and forced the gun down by Mad Dog's side.

When they arrived in Mellick Ben stopped the car a hundred yards from the station, forced Mad Dog out and marched him to the barracks in his vest and underpants. Ben Hanley had a tougher job refusing promotion this time but his determination was rewarded with the cult status of a national folk hero. He was now so familiar with the part he had created for himself that he correctly refused to be interviewed by the newspapers or *The Gay Byrne Show*.

Such landmarks eased the passing of Ben Hanley's first fifteen years in the force. And yet they did not glow as brightly as the fading memory of Diana Hayhurst in The Pub toilet. The only conscious decision he had ever made was to leave the mackerel boat and even in that he was following an opened trail. All that had happened to him since had simply happened to him, and as a consequence his creed was fatalism. While he was envied and praised by all for his individuality, his own assessment of himself was that he was mere flotsam. He might have bobbed contentedly to his destiny were it not for the obligation to visit his parents in Westport at Christmas. They were proud of him at home but not as proud as if he had been promoted to sergeant, detective or commissioner. And every Christmas brought its cargo of returned Paddy, all cock and cocky and dressed in flash gear. The English phlegm had surfaced again in the face of the IRA bombs as it had done during the Blitz and Paddy – who at least had a white face – was allowed to peep his nose out of the ghetto once more. With such competition Garda Ben Hanley was not the celebrity he should have been in his home village at Christmas. The competition was younger and it had more money.

THE LEAGUE AGAINST CHRISTMAS (II)

BATEMAN THREW IN the diddly club in the same spirit that Arthur Ellis suggested a carpet factory and Ernie Gosling the place where they make the paper hats. It is probable that at that moment among diverse gatherings all over the world and in various tongues Christmas was being denied and proposals as fatuous as those of Ellis and Gosling thrown into the ring. But the diddly club was ummistakably a sitting duck of a stand-in target for the intangible feast. Ellis raised his head out of his red beard and turned to Bateman. Ellis was smiling through the growth. He said: 'That's it.' Bateman was always happy that he could hold his own with the solo school in the repartee stakes and now he had again shown a touch for the apposite that was out of their league. Even Foster nodded slowly in agreement. There was yet room in the world for someone who had almost qualified as a Bachelor of Arts. Only a man steeped in Dickens could hit the bull's-eye.

For a few moments there was silence as the solo school contemplated the iconoclasm. Diana Hayhurst's vivacity froze into puzzled wrinkles on her forehead. Ernie Gosling licked a cigarette paper. A lark was what it was all about, they were on about having a right lark and Percy had the best idea because Arthur said 'That's it' and Mr Foster nodded his head. It was Ernie's pride that he always just about managed to catch on.

Foster tapped the card table with his wedding ring. He looked about him at the spectators and then leaned forward.

'Whose deal is it?' Foster demanded.

During the next week Foster wondered why he had not thought of it before: a hotel. He considered the doomsday situation. Suppose he popped off in his room in a hotel in Mellick? He would be discovered by the hotel manager who would call a doctor, a policeman and a clergyman, a committee to whom no credit would accrue collectively or individually by broadcasting that he had died in ladies' underclothes. It would not go beyond: MAN FOUND DEAD IN HOTEL ROOM. Too many people were found dead in hotel rooms for them all to have been reading Gideon Bibles at the end. Gladys would never know. Better still, she would have to wonder for the rest of her life what he had been doing in Ireland. Nick with his dirty mind would probably conclude that he had gone to Ireland in search of a whore. Nick would rally round Gladys. Kenneth wouldn't want you moping, Gladys, let me fix you a drink. Bottoms up.

Of course, if you looked at it that way he did not need Bateman or Ellis or any of them. Any hotel would do. He could do it in London. Book into a room and bring in his suitcase full of duds and strip off and dress up. Yes, that was quite logical. Why cloud the issue with an assault on Christmas? Somehow he could not see it as being that simple. Going off on his own, out of control like that, was the very stuff of mania – extreme like Ellis himself and his lino. No. He needed the anarchic cocoon of the solo school. That much he would concede. Propriety was a Sunday suit and he was as much entitled to his day in jeans as the next man. Or knickers. But it was the solo school had helped him see that. It was fitting that his investiture should be part of a solo school outing.

He was way ahead of them by the time Bateman suggested the diddly club. Not that Bateman meant anything by it. They loved to chuck ideas about when they were short of bombs. Bateman and Ellis, they would sit at the solo school and fantasise until doomsday. Unless he could expose their bluff and goad them into action. And no one knew better how to extract a performance from underlings. The yawning slackers who passed for articled clerks these days could testify to that. Yes, he would put a little bomb of his own under Bateman and Ellis. The more he thought on it the more he looked forward to flashing himself a little in the process – in something of the fashion that Gosling, with gasper dangling, liked to show how he could lift six glasses with five fingers. One carried modesty too far in denying one's talents altogether.

At the next meeting of the solo school Foster did not so much as allude to the proposal to sabotage Christmas though he was well prepared to push things along cutely if the topic was resurrected by anyone else. But, of course, as he expected, there was no follow-up. The Irish lacked tenacity; Ellis was sunk to the depths. And you could not anticipate leadership from Gosling or Hayhurst. Any time Foster did think to slip in a suitable aside that might turn their thoughts to Christmas, he was aware of the Guv'nor hovering round the table collecting glasses. At closing time Foster decided to put his toe in the water. Outside the pub he gripped Bateman lightly by the arm: 'I don't know if you've noticed, Bateman, but there are only fifty-six shopping days to Christmas.'

'I'm glad you told me.' But Bateman's raillery was

automatic. Foster was content that he had struck home.

Next morning Bateman made his tea and toast as usual, as foundation for the first cigarette of the day. On cue, as he exhaled into the smoke wafting from his fag, Foster emerged genie-fashion with his fifty-six shopping days to Christmas. Bateman felt the colour leave his face. He had battled Christmas for so long on his own that he had all but retired defeated. And then suddenly a week ago he had been afforded one glorious glimpse of the Transfiguration: himself with the solo school by his side taking on and defeating the feast. Only to have Foster bring him back down to earth with his command to resume the game. It had all been just so much bullshit like any other topic that cropped up between deals. Sober now and alone Bateman was conscience-bidden to recall that thievery was against all his breeding and education. He had never so much as ducked the fare on a bus despite living among a people for whom the fiddle was time-honoured. Stripped of ideology, robbing a diddly club was repugnant to him. These were daylight thoughts that accompanied Bateman on his jobless amble round the city, from the morning pint to the lunchtime sandwich and pint to the pre-evening meal pint. But later, at night, propped up by booze, Bateman saw daylight as an artificial stimulant to conformity. Christmas. He had earned his shot at the title. Take his evening meal. He knew the rasher was done when the bedsitter fogged from the burnt steam and holding his head back from the flying spatters he pressed the sausages against the pan with a knife to cook them on the outside at least. He could not cut the rasher with a knife lest it fly off the plate. He picked up the rasher with his fingers and bit it as though it were a stick of celery. This was the life of a once would-be Bachelor of Arts. When he ate out he did not have the confidence to stride into a hotel or decent restaurant and

dine on good food properly cooked. His low self-esteem
drew him to squalid cafés with fifties Pepsi signs over the
doors where he drank tea from plastic cups and cut fried
egg sandwiches with plastic knives.

On his nightly bar stool Bateman caught the ball and
sidestepped the Garryowen forwards and jinked his way
up the field past four Garryowen backs and went across
the line in the corner for the only score of the game. His
father and Frankie Timmons carried him off the field on
their shoulders. Up on the stand he received the under-
twenties cup from the branch president's wife and could
hear his name again and again through the babble. They
walked home in procession over the bridge behind Johnny
Bateman leading the goat. Disregarding the traffic the
throng continued up the main street singing:

> Beautiful, beautiful Thomond,
> Star of my life fade away.
> I sigh when I think of Young Thomond,
> For whom I played many a day.

His mother was at the bottom of the street with those
neighbours too feeble or feminine to have been at the
game. That night the doors of all the houses were open
and when the men came out from the pubs they drank
and sang sitting on the little walls of the small gardens
outside the compact houses. Children allowed up late
gathered to look at him leaning against the frame of the
hall door. Johnny Bateman climbed out of the celebrations to squeeze his shoulder with the sagacious: Don't
let it go to your head— There were senior cup days to
come . . .

Near closing time Bateman festered at the lack of
hearth awaiting him in the bedsitter. He would buy a
chicken and chips, and in the morning the bones would

reproach him and he would be sore across the navel . . .

He became a Bachelor of Arts and taught in his old school and captained Young Thomond to win the senior cup. At school he remonstrated with a Leaving Cert pupil: I never used language like that and I never met the man I was afraid of. He was picked to play for Munster and was the star of the inter-provincial series. But he was not picked for Ireland. Even on a bar stool at night Bateman was a realist. Ireland did not want anyone from a working man's club.

Home and life were now a bedsitter in a city where he did not have enough hands to twist enough ears while he remonstrated with the foul tongues of their owners. No one knew of his dreams, shameful fantasies that could not be shared. A man could drive himself mad sitting on a bar stool at night. Yet there was a reward in self-pity. The more Bateman indulged sorrow for himself the more the diddly club cried out to be done. Dare he hope that Foster's fifty-six shopping days to Christmas was anything other than a commonplace exchange? Was it hallucination induced by drink last night that led him to discern a conspiratorial weight in the remark? If the solo school did decide to take on Christmas he would have a sense of purpose for the first time in his life. He would be back among the comity of nations, at the top table, his glass of water as full as his neighbour's.

The solo school were dealing with a Diana Hayhurst bid of nine tricks in diamonds. It was Foster's deal so he took no part in the hand. Diana Hayhurst was trying to make up her bundle with a cold king of clubs and to this end she had interspersed her trumps with four decoy leads of low hearts, receiving each time a spade return which she roughed. Her second-last lead – a trump – confronted Bateman: he had the ace of clubs and the ace of hearts.

What to discard? Gosling and Ellis, and Bateman himself when out of trumps, had jettisoned clubs throughout the hand. And he could account for all but the king and the ace in his own hand. The queen of hearts was also missing and could have been held by Gosling, Ellis or Diana Hayhurst. Bateman reasoned that her four leads of hearts had not been decoys and accordingly he discarded the ace of clubs. Diana Hayhurst made her bundle. Her success called for a postmortem. Accusation was met with counter-accusation. Ellis claimed Gosling had given too strong a hint on clubs by discarding the queen, and both Ellis and Gosling turned on Bateman for not leading back the ace of clubs through Diana Hayhurst when he had got in on hearts. Bateman insisted it was a fifty–fifty situation. It was a case that demanded adjudication from the clear head of the non-involved dealer. Foster duly delivered:

'There are only fifty shopping days to Christmas.' The *non sequitur* provoked arched eyebrows all round. But Foster looked only at Bateman who held his gaze.

'I'm glad you told me.'

'Well then. Are you waiting for me to tell you there is only one shopping day to Christmas? Somehow I hadn't taken you for a waffler. I thought there was more to you than there is to Ellis, say.'

'I beg your pardon?'

Foster ignored Ellis. 'This diddly club, Bateman. Can it be done? Or were you being fanciful?'

'It can be done.'

Alf the barber arrived. The Guv'nor hung about. The solo school concentrated on the cards. When it came to Ellis's turn he dealt, and then sat back and thought.

With his braces, coloured shirt, corduroys, cap and beard, Arthur Ellis saw himself in the livery of a free soul and was proud that he had earned his manumission. And yet the vestigial Arthur Ellis of the NatWest feared that a day would come when he would have to pay the price, just as the patrons of the NatWest had to carry the cross of the thirty-six monthly instalments. He was fond of saying to the solo school: 'You see me, I did it.' But even as he boasted he was alert for the hand that would touch his shoulder, a Tammer with a scrip of authority rolled inside a rubber band: Thought you'd get away with it, did you? He had not expected the NatWest to take things lying down and knew damn well that higher management would have investigated, summoned Tammer, combed the books for the least nit of embezzlement. But he had not been a fiddler. They would have had to proceed further to discover a proper understanding of how such a canker grew within their hallowed hothouse.

He suspected that Kenneth Foster was an agent of the NatWest. What else could he make of the man? Alf the barber, the Guv'nor, the black and Paddy clients in The Lino Shop, Bateman, Ernie, even Diana Hayhurst herself, they were all of his new world. They fitted in. But the moment Foster took the cards in his hands – and taught himself how to play in ten seconds – Ellis recognised Nemesis. Foster's company might have handled some of NatWest's affairs. Certainly the NatWest did use accountancy consultants to recruit personnel, a shield against depositors of large sums using muscle to place idiot sons. The business of recruitment involved probing into backgrounds. The distinction was academic, the inference obvious: why not hire them to probe those with the death wish to be fired? They would have instructed Foster: All we have to go on is sudden infatuation with lino. Never any trouble. Sound as you could expect. With us since a lad. They might have given Foster orders to inveigle himself into the King's Arm's society. The NatWest would not have experience in investigating dropouts of the lino fixation variety. In common with other institutions such as the banks proper, the NatWest suffered a certain rate of attrition from dreamers going over the wall into the ranks of the poetry and artistic brigade. That class of defection was commonplace, anticipated and budgeted for in the recruitment and training allotment, and was no more remarkable than the provision for delinquent accounts. But in his own experience his case was unique – sufficient explanation in itself for their calling in Foster.

After a year of Foster in the solo school Ellis had decided it was time to shake off the monomania. The NatWest would surely by then have given up, written 'case unsolved' and closed the file. That was if the NatWest had ever opened it in the first place. And yet Foster did not fit in. And Ellis still feared a reckoning of some sort. And if this diddly club business was not St Peter running his talon down the ledger then Arthur Ellis was a monkey's uncle. Foster all for it. Only fifty shopping days to Christmas. Could the diddly club be done? Diddly clubs were limited to the tunes that could be played on them. You ran them or you robbed them. He remembered a couple of weeks ago Bateman suggesting the diddly club. There had been a golden glow in the solo school. But now his cynicism took a dive under the bed: he thought they were joking. He could have some understanding of Bateman's position. All that baloney about Savile Row suits and not having had his head kicked in. Nursing the wound until it festered Bateman might finally have lost the run of himself. But Foster? Was it possible that Foster was deranged? Taking a look from the point of view of a solid umpire of society, Ellis admitted that he himself could be classified as mad, ditto Bateman, certainly Diana Hayhurst was a weirdo and Ernie, well, Ernie was Ernie. Good ol' Ernie. Foster alone stood out as faithful to his standing in the community. And here was Foster running against form, going off the rails.

They would make a bollocks of it.

If he got involved he would be arrested, charged and found guilty. He could see the way he would be seen. First, good job chucked up in the air and wife abandoned. Then Tammer as character witness. Mr Tammer, when did you first notice . . . ? Psychiatric evidence of a split personality. Strong probability of degeneration into violence if allowed at large. They would lock him up with nutcases and give him electric shocks and pills that would make him fatter. That was the sunny side. That or be bunged into the Scrubs to have his arse raped.

They were playing a spread, Ernie's bid. Ernie had laid down a lone five of hearts, deuce and seven of clubs. His diamonds were impregnable. He had discarded the five of hearts on Foster's opening lead of a spade. By now Foster had managed to probe the five of clubs through Ernie drawing the deuce, and it was only a matter of time before Foster was satisfied that Diana Hayhurst was clubless when he would inexorably use the four or three to trap Ernie's seven. There would be no postmortem.

What would he do when Foster raised the subject again? He could opt out. But then he would lose his place in the solo school hierarchy. Maybe he was being premature. Foster's was only one voice. Outside of the view of a solid umpire of society the rest of the school were rational individuals. No: Bateman was for it and so was Foster, and that combination amounted to a controlling interest. He would look lovely out of it, presiding over the rump parliament of Ernie and Diana Hayhurst. And then he was the man in the middle and that ground had its compensations. After all, it was Bateman's idea in the first place and it was Foster who was pushing it through. It might be as well to remember that if he were obliged to turn druid's evidence, or whatever bottle-washer they had over there.

Ernie Gosling paid out glumly and yet he stood up for himself too. 'Go on,' he said to everyone in general. 'Go on, admit it, at least I took a chance, didn' I?' It was Mr Foster in particular whose absolution he sought. Mr Foster didn't approve of buck calls.

'If nobody never 'ad a go, there wouldn't be much lark to the game then, would there? Eh?'

At 'lark', Foster winced. There was as much necessity for 'lark' as there was for articled clerks to throw paper aeroplanes around the office. He switched back to Bateman. The presence of the Guv'nor and Alf the barber notwithstanding, it was time to deal with the first item on the agenda. That had always constituted his boardroom philosophy: Get down to it.

'Re that other matter, Bateman, I propose finesse. I'd go so far as to say I'd be impatient with anyone who didn't see eye to eye with me there.'

'Of course.'

'How's the shop these days, Ellis, run off your feet I expect?'

'I'll have you know, Foster, when you want something done, give it to a busy man.'

'Perhaps at some convenient moment we should have a head count. Your deal, Gosling.'

The Guv'nor never would get used to card talk. He went back behind his bar. Ernie Gosling completed the deal. Mr Foster touched his wrist and whispered: 'Are you with us?'

Ernie Gosling was not going to show himself up in front of Mr Foster by asking to have it explained. He figured it out for himself. What they were at was that they were going to find something to do that stood for burning down the factory where they make the paper hats because you couldn't really burn down a factory unless you wanted to spend the rest of your days in the nick. Mr Foster and Percy had something up their sleeves by the sound of it. There would be a right lark, and Mr Foster asking was he game. 'You can count on me, Mr Foster.'

The Guv'nor came out again. Mrs Dixon and Mrs Murphy arrived. It was not possible to progress beyond Foster's: 'I don't see it as woman's work.' To which Diana Hayhurst replied: 'Like fuck it isn't!' Bateman let it pass.

Foster smiled. They were all in. It was as easy as that. Slinky lingerie, lipstick, perfume, eye shadow: the vision brought a lump to his underpants.

During the week between solo schools Ernie Gosling liked to pause at Arthur's table and have a chat while Arthur entertained himself after his hard day in The Lino Shop by dealing four imaginary hands. Arthur was an easy-going bloke you could be yourself with whereas with Mr Foster you were inclined to watch your p's and q's. But even with Arthur he did not feel right about bringing up what his instinct told him was confined to a full quorum of the solo school. It seemed like one of those cases coming up in court that the papers wasn't supposed to write about. Neither did Arthur bring up the subject. The night before the next meeting of the solo school Ernie could not stop himself. Looking over Arthur's shoulder at the four hands he'd dealt, Ernie mumbled: 'What you reckon then, Arthur?'

'Reckon what, Ernie?'

'Mr Foster an' Percy. An' us all. What we gettin' up to then?'

'Oh that. Nothing much, Ernie. We're going to Mellick to rob a diddly club.' Arthur was matter of fact. Ernie nodded: 'That's how I figured it meself.'

It was a lucky bloody thing that he hadn't said anything to Linda or Betty.

Wednesday usually flew with the solo school to look forward to that night but today every time he looked at his watch he thought it was stopped. He always found something to keep himself occupied afternoons but now he didn't fancy anything somehow, not even a bit of kip in front of the programme Betty was watching. Around this time he should have been placing a paintbrush neatly on top of a tin and going into the kitchen to make Betty a cuppa. He found himself looking at Betty to see if Betty was looking at him, reading his mind, but Betty wasn't easily distracted from her programme.

There had never been a secret in the house. When he was bothered he discussed it with Linda and out of respect Betty was dragged in too even if it was something that at Betty's age she would not have a clue about. He could just imagine what would happen if he shared the diddly club with them. Say tonight when Linda and Betty would be watching the telly as usual while he washed up the tea things straightaway. Normally he'd sit with them a bit and have a gasper before he cleaned up but tonight he would be on edge, impatient to get to the solo school. Linda would notice: What's all the rush then? He might not answer because people often asked questions in front of the telly, and if they were glued to the programme forgot that they didn't get an answer or didn't take in the answer if they did get one. He might have it in his head to slide out unnoticed altogether but the bleeding ads would come on just as he was ready and Linda would turn round as he was holding his head back to get a last look in the mirror. He would have to bluff: I'll be off then.

He could see it all so clearly. It was raining now. Probably be lashing down after tea as well.

'Where you off to at this hour, Ernie?'

'Stretch me legs.'

'That's rain 'oppin' off the windows, Ernie, can't you 'ear?'

'You're right. Better take the umbrella.'

'Hold on. Just past seven, solo school's not till 'alf eight. Oy, an' you 'aven't done yer pools, you 'aven't.'

But he would have done the pools. He would do them now in a minute. That would help pass the afternoon when he stopped imagining.

'Yes, I 'ave then. Done 'em this afternoon, didn' I, goin' to put them in the litter bin now.'

'The wah? The litter bin?'

'Post 'em I mean.'

'How come you done yer pools this afternoon then? You never do pools afternoons, Ernie, you do 'em nights when we can all chip in. Bet you 'ave your daft QPR down to draw with Man. United.'

But he would not have put QPR down to draw with Man. United. He would do the pools now in a few minutes' time and he would leave sentiment out of it. Not that it would surprise him one bit if QPR did draw, United wasn't United like it used to be. He saw himself showing Linda the coupon.

'Sod yer pools, where you off to this hour's what I'm askin'.'

'I've a mind to stretch me legs an' you carry on's if it's a Scotland Yard job.'

Right, that was the way it would happen okay.

'Ernie, you stretch your legs right here by the telly that's what you'll do, you're not movin' in that weather me end up 'avin' to stay home feedin' you cough bottles. The ideas 'e gets, right, Betty?'

Betty wouldn't answer, it was just they liked to bring her in, show her respect.

'I've got the umbrella 'aven't I? Linda, you tellin' me now I can't 'ave a walk when I feels like it?'

'You walk from Land's End to John O'Groats you feel like it, Ernie. But not tonight when it's pissin' out as you can 'ear.'

'Linda!'

'Sorry, Betty, it's 'is fault.'

'How's it my fault you 'ave to be vulgar then?'

'Listen to 'im!'

'It's true for Percy, women don't 'ave respect for their tongues today.'

'That's a laugh comin' from a Paddy that is. Here's the programme, sit down, Ernie, an' no more interruptin'.'

That's how it would go. He would not be able to sit down. Suddenly he would let it out.

'What's that, Ernie?'

'Christmas.'

'Christmas?'

'Yeah, Christmas. But I don't spose you'd be bothered.'

'Course I would. Everybody's bothered 'bout Christmas, wouldn't be right an' they weren't. What about Christmas, Ernie?'

'It came up at the solo school, we're discussin' how to sabotage it.'

'Sabowho?'

'You 'eard.'

'Turn the sound down on that telly, Betty. Sabotage what again, Ernie? Sabotage Christmas?'

'You wouldn't understand, Linda. Sorry I mentioned it.'

'Bleedin' right I don't. 'E's 'avin' us on. Ain't you, Ernie?'

'Yeah, I'm 'avin' you on.'

'No, you're not.'

'I wish you'd make your mind up, Linda.'

'Come on, Ernie, it ain't funny. In front of Betty an' all.'

'Look, you take Uncle Albert, 'e makes me wear 'is paper hats Christmas, right?'

'Ernie, you're not on 'bout that again, are you, it's barely November.'

''E makes me an' you lot back 'im up an' I don't like it. That's me. Now you take Percy. Christmas 'e's locked up in 'is room all day drinkin' whisky an' talkin' to 'isself. You think that's right? Percy don't like Christmas an' I don't blame 'im. Arthur and Mr Foster, Christmas bothers them too. So we're goin' to get our own back for once. Awright?'

'What about her ladyship, Ernie? Why don't she like Christmas?'

He could imagine it all so clearly, the exact words Linda would use and he could hear himself being straight as usual like he always was with Linda and Betty.

'Diana 'asn't said. I don't think she's agin it, I think she might even like Christmas.'

'She odd then, Ernie, or what?'

'You're bein' sarcastic.'

'Me? Not me, Ernie. So how're you goin' to get your own back on Christmas then, eh? Christmas ain't the postman what you can get yer dog to bite, or kick up the backside or belt round the ear'ole. Christmas ain't any-thing, I mean anything you can say there it is I gotcha.'

'That's why it has to be symbolic.'

'Eh? Like how, Ernie?'

'It has to be somethin' that when we done it we can sit back an' feel better. Frinstance I suggested we find out the factory where they make the paper hats an' we burn it down . . .'

'Youwha?'

'But I wasn't agreed with . . .'

'I should bloody well think you wasn't. Betty, turn that telly off, turn the knob off altogether. Ernie, you want to burn down a factory, did I hear you say you want to burn down a factory?'

'Course I don't want to burn down a factory.'

'But you just said!'

'I told you you wouldn' understand. What I want to do's somethin' what's the same as burnin' down a factory. Arthur wanted we do a carpet factory, for another frinstance.'

'You're right I *don't* understand. Bet I know one thing though, the Irish bloke Percy, bet I know what Percy's suggestion was, right, Ernie? 'E wanted to blow up the 'Ouses of Parliament, right, Ernie?'

'No, 'e didn't, what a bleedin' thing to say. But what 'e did say is what we're all agreed on doin'.'

'What did Mister Clean Mouth come up with then?'

'Percy's got 'is old man still livin' back in Ireland. His old man an' 'is mate they run this diddly club, see? Percy figured we'd go over there an' knock it off.'

'Steal?'

'If you want to put it that way, yeah. But it's really Christmas we'd be doin'. The diddly club'd be standin' in for Christmas, see?'

'You losin' your marbles, Ernie? You standin' there tellin' me you're in a gang what's goin' to rob people's money? When was we ever robbers, Ernie, eh? You ever see me comin' home from cleanin' offices with an elastic band that wasn't mine?'

'Look, Mr Foster, 'e's an accountant, they don't come more respectable. Diana Hayhurst, she owns *Unipolitan*. Percy, I keep tellin' you he's educated, too educated for what jobs are goin', an' Arthur used to be top cat in the NatWest only 'e didn' fancy it. An' none of them don't see it the way you put it. What we're talkin' 'bout is

Christmas as wears us all down, is all.'

'We're talkin' 'bout me an' Betty goin' round Albert's first off an' then the Arms where the Guv'nor's goin' to hear what specimens 'e 'as for customers. An' soon as you can say up the IRA bobbies'll be all over the place so you stay in tonight, Ernie. Betty, get your coat.'

Taking it step by step that's how it'd end up. Anyway there was a half-hour gone just imagining. He'd do the pools now and then make a cuppa and keep his mouth shut tight about the solo school.

He rammed his hand up to his elbow into the postbox in an effort to retrieve the coupon. It didn't matter if your brother was the postmaster general or if you were the prime minister there was no way of getting it back once it was posted. It had to go to where it was sent, that was the rule. The coupon was filled in properly according to form and the tips of the experts.

No one could have been half the flibbertigibbet Diana Hayhurst showed herself in public and yet establish, develop and successfully manage *Unipolitan*. As in any business flair did have its place in the magazine – a poor second behind counting what went out and what came in. She was obliged to spend more time with her hand to a flushed forehead squinting at figures than nosing out 'Incest – The Last Taboo' or 'Ménage à Trois Rules OK', features which appeared to those not in the know as the fruit of a non-stop wallow in glamour. They were not to know that under such couturier creations every issue wore the same foundation garments. *Unipolitan* was established. Once it staked a claim to a given readership it had to continue with ninety per cent formula spiced with ten per cent fad and serve coated in unipolitanese, As *Time* magazine did. The patent gradgrind of the sweatshop was simply dolled up in designer drudgery.

Diana Hayhurst was wedded to *Unipolitan* a long time now and like a good husband did not notice that she was wearing of an ageing wife. The good husband tended his pigeons, stood for office, took up bowls, coached a schoolboy soccer squad, broke down a wall to allow open plan, drank, walked the dog or bought a video.

Once there were not enough hours in the day to devote to her magazine. Now, trundling under its own momentum, *Unipolitan* no longer needed her to work late at the office. Prime ministers took holidays and indulged the hedonism of an Agatha Christie on the bedside table; members of Parliament found time to be blackmailed by leather-clad flagellants. Mobsters went to church and extended their palms or slid their tongues out for the wafer. It was not ironic, it was of the scheme of things that Diana Hayhurst should find balm among her antitheses – the solo school. The men in the solo school were old-fashioned and had old standards and were a better inspiration than Hooper or Fyncham had ever been. She had discovered them on a whim and stayed on because they became her little pets. They were dull, rare, *amusing*. Reaction to any one of them would fill *Unipolitan*. They belonged in their chains – of which Christmas was the biggest link. What sort of a solo school would she have with men who had taken on and defeated Christmas?

On a Wednesday afternoon, a few months before the proposal to sabotage Christmas, Diana Hayhurst gave tea in the Ritz to an American film star. As editor and publisher of the magazine it was an occasion that could not have been hosted by even the most exalted of her plenipotentiaries. Also, he was a stud. His publicity touted him as thirty-seven years of age, and in the flesh in the Ritz he looked only thirty-seven. He was a fine man with a taste for England and things English. Despite his strong screen persona he exuded gentility. He held her chair out. He answered intelligently her tried, trusted and, therefore, inane questions. They got on. Over the éclairs the film star suggested: 'Diana, I have an idea. Why don't I give you dinner?'

Diana Hayhurst parried: she indicated the crumbs of the buttered scones. 'I have to watch my figure. Not another morsel today.'

The film star smiled. 'I don't know how to put it any more delicately.'

'You're doing fine. But haven't you a tight schedule?'

'I'm not flying out until nine thirty. Press conference at six. I'll give them an hour. Change, bathe. I shall await you in my suite at eight o'clock. How's that?'

Diana Hayhurst lit a cigarette and blew the smoke at the film star, rounding her mouth. She knew how to give studs a fitness test.

'I'll be there.'

She walked from the Ritz back to the pad over her Regent Street offices. She had a bath fit for a woman about to be fucked jet-set style, and then set about herself with the body freshener and deodorants taking care to apply a tasteful nuance to the nether orifice: studs loved to show what they could achieve with the tongue. She dressed in £487.50 worth of raiment inclusive of the ninety-nine pee Pretty Polly tights. The last item she put in her handbag was the tape measure with which she intended to take the length of his prick in action and at rest so that he would recognise decorations were being worn. She rang her usual taxi, arsed into the front passenger seat, hauling a wonderful view of her legs in after her.

'The Ritz, Pete.'

Pete tried to swallow his desire if not his curiosity. 'No card game tonight, Ms Hayhurst?'

Pete was already edging his way into the traffic.

'It's Wednesday?' She knew now it was Wednesday but wanted both of them to be mistaken.

'You must be rushed off your feet you forget the day of the week.'

She glimpsed the solo school without her. There were Foster, Percy, Arthur and Ernie and no need for dealer out. So she would miss one night. Pete was already at the Ritz and a gloved hand reached out from under the braided livery to open the passenger door. She could not go on Thursday night. She would miss out on a dose of the solo school designed to last a week.

'Pete, the King's Arms.'

As with the pleasure of those she consummated, the pain of the ride she missed soon faded. The only poke she would never forget was that from the barman whatwashisname in The Pub all those years ago. But she knew she had sacrificed a big moment for the solo school: she would not stand idly by now and let the solo school sacrifice the solo school. She would protect them from themselves.

Bateman was last to arrive. He went directly to the counter where he was served by the Guv'nor's wife. He vaguely heard himself being told that the Guv'nor was on a night off. Bateman's mind was on the solo school. They were not yet playing a hand, Ernie was dealing, yet Bateman could hear no banter. Even Ernie was obviously not at ease. He usually made a ceremony of concocting a cigarette and having done so, lit it, put it in his mouth and forgot to smoke it. Now Ernie puffed heavily, tense signals flaring from his nostrils. There was a poignancy about Ernie's paper hats *vis-à-vis* the heavyweight burdens of men of thought: it was tantamount to a corruption of youth to admit Ernie's uncluttered sensibilities to an adult seminar on destruction. Bateman strode to the card table and watched them play out the hand.

It was a straightforward bundle of Arthur's who Bateman could see held a certain ten tricks and so the play was mechanical. Yet the players were stiff. Arthur himself looked close to voiding his supper. He had six tricks made and still held three trumps and a cold ace. His normal form would have been to throw them in and exult: That's it. It was Foster who was always punctilious about playing a hand out. Now Arthur had lost his effervescence. And Ernie and Diana Hayhurst frowned in concentration as though the bundle could be defeated. They were rigid, the atmosphere so unlike the solo school that Bateman's enthusiasm began to dip before he got his sea legs as a conspirator. He sat down. Ellis was paid without a postmortem. Foster gathered the cards. At least Foster seemed himself, relaxed, the committee confidence of a zealot. Instead of dealing, Foster stacked the deck and put the cards to one side of the table. It was a gesture easily construed: the wonder of it was, Bateman thought, that he had not brought along a gavel and banged the table.

Foster's swivelled appraisal of the solo school lighted on Bateman. He opened softly.

'Over to you, Bateman.'

During the past week, at the thought of robbing the diddly club, Bateman used furbelowed imagery to tackle the shivering weakness in the calves of his legs: Back in time a base has been dug broad and deep for me so it's natural that I feel my bones a trifle old for the facile hurdle into apostasy. Stand not on the order of my going if that means what I think it means. Whether I swan from the high rock or slide ungainly down the grassy bank I will be as wet in the river from either approach. So here goes.

The solo school listened. Ernie Gosling lipped his

suddenly extinguished gasper to the corner of his mouth; Diana Hayhurst held her chin, an exemplar of attentiveness; Arthur Ellis raised his beard. Foster: it is quite tragic that Bateman should be unsound. They have a parliament and educational system more or less modelled on our own, they're white, Bateman passes for one of us. And yet the hairline crack of lunacy is merely dormant. Best to encourage him, keep him on the road to the hotel in Mellick.

McNamara's Bus

THREE-QUARTERS OF MCNAMARA'S bus on either side was reserved for non-smokers. Bateman was herded towards the rear with his fellow pariahs. The bus left the Gloucester Road coach terminal at eight in the morning and after a slumberous hour it arrived in Luton where the driver announced a fifteen-minute stop for those who desired to make 'a quick purchase'. Most of the passengers were unmistakably Paddies travelling home cheaply to stretch the Christmas spending money. Paddies, a few nuns, middle-aged knitting ladies and low class would-be dolly birds unaware that miniskirts were fifteen years out of fashion.

Halfway to Birmingham a woman in the smoke-free zone rooted in her carrier bag and opened a dainty tinfoil of sandwiches. She was immediately aped. Flasks of tea and milk, crisps, minerals and every oddity were consumed throughout the bus. Bateman's neighbour in the window seat – a grown man – gorged a chocolate bar. A group at the back, young, from the buildings, produced baby bottles of whiskey. They shouted: 'Yahoo.' McNamara's bus was well on its way.

Immediately across the aisle from Bateman a young

man with long hair and a longer scarf seemed at his donnish ease reading a book. His travelling companion, nearest to Bateman, was older and balding and wore a driving jacket over a hand-knitted pullover. They too shared sandwiches. The older man looked about him a lot, a fidget, a suspicion about him that he longed to be friendly. Bateman could not help but be drawn to watching them eating their sandwiches and was suddenly trapped by: 'Care for one?'

'No, thanks. Thank you very much all the same.'

'Go on, have a go. We've more than enough, expect to be sick of them, eh, nephew?'

The nephew looked over from his book and smiled at Bateman. Pleasant people. English. Odd to have Englishmen aboard. Bateman accepted. 'That's very kind of you.'

'Not at all.' The uncle munched on. A minute later, his mouth full, he mimed the offer of a second sandwich. Bateman raised his hand and shook his head. The uncle nodded, made a greaseproof parcel of the sandwiches and put them in his bag. He slumped a little in his seat and closed his eyes. Bateman allowed his own lids to droop. Decent sorts, hospitable without sitting in your lap.

Bateman nodded on and off. His companion in the window seat stared out the window all the way, now chewing pastilles. Across the aisle the uncle slept through Birmingham and an hour further on the road. The nephew read, raising his head now and then as though savouring the riches of literature. The back seat, oiled by the baby bottles of whiskey, gave birth to a poker game and a singsong:

> Her eyes they shone like the diamonds,
> She thought she was queen of the land.
> Her hair it hung over her shoulder,
> Tied up with a black velvet band.

The uncle woke, grinned at Bateman and turned his head to bestow approval on the music makers. Near Holyhead he broke out the sandwiches again, insisting Bateman have one. They reached the boat.

Bateman set out to drink his way across. He had earned his tilt at the bar after such a long bus ride. Earned his tilts at all the bars where all men with the entry fee were equal. The bars closed on Christmas Day. He hit off with a ball of malt to keep the cold out. He sat by himself with legs crossed and the glass on his knee. All round Bateman the passengers dug into their provisions. Whiskey did not fill the stomach as beer or Guinness did. He longed for another sandwich only because everyone else was eating. He debated going to the bar and paying a price for a sandwich that would compensate the shipping line for all the sandwiches brought on board by those who baulked at the line's sandwich prices. Just then the sociable Englishman passed, clutching the bodies of a pair of bottles, the glasses at a rakish angle on the necks.

'Good crossing.' The Englishman paused.

'Yes. It has stayed calm.'

'I say, we still have more sandwiches than we seem able for . . .' Bateman attempted to shake his head. 'No, I won't take no for an answer, I'll fetch some. Or better still, we're just around the corner, why don't you join us?'

Bateman was inept at refusing any offer with conviction. The uncle won easily.

'Blake. Harry Blake. This is my nephew John Taylor. Head always stuck in books.'

Bateman gave his own name and they formally shook hands. Offered the sandwich, Bateman was no longer hungry but accepted.

'We're on our way to New York to see my daughter, married out there. Rum, travel agent's best package is to fly from Shannon so we thought we'd spend a couple of days in Mellick.'

'I'm going to Mellick myself. I was born there.'

'Ah. There's a coincidence. Tell me, you know the hotel the Royal George?'

'Yes. I'm staying there this visit.'

'Fancy that, eh, nephew? You'd recommend it, Mr Bateman, would you? It's not that we're insisting on posh but it's all right, is it? You know travel agents.'

'First class.'

'Well, then. We're thrown together. You don't sound Irish, Mr Bateman, if you don't mind me saying so. Nothing wrong with sounding Irish I hope you understand, but I'd have taken you for an Englishman.'

'I've been in London twenty-four years.'

'Ah, that's it. Going over for the holiday?'

Bateman nodded. 'And some business.' Bateman thought he was quick there: it explained the Royal George without having to tell his life story. And 'some business' had a ring to it. Hollow.

'I see. I'm retired myself now. What line are you in, Mr Bateman?'

'Finish those.' Bateman pointed to the drinks. It was an escape available to an Irishman no matter how long he had lived in London. It was the Irish way of inflicting hospitality, no 'Would you gentlemen care for another' experimentation. At the bar Bateman set about finding a job for himself. You could not tell two strangers on a boat that you were idle. They would deduce that he had not the price of a sandwich, insist he have what was left in the bag. It would dampen their journey. Of course there was the possibility that the uncle would not pursue his career when he returned with the drinks, but he had to be prepared. None of the jobs he had worked at were fit to mention and yet even in fantasy it was a struggle to come up with anything better. He could not say he was an accountant: that dry profession was possessed of its own esoterics. He was more qualified to be a lino man. But the uncle might catch him out there. What the blazes did Arthur's clients use to put the stuff down? Tacks? Super glue? Could he become a potman? He was loathe to go outside the recruitment office of the solo school. The solo school was his only experience outside himself. Shamefacedly, he acknowledged that he did not have the character to become a potman: he was not sufficiently free of a scrape of snobbery to carry it out impressively. He did not *want* to be a potman. The job was beneath him. He had nearly qualified as a Bachelor of Arts. A lino man of NatWest provenance had caste but only such a lino man. And he knew nothing of finance, had never owned a plastic card. He could not pass himself off as Diana Hayhurst. Not that there could have been much more than neck to her niche. She had boasted during the solo school that she owed her success to looking into her heart and anticipating trends. Odd, he had been looking into his own heart all his life. He could give her more than a bucketful if hers ever dried up. There was a thought . . .

'Well, Taylor?'

'Seems a decent chap, Inspector.'

'Uncle. Uncle. You don't slip up when we're alone you don't slip up in company. Decent? Stock in trade, I should wager. Cool, I'd prefer to say. Calculating. We're not as on top of this as we used to be you know. Not since that night the Guv'nor gets back after a booze-up with his cronies to find the bar almost empty and the solo school in a huddle. Not a word from Ernie that night and not a word since even when we gave the Guv'nor his head to ask Ernie straight out whatever happened to that idea to sabotage Christmas.'

Bateman bought himself a pint of beer and a bottle each for the uncle and nephew. He stood at the bar reluctant to move while he polished his new promotion. The beauty of it was that it was not technical. He could say he was in Market Research. A Bachelor of Arts job. He would not need computer literacy. Those under him would be qualified in that disease. He would be above that, thinking big, looking into his heart. He ordered three whiskeys to go with the beer.

'Now, Mr Bateman, that is naughty of you.' The English liked to have their drink forced on them, conscripts where the Irish were volunteers. The nephew proved more English than most. He shook the head, pointed to the whiskey.

'Thank you ever so much but I can't touch spirits, don't agree with me I'm afraid.'

'Nonsense, nephew. Drink it up, do you good. Cheers, Mr Bateman.'

'Cheers.'

Bateman and Inspector Blake paid their respects to the taste of malt, allowing it to settle. 'Ahh. That's the stuff. But we were saying . . . ?'

Bateman jumped in. 'Market research consultant. You were asking my line of business.'

'Of course. Market research, eh? I know, you're with those Gallup Polls that forecast all the wrong election results.' Inspector Blake decorated the crack by nudging Constable Taylor's shoulder with his elbow and winked at Bateman. Taylor had risked the tiniest sip of whiskey and coughed at the interruption to its digestion. Inspector Blake slapped him on the back. 'Put hair on your chest, eh, Mr Bateman?'

'I'm with *Unipolitan*.'

'Oil company?'

'The magazine, uncle. The magazine, Mr Bateman?'

'Right. It's not as grandiose as it sounds, more a question of anticipating trends, looking into one's heart. The publisher, Diana Hayhurst, she insists on the title I'm afraid.'

'And quite right too. I don't believe people should sell themselves short. But you anticipate trends, look into your heart. How so exactly?'

Bateman looked into his heart. 'To give you an example,' he began hesitantly. The uncle nodded. An ideal guinea pig. Bateman felt dressed in a little brief authority. 'The way I see things it's a safe bet that tomorrow's people will be thicker than today's, given that today's crop are a damn sight thicker than yesterday's.' Bateman paused. They did not fall about. He was not contradicted.

'That's a hobbyhorse of my own, Mr Bateman, though nephew here would hardly go along with us. I follow you so far.'

'At *Unipolitan*, we believe what is considered meretricious today will in a short time be looked back on as old standards. We have to discover new depths to which our market could sink and cater for that market.' And still no deluge of rotten fruit. The uncle was shaking his head, sadly, in sad concurrence. There was even an arch of interest detectable in the nephew's eyebrow.

'Things are as bad as that are they?' the uncle pleaded.

Bateman's heart turned bountiful. 'In the short term, yes, I'm afraid so. But things are so bad they can't get worse and our prognosis is improvement developing at the nadir – America – and moving gradually across the Atlantic.'

'You really think so, Mr Bateman?' the uncle leaned forward. 'What improvement exactly?'

Bateman spread his hands. 'On all fronts. In a couple of years time, maybe as soon as twelve months, the prevalent fashions will embrace a return to short back and sides for men. Chastity before marriage. Respect for the old. And along those lines.'

'I'll drink to that, Mr Bateman. Go on, cheer me up some more.'

And why not? I can dream. The world wasn't always a cesspit.

'There will be a decline in drug addiction, a resurgence of manly drinking, a renaissance of the humanities and a worldwide reinstatement of the Tridentine mass.'

The nephew's eyebrow was stretched taut from its moorings. The uncle slapped the nephew on the leg. 'You listening, nephew? Mr Bateman's describing a world you never knew. And you say, Mr Bateman, you say all this will come from America. You could very well be right. I can tell you I was never one to knock Reagan. I've always liked the sound of what he says. But do go on. What else, tell us?'

Bateman's heart held a bottomless shopping basket of forlorn hopes. He threw out central heating and seated large families round an open fire reading books. He gave television the bum's rush. 'The moron's mirror I'm fond of calling it myself,' the uncle agreed. 'It keeps the kids off the streets, that's what the experts tell us. How many times have you heard me say nephew, I grew up on the streets. That's why the streets were safe, they were full of kids. We abandon the streets and then we wonder why there's nobody in the streets except winos and child molesters. My idea of a city is a place where anyone who owns a shop lives over his shop.'

Bateman nodded, too reverent even to breathe 'Amen'. He was pleased to observe that, young man as he was, the nephew too showed respect with his eyebrow strictly to attention.

They drank on, the boat sailed on, Bateman waffled

on. Abortion would die out. Divorce rescinded. The uncle blinked and nodded, the nephew's eyebrow arched higher still. Television, gaming and contraceptive machines would vanish from public houses. One would once again down one's pint in a palace of conversation. At last the whiskey that he struggled to finish emboldened the nephew to speak for his own grotty generation with a feeble: 'You can't turn the clock back.'

But the uncle could not get enough of it. 'Nonsense, nephew. Tell me more, Mr Bateman, tell me more. You're warming an old man's heart.' Bateman's bladder finally called him away to where in a toilet mirror he saw the face of an authority.

'Well, nephew?'

'I don't see it, Inspector.'

'Uncle. Uncle. You don't see what?'

Constable Taylor waved his hand. 'Short back and sides . . . chastity before marriage . . .'

'Neither do I. Pity. Although . . . No, you're right, Taylor. Still . . .'

'He's new to the job.'

'Don't be daft. No doubt about it now, eh? I tell you they have everything worked out nicely. Market research consultant. Bloody clever. Except we do happen to know that he was down the labour as recently as last week. You sleepy? Keep your eyes open.'

'It's the whiskey. They play cards together. It could be any group playing cards or meeting regularly for any purpose. One of them is out of work, another has a vacancy, it comes up in conversation. A lot of opportunities must arise that way, Inspector.'

'Uncle. He made out he'd been on the job for years.'

'Wouldn't it be natural for him to put on a bit of the dog? We're strangers to him, he might not feel obliged to tell us he just got off the dole. That would be natural.'

'Market research consultant. Bloody clever. Who knows what they do? Read tea leaves it appears. Let's stick with what we know, Taylor. Bateman, Ellis, accountable to no one. Foster, he can hide anything under the guise of business trips. Ditto Hayhurst. But not Ernie. Problem of logistics here. Ernie couldn't go to Southend on a day trip without the whole public bar, and the Guv'nor, and Ernie's wife and mother-in-law getting to know about it. Moving Ernie about would tax the brains of the brightest and the best, never mind this lot. So what do they come up with? According to the Guv'nor, two weeks ago when the Guv'nor hasn't picked up a tittle since he comes back from his night out, two weeks ago when they're shutting up shop and are having their night-caps, Ernie says Guv, there's a chance you might have to do without me a couple of nights near Christmas that's if it's all the same to you, Guv. The Guv'nor says, That right, Ernie, party-time with your Uncle Albert, eh? Not that, Ernie tells him, that's Boxing Night, this might be before Christmas. What's on then? the Guv'nor asks. I might be taking a trip to Ireland, Ernie says. Naturally the Guv'nor sits up and takes notice at that. Is that a fact, Ernie? says the Guv'nor and cocks his ears. And what is the Guv'nor told, Taylor, He's told the greatest concoction of lies you could imagine. It turns out according to Ernie that the solo school is playing away as usual when Mr Foster tells them that he's afraid they'll have to suffer the loss of his company in a couple of weeks, that In fact I'm visiting your country, Bateman. Oh, says the solo school. Yes, says Foster. Going over there on business, branch of a multinational client, in Shannon Industrial Estate, attached to the airport. I have an idea that's not far from where you come from, Bateman? Mellick, isn't it? And Bateman tells them Yes, Shannon's only fourteen miles from Mellick. When is that, Mr Foster? the Hayhurst item asks and Foster says it's such a date. Hold on, Hayhurst orders and whisks out her diary. I'm in Dublin that week. An appearance on The Gay Byrne Show. Apparently, Taylor, they have shows over there too that feel they can do with the likes of Madam Hayhurst. Ellis gets straight to the heart of the matter: Ellis says, We'll have to play with three. Bateman chimes in: You might have to play with two, Arthur, I was planning to go over and check on my father. Ernie – innocently, according to Ernie – Ernie says: There'll be more of the bleedin' solo school in Ireland than here. Ellis ruminates, Taylor. Hardly Ernie's words exactly but we're reconstructing. Ellis muses: Bateman, Ireland's up to its armpits in carpet by now I suppose? And of course Ireland indeed is so contaminated. Good mind to go over there myself and spread the gospel. Why not? As well off over there investigating as here with no game. And so there we are, nice as pie. All going to meet up over in Mellick and have a game. Just like that. Ernie. Ernie comes in: Lucky sods. You come too, Ernie, Ellis proposes. Like to, but enough to do keepin' body and soul together without jetsettin', Linda'd do her nut it's as much as she can do to get me to take her and Betty on a day trip. Be my guest, Foster points out. Don't take charity, Ernie stiffens. Never have. Did without first. I'm not giving any – frosty Foster – I'm taking my car, you can plank your bottom on an otherwise empty seat. Etc., etc.

'Now, Taylor, this is the story as we got it from the Guv'nor, as the Guv'nor got it from Ernie and as the Guv'nor has had corroborated by Linda. They had only one problem: how to move Ernie and they set about it with military precision – I'll amend that, paramilitary precision. Foster equals businessman equals business tentacles all over the place these days, shrinking world.

Check. Hayhurst equals trollop – all right Taylor, enough of the smirk – Hayhurst equals personality equals television any place, moron's mirror's voracious appetite for personalities. Next Bateman. No difficulty there, pivot of the fabrication. You can imagine them turning to Ellis, how to make it just plausible? Of course: lino. It fits in with their crazy pattern of coming together first day. And Ellis and his fixation add a touch of the fanciful. Can't leave poor Ernie out of it so spoon-feed the lot to Ernie and make him digest it so he can gurgle it up to the Guv'nor and Linda in a way that the Guv'nor and Linda will get the whiff of verisimilitude. Now the Guv'nor, true to his own genial nature as well as, you must remember, true to his capacity as our man on the spot says Well, Ernie, I'll just have to struggle on without you a couple of days, you enjoy yourself, Ernie. Don't know, Ernie says, haven't said it to Linda yet, she mightn't let me go. Come to think of it, Guv'nor remembers, you don't ever have a holiday without it's day trips, do you, Ernie? Course she'll let you go. And if Ernie needs an advance, the Guv'nor offers, mindful of Ernie's pride, Ernie has only to say the word and the Guv'nor will stop it out of Ernie's wages piecemeal. So the Guv'nor's a convert before ever we get to Linda. All set, Linda comes round but only after she's assured by Bateman, the Guv'nor and what Foster and Ellis know about it that Ernie won't be blown sky-high by a bomb, that the fire-cracker merchants are up north and Mellick's as safe as Cornwall. That's, Taylor, if any place is safe nowadays. Here he comes. You go and get the drink. Whiskeys. Make his a double, water ours to look double. We have to loosen his tongue and you stay with it – nephew.'

Bateman returned to find the uncle alone. The uncle sat over the table, smiling and shaking his head. 'Short back and sides. In my day you didn't get your hair cut you got a clip round the ear-hole from your old man. While we have the chance, Mr Bateman, let me thank you. Young nephew: much of what you say he's heard from me, not as well as you put it of course but he has heard me lament for the old days. But you're a much younger man than I am, coming from you he might just sit up and take notice. Chastity: there's an item not so fashionable these days. I don't mind admitting it in the least, I walked out with my wife for three years before we got engaged. There's a good lad. Nephew, I'm just telling Mr Bateman how I walked out with your aunt for three years before we got engaged. Three days now before they hop into bed, eh nephew?'

Constable Taylor unloaded the tray of drinks. He could not resist the boast: 'Three minutes if the disco is lively.'

'Hmm. Popped my head into a disco once. Popped it straight out again. Lucky not to lose the sight of an eye not to say almost having the eardrums burst. You wouldn't have any good news there for us, Mr Bateman? Discos on the way out? Cheers.'

Bateman obligingly enlarged on his vision. Discos were on the way out. It would soon be possible to distinguish once again the words of the songs sung on the wireless. The Arthur Traceys would come into their own. The uncle gulped: 'The Street Singer. An all-time favourite of mine, Mr Bateman. You hear that, nephew? None of your Beatles and Presleys any more. Tauber, Josef Locke. Vera Lynn. Gracie. *Saleee, Saleeeee, the pride of our alley . . .* Those were the days, Mr Bateman. Those were the days.' Books would have a beginning, a middle and an end without every second sentence spattered with four-lettered words. Comedians would learn to be comical without recourse to smut. Dance bands. Orchestras. The foxtrot . . .

In Dublin the McNamara's bus contingent reassembled, save those whose destination was Dublin. The bus stopped at Naas, Newbridge and Kildare for further 'quick purchases' of – they were on the Ireland side of the journey – liquor, a half-hour at a time. Constable Taylor matched Bateman and Inspector Blake watering hole for watering hole but, shopsoiled as he was from the long journey and the spirits, bottled beer finished him off as they approached Nenagh and he slumped in his window seat into a snoring sleep. At that stage Bateman had measured swords with the art movie and Constable Taylor was already befogged by the strewn corpses of Bertolucci, Antonioni, Bergman and the rest. Some chap called Errol Flynn was Lord of both the Forest and the Spanish Main and a Roy Rogers was singing a song about his own horse.

The uncle shook the nephew awake coming into Mellick. In the Royal George Hotel Bateman and the uncle finished off with one from the night porter's cache – the nephew staggered upstairs.

PART THREE

Mellick

FOSTER'S ORIGINAL PLAN had been to buy the duds in London, a city deficient in many respects yet a city where no purchase was remarkable, from a bottle of hair restorer to the most Byzantine sex aid. But as the deadline approached he was inspired to recognise that maybe on the other hand Irish lingerie would add spice to his debut. And over on that side of the water while he did not propose to rap imperiously with the ferrule of his stick he certainly would cough confidently and stand no nonsense. He dismissed any self-accusation of procrastination: he was simply a man who thought things out. No more.

He was bloody well glad now that he had not shopped in London.

Ireland has an incipient drug problem in comparison to the larger Western powers and it is probable that the larger Western powers would not be so much in the mire today if they had dealt as vigilantly with such incipience as do the Irish customs officials. Foster, Gosling and Arthur Ellis himself had their bags perfunctorily chalked and were through in good time when the strip of lino was spotted. Foster at the time was irritated by the unnecessary delay: his humour was always close to the surface where Ellis and his damned lino was concerned. Ellis explained to the Irish authorities that it was a mere precaution in case he encountered carpet and so on. Foster and Gosling stood by and nodded at the logic of the story they had heard so often. But one of the customs officials said: I see. And: Would you three gentlemen mind stepping this side for a moment?

They cut the lino into the narrowest of strips and the strips into the smallest of fragments. They discovered no contraband but having gone so far they turned on the already chalked baggage. Watching them pawing through his suitcase Foster congratulated himself on his foresight and deemed the contretemps auspicious. Given Ireland's reputation, a transvestite haul might have been more incriminating than a cello full of heroin. The officials apologised to Ellis and offered him a compensation form on which he contemptuously scribbled: NO COMMERCIAL VALUE.

When Bateman arrived at the barbershop he found his father where he had left him twenty-five years earlier – warming the palms of his hands from the heat of a filthy oil contraption. Frankie Timmons was on his feet lifting the lid of the kettle on the Primus. He believed this helped the kettle to boil more quickly and he was by no means a lone apostle of that creed.

'Oh,' Johnny Bateman greeted his son. 'What's all this in honour of?'

Bateman prepared to suffer his share. He intended to sidle into the diddly club with all the grace of an evening-suited cat burglar. He took off his raincoat and took a towel to dry the remains of the sparse mist that had nestled in his grey hair.

'Help yourself,' Frankie Timmons said.

As a double act his father and Frankie went back a long way. They were too old now to learn a new trick, such as making a civil remark. Bateman remembered the territory well. It was Fine Day equals What's Fine About It country.

'I'm here on business,' Bateman explained. He combed his hair. Looking into the mirror over the customer chair he could see them looking at each other, fearing the blow of good news.

'What business?' his father demanded. 'Weren't you on the dole two months ago?'

'Market research consultant with *Unipolitan*.' Bateman sat down on the waiting bench, making room for himself between dog-eared rugby magazines. 'It's the most famous woman's periodical in the world.'

'We never heard of it. How did you get that job? What would you know about a job like that?'

Bateman lit a cigarette. 'A friend of mine owns it.' He watched his father battling bitterly. He threw in a dummy: 'You must have had that kettle a long time.'

That kettle was a model that had seen service on picnics in the days when people hiked out of town to scenic river banks where they gathered sticks to light the fire and put the bottle of milk in the shade of the reeds in the river and you could practically *smell* the taste of the tea. This gospel of nostalgia was not doubted by Bateman: he could see the arse was practically burned out of the kettle. Frankie Timmons continued: 'They wouldn't even know how to light a fire today. We seen 'em gettin' into their cars. Fillin' up the boot with plastic flasks as big as breadbins full of lukewarm water. Off to the seasides where there's tables and chairs made of concrete all laid out for them inside a shelter and they pour the water into plastic cups with a teabag inside and they think they're drinkin' tea. On top of that they haul out a hamper full of cold chicken that they buy already cooked an' do you know what they think they'd be doin'? Twould make you laugh, they think they'd be roughin' it. Roughin' it. I ask you.'

Bateman watched Frankie Timmons' hand shake and the tea trickle out over the edge of the cup on to the saucer. Frankie scraped his bootlaced feet across the floor with the leaking cup and saucer to Bateman's father. 'You help yourself,' Frankie Timmons ordered Bateman who stood up and dug a spoon deep into the sugar bag. All served, Frankie Timmons sat down slowly: it was more of a landing, a careful landing. Both old men slurped their tea, his father's upper denture snapping after spillage on his chin. Frankie Timmons studied the floor.

'What's the job you said you had again?' his father demanded.

'Market research consultant. It's simply a question of looking into my heart, anticipating trends.'

'We know, cos we seen 'em,' Frankie Timmons continued. Bateman and his father had been speaking to the deaf ear. 'When we got the free travel you said to me, Johnny, you said c'mon away an' we go down to Kilkee for the day. I said comin' back, I said that's it, never again. Pampered kids sayin' the water was cold in the middle of July. From swimmin' all year round in hot water in the indoor pools. Peg Morrissey told us her youngfella had her pestered till she gave in and brought him to one of 'em an' what did she get for her trouble? The youngfella got verruca on his foot an' had his trousers stolen, they had to go home in a taxi an' he had to spend two days in hospital havin' it operated on. And what was on the bus an' we comin' back?' Frank Timmons shook his head at his confidant, the floor. 'A microphone. Someone started the singsong and they had a microphone on the bus. When they sang they didn't sing from their seats like normal people, they had to go up near the driver and sing into the microphone.'

'A man has a job looking into his heart.' Bateman's father did not sneer. He hissed. Angry that he should have to suffer such shame. The affinity between the two old men penetrated the deaf ear. Frankie Timmons looked up from the floor. With the benefit of the more favourable acoustics Bateman's father continued: 'How're you, Johnny? What's Percy doing these days? Percy? He has a big job over in London telling the future. When people come up to me and ask I'll have to tell them you forecast the future.'

Frankie Timmons nodded his 'I-know-what-I'd-do-if-it-was-my-son' nod.

'I suppose you'll be paying out the savings club soon,' Bateman probed lightly but if silver spoons had clattered through a hole in his pocket on to the ballroom floor of a country house he could not have twitched more guiltily. He reddened unnecessarily. The barbershop held three trapeze artists. While he bounced off the safety net Frankie Timmons flew through the air and gripped his father's ankles.

'How. How is what I'd like to know. How does he look into his heart? When people ask, if we could say this is the way he does it, at least that'd be somethin'. But just tellin' the future.'

'I didn't say I tell the future. I said I anticipate trends. You listen to the weather forecast, don't you?'

'What Frankie is sayin' is how do you do it. The weathermen have charts. They have satellites up in the sky that can show you the pictures of the weather coming along; what do you do?'

'It's like the tipsters,' Frankie Timmons contributed. 'I don't know how many times I've said it, if those fellas could give one horse, just one horse and it wouldn't have to be one horse a week but just one in their whole lives, do you think they'd be workin' for the newspapers?'

'They'd be over in Spain lying in the sun.' Johnny Bateman closed the case for the Crown and joined Frankie Timmons in glowering at Bateman in the dock. You asked innocently after a kettle and you were found guilty of microphones on buses, indoor swimming pools and Newsboy's failure to go through the card.

'When is the raffle in the Shakespeare?' It was the same question wearing new words. Bateman preened.

'Tomorrow night.' His father swept the answer out of the way: 'I suppose you know the winners.'

' . . . from lookin' into his heart . . .'

'I know one.' They stared at him. 'The name Johnny Bateman will come out of the hat.' Bateman smiled at his own dexterity. 'Now tell me if I'm wrong.'

'For your information it didn't come out last year.'

'Oh?'

'It came out for a tin of biscuits but what good is that?'

'I never won nothin' in it . . .'

Bateman's stratagem fought for elbowroom in the barbershop bursting with grievance.

'You used to take the money in my suitcase.'

'What does that mean?'

'The savings club. When you paid the savings club the same night as the raffle. Do you still do that – have them in conjunction?'

'For all that's to pay out,' his father said and he might have rolled a paper into a cone and bugled *du-du-du-du-du:* introducing Frankie Timmons!

'Save? Ask people to save today an' they laugh at you. Twenty-eight-twenty-seven, I forgot Sean Reilly pulled out, a man had a job and at forty-eight years of age he volunteers himself out of a job and spends whatever they gave him in one year: he went off to Spain on a holiday –

in February – off to Spain on a holiday in February an'
put in those aluminium windows an' bought a car an'
he's goin' round now with his hands in his pockets after
comin' to us to take out his savin's. A man that would
leave his job without bein' fired. Twenty-seven people
savin'. When one time we had a hundred and forty. What
about the day we went for a walk to see the new college.
Third level they call it. You can stay at school for half
your life. An' I'll tell you this: I don't blame 'em. There's
this queue outside this office an' a big sign written up
BANK OF IRELAND. We thought we were in the wrong
place but up above it a bigger sign STUDENT LOANS.
They were lendin' money to people goin' to school an'
givin' 'em chequebooks to pull out of their pockets when
they liked an' sign their name if they felt short. Ask
people to save? They'd think you were mad. I see them
out at trainin', a bankbook hangin' from every jacket.
Where are we goin' after, hold on till I see, it's okay I
have my chequebook. All we ever left in our pockets an'
we goin' out on the field was our teeth. They flash the
ball around, I shout at 'em, KEEP IT TIGHT. Do they
listen? They have ears but do they listen? Nancy boys.
Hair dryers. They come off the field an' have showers an'
dry their hair with hair dryers an' we're wonderin' why
people don't save. Save. With notices a foot high lendin'
money to schoolboys. I was in here with my father when
I was fourteen.'

An innocent auditor might have granted Frankie
Timmons his all too plausible contention. Certainly
Bateman's father did, plucking at a hair in his nose and
nodding. But Bateman had so much sympathy for himself
and his cause that he could analyse the outburst with
greater detachment. He put himself in Sean Reilly's shoes.
A forty-eight-year-old Sean Reilly was entitled to ask for
cards and his quicksilver gratuity while the redundancy

strain favoured a quitter's market, and if it was a sadly logical progression that Sean Reilly should blow the lot on aluminium windows and a Spanish holiday, well then every man to his taste and good luck to him and his time in the sun. And when he withdrew from the savings club to keep himself in the Woodbines to which he had always been accustomed did he not display the individuality of one who could do without bloody well waiting for Christmas? Tomorrow night – if it *was* tomorrow night – Sean Reilly would be in the Shakespeare with nothing to come, surrounded by Christians sagely observing that he had not minded his money.

All being well Sean Reilly would have a Christmas that no money could buy looking at Johnny Bateman and Frankie Timmons disgraced in front of 'People'.

Bateman did not allow himself to be diverted. 'I used to have to take my books out of the case that day. So you could collect the money from the bank in it. You brought the money back here to the shop to count it and put it in the envelopes and then brought it home and carried it to the Shakespeare that night. Maybe that's all changed now? Probably computerised?'

Bateman's father despaired of such a fool of a son. 'How can it be changed? What kind of a remark is that to make? That's the trouble today, we can count the money here with our own two fingers so that we won't be putting anybody out but what happens? The minute we go up to the bank some young one holds the whole place up adding it up on her adding machine. Then she has the cheek to say to the two of us That's correct gentlemen, as if it's a miracle we know how to count.'

Mental arithmetic will come back. 'Nothing's changed then, it's all done the old way?'

'It's all done the right way.'

Bateman nodded at the neat reduction. It was

important to hold on, not to listen to his father's gripe and even though it was Frankie Timmons' turn not to talk now, not to listen to the look on his face. Going into the shop the circumlocution available to Bateman was on a short lease and was all but used up now. Kettles, microphones, indoor pools, calculators, aluminium windows and STUDENT LOANS had eaten into the supply. Bateman was left with: 'So when is the big payout, is it with the raffle?'

'There's nothing big about it any more. It's even hard to get attention with the raffle. We could hardly hear ourselves last year. No respect for anything.'

Bateman decided he had as much as he could take and as much as he would get. The payout would take place tomorrow night, there were only twenty-seven members, it was all done the same old way. He stood up and reached for his raincoat.

'Where're you off to now? You're no sooner here than you're gone.'

Bateman flicked his thumb against the small stack of brown envelopes beside the sink. 'Twenty-seven isn't many, is it? Twenty-seven of these brown envelopes will be lost in my old suitcase . . . I have to go. My publisher is flying in, I've a conference . . .' His father wore the hurt expression. 'We have to look into our hearts,' Bateman expanded, throwing them a bone of humour. They declined to gnaw. They were hungry but not for that class of fodder. Without him they would be left to moan to themselves, a staple they must be weary of by now. ' . . . I was thinking . . . I'd like to take the case back with me . . . that's if it's all right . . . as a souvenir . . . I could call up tomorrow if it was okay with you . . . to collect it . . . ?'

'We'd be honoured,' his father sighed.

*

217

Ben Hanley and his partner patrolled O'Connell Street. Ben's partner proceeded with one hand in the pocket and the other inside the breast of the greatcoat, Napoleon-fashion. This was because Ben's partner was settled in his career and had always wanted to become a policeman since his father – who was now retired from the Force first told him that would be his vocation.

Ben's partner looked the part. Ben himself was content with the freedom of his tunic. His arms rose and fell in accompaniment and not in tandem with his feet. He kept his head straight but his eyes never rested. He was doing his job but his thoughts were far from that activity. They were on his vocation. He was a barman. It was coming up to Christmas again, that time when you had to go home and be welcomed as one who has not risen from the ranks. At home in Westport every Christmas, out of uniform, drinking in the locals, he was moodily aware of the countrified inelegance of the shelved women while having no bench-mark familiarity with even the poor best of the Mellick crop to sustain him – stopped short of commitment by the memory of Diana Hayhurst and the Sandras/Susans. Ben Hanley thought of London. Every Christmas in Westport you took your pint from the counter and sat back by yourself and tortured yourself with thoughts of London. You looked around you at what was accepted as service from behind the counter. The coloured cuff of a shirt extending sloppily from under any old pullover and the lemon slice lifted by the fingers. No necktie. Unshaven. Brown shoes that you could not see your face in. Any customer who felt the whim shouting Fuck! and no barman with the authority of proper livery to come out and whisper I think that will be enough of that now. No Sandras/Susans.

Ben and his partner pounded the wet streets illuminated by the Christmas lights strung overhead from building to building. It was a long time since Ben had shared his London with a partner. In the old days he was not believed and today he was likely to have his escapades topped by a tale from Paris or Corfu. They traipsed all over Europe now on four pee. As Ben and his partner slowed passing Woolworth's the rain fell again and they crossed the road to the sanctuary of the Royal George Hotel awning. They stood sentinel outside the Royal George for the statutory three minutes until Ben's partner spoke: 'Quiet tonight, Ben.' It was. But not as quiet as, say, Ash Wednesday night or any Monday or Tuesday after the pint got a belt in the budget. It was Christmas, the city thronged with latenight shoppers, the traffic bumper to bumper. But Ben understood that his partner did not speak comparatively. An earthquake taking place in front of them and Ben's partner would have said: 'Quiet tonight, Ben.'

'Yeah,' Ben conceded. 'You head off.'

'Sure? I won't be ten minutes.'

'Take your time.'

By himself Ben folded his arms and cupped his chin. Bus drivers did it. They climbed down from the wheel outside the city centre on schedule or not and nipped around the corner for a quick one or a gulped couple or three if it was the last chance before closing time. Ben did not have to be a detective – which he could have been – to know that. Any passenger with a nose could smell the driver's breath. I would never do it, Ben told himself, if it was my bus. His partner was swiftly around the corner, by now headed a block further towards the dock area where there was a side door into an understanding bar where he would be served in the hallway and where the drink might or might not be on the house. Ben did not know and he didn't care. He had never once said to a partner Quiet tonight. But then all his partners had vocations.

Ben watched the taxi triple-park outside two tour coaches. His partner would have chivvied the taxi around the corner but Ben did not have the zeal. It was Christmas, it was chaotic, what was a traffic jam among friends. The taxi man was around his car faster than a scrum half to open the passenger door to a fine pair of long legs that he escorted through the parked coaches to the canopied hotel entrance before returning to the cab for two pigskin suitcases. She wore a light subtly flecked autumn suit and a mannish single-feather bedecked angler's hat. She was not Westportish or Mellickish, more a touch of London, Ben observed, his mouth drying. That dimple. The way the lines are prominent on her fore-head . . . Ben's hand fell slowly away from his chin. It couldn't be. But she was no more than two feet away while she waited for her luggage and his eyesight was good. She took in the street, smiled at Ben staring at her, looked straight out at the taxi man coming with the cases. Ben's hands hung apelike, his chin slack. A porter took the cases in charge. The taxi man effused gratitude for a large tip, eyed Ben and ran back to his cab. Mercenarily inspired, the porter commanded: 'If you'd be good enough to follow me, Madam,'

Ben Hanley breathed: 'Diana Hayhurst.' She squinted at him. Those lines. The porter paused with the suitcases inches off the ground and glowered at Ben's insolence. 'You wouldn't remember me.' Ben elucidated. She tried hard, examining Ben's face under his cap. She put her finger to her lips. Ben said: 'Ben Hanley. You used to go into The Pub . . . it's fifteen years ag . . .'

'BEN!' Diana Hayhurst opened her arms. 'BEN, the best fucking barman in London!' She embraced Ben, stood back and repeated: 'The best fucking barman in London!' The porter rested his cases. Ben had never been a man or boy to cry but her accolade pressed two bucketfuls of happiness up under his eyes. 'Ben, you're a what – you're a copper, Ben!' Ben pointed to his uniform. He could not deny it. 'And I bet you're the best fucking copper in Ireland, right, Ben? Come and have a drink.'

She put her arm through Ben's but Ben did not move. 'I'm on duty.'

'Oh.'

'I'd be very happy to have a coffee with you.' Ben took off his hat as he was escorted past the porter holding the door open.

'You must tell me everything, Ben. A copper. A topper copper.'

A reunion is one of the raptures of life never better set than in the season of goodwill. In the lounge of the Royal George Hotel Diana Hayhurst and Ben Hanley were closer to each other than they had ever been in reality in the old days in The Pub. Ben told his everything over the first coffee. Out of Ben's mouth it did not amount to much. He was sacked, he came home, he joined the guards. And here he was. He made no mention of joy-riders, Mad Dog O'Dwyer, the IRA or the Scott Medal for Bravery.

'I'm so happy for you, Ben,' Diana Hayhurst patted his knee. She had taken off her feathered hat and had crossed her legs.

'It's a job,' Ben said. He could not tell her how he longed for his old niche. 'It's some coincidence,' Ben pursued the obvious. 'What brings you to Mellick?'

'What brings me to Mellick?' Diana Hayhurst weighed the question. She felt the material in the cuff of Ben's tunic. 'I'll tell you what brings me to Mellick, Ben,' she decided quickly. 'Ben, you might be able to help me? Would you, Ben?' She told Ben and Ben listened, on duty, over a second coffee. When she finished and asked 'Could you do that?' Ben did not hesitate.

'No problem.'

Ben's partner was waiting outside. Ben could smell the drink. 'Okay?', Ben's partner asked. Ben nodded and said: 'Quiet tonight.' Ben's partner did not catch on. Ben repeated: 'I said it's quiet tonight.' Ben's partner was puzzled. He did not understand his own code coming from Ben. So Ben had to draw a picture: 'Can you manage on your own?'

'Oh. Yeah, Ben. Sure. You take off, Ben, I'm okay.' Ben's partner's porter tasted better with Ben joining in on the act.

Ben returned to his flat, shaved, showered, changed into civvies and then went to the Shakespeare. He sat on a stool at the bar among the Post Office workers who were sleepily merry after another long day's Christmas overtime, the banking crowd who had forgotten to go home after dropping in for a couple before dinner, the regulars, the Young Thomond mob and the few seasonal strangers: the Royal George was just down the road and in a small world of intensive marketing a herd of Japanese alighting from a tour bus was no longer a novelty at any time. People from many countries came to Ireland not in spite of but for the soft rain. The GPO was around the corner and Ben was well known to all the clerks, sorters and postmen who were fond of clapping him on the back and demanding to know What'll you have? Long ago Ben had told the bar staff that the only drink he would accept was that paid for by himself. But the post office mob never stopped trying, not because any of them wanted to have a lock on him but because they were decent people. To make it up to them Ben talked to them and listened to them.

When Ben talked and listened in any company he was also able to almost lip-read the gist of conversations not intended for his ears. You caught a chance remark and married it to the shifty appearance, interpreted the emphatic movement of a hand. It was no more than detective work. A whole counter away from him Ben heard: 'So. Madam Hayhurst's arrived. The gang's all here, eh?' Unluckily, Bowler Downey, the singing post-man, had just made his entrance. He was known as the singing postman because he worked for the Post Office delivering letters and loved to sing, drunk or sober, early in the morning, midday or late at night and was ecumenical in his tastes – ballad, music hall, rock or opera. Bowler stood less than a medium-size man and had the habit of singing up; he liked to place his left hand on someone's right shoulder and sing directly to that single conscript. It was an inheritance from his boy soprano days, when to conquer nerves and shut out the audience he was taught to fix his gaze on a faraway blur on the balcony. Tonight Bowler chose Ben as his victim and because it was Christmas and he was nearing fifty, 'Mother Machree' as his song. *Sure I love the dear silver that shines in her hair*. So ubiquitous an entertainer was he that he did not expect and rarely received order. *And her brow that's all furrowed and wrinkled with care*. 'Good man, Bowler.' 'Shut up Bowler, you fuckin' ape.' Add to that that Inspector Blake and Constable Taylor were as gifted at not being overheard as Ben was at overhearing. Still, staring into Bowler's glistening eyes Ben caught ' . . . knock off the diddly club, no more no less . . .' *I kiss the dear fingers so toil-worn for me*. Ben had missed 'I think they're here to . . .' *Oh God bless you and keep you my Mother Machree*. Bowler was on the tips of his toes bawling the high note into Ben's face. Ben could not hear Inspector Blake say 'You can't see beyond it, eh, nephew? You can't or you won't. I'm not saying I can see beyond it but I'm damned if there isn't something there that we just can't see yet. She's on our floor. We saw her go into room one one two. Within a minute Bateman, Gosling, Foster and Ellis all join her. We creep along the hall. We cock our ears. What do we hear? I'll goabundle. I tell you, nephew, they're a weird lot. Bateman half an hour in the barbershop today. They all gather and what do they do? Produce the deck and play cards. Just like that. I think we should go back to the hotel. Be Johnny on the spot.' *Oh God bless you and keep you Mo . . . ther . . .* MA . . . CHREEEEE! 'Go aisy Bowler, me fuckin' head is at me.' 'Don't mind him, a hand for the singer.' 'More! More!'

Ben watched them leave. He had not heard much but he had heard enough.

It was a bundle of Foster's. He sat on one of the single beds in room 112 beside Ellis. Bateman and Gosling sat on the other with Diana Hayhurst on the dressing table stool. They played the hand on the breakfast trolley. Foster had the ace, king, queen of spades seven times, the king and knave of hearts and four medium diamonds to the nine. He could not have made the bundle playing against three blind mice. Worse, it was Diana Hayhurst's deal and Bateman led a club that Foster was obliged to rough: there was no prospect of sending them the wrong way. Foster looked at his cards again after taking the first trick. He could not understand how he had made such a bid. His mind was not on the game. How could it be. This ridiculous business, this diddly club nonsense.

This Mellick place was not as he had envisaged. He had taken a stroll, gone window-shopping. The shop windows were as large as you could expect to find in Oxford Street itself and the dummies as splendidly accoutred and coiffed, complete with eyelashed eyes that followed him whichever direction he moved. Dammit, to hell with it, it was only bloody Ireland after all. He tried

Penneys, a Primark outlet. He followed the signs. As the escalator crested to the landing on the ladies' floor his face warmed. The only man there, and he could not even pause to finger a decoy suit. The place was laid out in grids and aisles. You helped yourself. You put your bra and your panties on your arm and joined the queue at one of the checkouts where the cashier in her shop coat pawed your items into a bag and rang up her till supermarket style. So easy in theory but damned difficult to carry off on a moistened forehead. He had not thought it out, planned. He thought he was getting looks. He adopted a purposeful walk that took him across the floor through the lode of lingerie down the steps and out into the fresh air of the street. He crossed the road and saw TODD'S, part of the Switzer/Harrods group. He stood in the doorway, as if sheltering from the rain. He spied in. He saw an elegant assistant hovering in a pinstriped three-piece and a lady in white blouse and smart black skirt and high heels and red lipstick with her hands clasped in the service position. They were only waiting the chance to say: And how can I help you?

Foster moved off. He had brought with him some vague notion of imperious purchasing: no, he was not a fool, he had not expected a bazaar of goateed fairies cobbling or petticoated colleens laying wares at his feet begging him to buy for half-nothing. But it was not that long in comparative terms since they were a subject people. The march of empire out and back should have left some moraine of deference to ease the way of a man on a delicate mission. He walked on through the shopping district. DUNNE'S STORES. If he was not mistaken as much an emporium as any Marks & Spencer's. No point going in there. BURTON'S. Another reassuring symbol that he could have done without. He passed a WOOLWORTH'S, restaurant, a fabric shop, china merchant with prices on the crockery calculated to deter other than fat Americans in golf trousers. And then: BANK OF IRELAND. A sign to soothe, you knew where you were, no need for a malaria shot. FIRST NATIONAL BUILDING SOCIETY. Mellick was down from the trees a long time. ANGLO-IRISH BANK and what was this: BARCLAYS! He was well into the money belt now. The ROYAL LIVER INSURANCE COMPANY. Somebody Somebody & Somebody, Auditors & Accountants. As good a street for its size as you could expect any place. He was not thinking now of dressing up in female undergarments. The PRUDENTIAL: he stopped and looked up at the corporate identity. The figure of Prudence in the coat of arms of The Prudential Assurance Company. There was the familiar red ribbon across her forehead. He had complimented the Prudential people at the launch of their logo. Prudence, he had been informed at the reception, signified *wise conduct*. And he had raised his glass to that. He moved up the street past an IRISH PERMANENT BUILDING SOCIETY, a moneyman botanising in a financial garden. Next came a Georgian crescent of doctors' surgeries, dentistry, the legal profession. And then, suddenly, a theatre, intimate by the look of it, and worse, next door, the ITGWU – Irish Transport and General Workers' Union. It was time to turn back. He crossed the street and aimed for the Royal George Hotel. On this side a Jesuit church, COUNTY COUNCIL BUILDINGS, another bank, ALLIED IRISH, the NATIONAL MUTUAL ASSURANCE ASSOCIATION OF AUSTRALIA. The chamber of commerce building, auctioneers, more Somebody, Somebody and Somebodies, shoe shops, chemists, TV rentals and on to the jewellery concessions tucked under the hotel.

Foster went upstairs to his room. It had been a wholesome stroll spoiled initially by frivolous longing. Mellick high street just was not evocative of the stripper's desired ambience. Wise conduct – *wise,* not good – equalled admitting now that he could not buy the duds in Mellick. Facing the fact head-on, he appreciated the beauty of his own backyard. Why, all he need have done was send a telegram to Gladys to the effect that her sister was dying in Southampton. Pack her on a train, rush home and plunge into her drawers – and listen later in the pub and smile inside himself at Nick acting the Sherlock Holmes with his Whoever could have sent it, then. Cut your losses, get out of this inoffensive city. Another way of going about it now that he thought about it was to . . . the phone rang. Diana Hayhurst was in residence.

Foster's knave of hearts was topped by Bateman's queen. Bateman came back a club that Foster roughed and then sent out his diamonds to be slaughtered. He had only seven tricks made when his last card, the king of hearts, was gobbled up by Gosling's ace. To begin with, the inquest was a silent one. Bateman, Gosling, Diana Hayhurst and Ellis raised their chins and widened their eyes. Looking between Bateman and Gosling, Foster was drawn to a pair of shoes behind them on the bed. They were Diana Hayhurst's pair of Roland Cartier burgundy with the ankle straps.

'You had the bare seven tricks.' Ellis initiated the prosecution. 'I had a certain small one and you buck seven tricks.'

Foster turned slowly away from the high-heeled ankle straps to answer this lout in the red beard still tainted with *lèse-majesté* against the NatWest. 'You woke up, did you, Ellis?' A coroner would have countered: That's not the point, Foster, but Ellis slumped. His protest had been mechanical. Since the customs officials destroyed his lino Ellis had withdrawn from the League Against

Christmas. He sat in the back seat of Foster's car all the way down from Dublin and refused to speak, would not even acknowledge Ernie's turning his head to enquire: 'You all right, then Arthur?' And when Foster said: 'Ignore him, Gosling, let him sulk,' Ellis did the ignoring. He folded his arms around himself in the back seat contumacious of all consolation. He would indeed be insensitive not to recognise a bad sign when he saw one. They were heading for the rocks and there was nothing he could do about it short of refusing to serve. Foster would never be brought to recognise that it was their compass the customs men destroyed when they vandalised the lino.

'Yeah, Arthur's right, Mr Foster, you didn' 'ave no bundle there.' Foster paid out in his exact fashion. He had no defence but you weren't going to have cheek from a potman. 'Amusing myself, Gosling, putting myself in your shoes, having a *lark*, Gosling, Bateman's deal.'

It was good enough for Ernie Gosling but not for Bateman, Ellis or Diana Hayhurst, Foster did not put himself in people's shoes, he did not go in for 'larks'. It was no time to play a hand of solo, that was all there was to it.

'I called round the barbershop today,' Bateman said, making no shape to deal. They waited. 'They only have twenty-seven in the club.' Still they waited. 'It looks like we can proceed as planned.' Bateman made a helpless gesture as though apologetic that he hadn't a more complicated stratagem. 'So if you want to cut the cards . . .'

Bateman placed the deck in the centre of the table. According to the plan Bateman was not a candidate for the short straw. He would write the cracker messages to be inserted in the envelopes but one of the other four would do the stealing at a time when Bateman would be seen to have an alibi. For the moment now Bateman was relaxed. The deck lay on the table mesmeric as a snake, Foster, Ellis and Gosling staring. Once any of them reached out there was no turning back. Diana Hayhurst moved. 'Hold it.' Ernie Gosling was inspired. 'Highest or lowest?'

'Highest,' Ellis muttered, to have something to say.

'Lowest,' Foster commanded without taking his eyes from the deck. Diana Hayhurst's thumb and second finger lightly lifted a cut and turned up the four of spades. Ernie Gosling shot his hands up out of the cuffs of his blazer and exercised his fingers *à la* the safe-cracker. His bravado was rewarded with the seven of hearts. He brandished the upturned cut around the table and then rubbed the backs of two fingers under his nose. He joined Bateman at ease and enjoyed the staring contest between Foster and Ellis. They did not stare at each other. They were glued to the deck. A minute and a half passed. Ellis admitted the weaker character by stretching out his hand. He lifted the king of diamonds. Foster remained looking at the deck. Ellis did not try to hide his shoulders collapsing with relief. Foster took his time. And then with the premeditation of an orderly man he briskly turned up the deuce of spades.

The four cuts lay neglected on the table. The solo school was prorogued *sine die*. Bateman said: 'I better go and write the crackers.' Ellis looked up at him, gave him the go-ahead nod. Ellis was sitting on his winnings. He was afraid to say anything that might provoke Foster to lose his grasp of the sticky end of the stick. He could have sympathy for Foster. Poor bastard was hypnotised, the way he stared at the deuce of spades. Ellis tried: 'Could do with a drink. Ernie, we look up some pub? Eh, Foster?'

'You reckon, Arthur? Been travellin' all bleedin' day, if I can stay awake, why not? You comin', Mr Foster?'

'No thank you,' Foster said but he spoke with gratitude. Gosling's invitation had been sympathetic, a proffered gasper to a condemned man.

'Not now. Bateman, I think we should confer.' Foster stood up.

Ellis was already on his feet. He turned to Diana Hayhurst.

'Join us?'

She thought about it. 'No. Not just now, you go along and have a good time.'

From the Treaty Stone Bar, just off the main lounge of the Royal George Hotel, Inspector Blake and Constable Taylor had clear sight of the passing parade. 'What d'you think, nephew?'

'I don't see there's much we can do, uncle.'

'Madam Hayhurst. And you're just the fellow.'

Constable Taylor sat stiff on his stool. 'Me?'

'Yes, nephew. You know all about her. Her greatest fan on the chat shows. Say, at breakfast if we don't run into her before then. You rise, approach her table, autograph for your live-in girlfriend or what not, like you to meet my uncle . . . that class of thing. I don't need to tell you, you're a policeman, it's police work. Maybe they'll dine together, if it isn't Mr Bateman, etc., etc. Then a bow to the lady. And so on. Should be a piece of cake to . . . hold it! Hold it!' They watched Ellis and Gosling walk out the lobby. 'No. Let them off. The way I see it, Gosling's a pawn, eh? Best to stick around. Bateman's our fellow. Bateman or Foster. That's the leadership from what we can surmise. Have another.'

Ben meditated in the Shakespeare. One of Ben's partners from the Mad Dog O'Dwyer days was on duty now in the station. A sergeant. He had only pretended to believe

Ben. Bowler had moved down the counter to command a group of bank clerks in doubtful harmony: *In the evening by the moonlight you can hear the darkies singing.* Ben saw himself dropping in on the sergeant: You remember that bird I told you about, the one I screwed in The Pub toilet in London? She's in town, staying at the Royal George. If you like to come down there with me I'll get her to prove it . . . *It was my granny's twilight song . . .*

'What you 'avin' then, Arthur?'

. . . *That's haunting me . . . that memory . . .* That English voice, in contrast to Ben's daily dose of the Mellick accent, on top of having seen herself again grigged him. If he could only stand behind the bar of The Pub again, neatly turned out, his eyes alert to the wants of his customers, as it should be, as it was with him, as it never is in Mellick or any other part of Ireland.

'To the diddly club, Ernie.'

'Cheers.'

. . . *strolling in the moonlight, moonlight, moonlight, strolling in the moonlight, moonlight, moonlight . . .*

Ben did not think of it as a quid pro quo: what she had asked him to do would not stretch him apart altogether from the fact that it was in the line of duty. He could ask her. She could only say no. And he did not want to have her leave Mellick thinking of him as just a cop. There was more to him. For fifteen years he had had nobody to tell that to except himself. She would understand. With those two at the end of the counter there was a chance he might catch her alone in the Royal George and explain his position. He pushed the remains of his drink away.

'Bowler, give us one bar of "Juanita" . . .'

Diana Hayhurst stood naked in room 112 undecided between a faded blue satin cotton jump suit with an elaborately appliquéd top by Ventilo and a crushed linen dress khaki in colour and safari in style. No, the jump suit was inappropriate for sitting on a bar stool, it accentuated the mother-earthiness of her arse whereas through the slit in the dress she could let protrude a bounteous glimpse of thigh. The telephone rang. It was Ben. He had a rather unusual request, if there was the remotest chance she would oblige him. He was ashamed to ask her face to face and if she thought he had a cheek he would understand perfectly and it would have nothing to do with the other business, he'd see to that as promised, there would be no problem there. Diana Hayhurst lay back on the bed, hugging the telephone and playing with herself using two fingers. 'Now, Ben, listen to me,' she told him. 'I'd be only too delighted.' 'Really?' Ben begged. 'Why not, Ben? As a matter of fact I've a better idea, Ben. What do you say to this.' She trapped her hand between her legs and gave Ben the scenario and was only interrupted by Ben's breathing into the phone at the other end . . . Ben? Are you still there, Ben? But first, she told Ben, she intended to drop downstairs for a few bracers, that would give Ben time to fix up his end. 'Okay? What, Ben? Nonsense! I'd be honoured. Anything for the best fucking barman in London.'

Had Diana Hayhurst just heard of the sudden death of her magazine or of her disbarment from the solo school, her entrance to the Treaty Stone Bar downstairs would have radiated bounce. As it was she sizzled up to a place at the counter. Reflexively, the barman tried to comb his hair with two pushes of the palm of his hand. He was not the best fucking barman any place.

'I see what you mean,' Inspector Blake observed to Constable Taylor. 'On second thoughts, I'll handle it.'

With calm disinterest she watched the young barman try to control his horn while he served up her vodka and white. She smiled at the poor fellow, drenching him, and tumbled a couple of quid out of her purse. And then, inevitably, she was approached.

'We were just talking about you. If you'll forgive us.'

She flicked the flame of her lighter under the tip of her cigarette and pointed the fag out of the holster of her lips.

'We've seen you on the chat shows of course but we've had the most interesting crossing with your colleague, Mr Bateman.'

Diana Hayhurst smiled. 'Oh yes?'

'You don't mind us gate-crashing? My nephew John Taylor. Harry Blake. Actually, what was it, nephew, three hours on the boat? Six hours altogether I'd say, and seemed no longer than six minutes. Mr Bateman was so – droll, I'd put it – he was so droll on his job with *Unipolitan*.'

'Percival *is* droll.'

'Is it all right to join you for the moment? Nephew, pull your stool up. When he told us he was a market research consultant with *Unipolitan* at first I thought it was an oil company but nephew here said Uncle don't be dumb, it's the magazine. Then I thought: Of course. If you don't mind my saying so I think it's a wonderful policy. Better by far than all this technology. I'm willing to bet your Mr Bateman would get the general election right for instance. I said it to nephew, I said isn't that what everything is about when you get down to it: looking into one's heart. I congratulate you.' Inspector Blake lifted his glass of beer in tribute.

Diana Hayhurst was a sharp woman. She recognised the presence of two Englishmen who had travelled over with Percival and to whom he had a position with *Unipolitan* as market research consultant. She was also alert to the connotations of 'looking into one's heart', as indeed John Paul Getty might have been to the potential of a can of crude oil. She moved her legs to allow her dress fall apart but the uncle only smiled at her for more information. There were people who decided at a certain stage in their lives that sex was best left to other people. The nephew was human. She aimed her dimples at him.

'I hope Percival hasn't given away trade secrets.'

But the uncle still had the running. 'Well, if he did they're safe with us, eh, nephew? I can tell you Mr Bateman fair bucked a fellow up. Short back and sides. To a chap of my vintage that's the sort of thing one likes to hear. Expect the renaissance of the barbershop within a year, Mr Bateman forecasts.'

Diana Hayhurst held the cigarette aloft feminine-fashion and widened her eyes. Short back and sides were as attractive as celibacy. 'That's Mr Bateman,' she agreed, winking at the uncle. 'And what else?'

'Eh? There was so much. Nephew?'

'Chastity . . .'

'Oh yes. Chastity before marriage. I wouldn't have thought it you know but looking into his heart Mr Bateman assured us. I may be old-fashioned but I said to Mr Bateman, I said I'll drink to that, Mr Bateman. No more abortion either. Of course not taking away from your colleague one sees now that he's right, that it's more or less inevitable, I mean a country can only go so far to the dogs without catching on to itself.'

Discos, television, contraception, rock . . . Her instinct had sent her to protect Christmas from the solo school and to save the solo school from itself. She was rewarded already. She would nail Bateman to a *Unipolitan* desk. Chastity! The uncle was going on about his daughter or something. He was looking at her with a question on his face that she hadn't caught. 'Sorry?'

'I'm saying you're probably in Mellick developing your business, new markets and that.'

'We're already in Mellick,' the businesswoman asserted. 'We're already every place.'

The uncle nodded. But he was waiting for more. He had a cheek and she had had enough of him especially now that she could see Ben's face in the mirror. Ben was leaning against the entrance door of the Treaty Stone. 'So nice to have met you both, but I must rush.'

In Bateman's bedroom the League Against Christmas was reduced to a cast of two. As host Bateman had given Foster the chair while he himself perched on one of the beds. For the first time since the diddly club was proposed back in October Foster was obliged to give the matter the unqualified attention that he devoted to all his affairs. He listened to Bateman. Foster would have defended himself against any charge of racism: he would have pointed out that he was simply aware of the distinction between a master race and the irrepressibly quaint posture of a people not yet weaned from romance. That was all. You did not expect *gravitas* immediately from those just free of the yoke. No more. He did not hate the Irish. Neither by a long chalk could he be expected to bloody well love them. And yet, listening to Bateman's *enthusiasm*, if he was not quite turned into a Hibernophile on the spot he discovered in himself a more understanding warmth than heretofore. He was in Bateman's shoes, looking at it from Bateman's point of view. He became the neighbour dropping round to spectate at the painting of a door who's the one to notice the spot as yet uncoated.

'Bateman, I've had a thought. Unfortunately I could give it you with more confidence if I hadn't cut the deuce myself. I'd much prefer if it had been Ellis. No. I'll keep it to myself. You'd misunderstand me. You'd think I was looking for a way out.'

Bateman had to drag the thought out of Foster. Bateman examined the thought while Foster protested that he was withdrawing the thought, that it was only a thought. Foster left the bedroom unburdened. Bateman, alone, was now the League Against Christmas.

Foster did not give one damn what Ellis or any of them thought about him. All the more reason then for not letting fellows like that have a pot at you. Keep them in their place. Of course Gosling wouldn't have the nerve. But Ellis knew how to use himself. Having once been part of things and now out of it, Ellis had a cunning founded on familiarity with both sides, that is if you could call a wallow in insanity a side. Ellis would bring it up sometime, maybe not this trip even though he was doubly unhinged by the customs men ripping up his dirty strip of lino. In three months, Easter say, when Foster was conscientiously pointing out a flaw in the play, Ellis would let it slide out apropos of damn all: Smart piece of work you pulled ducking out of the diddly club, eh? No, now was the time to forestall that class of criticism. They were gone off some place, Ellis and Gosling, for beer. He might just look Hayhurst up, put it to her. In a way she was the most likely to understand, a logic of their own – women, almost Irish you could say, could reason quite progressively just so long as you began in midair, from a foundation of cloud. Cloud-cuckoo-land. Try her door for a start. And be authoritative, no need for apologetics. He rapped fimly calling out 'Hayhurst?' No answer. He rapped again. The door seemed to yield a little. 'You there, Hayhurst,' he called, trying the handle. It was unlocked. Typical of a woman. He put his head in. Clothes flung all over the place. He saw the high-heeled ankle straps where he had last seen them – on the bed.

The sergeant lifted his knee up to the edge of the desk and backed his chair on to its hind legs. He twirled the Biro cogitatively between his teeth. He looked up at the clock. Ben was some character. No one could ever accuse Ben of talking shop. At least not cop shop. As far back as the Scott Medal days, all Ben ever went on about was working in some bar in London.

The sergeant knew that Ben was on duty yet Ben had come in to the station in his street clothes and said: 'Synchronise our watches', the sort of guff you normally got only on those imported American detective series. The sergeant didn't have a watch so Ben had adjusted his in tune with the station clock. The sergeant was Ben's superior yet he had never given Ben an order. You worked with a partner rounding up Mad Dog O'Dwyer, raiding stills, purging the housing estates of joyriders, standing up to bank robbers, and you made sergeant while Ben just was not interested even though Ben had done it all and the sergeant just happened to have been along. When the sergeant wanted to give Ben an order the sergeant said: Ben, any chance you'd do us a favour? And it was not that the sergeant was not officer material. The sergeant was well able to order: You. You, you and you. Hop to it. The station clock was five minutes fast. Ben had wound his watch on accordingly and ordered: 'Listen carefully, here's what I want you to do.'

The Shakespeare was a thirty-second walk from the station. The sergeant looked at the station clock and started walking. He understood perfectly Ben's instructions – Ben could make himself understood – but he had no idea why Ben so instructed. He opened the door of the Shakespeare, looked up at the Shakespeare clock and saw he had two minutes. He excused himself through the crowd and had his hand grabbed by that little Bowler fellow from the Post Office who sang soulfully up at him: *We run them in, we run them in, we run them in, we show them we're the bold gendarmes*. The sergeant gently pulled Bowler's grip loose and continued down the bar. He beckoned the proprietor. The proprietor cocked his head into the whisper-listening position. The sergeant ordered him to lock the door leading to the toilets after the sergeant.

The sergeant stood at the foot of the short flight of steps and calculated that there was one minute to elapse. Sixty, fifty-nine, fifty-eight . . . At exactly ten o'clock the sergeant was to open the door of the ladies' toilet. That was all Ben could tell him, Ben told him. 'Trust my judgement, okay?' Anyone else coming to the sergeant with a proposition like that would have been told to scratch his boll . . . five, four . . . The sergeant stood on the landing . . . three, two, one . . . he opened the door.

The timing was not quite perfect but that was nobody's fault. As it turned out the timing was better than perfect. Fifteen years earlier when Ben was the best fucking bar-man in London he was no more than a youngster and had come immediately with the first contact of her pubic bristle with his bulb. Now they were both fifteen years older. They were in the Shakespeare toilet at two minutes to ten. They kissed first as people do who are capable of adding a touch of love to sex. They fumbled and soon the buttons of the safari dress were open and Ben's trousers unbelted. Her tights and panties were down and the cups of her bra were off duty like a welder's goggles round his neck. At ten o'clock on the dot they were both naked and Ben entered her just as the sergeant opened the door.

The sergeant understood now. But he had no instruc-tion as to how long he was to maintain his vigil. Then again the sergeant was a self-starter and took it upon himself to remain on duty. He was a witness for one and a half minutes longer than either Ben or Diana Hayhurst had anticipated.

With the threat of the short straw behind them now Ernie Gosling and Arthur Ellis could toast the diddly club in the Shakespeare. They were pub people, comfortable in a strange bar and the day was long since past when there was anything remarkable about an Englishman on the premises or, indeed, anything exotic about any species. Television had undressed the nations for the world no longer to wonder at, and even a bone through the nose or football-sized tits inspired only a yawn of familiarity. You could get lost in a packed Christmas pub anywhere now, your privacy sacrosanct. There was even a small chap roaring his head off singing one song after another and he was only so much distraction to the rest of the customers as an unseasonal fly that might cause you to smack lightly at your jaw.

'Beer's okay, Arthur,' Ernie Gosling acknowledged a sign of civilisation.

Arthur Ellis had swallowed without tasting. Now he held a sup in his mouth. 'Fine, Ernie.' But he relished a different prospect. His hotel room was carpeted, wall to wall. Not the Royal George's fault, no more than any place else's. All the best places were modelled on each other all over the world. People paid for knowing what they could expect. Nobody forked out for mystery tours. It was good to be thinking straight again, thinking lino. From what he could see the whole Shakespeare place was covered in lino, not so much as an offending mat, even if the lino was tattered almost to a death rattle. Leaning on the counter he had noticed the lino as his foot caught in a ripped segment. All he had to do was bend down to tie his shoelace. It did not matter the size of the piece he managed to tear off, it would be there on the floor beside his bed in the Royal George when he rose in the morning. If it only accommodated his big toe, so what? How did you measure a principle? 'Cover me a second, Ernie.' About the dimensions of a cigarette packet, he slipped it into his pocket as he straightened up.

'What you doin', Arthur?'

'Got me a piece of lino,' Ellis used American, the language of cover-up, to coat the theft of a piece of the Shakespeare. Robbery was robbery. He had begun to come round once Foster cut the deuce. He was out of it, thank Christ, safe in the Shakespeare with Ernie. It was all in Foster's lap now. And Bateman of course. Well, it had been their baby from the word go. What could go wrong now? All he was obliged to do from here on in was take his seat in the distinguished strangers' gallery. He must have been mad to risk it. Escaped from the jungle, carved a lino empire for himself, found freedom and then chanced it all on a cut of the cards. He could have ended up in jail. Mad. Anything did happen he would bloody well deny all knowledge. Without blinking, swear he'd never heard of no plot to rob any diddly club. Let Foster carry the can. He had been shit scared, nearly pissed in his trousers. That's the way it was when you knew a thing or two. When you had imagination. He was even willing to bet a pound to a penny that Foster was windy and Foster was as dull as they came. Only Ernie kept his cool. How did Ernie do it? Ernie wasn't dumb.

'Ernie?'

'Yeah Arthur?'

'Tell me, Ernie, were you hoping to cut an ace?'

'Knew I wouldn't.'

'How did you know you wouldn't?'

'Felt lucky, didn' I?'

'Yeah? How?'

Back that time when he forgot to put the coupon in

the litter bin after his narrow escape of nearly letting Linda and Betty in on it, he was edgy for four days. He thought the bleeding fire brigade would have to be brung to get his arm out the postbox. But he didn't click! And to cap it all QPR DID draw with Man. United! Away! But he had to live with the fear of the click for four days and on top of that the League Against Christmas, because it was the night he posted the coupon that Percy told them the plan and how they would cut the cards when they got to Mellick. Until on the Saturday the football results were flashed on the BBC and he hadn't even managed two draws! That's when he knew he was safe in the solo school and in the potman's job, and felt it in his bones that he wasn't going to draw no short straw.

The next few weeks they were all edgy in the solo school, he could sense it – except himself, he never once felt scared – and then he noticed something the night they had to arrange how to get them all over to Percy's country and have it seem natural. He was the big problem himself, he knew that and so did the rest of them. They got round it the way they did but the thing he noticed was that Mr Foster said: 'Ernie can travel with me in my car.' Dian wasn't going to spend hours in boats and buses or trains, *or* cars, she was a flyer, and Percy had to travel on ahead to check out the lie of the land. Mr Foster had said: 'Ernie can travel with me in my car,' and then: 'What about you, Ellis?' Arthur and Mr Foster always had a dig ready for each other right from the start-off, they all knew that but even so by rights Arthur Ellis should have been thought of first before Ernie Gosling. But Mr Foster had said: 'Ernie can travel with me.' Now one way of looking at it would be to say who was first in the solo school, who begun it? It was himself and Arthur, and Percy come along next and then Mr Foster. And Diana for dealer out. So one way of picking the team would be to say Arthur first, Ernie second, Percy third . . . But in real life Mr Foster was the boss, that was understood without anyone having to say it. If a giant octopus nabbed five blokes from all over the world, one from every continent, and dropped them on a desert island one of them would naturally turn out to be the leader whether he was first or last to arrive. When Ernie held an election in his mind he always picked Mr Foster first and Arthur second, Percy third and Dian fourth even though she was a woman, and himself last. But suppose there was a real election – they were grown men, things didn't happen like that – but just suppose Mr Foster was picking the team like the prime minister picking her cabinet. Mr Foster wasn't a bloke who'd feel the need to pick *anyone* after himself, he was that type, but if he had to by a rule that was there that obliged him to, who would he pick number two? He wouldn't pick Diana Hayhurst because she was a woman, no offence to women or anything and leavin' aside the prime minister which was one of those once-offs. So it was between Arthur and Percy. And himself. He was entitled to be considered because even though he was only a potman it wasn't the Archbishop of Canterbury they were trying to find, it was like in the Army – you never knew who'd show up tough on the day, it might be a bloke who was a chippy in real life instead of say, a bank manager. And this was just a solo school. Solo schools were made up of all sorts just like *This Is Your Life,* you could be sitting down waiting for a general or a film star to come on and instead it could be someone lost his two legs in a car crash and had two new ones fitted and went on to climb Mount Everest, and that'd be the very programme would turn out better than any general or film star. So he was as entitled to be in as anyone else. Mr Foster might have spotted how Arthur had the heebie-jeebies when they were cutting the cards and that was solo school business. Whereas *he* had kept his cool which Mr Foster must have copped on to as well. So in his head Mr Foster might say This isn't Miss Great Britain, this is the solo school, and he might draw a line through Arthur's name. That would leave Percy. Mr Foster sometimes made remarks about the Irish 'Your countrymen, Bateman' – that class of thing that you couldn't be sure was Mr Foster serious or taking the mickey, but no, he had got together with Percy first off about Christmas – he would pick Percy. That was fair enough. Mr Foster wouldn't be spiteful just cos Percy was Irish and rightly so. Percy would be number two. And when Mr Foster came to write down the next name he would put Ernie Gosling. He could trust Mr Foster's judgement, that was how he was able to keep his cool cutting the cards, because any time he thought about it he thought about it this way: There was five people in the solo school and the solo school was taking time off to fight Christmas through robbing Percy's old man's diddly club. That meant that five people were robbing the diddly club. Except that they only needed one person to actually do the job – that is, the way Percy wanted the job done. You could say the other four were minding the getaway car only it was a case of the getaway car couldn't move unless the fifth person was safely in it too, the same as if he had the keys or the can of petrol. Sposing the diddly club was a tin of beans high up on the top shelf of a small shop and of the five people who wanted to knock off the tin of beans one was a midget and there was no chair to stand on or ladder to climb up in the small shop. And they cut the cards and the midget won and got the job of nicking the tin of beans while the other four six-footers waited outside in the car for the midget who had the keys of the car in his pocket. The other four would quickly figure that unless they were happy to have the lot of them

be bollocked it would be a better idea to say to the midget
You were game ball but it's best if you drive the car.

If he had cut an ace back in Dian's room in the hotel
they would have all sat back with an air of that's it then,
only on all their faces there'd be written a doubt that he
might land them all up the creek. He could put pieces of
paper into envelopes and take money out of envelopes as
good as the next man but suppose something turned up
they hadn't bargained for. He just wouldn't – and he had
to admit it to himself – he just wouldn't be able to talk
his way out of it as good as any of the rest of them,
frinstance Diana could show her leg or let out a glimpse
of tit, that type of thing or whatever. After cutting the
ace they couldn't say it's okay Ernie you're not up to it,
you're a midget, Ernie, cos then he'd *have* to insist Who's
not bleedin' well up to it. So it would have to be done
subtle. Mr Foster would come up with something like:
I've been thinking, maybe we could use Ernie a better
way, Ernie might be more important to us ... Or Mr
Foster might come up with: There's something else needs
to be done but it's dangerous so I'll do it myself even
though it involves throwing darts and I'm not the best
darts thrower, it's actually a red-herring job but it's
necessary but as I said it's dangerous so I can't ask anyone
else even though I'd be much happier if I was a decent
darts player ... Of course everyone knew who was the
best darts player in the King's Arms let alone in the solo
school so Ernie Gosling would end up having to fight
them to be allowed to do the darts job dangerous or not.
What it was was that Mr Foster would be cute and save
him from the diddly club job but at the same time leave
him with his dignity. He would see through it but he
would go along with it recognising that was the way
things should be done to keep the peace and everyone
hold his head up. He knew this and it was better

knowledge than what you got at school because without it you couldn't get through life, it was how he got through the Army, the motor factors, how he landed the potman's job, how he could deal with Linda and Betty and the Guv'nor. The darts job or whatever would be a breeze. And that was why he felt lucky but he couldn't hardly tell that to Arthur, you just climbed inside your own head, that was all, but you couldn't explain it to someone else like Arthur because then he'd be inside your head which was one place there wasn't room for two.

'Dunno, Arthur. Just felt lucky, didn' I?'

Ellis did not probe the mysterious emotion. He savoured his beer. He had the lino in his pocket. He had lifted the king of diamonds. Fuck Foster, him and Percy could have it between them.

Foster closed the bedroom door behind him, and then brought the hand from behind his back to finger tip his glasses up the bridge of his nose. He fogged the lenses by blowing out his breath with the lower lip pouted. He had always imagined himself cocky in this much-yearned-for circumstance but now he was disappointed to think his penis limp. But it wasn't. As he would have known if he could reason. If he could reason he would reason that he'd want to be off his head, Diana Hayhurst might return at any second. But the logic of the libido had taken control. He wore glasses to combat myopia. He took a couple of steps forward and stood in front of the dresser mirror. Slowly he put his hands up to remove the glasses. He folded them methodically and laid them carefully beside a pair of crumpled tights on the dresser.

Foster slipped off his jacket and loosened his tie, all the time watching the man in the mirror. He took off his shirt and vest and administered a whistling-past-the-graveyard slap to his belly button. He unbuckled his belt and let his trousers fall to the ground. He thumbed his underpants down to his ankles. He was naked, apart from his socks. What had been only firmish now began to brush the inside of his leg. There were appurtenances of facial improvement on the dresser beneath the mirror. He picked up the lipstick. He pursed his lips, as he had noticed Gladys do, and daubed gently, sucking in as Gladys also did. There was a tingle to his penis as it hardened. He put the cap on the lipstick and replaced it carefully. He was not so accomplished with the green eye shadow, a dollop of which blinded him. He had to sit on the bed for two minutes and roll his eye around inside the closed eyelid. When he recovered he moved on to the compact: not a man to repeat an error, he closed both eyes as he patted his cheeks with powder from the powder puff. With his short sight, through the settling dust, he saw an image in the mirror in which he could take pride. The application was as judicious as Gladys herself could effect and Gladys had taste in that line, he had always thought her the best made-up woman in the pub on Saturday nights: all the more galling, her next to Nick, that he usually reeked of something salesmanly. Foster's penis grew into the mirror. He turned away and saw the Roland Cartier burgundy kid high heels with ankle straps lying on the bed. He sat down and tried to try one on. But he was a size eight. He stood up and held the shoe appraisingly. His first obstacle. Tentatively he hung the shoe by its ankle strap on the peg of his penis. Obstacle overcome he stepped to the dresser, opened the top drawer and lifted out a pair of burgundy panties. He slid them carefully over his toes and they came the whole way up until they were impeded by his penis bearing the shoe. He uncrumpled the tights that lay beside his glasses and moved back to the bed gingerly so as not to dislodge the shoe. The tights made it to within a couple of inches of the panties and he was blessed with a flash of his own white thigh. He eased back to the open drawer where he found a burgundy uplift bra. Never one to have gone in for anything as ludicrous as fitness, his underdeveloped musculature now came into its own: the bra fitted him. The shoe jerking, he returned to the bed and lay down, his head elevated on the pillow and surveyed his body. That fool, Nick Bentley, with his hand on Gladys's knee and his salesman's sanitised jokes, what did he know? Youth must have its fling, Nick Bentley didn't know what a fling was. Foster bent forward and kissed his exposed white thigh. His penis tingled again and he lay back. He should be able to look down his body without impediment, as though it was his wife's. But Gladys did not have a penis. There should have been some way to unscrew his penis and chuck it on the floor with his own clothes, so that when he looked down he would see a little hairy valley without any monuments of distraction. And it wasn't as if he needed the shoe, they all kicked off their shoes at the least opportunity: after shopping Gladys lifted them off after wiping on the mat and padded into the hall with the soft exclamation, My feet!

If he could only have a little hole like Gladys had. 'Don't poke about, Kenneth' was her response when he wanted to play in there with his fingers. He leaned forward and tried to push the penis out of sight behind his thighs. The shoe fell off. Had the penis been limp he would have had no bother but now the lad was ready to damn-well burst. He brought his knees up, secreted the penis and stretched his legs again. The rocklike erection was hidden. Now even a fly looking down from the ceiling would think he was all woman. This was only the beginning, these were only Hayhurst's things, wait until he was in business with Gladys gone shopping and her wardrobe and drawers at his mercy, and the earrings to really top things off. He had never had his penis under his thighs before. It was pleasurable. He was able to manufacture a gentle friction by lowering and raising his knees ever so slightly like lazy pistons, and suddenly he was gripped by a frenzy that could only be sated by clutching the bra and rubbing the cups all over his face until the off-stage penis could take no more and erupted.

On those rare nights that Gladys touched his knee conferring on him the freedom to turn her round and have a bit, Foster was as much a victim of postcoital depression as anyone else of his sex and this was never helped by Gladys gathering to herself more than her share of the bedclothes. And lest he might be tempted to bask in any afterglow of his imagination, Gladys would add a quiet lingering fart to the cocktail of exhaled gin and its and then snort off to sleep. But now Foster stood in front of the mirror in Diana Hayhurst's room and smiled at himself. Where was the heart attack? If he was to be attacked, now was the time. It would be inappropriate to be struck down after he had re-entered his own clothing. It was done. And it could be done again and again, and now that he knew how to hide his penis what refinements might not follow? Of course Gladys was past the child-bearing age but that did not mean he couldn't use tampons himself.

Ben Hanley knew better than to have brought Diana Hayhurst in through the public bar. Post Office clerks, sorters, postmen, the banking crowd and the Young Thomond mob were capable of reacting in only one way collectively to the presence of a woman of class. Get 'em off you, Ben. Even Bowler was likely to start kissing her from the knuckles all the way up her arm while he sang 'Your Tiny Hand is Frozen.' They just did not have the

London polish that enabled Ben to stay cool in the company of a hot woman.

When Ben's and Diana's bodies disengaged – his chest and her breasts parting with a suction plop – Diana smiled on the sergeant who was a Shakespeare client himself in his off-duty hours. Ben brought the sergeant out of his trance by closing the door on his disappearing nose and slack, salivating lips.

'Thanks,' Ben said, as he brought his trousers up.

'Thank *you*, Ben, thank *you*.'

There was no shyness on either side. If anything they were more comfortable with each other than in the act of fucking. Diana's bra had come undone. She pressed the cups to her breasts and turned around. 'Clip me, Ben.' Ben obliged, yielding to the temptation to kiss her gently on the back.

Ben combed his hair while Diana took out her handbag mirror to correct the damage to her make-up. They went back out the hall. Notwithstanding the variety of her sexual proclivities Diana Hayhurst had never had to greet the public wearing garments rumpled in the act. The safari dress was now a spent cartridge. She went back to the hotel to change into the jump suit and caught Foster in *his* act.

If you were any kind of a man, before you opened your door mornings you stepped into your armour. Failure to take this elementary precaution and you took a buffeting that shaped you into the village fool, a wino, crank, subversive or pederast. Bateman had never hit the street in his vest. Couldn't afford to as a non-diploma holder, a layman, a broad figure. But cloaked in the alb of scorn, he was proof against the men of action, the achievers, the specialists. The specialists. There was that child you seemed always to be reading about: incurable ailment, grief-stricken mother, half-a-million pounds to send him to that first-class man in Switzerland or America, plight touching the hearts of the readers, money pouring in, shots of postmen laden with sacks of donations, early days yet, difficult to be sure if operation one hundred per cent success till at last, one year later on child's birthday, photograph of toddler with full head of hair grown again engaged in normal child's activities. Bateman adjusted his vestments and saw only that the hungry cunt took the money: no fee, no foal. But in the workplace, the factory floor, the office, Bateman kept his mouth shut and his powder dry and agreed: Yes, it was wonderful about that young kid. Dr Bollix, may you be stung and wail for want of a dock leaf. Interest rates up, interest rates down, ninety million wiped off the stock exchange: what was it all about? Economists noticeably with the arse of their trousers intact. Without the scorn your head would ache with the pain of not being able to understand. You had to award yourself a degree in good manners and look down your nose at all the other disciplines, chuckle merrily at the innocence of the certainty all around one. Around one who had chosen the better part.

This is all very well and effective at the height of battle but what of our champion in winter quarters? Loafing around in the long johns of reality comes the unbidden glimpse of self-recognition. Layman = good for fuck all. Broad figure, Renaissance man = you must be joking, poor soil sprouting a variety of weeds of the genus good manners, a peasant accomplishment.

It was way past Bateman's drinking time and yet he remained in his room in the Royal George Hotel after Foster left. He was perplexed, but by what? He was alone, the lorgnette of superiority off duty, reduced to the hard-boiled vista. There was no doubt but that Foster had been on the ball, but you would have put your money more confidently on Arthur Ellis to discover that it was inapposite for Bateman to have an alibi; that, further, not alone should Bateman do the job on his own but that he should be more or less *seen* to do the job; and that if the consequence was that he do jail, then so much the better.

Of course Foster was right. It was logical, always bearing in mind where you started to reason. Bateman was not afraid: fear would have sent him downstairs to the bar. And yet he sat there, puzzled. Where was the euphoria? The twenty-four-year-old thirst for revenge? He was conscious of a weariness of his father, of Frankie Timmons, of the smug and the certain, of that money-mad prick of a doctor in Switzerland or America: best to let it all wash over you, shrug it off. That came with middle age. Maturity, to give it its euphemism, when you had lost your go. Percival Bateman? No longer the hungry fighter? Paunched perceptive? Flab on the fine anger? If you weren't bitter then you had to be sweet. And that was it: he stood up, ready to attack the drink now. It was happiness, of all things. In of all people, happiness. It was Ernie, it was Arthur, Diana and Foster. The solo school had changed him from a grump in disguise to a man of camouflaged contentment. He was happy. Jesus, I'm happy! Christmas was no longer a threat. I'm happy, the best armour yet.

'Oops,' Diana Hayhurst said. 'I do beg your pardon, Mr Foster, carry on.' She stepped back out into the corridor. She was not outraged. She did not need an explanation. Not even for her jump suit would she be so vulgar as to interrupt a consenting adult indulging his predilection. But my, my – Foster! It was better than . . . it was better than being fucked by Ben. She could hardly count her winnings as she thrust her leg out going down the stairs. She breezed into the Treaty Stone Bar, ignored the 'Ah' from the uncle fellow at the counter and continued into the ladies' where she examined her treasure: the League Against Christmas was scuttled; she was about to capture Bateman for her *Unipolitan* house plant; and by fuck did she have Foster where she wanted him. And she had done Ben a favour in the Shakespeare toilet. And it had all happened in one night. 'Ah,' she was greeted again when she re-emerged, but she held up her hand and smiled: 'Mine.' She owed this uncle and nephew. They had delivered Bateman. She sat up, exposed the leg, settled in to drink and look charming at whatever nonsense the uncle was prattling.

'. . . not a bad hotel but I said to nephew here for local colour you don't sit still in your hotel, you move out, mix with the people . . . stretching the legs just a block up the road and there leaping out at us, you can just imagine how comforting, splendid sign-writing, THE SHAKE-SPEARE. I said to nephew: in here, surely feel at home, packed out, singing their heads off, just the type of thing your Mr Bateman predicted on the trip over. I said to nephew this is the way it used to be, gather round the piano in the old days and a right knees-up – ah, there he is, Mr Bateman, man of the moment. Move round nephew, that's it, what's yours, Mr Bateman?'

Bateman had stepped warily down the stairs as though breaking in a new limb, a pair of happiness legs. It was true, it was happiness. Discontent was like virginity or an umbrella after all – designed to be lost. Here was more of it, Diana and the uncle and nephew all turned towards him with a welcome.

'It's mine, uncle. Percival, look into your heart and name your poison.'

Bateman blushed. He was a fool. He should have put two and two together. He was thinking: had she explained to the uncle, Mr Bateman doesn't work with

Unipolitan? The uncle and nephew would look down on him. She slapped the counter and called 'Whiskey!' without awaiting his choice.

'You didn't tell me, Percival, you never said we had such a fan. Uncle Harry says you have a wonderful heart. And so say all of us. Toast, To Percival's heart!'

She clinked her glass against the uncle's and nephew's. The uncle said: 'Cheers, Mr Bateman.' The nephew echoed: 'Cheers.'

'And now,' Diana Hayhurst prodded her chest, 'to me. To the lady who discovered the man with the heart.' Bateman's whiskey was on the counter. The uncle passed it along. Bateman joined the uncle and nephew, the uncle the spokesman: 'To Diana Hayhurst!' Bateman raised his glass.

'And by the way, Percival, in case it slips my mind – excuse the shop uncle – the first day back be in my office at eight, something's come up and I need you *badly*.'

Peripherally, the uncle and nephew were impressed and straight in front of Bateman's eyes the lines on Diana Hayhurst's forehead and her dimpled smile told him she was offering him the job. The happiness of the happiness and now the happiness of a position, it was rich. Bateman drank to himself. The uncle was off again.

'Just saying, Mr Bateman, bar up the street, the Shakespeare, attracted by the name naturally, place after your own heart I should wager, singsong in full throttle and no television, I saw a sign up tomorrow night Christmas Draw, I said to nephew put me down for that, bet that will be a song night, I said nephew you'll have to go along with me there, age before beauty, dammit I don't recall when I did last hear a bit of singing in London . . .'

Bateman caught Diana Hayhurst's thin smile. Of course she could not know that he had changed. He was a happy man. He was no longer driven by the confiscation of his

Canadian dollars. He saw the climate of opinion of those days and understood his father's need to put on the dog going to London for the fitting. His father's faults were not his father's fault. It was the age, pride in manliness, shame at cowardice. They did not have education, could not grasp the world outside of the physical. Or some such explanation. He did not want to do the diddly club. He did not want to hurt his father or Frankie Timmons or anyone at all any place. He had happiness to spare. And yet if he backed off he would lose the respect of the solo school, lose the job as market research consultant. There had to be a way out. He was only on his first whiskey but even so judgement was clouded by the feel of a glass in his hand. He might rise a different man in the morning, his old self, hatred, self-pity. He could put it to them in the morning just as Foster had come with his thought earlier that night. He could put it to them that it was inapposite as a Christmas surrogate if he himself no longer saw the diddly club so. Hadn't they spent two years telling him that he was off his head to be bothered by what bothered him?

' . . . isn't that so, Mr Bateman?'

That Arthur Tracey didn't need fourteen electricians to help him sing over a clothesline.

Foster took off the panties and tights and began to put his own clothes back on again. His first instinct was to deny everything. In that he was not remarkable. The best defence, anything else plea-bargaining. But it would not hold up. There was no denying it to Hayhurst, a specialist in that field. So he did the next best thing. He admitted everything, to himself preparatory to approaching her with his hands up. At the same time you damned well didn't lose your authority overnight. In all those black and white fifties prisoner-of-war films the British officer class looked down the nose at their inferior captors. He would stand no nonsense. On the other side of the ledger, he was indebted to her. There were no heart attacks involved – he had cleared his head of that rubbish. You simply got into the duds and did your business and then stepped back into your street clothes like a bus driver coming off shift.

He went downstairs hoping to catch her in the bar. There she was exposing her leg to the whole place, Bateman with her and two fellows yapping away. The best of British luck to Bateman in his mad escapade but he was damn glad to be out of it, his own mission accomplished. It was bloody amusing to see them making up to the locals, the first thing the dumbest policeman asked was Did you notice any strangers in the vicinity? And it would be a case of Come to think of it there *was* a woman waving her leg around all the way up to her fanny. He decided on the other end of the bar but of course he should have expected it.

'There's Mr Foster. Over here, Mr Foster.' His name, coupled with her flagrant self-advertisement for all to hear. He changed direction and put on the best public face as he heard himself introduced to two Englishmen, Uncle Harry and his nephew John – overfamiliar with it. He had to allow her to buy him a lager and listen to the Uncle Harry fellow.

'I take it you're with *Unipolitan* too, Mr Foster?'

'Yes, Mr Foster's our accountant, breathes down our budgetary necks, right Percival?'

Bateman nodding. Some juvenile concoction of theirs, unnecessary of course, explaining their appearance as a group. She probably had Gosling down as tea boy for when the need arose and Ellis ticked off as fashion correspondent. Fool of a woman. If he could trust his ears according to the Uncle Harry fellow Bateman had become a prophet, seeing into the future on behalf of that rag of a magazine And this epidemic of indiscipline had broken out while he was upstairs togging off. Without a word of consultation. The wonder of it was that they hadn't actually told the garrulous uncle and his nephew about the plot to rob the diddly club. When he was able to yank his attention away from the uncle's hypnotic series of rhetorical questions Foster easily caught Diana Hayhurst's eye: she had been staring at him. The bitch contorted her face into her innocent did-you-call-me-Mr-Foster? expression. Foster moved his head: 'Could I have word with you?' He indicated a corner of the lounge.

'Duty calls,' she beamed at the uncle and nephew.

As he took his drink away Foster could hear the uncle explaining to Bateman: 'Never off duty, eh, Mr Bateman? Conscientious fellow, I'd say.'

She had the brazenness to sit down and be attentive as though she were his secretary, even covering her damn leg for once.

'I don't know what you're at, Hayhurst and frankly I don't much care to know.'

'Yes, Mr Foster.'

'I'll come to the point. You probably have some idea in your head about my presence in your room just now—'

'Not at all.'

'Please. If you haven't already done so I don't see the necessity to broadcast your findings. If you understand me.'

'Of course I understand. You want it to be our secret.'

'If that's how you like to put it,' Foster was obliged to agree. She held all the cards. He was satisfied that he had carried it off as best it could be done. She would always be a threat. He would just have to bluff it through as long as necessary.

'No problem,' Diana Hayhurst said.

Foster looked at her again. It was a new world to him, Shepherd's Bush, the solo school, here in Mellick robbing diddly clubs. He was still an apprentice among the shiftless. Did they take everything as lightly as that? Supposing he had summoned a meeting, announced by the way, I thought I'd bring it to the notice of the members, I've taken to dressing up in ladies' underwear, you know? Ejaculation and what not with my make-up on, slobbering the cups of my bra all over my face. Would Ellis say: By Jove, Foster, congratulations. Wouldn't be one damn bit surprised if Ellis didn't add I hope you do it on lino, Foster. And why not? Maybe Hayhurst was capable of depth after all. Maybe her understanding was founded on something other than the prevailing laxity. Unlikely, but just in case he may as well unbend a little, put on a show of interest in her tawdry affairs. He waved the back of his hand in the direction of the counter.

'Those fellows, are you caught there, having to justify yourself or something?'

'Uncle Harry? Percival fell in with them on the boat, it's the most wonderful thing. He told them he was a market research consultant with *Unipolitan*. Gave them the benefit of his thinking, his ideas for the magazine. And do you know what, Mr Foster? His thinking is fucking marvellous. It so happens I need a man like that, so it will turn out he wasn't fibbing at all!'

Foster could not let it pass. 'You know nothing of Bateman. Are you telling me you intend to appoint a mystery man?'

'Of course I know Percival. He's in the solo school.'

'You don't hire a chap out of a solo school.'

'I do. I will.'

'I suggest you think about that. I think you should wait

until this diddly club business is over and done with. I say so in my professional capacity.'

After Ben Hanley had escorted Diana Hayhurst back to the hotel entrance he returned to the Shakespeare to finish the night with a few well-earned pints. The two diddly club merchants were still there as was Bowler, the voice croaky now from fags and an overextensive repertoire. In the privacy of the packed and noisy public house he was back again in The Pub, responding to Leonard Hooper's little finger, the best fucking barman in London. His ex-partner had seen him in action tonight and Ben was certainly not swearing him to secrecy. And anyone else who did not have the faith, Ben would tell them: Ask the sergeant if you don't believe me. But now that would no longer be enough. He'd had a taste of it again tonight, a taste of a London woman. The fug of the metropolis would cling to him all through the Christmas. It was five to eleven. Those two were leaving and it was also his time to go. It had never been his policy to be in a pub for even the suspicion of one more than the last drink. It was time for him to go get his fish and chips in a small town.

He watched them walk down the road in front of him and though he did not catch the words he did their London cadence. He would have liked to run on and put his arms around their shoulders and say Hey mates, I'm a London bloke myself at heart. They turned into the Royal George. Ben trailed them as far as the main glass doors. Diana was in there somewhere. He could always stroll in as though he wanted to use the toilet – to piss in – although management did not encourage the mentality that saw the hotel as a public convenience. He could be going upstairs to the disco. He could be pretending to be waiting for somebody. He saw them turn into the Treaty

Stone Bar. He followed on and just at the door to the bar he could see her with another one of them and he heard: ' . . . think about that. I think you should wait until this diddly club business is over and done with. I say so in my professional capacity.'

Ben edged back out to the street and went for his fish and chips.

'Well, Taylor?'

'Inspector?'

'Uncle. Only one day to go. D-day. D for diddly club, eh? Taylor, you're looking – what's the right word? – Taylor, you're looking . . . *un*enthusiastic. Am I to be congratulated on my detection there?'

'It's the feeling of impotence, Insp— Uncle.'

'Eh? Oh. I understand. Here's your brother. We didn't gain anything tonight did we? Let's go over it again, pound the beat, knock at the doors. They all gather in Madam Hayhurst's room and we creep along and what do we hear? I'll goabundle. We nip out to the Shakespeare. We've left the five of them back at the hotel playing solo in her room, so we decide the Shakespeare isn't where it's at if I may be allowed my colloquialisms – I don't know why you smile like that, Taylor, I'm not exactly Neanderthal man you know – and we double back to the old place and establish our crow's-nest in the bar downstairs. First we spot Gosling and Ellis leaving the hotel. Remember, one minute they're upstairs playing solo, next, comings and goings to beat the band. Gosling and Ellis off who knows where up to what we can't imagine. Then, zing, the Hayhurst item comes in looking ready for a beach party— eh? What's amusing you now, Taylor? Anyway, she comes in, I do my stuff. We have it confirmed that they've concocted this market research consultant sinecure for Bateman by way of covering all angles, etc. Then, suddenly, she hauls her leg off the stool and vanishes in a hurry. That's herself, Gosling and Ellis out in the great unknown before you can say Bob's your uncle. We decide to hang tough and sit it out. And what's our reward? The return of Madam oozing good-will and standing her round like a trooper. Noticeably on a high, if that's what they call it, since we've last seen her which leads us to suppose that something's been accomplished, groundwork laid for instance. Enter Bateman. Drink for Bateman, I'm suddenly her Uncle Harry, next thing we're drinking a toast to the fellow. And then a toast to herself for discovering him. They were toasting something all right, Taylor, and you can be damn sure it wasn't themselves, it was their plot. I kept the pot boiling – that comes with experience, Taylor, the ability to converse and keep the eyes peeled at the same time – and while I'm doing my bit I see them giving each other the nod. Now we're joined by Foster to whom we are introduced as Uncle Harry and his nephew John. A glass of lager man, Foster. Ever see a snap of Beria, Taylor? No? I suppose you wouldn't have. Or Himmler? Hatchet men. That's Foster for you. The same tight look. Cold. Professional. Fanatic. Doesn't even speak, let alone bother with the social niceties as Bateman and Hayhurst make such a point of. Our accountant breathes down our necks at *Unipolitan*. And then Himmler says Could I have a word with you? and she obeys like a shot. Of course we both know, Taylor, that Foster has never been within an ass's roar of *Unipolitan* but even if we didn't know we know now because accountants don't click their fingers and have tycoons like Lady Diana coming to heel just like that. Foster, Taylor, is the chill factor in the organisation. So we're there dragging the future out of Bateman, and herself and Foster are across from us and I can see the ruthless map of his frozen face while they're at whatever they're at and enter Gosling and Ellis who without thinking take a look in the direction of Foster and herself, and I see her shake her head just like that and at the same time roll her eyes in our direction and they catch on immediately and go lonesome to the other end of the bar as though they know no one. So we're getting no place fast, Taylor, and I'm obliged to be inspired to announce that I've an early day tomorrow and suggest to you, Coming nephew? And you get my meaning and we bid good night to Bateman and Hayhurst and Foster on the way out, and I can sense from her and Foster's lukewarm good night that they're relieved to see the back of us. And there we are. We come up here to our bedroom and I give you instructions, Taylor, after only five minutes I tell you to nip back down and go out in the street and take a turn round the block to clear your head manoeuvre and what do you notice on your way back in? Bateman, Foster, Gosling, Ellis, Hayhurst, all together in the one group at the bar with their glasses raised and a chorus of muted voices intoning: "To Christmas." Now, what do you make of that, Taylor, eh?'

'They're here to rob the diddly club.'

'How? When? Where? That's not good enough, Taylor, we're policemen, it's our job to know, to anticipate. Shall I tell you something, Taylor? If I could only be sure it was only the damn diddly club. I'd like to knock them up in their rooms and ask them, Say, I beg your pardon but are you only here to rob the diddly club? and if they could assure me Yes, that's all, then I would wish them well and sail home. Taylor, up early, we may have to split forces, every movement must be followed from the minute they brush their teeth.'

Diana Hayhurst saw off Uncle fucking Harry and his fucking nephew with 'Good night, good night.' She and

Foster and Gosling and Ellis gathered round Bateman at the bar. Ernie Gosling said: 'Well, 'ere's to Christmas then.' After any toast, in the rowdiest gathering, there is a hiatus until the figure of authority taps his glass with a spoon preparatory to moving proceedings along. And now a quietude descended upon the League Against Christmas. They looked at each other uncertain who was the master of ceremonies and at the same time avoided each other's look. Until the force of his personality and his unconquerable good nature could no longer contain Ernie Gosling's: 'Percy, I hope all works out for you an' Mr Foster tomorrow.'

They were unaccustomed to standing around the bar of a strange hotel. A deck of cards was the medium of their communication and without it they were vulnerable. The diddly club was exhausted as a catalyst of camaraderie. Worse, now that the deed was almost upon them, the diddly club was an impediment to even the most commonplace of exchanges. Anything they might say would have a hollow sound. Unless of course someone volunteered the obvious: Let's go home while the going is good. But it was a case of who was going to be first to be seen ceasing to applaud the dictator. Except for Diana Hayhurst, they were in thrall to their own thought police. Foster could see no good in telling them that Bateman was going it alone. He could predict the consequence of that. Ellis would seize his chance to espouse another crusade and insist on leading the charge, provoking Bateman into a fit of even greater obduracy than he had thankfully displayed in his hotel room earlier that evening. Best to leave well enough alone. Best, on a personal basis, to quit the whole bang shooting match. Foster placed his glass on the counter and embraced his inferiors with a single 'Good night.'

He withdrew quickly and was already out of the Treaty

Stone Bar and into the lobby before Ernie Gosling blinked himself alert with the afterthought: 'Night, Mr Foster.' He shook the dregs in his glass with a stylish wrist movement and finished his beer. 'Reckon it's time old Ernie hit the sack an' all.'

'I'm with you, Ernie,' Ellis said. He squeezed Bateman's arm lightly, nodded and winked at Diana Hayhurst.

Alone with Diana Hayhurst, Bateman could not stare at his shoes indefinitely. He had his explanation ready. The uncle had asked him his line and it would have been wearisome to go through his whole career to date so he had delivered the first lie to come into his head. But when he did look at her she said: 'Right then, Percival, can you start on Monday?'

As the Guv'nor and Ernie Gosling knew before him, there are forms to be observed in these matters. What he should have done was protest his lack of qualifications, point out to her that it was all a giggle, go through the bureaucracy of having her insist he could do whatever it was she intended him to do. But that would have been unworthy of both of them. This was virgin territory. Bateman, with his degree in etiquette, understood that there was a better way. 'Do you give luncheon vouchers?'

'Yes, Percival.'

They were adult, mature people. When necessary – economy of expression, every word fit to take the field – they could function without flimflam. It was really true. She was giving him a job. And yet it was too spare for him. He needed that extra padding of collateral.

'Looking into my heart?'

'Exactly.'

She was a different woman than he had known inside the solo school. She was levelling with him. There it was: the job. She would not deign to elaborate. If he asked another question he would get another, straight answer. He would be immature to press it further. Good manners dictated one last statement and Bateman was not surprised that tears, that wet water that he had shed so often in sadness, that tears, now of happiness, were gathering inside him as he said: 'I don't know how to thank you.'

Diana Hayhurst slid off her stool and touched his jaw with the palm of her hand. 'Good night, Percival.'

He ordered a pint and a large whiskey and lit a fag. It was all part of fate, destiny, God's plan, that he should have been saved from the conventional. His father's winning a Savile Row suit in Young Thomond's ruby anniversary raffle was the start of a trail that led him to be appointed market research consultant for *Unipolitan* in the Treaty Stone Bar of the Royal George Hotel. It was part of God's plan that he should have four solo school friends plus the uncle and nephew: the way was open for him to be himself among strangers on a bus or boat or anywhere and he would be accepted as a hail-fellow-well-met. Deliverance had come as a place at a new table, his chips piled as high as his peers'. He was ready to play again.

D-DAY

THE SERGEANT HAD never questioned any of Ben's instructions before and this morning Ben was authoritative and sure of himself. Ben disarmed the sergeant by needing the sergeant in the first place. The sergeant was off duty. But only he would do Ben of all Ben's previous partners, Ben said. And Ben did not want to recruit from higher up. And for once Ben was telling the sergeant everything he knew, Ben swore. There was a group in town from London, intent on mischief. Ben's informant was one of the gang themselves. The sergeant nodded. That was typical of Ben, getting it from the horse's mouth. What the gang were up to Ben could not say because he did not know, his informant was adamant that the objective was an irrelevance and Ben had reason to trust his informant better than he trusted himself. Their job, the sergeant's and Ben's, was to protect the gang from themselves. They were a harmless lot who were innocently unaware that their contemplated prank was felony in the eyes of all but themselves. Rather than allow them to proceed and nab them with their pants down it was by far more ethical to intervene and administer a metaphorical cuff round the ear. That was how it had been put to Ben by his informant and that was how Ben saw it and he was confident the sergeant would agree with him there. The sergeant nodded. Obvious.

'So what exactly do we do, Ben?'

'Arrest the lot.'

According to Ben's informant it would only be necessary to lock them up this morning until around ten o'clock tonight when the target would no longer exist.

'What if something goes wrong?'

'Wrong? Why should anything go wrong? Has anything ever gone wrong before?'

'No, but you always held something back from me that I understood after when you let me in on it. All you have now is an informant whose reliability—!'

It was her all right, Ben admitted. It was Diana Hayhurst whom the sergeant had not been able to believe had been fucked by Ben in a toilet years ago in London when Ben was a nobody barman. But he had to believe it last night when he saw her nude from the knockers down to her ankles and Ben ramming her in the Shakespeare jacks. The sergeant, as a mere sergeant, had to trust an informant of the stature of the world's most famous magazine publisher. But as a man with a humble opinion of himself he thought it incongruous that she should be giving barmen a free lick as though twas on the National Health instead of prick-teasing all comers except maybe film stars or millionaires the way all the really hot things did. Finally the sergeant was no more able to go against Ben's track record than he was capable of discoursing on theology with the Pope's top adviser.

'Okay, let's go, Ben.'

Inspector Blake and Constable Taylor were standing under the canopy outside the hotel entrance. It was a soft morning of a warmth year after year dubbed unseasonal.

Inspector Blake stretched his arms and gaped, trying for the yawn that indicates the citizen freshly risen from a blameless sleep. 'Well, nephew?' Inspector Blake had just observed when they were accosted by one of those Irish *gardai*, as Inspector Blake had said they were called.

'Sorry to bother you, Gentlemen, but would you like to help us in the course of our duty?'

'Eh?' Inspector Blake threw back his head.

'We'd be so very much obliged if you would accompany us to the station.'

Inspector Blake and Constable Taylor exchanged looks. Constable Taylor's eyebrow was arched again, awaiting guidance. Inspector Blake recovered: 'Of course, Garda my dear fellow. Honoured.'

Ben extended his left hand. 'Just around the corner and thank you for your assistance.'

'Not at all. As I say, honoured. Nephew.'

They turned off O'Connell Street. About twenty yards down the block Inspector Blake stopped. Constable Taylor stopped. Ben and the sergeant stopped. 'Is that the way you do it here?' Inspector Blake asked out of professional interest and continued prankishly, 'We could just as well tell you go and take a running jump, *Gardai*. *See*, I know my plural. But shouldn't you give us an inkling, accuse us or what not, that class of thing?'

The sergeant admired Ben's style.

'We know who you are,' Ben smiled, putting a firm hand on Inspector Blake's shoulder.

'Ah. Hear that nephew? Good work, *Gardai*. On your toes. Good show.'

Ben opened his hands modestly and took a slow first step forward. All fell in together and continued to the station. Inspector Blake was too impatient to hold in. 'The diddly club?' he winked at Ben Hanley. Ben nodded. 'First class. First class.'

They ambled into the station past the desk, past the stolen bicycles, past *gardai* nodding, 'Hi Ben, Hi Sarge.' Ben led the way into an open cell followed by the sergeant and Inspector Blake and Constable Taylor. Once inside Ben turned round and walked out again followed by the sergeant who closed the cell door and turned the key.

'Eh?' Inspector Blake grinned. But the *gardai* walked away.

'Well, Taylor?'

'Uncle?'

'Uncle my arse. Inspector, thank you very much. Where are we now, Taylor? Eh? Where are we? In the lock-up. That's where we are now comfortably ensconced. It's gone far enough. I'll try again. Out of the way, Taylor, out of the way.' Inspector Blake gripped two of the bars, inhaled and shouted. 'I SAY! . . . I SAY! . . . LET US OUT OF HERE . . . BLAST IT, WE'RE POLICE OFFICERS! . . . I SAY! . . . ANYBODY BLOODY WELL OUT THERE LISTENING?' Frustrated, he shook his head and turned back from the cell door. 'I don't know . . . TAYLOR! Are you amused, Taylor? Eh? You find it funny, do you? We have to relax, Taylor. We have to – keep – our cool. Let's go over it again, Taylor. We rise. We wash, we shave, we dress. We descend to breakfast. Over my boiled egg and your rashers, Taylor, we wave a genial good morning to that gang of anarchists, right? I point out we can't risk losing our quarry. While they're still idling over the orange juice we man the exit ready to greet all or any as they emerge and wear the newspaper over our face as we stalk the quarry on the last day. Before you have time to tongue the rind of the rasher out of your teeth, Taylor, we're jumped upon and not in your straight-out London bobby style, *oh* no: sly servility, the bloody hallmark of your Paddy. It can't be happening,

Taylor. Hold on, I'm not standing for it . . . I SAY. . . I SAY, ARE YOU ALL DEAF OUT THERE?'

The sergeant was proud of his judgement. 'I knew you were holding out on me, Ben, I just knew it.'

'Only that. I told you the lot except the diddly club. There was no point unless it was necessary. And I didn't tell you, our friend did. Can you beat it? They come all the way from London to knock off Johnny Bateman's diddly club. We better get the rest of them.'

'Ben?'

'Yeah?'

'Why is he roaring in there that he's a police officer?'

Ben Hanley tapped the side of his head. 'Why does he want to rob a diddly club? Why are there three Prince Charles's above in the asylum?'

'I SAY! . . . BLAST IT OUT THERE . . .'

' . . . too late now but in retrospect . . .'

'Eh?'

'I think we made a mistake there, Inspector, travelling incognito.'

'Taylor, what you're saying is I made a mistake. You're right. I did. I said no ID. I was thinking of you, Taylor. I wanted you to shed your bobby trappings completely. Incognito is incognito. But, Taylor, *they* mightn't listen to us but that doesn't mean we're not policemen. And here's one for you, Taylor: those two who walked us in here and left us on our tod, they're not policemen. They're in on it, Taylor. Dammit, they don't operate like that in Spain. Turkey, even. *We* don't operate like that ourselves under the PTA, for heaven's sake. They may wear the uniform but they're bent. They're *sympathisers*, Taylor. But the whole damn *gardai* force can't all be in on it. There's a straight cop out there . . . I SAY . . . CAN YOU HEAR ME, YOU PARCEL OF IDIOTS? . . . someone's coming, struck oil at last Taylor. HERE, I SAY, HERE . . .

buck up, Taylor, look honest . . . AH, there you are, good chap, now listen carefully—'

'I'll have to ask you to listen carefully to me, Sir. You'll have to stop all this shouting and roaring now—'

'BUT YOU DON'T UNDERSTAND!'

'Keep your voice down, please, in your own interests now, Sir.'

'BUT DAMMIT, sorry, but dammit man, listen, we – are – police officers ourselves. London. Shepherd's Bush. Here, will you just ring this number, say you're ringing on behalf of Inspector Blake?'

'Now, Sir, if you'll only be good you'll have your dinner soon the same as I'll be having myself and it's only until tonight and you'll be out that door. For your own good, you understand.'

'But dammit man – Taylor – Taylor, tell the fellow — all you have to do is ring that number, one simple telephone call, surely we're worth a telephone call? Eh?'

'I'm afraid that's something I can't do just like that, Sir. Cutbacks. Trunk calls must be logged through my superiors, Sir.'

'I'LL PAY FOR THE GODDAMN CALL, YOU FOOL. HERE—'

'Bribing a *garda* is considered a very serious—'

'JESUS!'

'Now that'll be enough, thank you, if I have to come back again you'll do without your dinner, Sir. I hope you understand me.'

'Please, come back . . . come back . . . COME BACK, YOU DOLT!'

Foster slept well and rose early. Whoever would interfere with his seven hours it was never going to be a member of the solo school. A modern-day articled clerk, imprisoned in a collar and tie, breeding pimples in the hothouse office, had about as much chance of disturbing Foster's equilibrium. But he was a man who saw things through. He consulted his mental diary. His own business was accomplished, in-tray empty. In fact, Bateman's was the only department trading today, that small matter of robbing his father's diddly club. Foster was out of it and his function consisted in damned well staying out of it. There was only the one danger: Ellis. Ellis was as yet unaware that Bateman was operating alone. All Foster had to do was keep Ellis in his ignorance until Foster would have put himself out of reach of a last minute change of plan by bolting his breakfast and disappearing for the day. Ellis and Gosling were sharing. Foster knocked at their door. He heard: "Ang on.' Ernie Gosling answered, wearing a Woolworth's dressing gown, Foster noted, a fellow you would have expected to sleep in his underpants, brand-new, poor chap probably bought it for the occasion, or had the lower orders abandoned their image entirely?

'Mornin', Mr Foster.'

Foster walked past him. Ellis was asleep, the bed-clothes chinned up under his red beard. Foster pointed: 'Wake him.' Gosling shook Ellis by the shoulders. Ellis yawned, made Three Stooges' lip sounds, blinked.

'Just a small precaution, Ellis. At breakfast. Best if you and Ernie stay together. We don't want that uncle and nephew on top of us this morning, having to explain your presence. It's not as though we can place you in *Unipolitan*.'

Ellis swung out of the bed, putting his feet on what looked like a scrap of lino. Ellis slept in his underpants. That was lino-loft life for you. He scratched the hairs on his chest and yawned again. Foster turned his head. Slob.

'Foster, anyone would think we were dealing with

two policemen liable at any moment to dig out their notebooks and demand our names, addresses and occupations. And why can we not be placed in *Unipolitan* if it comes to that?'

'Your appearance is against you, Ellis.'

'Is that a fact?' Ellis pulled on his corduroys, thumbing the braces over his shoulders, searching for his garish shirt. 'What's wrong with my appearance, Foster?' Ellis was boiling but he smiled at Foster, something he had never before managed: he would get back at him another time but today there was no profit in disturbing the arsehole.

'You don't look like a *Unipolitan* man unless it's that you're our lavatory cleaner. And then you wouldn't be travelling with the publisher, accountant and market research consultant.'

'I suppose you do have a point, Foster. But what about Ernie? Ernie dresses well. Can't you find a place for Ernie?'

Dressing gowns, rolled cigarettes, hair oil, a pair of ponce's crepe soles.

'Of course Ernie would fit in. But we can't have you dining alone, Ellis.'

Foster thought it a good early morning's work. There was no place for Ellis anywhere outside of the solo school. Quitting the NatWest a fellow thought he was cutting loose when all he achieved was a step into the gutter. It was one's obligation to let a fellow know that. The white man did not walk away from his burden.

'Ernie?'

'Yeah, Arthur?'

'Pinstriped prick. I changed my suits twice a day at the NatWest. Different suits every day. Foster wears the same suit every Wednesday to the solo school. And unless tailoring's gone downhill his is off the rack.'

Of course Ernie would fit in, Mr Foster had said. Like

he'd thought: Mr Foster was cute, he could rely on Mr Foster's judgement.

Foster relaxed: without Ellis and Gosling at the table a chap's urbanity wore a looser sleeve. One could look around the dining room confident of one's position. When the uncle and nephew couple waved – imagine having to suffer them on the ferry – Foster cut them with a nod although Hayhurst, what else, waved back with a big false smile and a 'Morning, Uncle Harry, morning nephew.' Bateman too raised a greeting arm but raised it slowly, a drawbridge of woe. The fellow looked in danger of cracking. It was an occasion for the calculated risk in so far as an Irishman's mood could be gauged by any earthly agency.

'Bateman, you got the better of me last night but this morning I won't have it. I can't let you act on your own. My idea, I admit, well meant, but unwise, I see that now. Hayhurst, I'm counting on your support here, your good sense' – butter her up a bit – 'last night, Hayhurst, it seemed like a good idea at the time that Bateman should pull it off on his own, more appropriate to achieve his own personal redress and so on. Nonsense of course but I'm afraid Bateman here jumped at it.'

'No.'

'Come, Bateman.'

'No. I operate alone or I don't operate at all.' Deliverance! Foster would pick up his cue: Well then, Bateman, don't operate, I forbid you.

'As I feared, as I feared. You're a stubborn fellow, Bateman. My grudging admiration, I must admit. Pluck I suppose I'd call it. I'd call it pluck, Hayhurst?'

She was not sitting there in her jump suit today without having been quick on the uptake all her life. Foster was some merchant.

'*Unipolitan* pluck.' Diana Hayhurst closed her fist and

lightly touched Bateman's jaw. 'Right, Percival?'

No smiler at the best of times and now with his nerves knotted, Bateman forced a rictus of self-deprecation. Tea and toast was as much as he had risked and the toast was stuck in his throat uncertain whether to go down or come up. He chafed at his lack of assurance. For once better to be a blunderbuss prick unconscious of where he trod; better to be a doctor in America or Switzerland performing miracles for miraculous fees. Better to shit or get off the pot. Go down on the ball or fly-kick. Fuck them. Fuck everyone. Like an old woman sitting at the table. Get up and go. Do. Act. Be a hero to the solo school. The solo school was everything to him now. Everybody had something that came first, Diana Hayhurst had her magazine, Arthur his lino, some their mothers came first, some their wives. His cancer was putting the whole world first, Mother Teresa's crowd, potbellied black babies, boat people, they all came whispering in your ear if you tried to treat yourself to a penny lollipop, they spotted you as a soft touch. The thrill of a new pair of shoes on their first outing didn't even last till you reached the pub. On your way you saw some poor chap on crutches with only one leg. Fuck you, leave me alone.

Bateman drew the paper napkin across his lips: hotel procedure, everybody did it. Only kings ate with their fingers and belched. The middle class had each other by the balls. Etiquette they called it, going around in a corset of mannerism, washing your hands after handling your mickey as though twas a leprous clapper you pissed out of. Bateman's rage began to rise. What was Christmas? Only the high priest of suffocation emerging after the kings had gone to bed.

'You'll excuse me,' Bateman said, rising, tucking in the chair. 'I must be about my father's business.'

Foster looked after Bateman. He shook his head in what he hoped was the sad and weary way of one who has done his all to protect the innocent from the lash of life, and failed. Hayhurst stabbed the prong of her fork into a piece of egg, rasher and sausage and chewed the confection without a burden to inhibit her appetite. Unless he was a fool she was acting a part. You didn't tuck in beside a chap who had jerked off dressed in your clothes the night before. Then again what exactly constituted the rubric of a fair cop? It was damnable, a woman like that having the high ground over you. He was willing to play his part if he only knew what his blasted part was. It was unnatural to sit there and not talk and it was unnatural to sit there and utter a commonplace. He could not look around the room all morning taking in uncles, nephews, Goslings, Ellises. He couldn't eat. He was stripped, defenceless, without her firing a shot. He turned his head back to the table. Her fork poised, she looked up from her plate.

'Mr Foster?'

He answered as though admitting to his own name. He croaked: 'Yes, Hayhurst.'

'I thought I'd do some shopping.' She sipped her tea. What was she at? 'Should take me the best part of an hour at least.' She was moving her chair back. She was standing, leaning over the table towards him. 'I forgot to lock my room, why don't you have a good time.' She was smiling, pinching his jaw. His prick was jumping.

Outside the warm rain was falling again, a good excuse for Ben and the sergeant to stand in under the hotel awning. Diana Hayhurst said, 'Ben,' and smiled at the sergeant and added, 'I was just about to ring you, Ben.' She linked arms and drew Ben out of the sergeant's hearing. The sergeant observed Ben listening and nodding while she fingered his tie and cooed her information up at him. Maybe Ben had a prick as big as a black's and there was going to be a matinée performance in a jacks someplace. They weren't making a song and dance about it, she was moving off now, pausing only to arch her head back to take in the sergeant and bid 'Byeee!' The sergeant flushed but showed his breeding by tipping his hat. Ben came back and stood beside the sergeant.

'All right?' the sergeant asked. Ben nodded.

'I'm goin' out see if I can't get the *Star*, Arthur. All they 'ave 'ere in the lobby is Irish papers and *The Times*. Comin'?'

'Sorry to bother you, gentlemen, but would you like to help us in the course of our duty?'

'You wha', Guv?' Ernie Gosling's bewilderment spoke of unshakable innocence. Less convincingly, Arthur Ellis echoed: 'I beg your pardon?'

'We'd be so very much obliged if you would accompany us to the station.' Ben franked his courteous request with an affectionate hand around Ellis's shoulder and the small impetus thereby imparted was sufficient to set them moving away in front of the hotel. Ernie Gosling shrugged, fell in with the sergeant, asked: 'What's it all about then, Constable?' The sergeant put a finger to his lips and winked. Round the corner Ellis stopped: 'I've left my lino back in the dining room.' Ben grabbed his sleeve. Ellis pulled. 'Just getting my lino.' Ben held on. Ellis jerked. Ben's fingers lost their grip on the shirt. Ellis ran. Ben and the sergeant were partners of old: the sergeant ran after Ellis, Ben motioned Ernie Gosling on towards the station.

The sergeant was no longer a man who could leap into the air and catch a Gaelic football. Though he was in his early thirties, he lived in the post-indigent age and could not remember when his belly touched his back with the hunger. Only joggers were slim and fit now and they hadn't the price of flab anyway, their disposable income more or less directly debited to torn ligament specialists. The sergeant was in no way remarkable in putting his health before his ability to catch a bus. And besides, all the criminals travelled on four wheels these days. Neither was Arthur Ellis a speedigonzalez. So it was a race of jowls and dewlaps. Back around the corner past the Royal George Hotel, left around the next corner and left again at which stage both Ellis and the sergeant were knackered as Ellis, come nearly full circle, ran straight into Ben's outstretched arm. 'No need for it,' Ben commented. The sergeant leaned against the wall, took off his hat and wiped his forehead with his tunic sleeve. Ellis was bent over with his palms on his knees, panting. 'All right,' Ben ordered and herded them across the road.

The station was a modern one, designed to accommodate members of the IRA held for questioning under the Offences Against the State Act. Ellis and Gosling were directed towards a cell in the wing furthest from where Inspector Blake and Constable Taylor were detained. Outside the cell door Ellis found his breath. 'Please—' he began, but Ben chested him inside and flicked thumb and forefinger at Gosling to follow. 'Now,' Ben said, 'I don't want to hear any of you shouting that you're policemen, fair? It's only the diddly club so no messing.'

'IT'S NOT US!' Ellis shouted.

'Calm down.' Ben backed out of the cell but Ellis grabbed him with two hands by the collar.

'We've nothing to do with it, it's Foster, he's the one, we're not involved I tell you . . .'

'Mr Foster will be here before you know it,' Ben spoke into Ellis's eyes as he freed his tunic and locked the cell door.

'Hold on. Listen, I'm the London – rather I *was* the London Area Manager of NatWest Finance, if you want to check my credentials. We've nothing whatsoever to do with this diddly club business, this is my colleague Ernie Gosling – Ernie, tell him, explain that we're not in on it, tell the man that it's Foster he wants, come on Ernie, speak up . . .'

All your life it came natural to you to say Morning, Constable, if you ever met a copper because there was a golden rule that a blind man could see that it was a waste of time acting the smart aleck with the boys in blue and on top of that you were brought up to believe that you had nothing to fear from English justice if you were innocent apart from an odd freak case where they topped the wrong bloke for doing away with all those women, that whatsisname character that they made a picture about with Richard Attenborough in it. So with nothing to hide it was easy to be cool and calm saying to yourself It's a case of mistaken identity, soon sorted out, apologies all round, have-a-laugh-about-it-over-a-cuppa-and-enjoy-your-stay-in-Mellick-Sir-type of happy ending. But suddenly it came into your head that there was queer things happening with the latest technology: they could take the coat off your back and examine it under a microscope nowadays and find a speck of dirt that was the same as what was found where some bloke had gone berserk with an axe and done half a dozen in. Your coat could have been in the cleaners' same time as the axe bloke had his trousers in, and you could end up guilty over some mad professor and his magnifying glass. But before he had time to get the wind up there was this Ben rozzer as someone had saluted him on the way in, there was this Ben saying he knew about the diddly club. And if that didn't take some beating. It was time then to act dumb but put the thinking cap on pronto. Lucky there was space for a breather with Arthur hogging the limelight, losing his cool. Figure out how they tumbled to the diddly club later – if there was going to *be* a later – but stick with they *had* tumbled and no more about it. Question now, what's the best tack and there was no doubt so far: keep the mouth shut and the ears open. They were picking Mr Foster up next and that was a good sign because promoting himself in the solo school was a lot of wishful thinking really. If you were charging the solo school and knew the situation you'd see that Ernie Gosling wasn't no ringleader.

'. . . Ernie, tell him who I am, who we are, explain to him it's Foster. . .'

If you told a copper what the copper knew already what would you get for it? Sweet fanny adams. You'd be squealing, and in the big league you'd get done in by your mates afterwards. The cops themselves didn't appreciate squealers, they used them but they didn't give them no decorations. Anyway the thing to remember was that even after they brung Mr Foster in there'd still be Dian to notice as everyone was missing and start making enquiries. First place anyone asked was in the cop shop, and then it would be a question of I'm the publisher of *Unipolitan,* these are my friends, how in the name of fuck – she'd probably come out with it like that too – how in fuck can you arrest people for what you think they intended to do? How ever the Ben rozzer and his sergeant mate got word first off, probably someone doing a bit of overhearing when we were off guard. Best just get out the making of a gasper and stall. Didn't much matter, there they was moving off, not even listening to Arthur . . .

Something was bothering Ben, the sergeant could see. On the way back to the Royal George Ben suddenly stopped. He gripped the knuckle of a finger between his teeth. Ben was not a man for talk when he was in action. When the dust had settled and the case was closed Ben liked to unwind over a pint and talk – then, and not before.

'What's up, Ben?'

Ben shook his head. 'I dunno. Sarge, we never arrested people like those before, did we?'

'In what way, Ben?'

'They all admit it's the diddly club, they admit they're guilty and yet they try to wriggle out of it. One of them roars out he's a police officer, next guy tries to shop Foster. God only knows what kind of reaction we can expect from this Foster character.'

The sergeant took a step forward so that he could turn and look into Ben's face. 'Ben, you know something. You know something about Foster, whoever he is? Come on, let me in on it.'

Ben put his hand on the sergeant's shoulder. 'I'm curious, I have my instructions about him but I don't know anything. But I'm curious. Let's go.'

Without knocking, Ben quietly turned the knob in the door of room 112. Ben had an advantage over the sergeant in that Ben was a London veteran and also Ben had the benefit of Diana Hayhurst's instructions outside the Royal George earlier. So Ben kept his sang-froid. But the sergeant had led a sheltered life. 'Fuck me pink,' the sergeant said out loud.

Foster was wearing the khaki safari dress last seen by the sergeant down around Diana Hayhurst's ankles while Ben was riding her in the Shakespeare jacks. He was standing in front of the mirror with his elbow crooked and his hand resting lightly on his hip the way models pose. His arse was arched backwards and his skinny leg was thrust forward out of the dress. And he had a prick on him solid as a banana in a freezer.

'Sorry to bother you, but would you like to help us in the course of our duty?'

Foster was astonished at his phlegm. There were two policemen in the room with him and he was wearing Diana Hayhurst's dress. Yet he was aware of this unusual gathering in a detached way only. Because yours was a solid life did not mean that down the years you did not try to understand the basically incomprehensible. You read of people who took drugs and then indulged in orgies, of millionaire rock singers getting so paralytic that with all their money and – prestige, if that was the word, their idea of passing the time was to sit around and watch women copulating with Alsatians or beer bottles or each other, varieties of erotica that made you shudder despite your best effort to bridge the decadent gap. And the next day, shorn of stimulants, they went about their business, appearing free of charge in concerts in aid of the Third World, probably with no exact recollection of the depths to which they had sunk previously. He had come into the room at what he interpreted as the behest of Diana Hayhurst herself, and when he saw the dress flung across the bed he behaved as a man following arrows. He was aware yet unaware that he was sober yet had the licence of the drunk, that he was drugged yet capable of standing outside his experience, that he was in the grip of release. Apart from straightening his leg, allowing the flap of the dress to veil his tumescence, Foster made no effort to act the guilty party.

'And what can I do for you?' Foster heard his voice, the voice of the bulldog breed, boom letters of credence. If Nick could hear me now.

'We'd be so very much obliged if you would accompany us to the station.'

The disembodied Foster considered the tableau from outside its membrane. His spirit wore a beret and pencil-slim moustache. He directed himself in an arch comedy of manners: 'Would you indeed? And I'd be obliged if you would close the door quietly on your way out. There's a good chap.'

Ben knew, the sergeant decided, looking at Ben's casual smile. Before we came up here, Ben knew what to expect, the bastard can't help holding something back all the time.

'Come on, Foster, it's only the damn diddly club.' It was a case the sergeant would not forget in a long time. Fucking in toilets, people roaring out that they were policemen, grassing on each other, dressed up as women. And now this fish.

'How the devil . . . ?' 'Diddly club' had ruptured Foster's protective balloon.

'Come on,' Ben repeated, picking up Foster's jacket and putting it around his shoulders as he urged him towards the door.

'Ben?' the sergeant pointed a finger down at the dress.

'No.' Ben explained. 'He has to come as he is. Instructions.'

'He's barefoot, Ben. It's raining!'

Ben considered his instructions, then nodded. The sergeant got the shoes, knelt down in front of Foster who stepped into them. The sergeant tied the laces. Foster said: 'This is outrageous . . . !'

Ben and the sergeant brought Foster down by the fire escape and exited at the back of the hotel. They crossed the road diagonally and entered the station.

Earlier the day duty officer had looked up from his sports page when the sergeant and Ben brought in the first batch and guessed: Selling Lines Without a Permit, but before he could weigh that deduction against Hit and Run one of them was roaring out of him in an English accent that he was a policeman, and a detective inspector at that. Then the sergeant came out and explained – if you could call it an explanation – that they were being held for their own good until tonight. So the day duty officer's money went on: Ducked Out of St Joseph's, Nurses to Call Later. It was tragic, they looked good types from decent families, but there were signs that the whole world was cracking up – this thing Stress that everyone was on about, there was none of that when people had nothing and made their own amusement, now you had the chairman of St Vincent de Paul telling the papers about the New Poor coming to the society for the money to pay their electricity bills or their mortgages when they were wired up with the last word in immersion heaters and fridge-freezers and whatnot and the houses themselves were bungalows the size of you'd see in Spain or Texas, while he lived himself in a council house that he was only now thinking about buying from the Corporation if he could afford it. The sergeant and Ben went off and the day duty officer leaned his elbow back on the sports page and tried to concentrate on his business – the first thing you were told in Templemore was not to fall in love with the patients – when next thing the sergeant and Ben were back again with two more, one of them a chap togged out like Burl Ives in *The Big Country* but who insisted he was the London Area Manager of NatWest Finance and that it was a fellow called Foster they wanted in connection with a diddly club business while his mate, a spiv straight out of one of those wartime pictures, sang dumb. And then Ben said something about Foster would be here soon. Unless there was a mass escape from the quare place . . .

Here was the sergeant and Ben back again with – It was a man, it was definitely a man, the day duty officer could swear, but unless they gave out funny uniforms up there nowadays the man was wearing a dress, you could see his leg coming out through the slit and after they passed you could see the backs of his hairy legs and they were solid men's shoes. Jesus!

Ernie Gosling had rolled his gasper. There were no signs up saying NO SMOKING like there were all over the place no matter where you went these days. It was something to do to pass the time, Arthur just sitting there staring at the floor, not answering when Ernie tried to cheer him up: 'You'll see, Arthur, Diana'll sort it all out.' Suddenly Arthur jumped up and was clutching the bars: 'Foster! Foster, tell them we're not involved . . .' It was Mr Foster all right, but blimey if he wasn't togged out in one of Diana's dresses! What must have happened was something like Mr Foster having a bath and the raid happened and he was took as he was and Diana rounded up too at the same time only she probably escaped somehow and the rozzers said Here throw this on, the whole thing was done in some panic. They were leading Mr Foster past the next cell with Arthur yelling 'For Christ sake, Foster, tell them we're not involved,' but again same as if they was deaf the rozzers just clanked the door shut and pissed off just as they done earlier.

The sergeant was not obliged to tell you much if anything and while Ben did not have the same authority, at the same time Ben was Ben, Scott Medal and so on and the day duty officer was not up to demanding information from Ben as an equal. Still, you'd be neglecting your job if you didn't display a proper curiosity. As they passed out the day duty officer ventured: 'That the lot?' He asked this of the sergeant and he noted that the sergeant looked at Ben. 'That's it,' Ben answered, 'just keep them happy until tonight.'

Ben unwound. He and the sergeant went to the Shakespeare for morning coffee. 'Well, Ben,' the sergeant said, 'what are you holding back on me now?' Ben shook his head. He told the sergeant all he knew. Last night while Ben was on patrol he stood under the Royal George awning out of the rain. A taxi stopped outside the hotel and from it and from the London past emerged Diana Hayhurst. He went inside with her and had coffee while they compared notes and brought each other up to date. And then she asked him if he would do her a turn.

'I told you about her years ago, but you wouldn't believe me.'

'Sorry about that, Ben.'

'Anyway, you saw for yourself.'

'I sure did, Ben.'

'She told me that she played cards with friends of hers once a week in London and that they were a collection of lovable eccentrics. One thing they had in common – the eccentrics – was that they all hated Christmas for one reason or another, right?' Ben held up a finger.

The sergeant nodded, then shook his head. 'Why would anyone hate Christmas, Ben?'

Ben looked around the bar by way of not looking at the sergeant. He could understand only too well how someone could get pissed off Christmas. The past brought understanding and Ben had a past while the sergeant was innocent. There was no point in educating the sergeant.

'Who knows?' Ben equivocated. 'The fact was that they didn't like Christmas and decided to do something about it. They knew there wasn't much they could do about Christmas so they decided to find a substitute for Christmas and attack it. For a reason she was not at liberty to explain to me they picked on Johnny Bateman's diddly club and decided to knock it off.'

'How'd they happen to pick on Johnny Bateman's diddly club, Ben?'

'I told you, she couldn't say. And I . . .'

Ben remembered, she had leaned towards him and placed her hand on his knee and he caught a taste of the mood when your prick is out of your trousers and it's lunging into one of the finest women in London. She said 'Trust me Ben, don't ask me how it came about that we settled on the diddly club here, please, Ben?' And at that point the seed of a small hope was planted in Ben's trousers but he couldn't explain all that to the sergeant.

'That doesn't matter, the fact is they did decide on the diddly club. Of course, she was against the whole cockeyed idea herself, but she had to pretend she was as keen as they were so that she would be on top of what was happening and could thwart them. She didn't rightly know how she was going to do it but as things turned out I turn up and her problems are solved. I said "What do you want me to do?" She explained that the simplest way would be to arrest everyone, she said, "I want you to round up all five, that way no one will be suspicious of anyone else and won't have a clue what hit them." "Well," I said, "I don't see any problem there." And I didn't because from where I sat I was acting on information received and doing my duty. She said the problem was how she would point them out to me without them knowing she was shopping them. I told her to leave the police work to the policemen, that I'd point them out to myself just as I have done. And that's it, Sarge, you have it all now, job's done.'

'How did you finger them, Ben?'

'As it happened I didn't have to. I didn't want to bother the manager. It was going to be the receptionist or the night porter, does it matter? I changed and came in here for a couple. That headcase Bowler was singing all his songs so that you could hardly hear yourself think. But there are these two strangers at the other end of the counter and I catch them saying "Madam Hayhurst's arrived, the gang's all here." And a minute later: "Knock off the diddly club." So I said that's two I don't need to enquire about. I'm not over congratulating myself when they shove off and two more arrive. They buy a drink and raise their glasses and one of them says "To the diddly club, Ernie" and the other says "Cheers." So that's four. Later, after Diana and me – after you were around yourself – I came back for another drink and they were still here near closing time. When they left I left. I followed them into the George just far enough to see Diana with the bloke who turned out to be Foster and I heard him say something about waiting until this diddly club business was over and done with. So I didn't finger them, they introduced themselves. Eccentrics? Incompetents! Just shows how right Diana was.'

'Ben?'

'Hm?'

'This Foster. He was wearing a dress. Her dress. And we took him in it. Instructions, you said, Ben?'

'That's right. Outside the hotel, Diana told me to pick up Foster in room one one two and take him just as he was. She was specific.'

'Why was he wearing her dress, Ben?'

Ben opened his hands: Search me. But Ben had thought about that. It was something the sergeant just would not understand. When you were minding your own business as the best fucking barman in London in the swinging sixties even if you never earwigged you couldn't but be aware of the fact that there were people with certain predilections. When you didn't have excitement every minute of the day there were times when it seemed a dull old world. It was the difference between the Irish and the English. The Irish – those like the sergeant who hadn't travelled – they thought the English didn't know how to enjoy life because they didn't get pissed and throw up down the suit and eat takeaway night feeds and go to Gaelic football matches and beat up the referee. They saw the English temperate in habit. On the subject of pleasure the Irish thought the rest of the world could not see the Irish arse for dust. They scorned the English family of two point one children – or was it one point two? – compared to the Irish average of seven point nothing. But they were wrong. It was just the English didn't mouth. They acted. Witness World War Two, the Falklands: they said to themselves Right, let's be having you, and acted. And so when John Thomas sounded reveille they swept their feet out of the bunk on to the floor pronto. As far back as the non-swinging fifties – when Foster would have learned his etiquette – they didn't Brylcreem the hair to go to the palais to get pissed on light ale and paw the floor with their winkle-pickers. They went for the ride equipped with Durex and clicked, and next day felt no need to run to a priest and tell him all about it. They frowned on murder, robbery (apart from the fiddle), queue-jumping and layabouts. These reservations aside, they acknowledged different strokes for different blokes. So Foster liked to dress up in women's clothes? His business entirely. He was a lovable eccentric according to Diana and she accommodated him. Ben wished he was back there, in London, part of the judicious tolerance of the metropolis.

'I think he's probably a pervert, Ben.'

Ben let it go. Otherwise he would have to explain to the sergeant that a pervert was a barman who neglected to polish his shoes.

The sergeant left but Ben dawdled on over the cold coffee. In a moment he would ring Diana Hayhurst and the praise would come melting down the line, tingling him to the point of misery. Tonight he would release her eccentrics and tomorrow they would all return to London. Better that she had not turned up in Mellick at all; he had been reconciled to his lot but now his lot was more miserable than ever.

Ben took out a pair of ten-pee pieces. He was ringing from the Shakespeare and while that limited his vocabulary he would not let it cramp his style. 'All no longer present but accounted for,' he reported. And it hurt him to hear: 'You know what you are, Ben? You're the best fucking copper in Ireland, Ben.' He closed his eyes against the cross.

'Now listen to me, Ben. I thought to have lunch first but it's probably best if you take me now.'

Ben held the phone away from his face and grinned. She wanted more. By Jesus, he was her obedient servant.

' . . . cause less suspicion if I'm brought in more or less at the same time as everyone else . . . and make sure I'm taken past Foster's cell, I can put on a show – Sorry, what's that, Ben?'

'I said, what are you talking about, Diana? Are you saying you want me to arrest you?'

'Of course, didn't you listen to me? if I'm not nabbed it will be obvious I ratted, right, Ben?'

'I suppose so.'

'Suppose? There's no doubt about it, Ben. And just to make it the real thing, proper and formal, I don't think we could keep straight faces, the two of us: why don't you send the sergeant, tell him to act stiff and copperlike so Foster can't read between the lines . . .'

When Ben handed someone a gin and tonic in The Pub it was because they ordered gin and tonic and if they said Ben, I ordered gin and white lemonade, Ben let it go and pretended he was fallible. Arrest all five, he distinctly remembered her saying. Admittedly she also said arrest everyone. Slip of her tongue of course. You always played cards with six.

On the sergeant's way to the hotel he went over his last exchange with Ben. 'Who's next Ben, eh?' which was only natural in the circumstances. 'What if it turns out she says, By the way, I forgot to instruct you to arrest the manager of the Royal George? I mean, this is like Russia, Ben, no one knows who's next.' Ben's answer which was like no answer he had ever taken from Ben before: 'Look, why do you have to ask so many questions? Just go and do what you're told.' And: 'So I forgot, so I slipped up for a minute for fuck sake.' Worse, Ben said this in the hearing of the day duty officer who looked up from his paper. The sergeant had had a good mind to draw Ben's attention to his rank, Scott Medal or no Scott Medal. But the sergeant had kept his temper – he was committed, in Ben's hands.

The day duty officer meditated: Ben giving orders to the sergeant like that! 'Go and do as you're told.' You couldn't speak to your own children like that these days, you had to come up with a reason, otherwise they wouldn't respect you. It was all part of a new psychological way of bringing them up that included standing around clapping your hands if your child ate his dinner instead of fonging him in the hole if he didn't.

'. . . outrageous! I can tell you flatfoot, my MP's ears will be ringing when I get out of here and you'll be out on your arse, you Mick prick—Ernie! Arthur! What's happening here?'

'Go and do as you're told' the day duty officer had heard Ben order the sergeant but the day duty officer had also been told by Ben that that was the lot. Now here was the sergeant with a woman swearing like a tinker except she looked more like gentry, threatening to get on to her MP.

'Mr Foster! You too?'

'If you'd please move along, Madam.'

'Take your fucking hands off me!'

Gentry or no gentry, the day duty officer was on duty and it was clearly his place to go to the assistance of the sergeant. Between them they managed to push her into a cell, with the man in the dress standing up holding the bars looking on and the fella with the red beard roaring out of him 'Diana, tell them we're not involved, tell them it's just Foster.'

There was a large, scattered constituency of which Bateman was in no doubt he was the most fitting representative. They were his people, their faces turned up to him now. He was their champion down through the years. He stood for the patrons of the New York singles' bar. He carried the banner of the timid. Under his umbrella traipsed the motley battalion of social cripples keeping their spirits up with lonely airs. All the old arguments against Christmas stood up.

There was a middle-aged man somewhere, seated on a functional chair, the waste bin upturned for a footrest, the library book on his lap closed against the dimming typeface, serving his lengthy sentence for some short sin of the past. In another room, brightened with curtains, flowers and a cloth on the table, a lady of humble savings and accumulated frugal tastes, her hair permed, skirt well below the knee, blouse buttoned to the neck, past menstruation, born too soon, fastidious in an age of abandon, wrapping the Christmas present to take in a few days time to the dinner in another room brightened with curtains, flowers and a cloth on the table with another lady with whom she had kept in touch. She pushed through the crowd and on tiptoe inserted a forget-me-not in his buttonhole.

There was a young man studying Newsboy's form in the *Daily Mirror*, meaning well, chafing at prosperity's ponderous tread, caught by the irresistible two-mile chase with only four runners. This is for you, Ma. This is for you, Da. Spotform's heavy round mark opposite the favourite. Six to four on. A case of buying money. Shit or bust, otherwise the brown envelope turned upside down empty on Boxing Day. Three the winner; outsider, twenty to one. Newsboy nowhere. Owner, oddly enough, pleased. Top weight, needed the run, aim all along Cheltenham in March. Envelope upside down empty. How to get the jacket out of the cleaners.

Is everybody happy? What's the matter with you then. Am I talkin' to myself or are you listenin'? Nothin's the matter? I should bloody well think there wasn't, it's Christmas you know, your Aunt Ivy's comin' round in half an hour so try and look lively, all right? Eh? You were just thinkin' of what? Chuckin' it? Chuckin' what? Chuckin' your business studies? You're some trump you are! You don't let your mother hear you talk like that, nice Christmas present that'd be, after all we done. What's got into you of a sudden? What you mean you don't know? What kind of answer is that? I see. It's not you. Listen, I was your age there wasn't no business studies. There was and I could have gone I'd have jumped at it. What do you want then? Hang on, people been botherin' you? No? Sure? Well then, go on, let's have you, what do you want? You dunno. You dunno what you want but you know what you don't want. You know what you want don't you, you want a good kick up the arsehole you do.

Yes, all the old arguments stood up. Bateman stood up and looked out the window of his hotel room at the street of bulbs and decorations and the oppressive scurry of the well-off. Out of our way, we're shopping. Christmas shopping.

Every year they said it, the suicide agencies: 'Numbers up.' It was their busiest period. They appealed. Look in on that elderly neighbour of yours, don't wait for the accumulation of milk bottles outside the door, see that everything is hunky-dory, we can't have people doing themselves in at Christmas and it isn't as though we can do away with Christmas just to save a life. So keep your eyes and ears wide open at Christmas, we know from our records. Hello? I see, your late husband's anniversary. Pardon? *Tenth* anniversary. I understand, you want to donate his clothes to the needy. That *is* thoughtful of you, Madam. I can well believe it, I can well believe the suits are as good as new. Just one second now I'll get a pencil. Em-a-oi-d-a. Just one more second now while I put my hand over the phone. Listen, old dear down Maida Vale way, classic symptoms, late-hubby's-clothes-for-the-needy caper. Nip down there: if it makes her happy and you see anything that fits, bottoms up. Otherwise, *you* know – tell her hang on to clobber until after Boxing Day, needy all gone off on holiday, begging all done, or whatever. I'll try and keep her talking. Check for pills, bottles, razor blades, the usual. Just you make sure she'll hang on over Christmas.

Bastards. Specialists. Swiss surgeons. The Pope out on the balcony: I love you all. The Queen, weighed down by jewellery, reading her speech out through the television, the President of the United States of America – Give us your hungry, your poor and your fund-raising cripple for our specialists to operate on. Egypt, France, can you hear me over there? Greetings. Even the fucking rabbi prodded on to the box to voice his bearded salutations.

The deputation, resting its case, was puzzled to see

Bateman equivocate. What, the Member for the League Against Christmas? Surely no. Why? Because— because he was no longer one of them. He would never lose the sensitivity to spot the species no matter under what camouflage they squirmed. But he himself was out in the open, no longer skulking in the undergrowth. Now he could see robbing a diddly club for exactly what it was: robbing a diddly club, In evidence, he saw Ernie and Arthur terrified when the cards were being cut, and Foster unveiling his draft dodger's proposition. He himself had been deluded to the precipice by the picaresque of the solo school. But now he saw that crowds gathered. Your own crowd. They came together and they drifted away and you were left on your tod, taken in charge. That was robbing a diddly club. No more. No less. He was sorry, but he couldn't help but see what was in front of his nose.

The spurned species turned away, looked back again. They shook their heads. They began to move off but Bateman caught the whisper: 'It's the oval ball coming down out of the high sky again.' No longer one of them! How could a decent man be content? Happiness was the speciality of the specialists. The poor bastard's afraid. Come on, we may as well shuffle off – what else is new? Guerilla turned statesman turned Coca-Cola importer. It's hard to blame him. New job, friends, confidence: already he has the idea of booking into one of those hotels that lay it on at Christmas, bar open where he can entertain uncles and nephews looking into his Dickensian heart. We've waited a long time, we can wait longer.

What could be summoned could be dismissed. Bateman pressed a button and dissolved the allies of his imagination. There was nobody out there whose lot would improve an iota by any action of his. Nobody needed him as he had needed them down through the years. Pfft. Hop it. Off with you. It was comical, a man listening to his own imagination. Bloody dangerous to give your Frankenstein the run of the house.

Downstairs in the Treaty Stone Bar Bateman had two pints before lunch. Every time the door opened he looked in the mirror to see Ernie, Arthur, Foster or Diana, or the uncle and nephew. But the two pints went down and nobody appeared. He would tell them over the soup.

When he had finished the coffee and the cigarette began to burn his fingers Bateman accounted for the uncle and nephew by placing the sociable uncle with a kidnapped audience in a downtown bar. It was, after all, Christmas when conviviality broke out among the vested interests. They skirted the gaunt face and the thin wrist holding the mendicant tin can and shook the snowflakes off the overcoat as they closed the door of the warm hostelry behind them and greeted jollily Merry Christmas All. This is mine/No, I'll get it/It's on me, I insist. Good luck who stood. Cheers. The annual battle to beat peers back from the till, content that the assembly line of one's fellows queued up to reciprocate. The door opens shiftily and enter in frayed cast-off and cold blue nose in want of a hankie, a rheumy-eyed spoilsport, but the day saved by on-the-ball landlord lifting his counter and emerging with the eviction grip.

Christ, where was I? The uncle and nephew. They might have bumped into the solo school in the street, that would account for the two birds with the one stone. Which was the easy way of doing things. Otherwise where was the solo school? But if they were all well shod in out of the cold having a grand Christmas time wouldn't one of them think of ringing Percy to tell him where they were, so that he could join them in the fun? It was what he would do himself if say Ernie were back on his own at the hotel, wondering where everyone had gone. Unless they were ducking him. Not necessarily a collective decision of theirs but suppose individually they thought it prudent to shun his association until the dust settled? – as he suddenly now found perfectly understandable.

Do you? Do you find that understandable? You're settling in quickly, to the manner born.

The waitresses were paid by the hour whether the hour lasted fifty or seventy minutes. They were giving Bateman the eye. He wilted and went back upstairs to his room. He lay down on the bed. The cosy entity of the solo school disintegrated. Ernie Gosling thought for himself and said: Sod Percy, it's dog eat dog an' every man for hisself. Careful, prudent Foster was not the man to stand shoulder to shoulder with a diddly club robber. Arthur Ellis, a lino man, knew when to fade. Diana Hayhurst, giddy, soft, coarse, feminine, was not immune from the taint of social leprosy. She could distinguish between the cachet of the divorce court and the criminal court.

So what? They left you like you left us. How does it feel? No, we won't go away, we're never going away, we'll be with you in your hotel on Christmas night, every second of your new-found contentment we'll barge in and we'll tweak away. We'll never let you rest, never let you alone and what's more you know it. Now, angry as you are that the solo school has deserted you, knowing how we feel, you know what you have to do, you know what has to be done.

Bateman turned the key in the front door and walked in the hall. He opened the kitchen door and looked in at his father sitting down at his tea. It was his first time in the house with his father in twenty-five years. Bateman stood holding the door handle, waiting for a welcome.

'Will you come in if you're comin' in and close the door.'

The fire was lighting. It was not banked up red-hot as Bateman remembered from the past. It was the fire of a man who lived alone, only lighted when he came in off the street, not tended all day long. But it was a fire, with flames however pallid, not an electric or gas job. The table was laid without a flourish: plate, cup, saucer, knife, fork. The sugar bowl, at least, was a symbol of not going around with the fly open but the sliced pan stood up in its wrapper – nobody living alone could be expected to lay the bread out on a plate. His father was picking at his last bit of liver.

'I forgot you'd be comin' and might want a bit, I only buy what I use up but there's two eggs there I'll do them for you the pan's still hot.'

'Stay as you are, I'll do it. I'm used to cooking for myself.'

Bateman went to the pantry and found the two eggs where he would have expected to find them in the dresser twenty-five years ago. He lit the gas and cracked one into the pan. He had never known his father to cook. His father said: 'Heat up the kettle, the tea might be cold.'

Bateman looked out from the pantry at the case on top of the radio. There was always something on top of the radio, his mother's sewing basket, a box of buttons, the rent book. As Bateman tried to turn the egg it broke and he had to use the knife to keep it flicked into one piece. The egg was destined to go between two slices of bread. Bachelors learned early the futility of trying to dress a plate. He sat down on the same chair at the same side of the table that was his place when his place had been in the house.

He poured out a cup of tea and cut the fried-egg sandwich in half. It was too late now to realise that he had come too early. What was he supposed to talk about to this strange father across the table. He was disap-

pointed to have to use the milk directly from the carton –
an abomination of an invention for which the discovery
of any amount of antibiotics would never compensate.
One good thing: the salt was still in an egg cup,
accessible, not trapped behind clogged holes.

'Why don't you pour the milk into the jug?' Bateman
pleasantly asked his father, and would have bitten it back
if he could.

'Because if I poured the milk into the jug I'd still have
to pour it out of the jug into the cup. You come all the
way over from England to ask me that.'

'When Mam was alive the milk was always in the jug,
even though we had bottles then instead of those cartons.'

'Do you use a jug yourself over in England?'

Bateman was startled. It was the closest he had ever
heard his father come to debating a point.

'No.'

'So why does it bother you what I do?'

'It doesn't.'

'What did you say it for so?'

'I was just making conversation.'

'Hm. You'll never get your own television show do
you know that.'

Johnny Bateman stood up and carried his plate, cup
and saucer out to the pantry. Bateman ate his sandwich.
He was unexpectedly at ease in his father's house. He
could hear the water being poured into the basin and the
noise of the plate, cup and saucer being washed. And he
could hear his father say: 'Tis no wonder you're still single
if that's the way you talk to people.' Bateman was at ease
in his anger as the recipient of such cruelty. He carried
his own plate, cup and saucer out to the pantry. He went
back for his own knife, his father's knife and fork, the
one spoon. He took the tea towel and did the drying.
While his father put the crockery in the dresser and the

cutlery in the drawer Bateman cleared off the table. He did not notice that the butter was not in a butter dish.

Bateman's father sat down by the fire. Bateman sat opposite him, took out his cigarettes, offered one.

'I gave them up seventeen years ago.' There was no answer to that. In fact there was more to come, always was nowadays. His father watched him light up and completed the formula.

'You'd want to cop yourself on and think about givin' 'em up yourself. They were never any good to anyone.'

The greatest lie ever propagated every day by converts. Outside of death by lung cancer the fag was the greatest comfort known to man, lonely man. But here was not the time or the place to argue that toss. And besides, Bateman realised they were almost communicating. He pointed to the radio as he rose.

'My school case.' He took the case down, lay it on the table, pushed the case open with his two thumbs. 'How many did you say, only twenty-eight?'

'Twenty-seven. Sean Reilly pulled out.'

Bateman closed the case. He sat back by the fire. 'So he'll have nothing to come tonight.'

'Good enough for him.'

Elbows on knees, Johnny Bateman held his fingers extended in the toasting position. It was the way old men sat by fires.

'You'd feel sorry for him,' Bateman said, 'especially Christmas.'

'Forty-eight. What kind of a fool thinks he can stop work at forty-eight. He couldn't get rid of it fast enough. He had to go to Spain on a holiday in a February, he had to buy a car. That's gone too and the money he got for it is gone, that's if twas ever paid for first day. He had to put in those aluminium windows. We asked him why he put in the aluminium windows and of course twas they were guaranteed for fifteen years and he wouldn't have the trouble of maintenance. Imagine a man dreaming of not having to paint the windows of his own house. If there was glass came with the windows that washed itself and his wife wanted to buy it he'd probably kick her around the house. But he's too big to paint windows all of a sudden. Frankie saw him downtown with his three boys and heard him givin' the order: "Tog the lot out." Shoes, anoraks and two suits for himself. A man used to dealin' with the Provident all his life. And while he was at it he sent Maisie into Hélène Modes to buy fur boots and a coat with a fur collar and handbag to match, she stickin' out like a sore thumb at bingo. And a sheepskin coat for himself to go to the rugby matches instead of his old gaberdine. He wasn't long landin'. Brandy he drank for a while. Brandy! His belly out an' his sheepskin coat on him an' it roastin' in the pub and the brandy and Throw me out twenty Churchman there, thank you.'

Bateman watched him chewing on his anger. 'He lived it up?'

'He was a fool. He'd put his foot on the rail in the pub and pull his pants up an inch as if not to bulge them at the knee when what he was really at was showing off his shoes. Someone was bound to say I like the shoes, Sean. That's when he'd start the old game of Guess how much I paid for those shoes now. Brown brogues with the toecaps and him coming out with the line Those shoes will last me fifteen years, as if they were aluminium windows. Fifty-three pounds but worth every penny he claimed. Better than buying four pairs for thirteen pounds each. That class of guff. It made me want to puke.'

'He thought twould never end?' Bateman wanted to keep the communication going. He liked the account of Sean Reilly's glory days.

'He bought a pair of binoculars to go out to the races.

A meeting once a year and suddenly he needs binoculars, and you think he carried them in his sheepskin-coat pocket? He wore them around his neck bouncing off his belly.'

'He seems to have gone in for it all right.'

'When there's little left tis easy add it. It took him fifteen months before he was back on the pint and announcing that idleness didn't agree with him, were there any jobs going that he might be interested in? This to a crowd wearing bum-freezers, half of them idle and businesses closing down every week and all he was ever able to do was work in a factory.'

'He couldn't get a job?'

'Of course he couldn't get a job at nearly fifty after chucking up one at forty-eight. Job gone, money gone, stamps gone, he wasn't long learnin' his mistake on the dole. I said it to Frankie when he came in for to take out the club, I said I saw it coming.' His father looked as pleased as any prophet whose predictions are fulfilled. But Bateman – ever alert – sought the nerve centre.

'How did he take it, coming down in the world again so quickly?'

'People like that never learn their lesson. He has half the town tapped trying to live up to what he never was. I can't wait to see his face tonight when everyone is gettin' their money. I'll tell you one thing, you won't see him going to the races with his binoculars this St Stephen's Day.'

Bateman quelled the clamour of his constituents. All right, I'm not blind, so I have to do it for a poor binocularless bollix.

There was more but not much more, punctuated by his father going to the pantry to shave out of the basin and going to the toilet in the backyard and while his father was out there Bateman switched the envelopes in the case. When they were leaving he took the case off the table and said: 'I'll carry it.' His father began: 'There's no need—', but Bateman cut him off: 'Can I just carry my old school case for old times' sake, do you mind?' They called for Frankie Timmons. Bateman fell into their shuffle as far as the Shakespeare where he remembered that he had to make a telephone call. He handed Frankie Timmons the case. 'I won't be two minutes.'

Over the same bridge that his father had thrown the goat Bateman let the twenty-seven envelopes containing £7500-odd fall down into the river.

Inside the Shakespeare Christmas tugged at Ben Hanley. But Ben was unresponsive. Bowler sang:

> Oft in the stilly night,
> Ere slumber's chains had bound me;
> Fond memory brings the light,
> Of other days around me.

The Joker O'Brien accompanied softly on the melodeon. So-called because he was made in the shape of one who never smiled. Bowler was as yet only half-drunk and his voice was at its best. The fire was lighting but Mrs Quinn sat with her black overcoat on, her black hat and her black handbag clutched on her lap and on the table in front of her a large sherry compliments of the house. The lugubrious Joker tapped slowly on the floor with his foot as his fingers sought the subtlety to complement Bowler. Her head moving slightly from side to side, Mrs Quinn hummed her song equally unobtrusively.

> The smiles, the tears,
> Of boyhood years,
> The words then softly spoken,

> The eyes that shone,
> Now dimmed and gone,
> The cheerful heart now broken.

Beside Ben, with his hand resting on the counter, stood Sean Reilly. His head was respectfully turned towards the singing. Bobby Neville sat at the bar by himself studying the overnight declarations in the *Evening Press*. A quiet man, he sat and picked his horses, happy in his own company. Yet even Bobby Neville was drawn to lift his head in response to Bowler's magic. Dan Reddan, a self-made man in the motor business, wore a blue pin-stripe of old-fashioned cut, the jacket open to show a well-fed stomach. He held a brandy in a brandy glass – not necessarily an inevitable concomitant given the quality of bar staff in Ireland. Dan wasn't sitting or leaning on the counter. He stood in the middle of the bar with his spare hand in the trouser pocket. His eyes were as attentive as his cars. Ben had heard it a score of times: Dan Reddan never forgot where he came from. When they were building the Young Thomond pavilion Dan Reddan got out of his Mercedes and mixed cement with the best of them. Ben heard the fire spark. Dan Reddan heard the door open. His hand came quickly out of his pocket and a pre-emptive finger to his lips to shush the two Miss Houlihans and Peg Morrissey as Bowler began to finish where he had begun:

> Fond memory brings the light,
> Of other days around me.

There was sincere clapping from everyone. Dan Reddan called: 'Fair play to you, Bowler. Donie, give him a pint.' And added to Sean Reilly: 'My mother used to sing that.'

'I often heard her.'

'Sean, you'll have a drink. Ben, will you have something? You will, you'll have this on me or I'll be insulted.'

And 'this', by the proprietor's translation of Dan Reddan's wink, was a pint and a large whiskey.

Dan Reddan put his arms around the two Miss Houlihans, dressed in their best, and hugged them while they blushed through their make-up. He gave Peg Morrissey a more worldly kiss on the jaw, called for two lemonades for the two Miss Houlihans, failing once again to overcome their abstinence, and a large vodka for Peg Morrissey. He ushered them towards the seats near Mrs Quinn, behind Bowler and the Joker O'Brien.

Sean Reilly demanded: 'Come on, Bowler, give us another one.' And the proprietor brought the pint out to Bowler. The singer took a gulp and wiped the froth from his mouth with the back of his hand. He suggested to his accompanist 'Sweetly she sleeps'. Ben could think again. *Sweetly she sleeps my Alice fair . . .*

What it is, Ben thought, is that I have lost my innocence. A singer, a song, a melodeon player, a fire; gentle ladies; decent men; decorations looped along the walls. Young Thomond country. People who care passionately about the result of a rugby match. They like to wear their good side and use Christmas to laugh off their good turns with a Not at all, not at all, nonsense. They're not unique there, up in Westport the same crack is going on only with a little more awkward graciousness and even in Kilburn they're at it.

> Her cheeks like the roses' dew.
> Sweetly she sleeps, her golden hair
> Lies soft on the pillow there.

The more people in the bar the more attention Bowler received. When the door opened now more than one head turned and more than one finger was raised to caution the new arrivals. I should be happy saving the diddly club for these good people and I am. But I am not as happy as I should be. I should be happy to have nabbed Mad Dog O'Dwyer and of course I am. But I'm not as happy about *that* as I should be. And the joyriders and all the rest of it. And there's more to it than that I just wasn't cut out to be a cop.

Take this night of nights as the pub fills up. In the fifteen years of Ben Hanley's patronage the order of proceedings had not changed. Bowler came on like the ponies in the circus while the customers took their seats. When Bowler was at his best nobody sullied decorum by singing in his immediate wake. But decorum had been observed and now the Joker sang a medley that roused the whole pub into chorus.

Will you join in the van
Like a true Irish man,
We're going to fight the forces of the Crown.
Will you march with O'Neill
To an Irish battlefield,
For tonight we're going to free old Wexford town.

The joker slid like mercury from one box standard to the next while the door opened more often and more and more came in and the last of the lines were sold. Ben Hanley cynically pressed the fast-forward button. The place will soon be packed with people and smoke. Backs slapped. Happy Christmas. Many Happy Returns. You're looking well. You're looking well yourself. What'll you have. The Joker will glide into a reel that will propel the flushed Dan Reddan to seek the nearest tanked woman and make space to display a few obsolete steps. Good man, Dan, you never lost it. And so on, on to the raffle itself after the diddly club pay-out. Bobby Neville: a ham. Hooray! Well done, Bobby. Ben did not buy a line. Nobody noticed that he never won nor ever bought a line. Not having a vocation he had to watch himself that bit closer. Hamper, box of biscuits, bottle of brandy. The last time Dan Reddan won – turkey – he had put it up again on the grounds that he had already received presents of two birds. Liar. But fair play to him. The raffle over, some of those who didn't win and could have done with a win, feeling the letdown, the pre-post-Christmas depression.

After the raffle Bowler will appoint himself master of ceremonies and call upon one of the Miss Houlihans to sing 'The Old Refrain' and after a lady a gentleman, Dan Reddan to do 'When the Sergeant Major's on Parade' and another lady to oblige with 'Juanita', and soon on to the younger crowd who will put the Joker off key by all shouting together something from the Golden Treasury of Eurovision Song Contest hits.

And it is all so— so oppressive as I sit here not cut out to be a cop. As the singing and the music and the shouts grow louder and the smoke thickens and my discontent is hidden in the fogged mirror, I am no longer cut out for this simple decency.

'Here's the two boys,' Sean Reilly indicated Frankie Timmons and Johnny Bateman coming in with their case. The pub was as yet marching with O'Neill to an Irish battlefield so Peg Morrissey and Mrs Quinn and the two Miss Houlihans were not out of order in snaking through the chorus to be near the pay-out. Frankie Timmons and Johnny Bateman stood immediately inside the door glaring at the occupied seats under the window and the laden table where they always administered their business. Dan Reddan winked at the proprietor 'Donie, the club.' Ben caught snatches of people being wheedled out of their seats – ' . . . only take five minutes . . . let the old boys sit down'.

Dan Reddan delivered a speech. He called for order. 'Order please. Ladies and *gentle*men, if I could have your attention.' Sean Reilly echoed: 'Come on, a bit of order now.'

As they all knew, Dan Reddan told them, it was Young Thomond's diamond year and if he was allowed to so put it they were privileged once again tonight to have in their presence two gems, Johnny Bateman and the one and only Frankie Timmons. ['Hear, Hear!' Sean Reilly, leading the applause.] 'While things mightn't seem as bright these days as we anticipated when we were trying to make our way, yet there were times when things were an awful lot worse. In hardship and want Young Thomond always had a tradition of mutual assistance and I defy contradiction when I say that no two people embody that tradition more than Johnny and Frankie.' ['Hear, hear!']

Jesus, it's choking me. There's a world out there that none of them know.

'Today we have credit unions doing good work and the financial institutions where it is easy enough to borrow – although as any businessman will tell you easy borrowing is hard saving. But there were dark days when people of our background either had or had not and the temptation was to live for the day. But thanks to the likes of Johnny Bateman and Frankie Timmons we allowed ourselves to have a little of our lot prised out of us so that at a time when we needed it most whether we knew it or not we had it. To me Johnny Bateman, Frankie Timmons and Young Thomond are synonymous with Christmas itself. I ask you to join me in raising your glass to Johnny and Frankie and Christmas.'

I'm some hypocrite, clapping with the rest of them and

toasting the two old duffers. All the same I am glad I saved their diddly club. It was Diana saw what needed to be done: a metropolitan, like myself.

All the people involved moved up the bar to watch the diddly club being paid out. Dan Reddan – in the van like a true Young Thomond man – was a step ahead of Mrs Quinn, Peg Morrissey and the two Miss Houlihans. Some of those not involved watched with the curiosity due to a relic of the past, those for whom diddly clubs belonged with washboards or their grandfather's long johns, those who had reached their apotheosis at a time when thrift was not so much unfashionable as unnecessary – especially saving that advertised poverty, as distinct from investment that bespoke surplus. It was quaint to see the old ways not altogether died out. But like Bowler's songs they wouldn't do all year round.

'Raymond Beegan,' Frankie Timmons announced alphabetically, reading from his exercise book as Johnny Bateman opened the case. Ben Hanley was amused to note the self-conscious way Ray Beegan edged up the bar to collect. Humble people, unsteady in the limelight. Frankie Timmons was standing up looking down at Johnny Bateman; and Raymond Beegan, Dan Reddan, Mrs Quinn, Peg Morrissey, the two Miss Houlihans, the proprietor inside the counter, Sean Reilly and Ben Hanley were waiting, not realising there was a hitch as Johnny Bateman blinked and sorted the brown envelopes with no names written on the outside. Ben Hanley noticed puzzlement on the faces of his fellow watchers. The whole business usually took less than ten minutes. Frank Timmons called out a name, that person came up, got his envelope. Suddenly Dan Reddan was stepping forward and holding out his hand and reading a piece of paper, passing it along the bar, holding out his hand again, and it was like people sharing snapshots except that there were some puzzled, nervous laughs. Sean Reilly stretched his hand over Ben's shoulder and said 'Jesus, what's goin' on' and handed the cracker message to Ben. FUCK CHRISTMAS. The next read: UP GARYOWEN. Ben was already in action, pushing through.

Dan Reddan had taken charge going through every single envelope. 'What happened?' he asked, putting another message on the counter. YOUNG THOMOND – THE HOME OF IGNORANCE.

He yielded precedence to Ben's authority but all Ben could do was repeat Dan's 'What happened, Mr Bateman?'

The whole bar pressed forward including Bowler and the Joker. Johnny Bateman and Frankie Timmons sat surrounded by people looking down at them.

'Mr Bateman?' Ben Hanley pleaded.

Dan Reddan edged in front of Ben and put his hand on Johnny Bateman's shoulder. 'Johnny, Ben's talking to you, Johnny.'

But Johnny Bateman did not lift his head. He stared at the empty case as down the line Sean Reilly opened another cracker and read softly to the bystanders UP YOUR DIDDLY CLUB. Johnny Bateman's eyes were wet and tears began to dribble down his face. Dan Reddan shook him gently: 'Johnny?' and turned to Ben Hanley. All that was left in Ben's locker was to shift his gaze on to Frankie Timmons. Frankie Timmons was transfixed looking at Johnny Bateman staring into the empty case while around the bar voices asked 'What's going on?' and were answered 'Shh a minute, I don't know. Look at this one, Jesus, BATEMAN THE BOLLIX, what kind of a bastard would do this? If Garryowen are behind this I won't be responsible . . .'

Frankie Timmons sank down on the seat. He put his hand around Johnny Bateman's shoulder and leaned his head forward to try to get in his line of vision. 'Are you all right, Johnny?' Johnny Bateman nodded ten times but he was still crying and his eyes were still fixed on something and it was plain to Frankie Timmons and anyone with an eye to see that Johnny Bateman was not all right. Frankie Timmons kept his hand around the shoulder as though they were there alone and a whole crowded bar was not looking on. Behind him Ben could hear someone whisper and he could imagine a hand up to a mouth: He hasn't been himself for a while you know. Ben Hanley had never been in a situation where he had not been able to deal with that situation but now he was too limp to invoke the rule book and sort the simple mess out by rote. Dan Reddan said: 'Talk to us, Johnny,' and as he spoke he looked at Ben and Ben read: You're supposed to be the detective around here, do something.

Ben tried.

'Mr Bateman, could you just tell us what happened? We can look after everything.'

'He doesn't know what happened,' Frankie Timmons barked. 'If he knew what happened he wouldn't a let it happen. Leave him alone. You all right, Johnny? Will I take you home?'

Johnny Bateman's fingers closed over the rim of the case while he uttered a short convulsive sob. Frankie Timmons tightened his grip around the shoulder. The people stood there. Dan Reddan tried to think of something to say, muttered aside to Ben: 'I wonder should we get a doctor?' But Frankie Timmons heard.

'He wants no doctor, he wants to be left alone.'

Frankie Timmons eased Johnny Bateman to his feet. Dan Reddan stood back, moving Ben and the crowd back to let the two old men out. Frankie Timmons picked up the book and the case but Dan Reddan said: 'Frankie, leave the book, I'll take care of it.' He moved closer to

Frankie Timmons and said urgently: 'You hear me? I'll take care of it.' And then realised he should add: 'Hold on, we'll get someone to drive ye.'

But Frankie Timmons supported Johnny Bateman towards the door and refused: 'We're all right, leave us alone.'

Not in the mackerel boat as a kid, certainly never in his capacity as the best fucking barman in London, and never up to now as a cool cop had Ben Hanley felt impotent. Dully, he heard himself being given orders. 'Ben, you take the book, just call out the names. All right everybody. We'll just carry on as normal, okay? Ben and I are doing the honours. Right, Ben, just call out who's first.'

Ben opened the book. Ray Beegan was no more than two feet away but Ben called out as though to be heard at the back of a church: 'Raymond Beegan.' Ray Beegan had only to move forward a pace. Dan Reddan had his cheque book open on the table and the top off his Biro.

'How much, Ben?'

Ben read the amount opposite Ray Beegan's name. 'Two hundred and fifty.'

'That right, Ray?'

'That's right, Mr Reddan.'

Dan Reddan wrote out 'Raymond Beegan' and 'two hundred and fifty pounds' and put the cheque in the envelope and handed Ray Beegan his due. It was all accomplished with a grim determination, twenty-seven names and amounts, twenty-seven cheques, twenty-seven recipients. All done to a background of whispering and conjecture.

Between calling out one name and the next Ben Hanley watched Dan Reddan write out the cheque and insert it in the envelope, and while Dan had begun stiffly reflecting the hole in his account, he eventually settled into a flourish and the smile on his face handing over the envelopes settled into good will and there was no doubt to Ben but that Dan Reddan was enjoying his sacrifice. Ben counted up to roughly seven thousand pounds. The two old boys kept their book neat. Opposite every name was the weekly amount grand-totalled at the end of the line. Ben Flanley called out the last name before he noticed that the contribution only went halfway across the page.

'Sean Reilly,' Ben called.

All those who had collected their cheques had withdrawn from the front line. The hilarity had gone from the night to be replaced with what the hell happened and wonder that the world still held such decent men as Dan Reddan. There were only a couple of non-diddly club members between Sean Reilly and the pay-out and though he was bewildered by the sound of his own name coming from Ben there was nobody in the way of Dan Reddan looking up from his chequebook at the delay and calling: 'Sean? Come along.' It was bad enough to be skint without having to shout it down the bar. Sean Reilly walked up and bent down and whispered to Dan Reddan and Ben.

'I pulled out in the summer, they musn't have marked it off.'

'I see it.' Ben put out a finger. 'Here.'

Dan Reddan turned his head and looked down at the book. It was there all right, marked 'paid', a withdrawal of £145. Dan Reddan looked up at Sean Reilly and Sean Reilly nodded now that everything was sorted out and turned to go back to his pint. Dan Reddan grabbed his elbow and glanced over at the entries opposite Sean Reilly's name. He calculated what Sean Reilly would have had to come if he had stayed in the club and then still holding Sean Reilly he wrote out [Pay] 'Sean Reilly' and 'two hundred and fifty pounds'.

'There. Happy Christmas!'

'You don't understand, Dan—'

'Shut up.'

Sean Reilly stood there holding the envelope, not knowing what to say. 'Dan, I don't know what to say . . .'

'Don't say anything. Listen, get that melodeon going.'

Sean Reilly thought of something. 'Thanks, Dan.' And he moved back down the bar, calling: 'Joker, music, Maestro. Dan said get cracking.' And then he added: 'Bowler!'

Dan Reddan and Ben Hanley remained sitting at the pay-out table. Dan Reddan called: 'Donie, push down our drinks.' Ben watched him hold his coat open and push the chequebook back in the inside pocket.

'I'll have to transfer funds,' Dan Reddan smiled at Ben.

Rockabye your baby, with a Dixie melody.

'That was decent of you,' Ben said at last.

'It had to be done.'

'I'd better get about my business. See if I can get the money back.'

Dan Reddan held him. 'Don't bother, Ben. You heard Frankie. I don't know what happened. You don't. But I've a feeling that whatever happened didn't happen. I don't know and quite honestly I don't want to know. I don't want no one to know. If we're to find out we'll be told and if we don't hear we'll forget about it. Anyway, I won't starve. Go down on that.'

Dan Reddan spent himself on the rest of that night. When he thought there wasn't sufficient liveliness about the proceedings he abandoned Ben and went among the crowd and put his arms around shoulders and lifted his and their voices in chorus. He forced the diddly club into the background. He decided it was time for the raffle. He and Donie called out the names and the matching prizes. When the raffle was over he called on Bowler and Bowler called back: 'Yourself.' Dan Reddan sang 'When the Sergeant Major's on Parade'. Ben watched and thought: There's one man with a happy Christmas.

Bateman walked back over the bridge and up the town. The shops were open late and the streets were festively illuminated and crowded but Bateman was unaware of his surroundings. Block after block passed him by without his noticing their progress. The Royal George was behind him and he had not seen it as he passed. And so was the turn-off to the Shakespeare and he had not thought of the Shakespeare. He was empty of rationale and full with the giddiness of a weight lifted. Years of tension seeped out of him and left him clean like a cured leper. He went into the house as naturally as he had used to as a child and he sat down to the fire and poked the coal and rested and smoked his cigarettes until there was a pool of ash at his feet, and not alone did tears not come but he was elated. He was carefree, he was at peace with himself and the world. He had good will for all men including the guards when they would come for him. He would smile at the judge and admit, No, Your Honour, I have nothing to say in mitigation. The fire was warm and he would have that job and he had the solo school, however imperfectly he realised it was constituted. He was calm.

Bateman listened to them shuffling in the passage. He heard the front door open and then the kitchen door and saw his father and Frankie Timmons linked. Bateman looked to see the guards behind them, come to demand an explanation that they could not possibly understand. But Frankie Timmons closed the front door with his free hand and escorted Johnny Bateman to the seat by the fire. Frankie laid his burden gently on the chair. He did not look at Bateman. He continued out to the pantry and opened the bottom of the dresser and came back in with a bottle of whiskey and a glass. He poured a good measure and held out the glass.

'Get that into you, Johnny.'

Bateman senior, bent over the fire opposite his son, accepted the glass and held a mouthful and swallowed. Frankie Timmons went to the pantry and came back with a glass for himself. He filled his glass and dragged a kitchen chair over to the fire and sat beside Johnny Bateman. They drank and stared into the fire and did not speak. Bateman watched them. He had to light another cigarette to battle the silence.

'Where's the money?' Frankie Timmons said into the fire.

'America.'

'What's that supposed to mean?'

'I threw it in over the bridge. The tide's going out.'

Frankie Timmons looked up from the fire at Bateman. Bateman's father looked up from the fire at Frankie Timmons. Frankie turned back and looked at Johnny Bateman and then both of them looked into the fire again.

'There's only one thing he wants to know. Tis the only thing we all want to know. You took the money and now you say you threw it in the river. And twas you wrote those things on the pieces of paper. We only want to know one thing. Why? That's all we want to know, why?'

EPILOGUE

BEN HANLEY WALKED up and down the Kilburn High Road, baffled that he could not find the Emerald Staff Bureau. He stopped a stranger who looked Irish and asked: 'Is this the Kilburn High Road?' The Irishman answered: 'Bull's-eye, Guv'nor.' Anyway Ben had seen it written up on a wall at the start of the block: Kilburn High Road. He tried a pub where he was told that there was a travel agency there now and that business was transferred to the church in Quex Road. When he arrived at the church he could find no sign of the Emerald Staff Bureau. He went inside and knelt down as though he were saying a prayer but his eyes darted around the church at a scattered five or six parishioners. When he saw an elderly woman leave he followed her outside. She did not know of an Emerald Staff Bureau but round the back there was the overnight hostel if that was any good to him. Ben went round the back to a prefab extension and what looked no bigger than a hut with a sign that read: MARIAN EMIGRATION CENTRE. There were two young blokes sitting on the steps outside the hut. They were unkempt. Each of them had a duffel bag at his feet. Their hair was long and stringy. Parka jackets coming off the assembly line look as if they have been slept in and theirs were also torn under the armpits. They both wore runners. Ben could see that they were feeling the cold. They sat and stared at the space of step between their legs. They didn't look up at Ben. Suddenly one of them stood up and shouldered his duffel bag. His mate said: 'What're you doing?'

'I can't face that mad bastard again.'

'Hang on. It's just for one night.'

'I don't care. I might belt him one and then I'd be locked up. Come on, we'll kip out. Once more won't kill us.'

They walked off. A minute later the door of the bureau opened and a young tramp with a docket in his fist came out. A voice called: 'Next, and keep the door shut.'

Ben had his best grey suit on and a blue shirt so light it might also have been grey, a maroon tie, polished black brogues and a navy crombie. Mr O'Donovan looked up from his little desk at the splendour. He had grown older. His hair was thin and grey and swept back severely in the square fashion. The frames of his glasses were officiously cheap.

'Mr O'Donovan,' Ben said.

'Yes?'

'I suppose you don't remember me.' Mr O'Donovan pulled his head back to appraise Ben standing. 'Hanley. Ben Hanley. I had a few jobs through you years back. In The Pub. You placed me in The Pub.'

'I suppose maybe I did. I placed so many in so many pubs.'

'This was *The* Pub. The Pub was the name of it, the time of the bombs—'

'Ahh, Hanley. Of course. Now I have you.' Mr O'Donovan came out in front of the desk and offered his hand. 'Yes, Ben Hanley. I do remember indeed.' Mr

O'Donovan rested his spare hand on the shoulder of Ben's crombie. 'You've made good, I can see that. Take a chair, make yourself comfortable.' Mr O'Donovan went back behind his desk and looked out at Ben. 'Those were the days,' he said wistfully, 'but you've made your way, I can see that. Good of you to drop in. Not many do. Hold on.' Mr O'Donovan went to his cabinet and found a dog-eared card. 'Yes, last heard of in that place I sent you to in Kilburn, right? Then upped and disappeared. That was naughty. So what have you been up to?'

'I went home.'

'Sensible fellow. That's what I tell them all. Go home. I told them that then and I tell them that now. Go home. Go back. What do I get for thanks? I wouldn't like to tell you the type of article I have to deal with these days. But never mind. Tell me, I'm all ears.'

'I joined the guards.'

'Did you? Good man.'

'But I wasn't cut out for it.'

'Oh. Well, maybe everybody isn't. That's understandable. So you joined the guards, you left the guards. Go on.'

'I didn't leave them. I stayed on. That's what I've been doing the past fifteen years.'

'Well done. You stuck to it. And it looks as if it suits you.'

It was a relief to Ben to sit once again in Mr O'Donovan's presence. Although Ben had been marking time for fifteen years they were both essentially in the same line of business: service. And Ben had bottled it up all those years, never had the opportunity or the right company in which to bare his wound. But Mr O'Donovan was a fellow professional even if he sat at the other side of the desk. Ben paused and sought the best avenue of approach to Mr O'Donovan's understanding. He thought now that he could tell anything to Mr O'Donovan, even the truth. Mr O'Donovan had shaken his hand and given him a chair.

But Mr O'Donovan too had need of a sounding board. 'Yes, I can see that it suits you. Can't say I'm in the same boat— Ben. I can call you Ben, I suppose? I hung on as long as I could. Until there just wasn't any point. Three years ago I was paying the rent out of my own pocket, out of savings. And that was a year after having let the receptionist go. Before that I cut back on the chap I used to have in to do relief when I took a holiday or when things were busy and I simply needed to go out for a meal. I finished up sitting there over a sandwich waiting for the phone to ring. Do you know what I do here, Ben?'

Ben shrugged, puzzled. 'Same line, isn't it?'

'Not unless you equate giving winos a doss for the night with the operation of a respected agency. They come over here with their faces washed or as smart as you can expect coming off McNamara's Bus, and they sit down where you're sitting *full* of themselves. I tell them go home. They sneer. They're entitled to one night. They leave in the morning and they leave behind a complaint that the tea was cold or they only got one sausage with the bacon and egg. You see some of them again three days later. Some last a week. A month. Having stopped short of nothing bar selling themselves on the street. Oh, they say to themselves in the beginning when they lay down in the prefab bunks with the crowd going back, That lot didn't try, I'll have no problem, I'll start off in a bar. As you know, Ben Hanley, if there was bar work the Emerald would have it. But do they listen? I'm on salary here. Parish priest asked me. We were always more or less in harness so when I folded he asked me. And he didn't need me in particular. A robot could do the job. But he's a decent skin. At the same time it's parish work and can you tell me who ever heard of a rich parish? So I'm working for a salary. A small salary. It's a small job. When once I had three lines to my telephone.'

'I'm sorry to hear that,' Ben said and he was sorry, in a detached way, as a subtitle to his regret that Mr O'Donovan might not be in a position to help him.

Mr O'Donovan nodded. 'Garda Ben Hanley, eh? Tell me, what rank?'

'Just *garda*, Mr O'Donovan.'

'Oh. After fifteen years? That doesn't sound like the Ben Hanley I had on my books.'

Here was Ben's opportunity to impress Mr O'Donovan and also a natural lead-in as to why he was sitting opposite Mr O'Donovan at that moment.

'I could have, Mr O'Donovan. I turned down promotion, what, four or five times. The first time, I was after getting a Scott Medal and . . .'

'A what? You got the Scott Medal for Bravery? Wait a minute. I know. I remember it. Hanley, I never connected, didn't you round up Mad Dog O'Dwyer?'

'That's right.'

'I knew it.' Mr O'Donovan tapped Ben's file card. 'Nobody from my academy could spend fifteen years at anything without advancing. You turned down promotion?'

'I wasn't cut out for it. I thought if I went up the ranks then I'd never be able to make the break again. You see, Mr O'Donovan, all I ever wanted was to be barman. I've never let that dream go.'

'Rot. Absolute nonsense. You should thank your lucky stars. And you know better too. Take my advice, next time you're offered stripes, you accept and hop to it my lad. Get a grip on yourself.'

'I won't be offered promotion again.'

'How can you know that?'

'Mr O'Donovan, I resigned. That's why I'm here.'

'What???' Mr O'Donovan's hands were on his desk. His backside lifted off the chair. He sat back. He bent his head to look searchingly at Ben. He read Ben's file card again.

'Have you blotted your copybook?'

Ben thought about it. 'Something did happen that finally convinced me.'

'Out with it.'

'Even though I didn't want to be a guard, I took pride in doing my work as best I could.'

Mr O'Donovan nodded.

'But it happened that through my fault there was a reflection on the sergeant at our station. He lost his stripes. But it was really my doing. After that I knew it was now or never. That's how I'm here.'

'So what did you do to cost this sergeant his job?'

Ben got word, Ben told Mr O'Donovan, of a gang in town to rob a savings club. He persuaded the sergeant to lock them up. Prevention better than cure. They failed to lock up one of the gang. The savings club was robbed. Two of the people they did lock up didn't belong to the gang. The sergeant had to carry the can.

'I'm not a policeman of course. But if you'll pardon me saying so, that doesn't sound horrendous. You did your best. Can't nab everyone. Perfectly innocent people are detained by the authorities every day. Nothing to fear if they're innocent. That's what I tell our people here when they're hauled in under the PTA. The sergeant can't have got the boot for that.'

'Unfortunately, the two we picked up were a detective and constable of the London Metropolitan Police.'

Mr O'Donovan's chin fell on his chest. He looked out over his glasses. His eyes fell again on the file card. It was all there: serviced a woman in the ladies'. He had not understood that then. He did not understand it now. It was not to be understood. He had always regarded his placements as foot soldiers. In Mr O'Donovan's eyes the crombie vanished from Ben's back. The 'Ben' fell away. Back then Hanley had disgraced the flag. At a time when Hanley was in such a good position. The Emerald's pride. And now, though it sounded pure daft, Hanley had done it again. Another cockup. Mr O'Donovan had had enough of failure – Hanley's, his own, anybody's. Dealing with hobos morning, noon and night. He wasn't getting much of a salary from the parish. Working for a salary! But he had a job to do and he did it now.

'I see. I'm sorry about that— Hanley. But you resigned? You weren't cashiered?'

'I left of my own free will.'

'Well go back of your own free will. That Scott Medal, they'll take you back. Tell them you found nothing here. If it's necessary I'll— I'll give you a reference. I'll go that far for you. But go home like a good lad. Go home and have a bit of sense.'

Mr O'Donovan was used to telling people go home. When to have advised them otherwise would have been an abuse of his position. He was accustomed to the sullen reaction, the ingratitude, sometimes the abuse. He was steeled to look across his desk at the faces of disappointment. Of course some of those who ignored his voice of experience did find jobs of a sort. But what sort of employer leapfrogged the agencies? Guv'nors and subbies coining it out of the Irish slave traffic. No stamps, no cards. Exploitation. At least Hanley wasn't sullen. Mr O'Donovan could read the disappointment but he thought his practised eye also saw resignation.

'You won't help me?' Ben spoke softly.

'Won't? Not won't. Can't. Damn it, Hanley, I am helping you. I'm saying go back to your good job. You have fine clothes–' Mr O'Donovan pointed out his window at the prefab. 'Do you want to see how they're dressed in there? They wouldn't listen. I've taken abuse. One young pup stood with his hand on the door after I gave him the benefit of over thirty years in the trade. He had seven honours in his Leaving Certificate. He wanted to rough it, he claimed. Wanted to see how the other half lived. A job working a lift he thought he wanted. I was as considerate with that boy as if he were my own. That pup stood at the door looking back at me and he shook his head. He grinned at me. He said: "You crazy cunt." He wouldn't listen, Hanley. He wouldn't listen.'

Ben listened, attentively. He eased up out of the chair and put out his hand. 'Mr O'Donovan, I know you mean well and I thank you. Believe me I am grateful for your interest. But I can't go back. It's— I can't explain it, I have to do this. I'm a barman or I'm nothing. Even more so, I'm a London barman or nothing. The best barman in London or nothing.'

Mr O'Donovan looked at the proffered hand. He jumped up. 'You don't believe it no more than the gurriers. Right then. Sit down. I'll show you. Put your fingers in the wounds.'

He went to his cabinet. He sat down again holding a sheet of paper with a finger and thumb at either side.

'This arrived a week ago. It was sent to the Emerald. There's a travel agency there now, they forward anything that still trickles in. This letter is from a Guv'nor who wouldn't give me the time of day when I canvassed him in better times. But he must have kept some record since he still had my address three years after I went out of business. It turns out, Hanley, that this Guv'nor does have a position and that's why he wrote to me. To the Emerald Staff Agency. And what is the position? What is he writing to the Emerald Staff Agency for? A potman,

Hanley. A potman. I may be down and I may be out, Hanley. But my God, a potman! Anyway, Hanley, I didn't throw it in the bin. I didn't write back as I might have done and tell him what to do with his "position". I owed it to the Emerald Staff Agency to show him we were never niggardly with courtesy. I telephoned him. And I'm glad I did, Hanley. Because I have an illustration for you that should be more vivid than any words of mine however well meant or well chosen. The Guv'nor had a potman, Hanley. A good one by all accounts, although how merit is measured in that trade escapes me. His potman had a success in the pools. And he couldn't very well have a pools winner for potman. That of course I could understand. But do you know what this Guv'nor told me? He had trouble getting rid of his potman. This potman fellow begged to be allowed stay in his job. Am I getting warm, Hanley? That's how tight things are. And it gets better. Any old potman won't do this Guv'nor. He's been used to the best, you see. He thought of giving me a "turn". I held on to my temper. I could hardly trust myself to speak. I mumbled that I would give it my best attention, be in touch. I haven't got round to it yet though. After Christmas is always our busiest week here. And I need time and a cool head to phrase with dignity the Emerald Staff Agency's umbrage. So there you have it, Hanley. If that doesn't convince you to go home to your good job then I honestly don't know what will.'

Mr O'Donovan was content that he had struck home. Hanley was not a stupid fellow. Mr O'Donovan almost felt sorry for him. The carpet had been swept from under him, his juvenile dream shattered and a good thing too under the circumstances. Ben Hanley bent forward and placed his hands on Mr O'Donovan's desk.

'Mr O'Donovan, could you get me that job?'

'You're joking?'

'I'm not.'

'A potman? Hanley, have you lost the run of yourself completely?'

'Mr O'Donovan, please. If you get me the job I'll always remember you for it.'

'I dare say you would. Enough is enough, Hanley. There are depths beneath which I will not sink and a potman is one of them. Go home. I beg you. Go home.'

'Mr O'Donovan, if you can't get involved yourself, would you tell me where it is? I'd just like to give it a try.'

Mr O'Donovan shook his head. He sighed. 'The King's Arms. In Shepherd's Bush.'

'Thank you, Mr O'Donovan.'

Ben Hanley backed out a few steps, turned towards the door.

'HOLD IT! Hanley, come back here. Sit down . . . Sit down, sit down.'

Mr O'Donovan was up and at his filing cabinet. 'No matter what I say you'll go after that job?'

'Yes, Mr O'Donovan.'

'Right. Then I'll handle it. Do it properly if it must be done. It's part time, by the way. Worry you? I can see it doesn't. Part-time potman. Live out, have you thought of that? No bed, no board. And no livery worthy of the name. A jacket, Hanley. A red jacket. Part-time potman, red jacket, live out. But I'll try for a stamp. I'll insist. No Emerald man ever worked for the lump. If you're going to degrade yourself, Hanley, we may as well all be degraded together. But it will be done right, the agency way.' Ben Hanley, erstwhile cool cop, became emotional. He vowed to Mr O'Donovan: 'I'll be a credit to you. I'll work at that job till I become the best potman that ever lived. Whatever that Guv'nor wants I'll have it done before he knows he wants it. I'll work my way up, Mr O'Donovan. I'll end up running that bar for that Guv'nor.

And when I'm finished there I'll move on back into town. I promise you: that Guv'nor will be on to the Emerald for more staff after I show him what I can do. I swear it, Mr O'Donovan, I'm going to become the best fucking – sorry, I'm going to be the best barman in London.'

And Mr O'Donovan saw it too. Why not? It was starting all over again from the bottom. The way it had all started before. He would place Hanley. He believed Hanley. Hanley would rise. Hanley would rise and lift the Emerald with him. In time Mr O'Donovan would not have to work for a salary any more. Abandon this doss-house. His nerve had failed, that was all. It took Hanley to come along and show him. Of course he would get him that potman's job. If by any chance the job was gone he would get him another, if it meant bringing him by the ear around every pub in London and demonstrating how Hanley could lick the floor.

'Right. Those clothes, they won't do. Too good. You'll have to strike the right note from the beginning. Cleanliness, of course, I need hardly mention that, is essential. But clean old clothes. Go to one of the second-hand shops. A clean shirt with maybe a slightly frayed cuff – you have the idea, Hanley? Shoes polished, shining always. Soap and polish are within everyone's reach though you'd hardly think it to watch the parade passes through here. And, Hanley—'

'Yes, Mr O'Donovan?'

'No slip-ups. No servicing anybody in the ladies'.'

'Yes, Mr O'Donovan.'

But when Ben Hanley had gone and Mr O'Donovan had telephoned the King's Arms and soft sold the Guv'nor, Mr O'Donovan was ashamed of his parting admonition. He felt warm towards Hanley who had brought the light back into his life. He regretted it all the more when he considered that if he could ever be sure of anything again, he was confident that in these disease-ridden times there could hardly exist such a trollop as would demand service in the ladies' from a potman.

'Taylor?'

'Yes, Inspector?'

'I'm the last man to interrupt a chap looking out a window but come here and have a look at seven down.'

'Seven down. Fuss. How many letters, Inspector?'

'Six. And we have R-blank-blank-F-L-E.'

'Trifle, Inspector?'

'A bit loose, Taylor. A bit loose, but that wouldn't be an impediment to the setters these days. It *begins* with R, Taylor. Four across: Companion of Robin. Marian, Taylor, right? Not much doubt about that, is there?'

'Unless it's Batman, Inspector? Then you'd have seven down beginning with T. I'd say that's it, Trifle.'

'Hmm. That would account for . . . everything else would fit then. Looks like you're right. Taylor, England: Companion of Robin equals Batman. In England. *Mirror*'s gone to the dogs. Poofs everywhere, bloody crosswords aren't safe any more. Thank you, Taylor. Go back to your window.'

'Inspector.'

'Hmm. Palindromic Irish town.'

'Quick, Inspector, quick.'

'Navan— What's that, Taylor?'

'It's him! Inspector, look, quickly. Quick before he's gone.'

'It's who Taylor?'

'Across the road. It *is* him, isn't it? Inspector? I'm not seeing things? It's that Hanley *garda* chap who nicked us.'

'Yes, there is quite a likeness, Taylor. Excuse me,

my puzzle calls. Only short three now.'

'He's heading towards . . . he's going in. Inspector, he's going into the King's Arms!'

'Inspector.'

'What is it, Taylor?'

'Seriously, Inspector, stop pretending. How can you sit there? It is him. He's here. And in the pub.'

'It's a free country, Taylor.'

'Please, Inspector, come on. What can be happening?'

'Happening, Taylor? A chap walks down a street and decides to go for a drink and you're looking for a "happening"? Inclined to exceed our brief, Taylor, eh?'

'He locks us up. Won't even listen to us. Locks us up. Locks us up with half the gang but not all the gang, Inspector, and the diddly club is robbed. And nobody arrested for robbing that diddly club. And now the *garda* is here and gone into the King's Arms where the gang has its headquarters. Inspector, it's stretching it a bit to accept that as coincidence.'

'I don't see that it is, Taylor. Didn't you tell me, Taylor, although I told you I didn't want to hear one more word about that damn pub or anyone in it, didn't you tell me that the Gosling chap had a second dividend? Even though I put my hands to my ears, you insisted on telling me that he got fourteen thousand-odd and that the public bar merchants queued up to the Guv'nor looking for Gosling's job because they assumed he'd be jacking it in after his click and even though I begged you to stop, you informed me that this Gosling wanted to hang on to his ministry but that the Guv'nor realised it would cause disaffection in the public bar and that then there were so many looking for the blasted job that he was going to go outside for an outsider – didn't you nearly give me a brain haemorrhage telling me ALL THAT, TAYLOR?'

'I was only doing what I thought was my duty, Inspector.'

'According to your doing your duty, Taylor, the Guv'nor is in search of a potman. So this is how I see it. I gave the Guv'nor the bum's rush. He arrived on our doorstep to report on the return of the solo school from Ireland but I ordered you to shoo him off the premises; you told him thank you very much on my behalf but case closed. Now, supposing the Guv'nor has become cop-happy – you know, Taylor, loves our company. It's not uncommon. He needs a potman but he doesn't come to us because we're not talking to him or else for some reason he thinks we won't jump at the chance to turn potman. That's right, Taylor, grin away. So he thinks of Ireland. Assumes they have cops over there. It's easy to follow it. He gets in touch with the *gardai* and they put a red alert out among their members. Potman wanted in England. And our Ben Hanley jumps at the career opportunity. That's how I see it, Taylor.'

'Inspector.'

'What to wear if it fits. Three letters. C-blank-P. Cap. And that's it— Yes, Taylor?'

'Would you allow me to speak for one moment as an equal, Inspector? Or even let me say something in the manner I would adopt if by chance I was your superior and was out for your own good? As an exercise, Inspector.'

'Speak.'

'Snap out of it. If I were on peer terms that is what I would feel obliged to suggest, Inspector. Snap out of it for your own good. You're bottling it in. I know you are.'

'Snap out of it, eh? I wouldn't have minded, Taylor. If we could have walked out of that blasted Paddy hoosegow and cut our losses. Suffered our bruises and nipped back home without anyone the wiser. But no.

Superefficient Paddy had to ring up Shepherd's Bush to check our story before releasing us with a hundred thousand Irish apologies. We end up on the carpet. Amendment: *I* end up on the carpet as your superior. My superior is there with the hands clasped behind the back. "What's this, Blake? Locked up by the Paddystone Kops?" I state my case as best I can. The judgement: "One, Blake, Ireland is outside our jurisdiction as is Cornwall for Christ bloody sake, Blake. Two, acted without any authorisation. Three, fell into the arms of the enemy." As I say, Taylor, I made my case. I pointed out that there was a robbery. I should have kept my mouth shut. "Robbery? A few pounds from a diddly club? Haven't we more pressing problems here in London, Blake? *Within* our jurisdiction?" Taylor, when I put forward the perfectly logical and reasonable explanation that I was fearful for the House of Commons, what did I get for my detective work? I'm asked if I've had my usual checkup this year. I'm led out of the office with his hand on my shoulder. A suggestion that if I have leave coming and feel like a holiday, that he'd see if the office could struggle along without me for a week or so. Taylor, I've unbottled. Satisfied?'

'I'm sorry, Inspector.'

'Taylor.'

'Yes, Inspector?'

'I'm damned if I take it lying down.'

'Yes, Inspector.'

'It was Hanley, wasn't it? Both of us can't be seeing things at the same time. It's obvious he's in on it. Send for the Guv'nor, Taylor. Another solo school member drops in out of the blue. Unless of course he turns up as potman. Good to see you grinning. Seriously, Taylor, I wouldn't put it past that lot.'

They were playing dealer out, and it was Ernie Gosling's turn to sit back and think and roll a gasper. The association of ideas proceeded from the smoke. Linda, saying: 'Ernie, we ain't exactly so poor now that you can't treat yourself to a packet of tailor-mades, are we, Ernie, never could stand to watch you fiddlin' about.' The very gasper threatened. The QPR goalie savin' a bleedin' penalty with two minutes left. To bring about a scoreless draw against Liverpool. At Anfield. Against all her better judgement and against the tips of the experts Linda gets sentimental cos I'm away over in bleedin' Ireland when we was never parted before, the war aside, and goes all soft and puts in QPR cos it's my team. Posts it. In the letter box. A bleedin' second dividend. Everything cocked up all because of a bleedin' second divvy. All right if it was a half-a-million click.

Mr Foster gone a spread – Mr Foster as we thought we'd never see again – Arthur pokin' low ones through him, bound to catch him with his lone seven of clubs – and feared for a while Arthur wasn't goin' to turn up no more neither. Fourteen thousand. That was what a normal bloke would have put by at my age if he'd got only half the normal breaks. Funny, pissin' in the pants for years in case of the big click and suddenly down in the dumps cos it was only a second divvy. The way the Guv'nor went about it though. 'Ernie, can you spare a minute?' Guv'nor never did give orders direct. 'Now that the novelty's worn off, Ernie,' the Guv'nor feelin' his way, 'have you given any thought to treating yourself, Ernie?' Me actin' cagey, 'How so, Guv'nor?' 'A holiday for instance. Treat the missus.' As if it wasn't to be expected. Guv'nor sayin' it was *his* missus 'appened to mention it, that it just didn't seem fittin' 'avin' a pools-winner potman with all the blokes around down on their luck.

His missus, 'e says, brung it up – as if everyone didn't know the Guv'nor wears the trousers in that neck o' the woods. Couldn't say much, didn' want to sound greedy, said it wasn't the money, I'd be 'appy to do it for sweet fanny adams. Baffled 'im, that did, but didn't change 'is mind none. Asked me to put meself in 'is position with Fred comin' up to 'im – Fred, me own mate from the motor factors! Fred was first stakin' 'is claim, only leadin' the charge, the 'ole public bar lined up behind him. Reckon if I'd a died the service wouldn't finish 'fore a queue'd form for me potman's job. I stuck up for meself with the Guv'nor. I said: 'Sod Fred.' But the Guv'nor says: 'Forget about Fred an' the boys and look at it this way. You enjoyin' your solo school, ain't you, Ernie, with Mr Foster and all the crowd, you enjoyin' it, ain't you?' I said: 'Course I'm enjoyin' it.' 'Well then,' Guv'nor points out, 'Mr Foster, you take Mr Foster, Ernie, he's by way of bein' a gentleman from where we sit, right, Ernie?' I agreed 'e was that. 'Mr Foster,' the Guv'nor figures, 'Mr Foster don't want potmen at his card table, do he, Ernie?' I said Mr Foster always treated me with respect same as anyone. Guv'nor claims Mr Foster'd treat me as an equal, have to, if I wasn't potman no more but just solo school player like the rest, not 'avin' to be 'oppin' up every minute collectin' glasses an' the like. The Guv'nor always was a sound bloke an' I got to see his way of thinkin'. He 'ad a point. Then he come back to Fred just to prove the point. It was never in 'is 'ead to even consider Fred for potman nor none of the public bar crowd. 'You see, Ernie, you was one in a million. Fred could no more do potman right than he could be prime minister, same as the whole lot of the rest of them weren't cut out for it neither.' So I said 'What you gonna do then, Guv'nor, have no potman?' I didn't like that, it'd be as though all the work I did wasn't needed to be done in the first place.

Twice Arthur's put a low one through Mr Foster an' 'asn't caught him. Seems Percy has all high clubs. Have a job puttin' Arthur back in. 'Course I'll have a potman,' Guv'nor insists, can't figure how he ever got on without one. Anyway, Guv'nor says, it's a bit of posh 'avin' a potman an' he feels entitled to a bit of posh as good as the next. He's goin' outside, through an agency. Bloke's startin' tonight, interviewed today an' come through. Guv'nor asked me keep an eye on 'im. I said I would, see that Fred or the darkies don't take the piss more than is allowed. So when I thought about it, Guv'nor not recruitin' from the public bar, saw that meant 'e means it when he says I'd be better off in solo school without bein' potman. 'An' maybe he's right,' Linda agrees but then I seed that comin'. I should be bleedin' thankful to still 'ave a solo school I reckon. What with the way everything fell out. Oh, oh, Dian's in now, job gettin' Arthur back in the drivin' seat again. Better get me thinkin' done 'fore the postmortem. What was it all about? I ask meself. Still ended up at Albert's Boxing night party, paper 'ats an' all. The presents we brung cost a packet, Linda said 'Why? Cos it'd be expected of us that's why.' I said 'We do it once it's expected every year', she said 'No it isn't, only while we can afford it', I said 'So that's it, we spend the lot on presents for bleedin' Uncle Albert an' the gang', she come back 'Don't you talk like that about Uncle Albert.' A row. Straight off, a row. An' can't even roll a gasper in peace. How did they find out about it though, the rozzers? Nabbed us all 'cept Percy an' he went an' done it. An' then let us go just like that. Mr Foster walkin' out in the dress an' Arthur not sayin' one word. Mr Foster checks out of the 'otel and drives home leavin' me an' Arthur on our tod only Arthur does a bunk too an' flies home. Lucky I got Percy to sail back with, I filled 'im in an' he filled me in. Dian, of course, on her plane, says

Arthur was on it an' wouldn't look at 'er.

I told Percy on the boat all about us bein' lifted an' only thing *he* could make of it was that one of us must 'ave ratted. But which one? And for what reason? An' why were we all let go then? Percy had that figured but didn't want to talk about it. What got Percy going was when I told 'im about Mr Foster arrested wearin' Dian's dress. He thought about that a long time. I said: 'What you reckon then?' An' what he told me give me the 'eebie-jeebies an' I still don't know whether to swallow it. Percy said there wasn't but the one way to explain it. Said Mr Foster was just one of those blokes that have a secret wish to do it – dress up in women's clothes – an' he must of got his chance there in the 'otel an' took it. An' he went on to say what nearly turned out true, that it wouldn't surprise him if we didn't see Mr Foster at the solo school no more. I remember the first thing that come into me mind, and bein' ashamed of meself for it, was thinkin' we'd still have four, it'd just mean not 'avin' to play dealer out. Then Percy kept askin' me to tell him Arthur's exact words when he was roarin' out of hisself in 'is cell. An' Percy kept goin' Hmm. I didn't think much about that then but I did after when there was no sign of Arthur. Not even in his lino shop for a while.

First Wednesday after Christmas lino shop's still closed but Arthur could 'ave decided on a bit of an 'oliday even though he was back open earlier last year. Wednesday night an' it's gettin' on, I'm there an' Percy comes an' then Dian. And that's it. Mr Foster don't show. No Arthur neither. We didn't even have the heart to play with three. There was no talk about it, same as if it might have been unlucky if we 'ad talked it out. I think we was all thinkin' that Christmas wasn't properly over, followin' week everything might be back to normal an' we might regret sayin' whatever we might 'ave said an' it'd be hangin' over us.

As it 'appened, next week flew what with all the talk about me been asked to jack me potman position an' that. But Arthur come back on the Monday, lino shop open same as usual. Thought I'd see 'im in the pub that night but he didn't show, so Tuesday I charged straight in and went to see 'im. He was quiet, like. Business was practically down to nothin' but that was expected. Arthur don't have sales. When I mentioned that last year he jumped down me throat, said only way 'e could 'ave sales was to give the stuff away plus a balloon free with each free roll. But 'e was quiet an' I guessed why too. I told him how we 'ad only me an' Percy an' Dian previous week and no game. 'He didn't turn up,' Arthur said quietly – he meant Mr Foster. I said no he didn't and then I asked, 'What about you, Arthur, you been away?' I could see there was nearly tears in his eyes. He said: 'Ernie, I let us down, didn't I?' 'How's that, Arthur?' But I knew but pretended I didn't know what 'e was on about. 'I'm a coward, Ernie, I couldn't hold it in. I was afraid, as simple as that, afraid, and you all heard me. Foster heard me.' I said: 'Arthur, you're no coward, you're talkin' daft just like Percy used to.' But he shot back at me: 'Percy is no coward, he pulled it off. By himself.' I agreed there about Percy. I told him: 'So what, Arthur? That don't mean you can't come to solo school.' He said: 'Ernie, everyone isn't as good-natured as you.' I got to thinkin' an' decided to take a chance hopin' it wouldn't somehow get back to Mr Foster. I said: 'Arthur, Mr Foster, you saw how Mr Foster was got up when he was lifted.' Arthur just said: 'So?' Then I come out with it same as if I was a psychiatrist so sure of hisself I could prove it. I said: 'Don't beat about the bush, Arthur, caught with 'is pants down, wasn't 'e?' I said: 'Mr Foster's bent, Arthur. Different strokes for different blokes.' I said: 'I don't 'ave to spell it out do I?' Arthur said again: 'So?' I said: 'If Mr

Foster don't let it bother him an' he's willin' to play, then why should you stay out, Arthur?' I was thinkin' as I was goin' along an' just before Arthur asked, I 'ad the answer. Arthur said: 'He wasn't there last Wednesday.' I said: 'He'll be there tomorrow night.' How did I know, Arthur wanted to know. Well, I didn't, did I? That didn't prevent me tellin' Arthur: 'Cos I rung him today, Arthur. Says he'll be along, says his New Year resolution is to stamp out all bad play an' we better 'op to it.' I don't rightly know where I got the idea from for that last bit but it did the trick. Arthur says: 'He did, did he?' Then Arthur says 'Fuck Foster! Ernie, he turns up, I'll be there.' Then I don't want to push it so I tell Arthur 'bout my winnin's. He was all interested so that passed the time. Now I had to do the next thing: Ring Mr Foster. I found it after combin' the book for accountants, took me 'alf an hour. I go an' get me coins and ring 'im. Was 'e chilly! When I got through all I get is: 'What is it Gosling?' I tell him we missed him, wondered if 'e was laid up or anythin', not like him to miss out. He was bluffin', I could tell, he liked me to know that he was a busy man. So I apologised. He said 'That's all right, Gosling.' I just went on, 'Yeah, we was all just wonderin', Arthur, Percy an' Dian an' me.' I could hear him take his time. Then suddenly he thanked me for ringin' an' said 'e 'ad to go. But I was quick in with: 'Will we see you then tomorrow night Mr Foster? Somehow we all feel we get on better with dealer out than 'avin' just the four.' He said he'd 'ave to see his diary. An' that's how we left it.

Then tonight I was all nervy what with the new potman expected an' all an' wonderin' would Arthur an' Mr Foster appear. Percy come first, then Dian but I don't say nothin' about my part in anythin'. But it worked. They were late but better late than never. Probably they was both stood outside watchin' to see who was turnin'

up an' then saw each other an' both come in together, an'
we're playin' now same as before. I can't help feelin'
satisfied meself. You could say I saved the solo school. In
a way I nearly am the solo school now.

I'd better watch it, I'll be asked in a minute an' I better
'ave somethin' to say cos it's plain Percy's a job now to
try an' get Arthur back in. They'll be at each other's
throats seein' 'oo's to blame an' Arthur won't like it if it's
'im what with Mr Foster sittin' back bein' amused like he
always does when Arthur makes a call he shouldn't.
Why? That's what Percy kept sayin' on the boat the
drunker he got, why? Why, why, why. I said: 'You what,
Percy?' and then he explained it to me. What about Mr
Foster though? Before we started tonight, everyone was
cagey an' sat down to the game an' there's these two
empties on the table not gathered up. There's a cloth we
use always kept under the table cos Mr Foster insists on
a clean surface – course he's right, nothin' worse than
sticky cards. But he gets out the cloth and points to the
empties an' just says: 'Gosling.' So I tell him about my
second divvy an' all but 'e just raises his eyebrows like. I
explain I'm not potman no more an' so on. I say as a kind
of a joke, lightly like, as any bloke would, I say 'I have to
act the gentleman now, Mr Foster.' So what does he do?
He takes the two empties himself and walks up an' plonks
them on the counter an' comes back an' looks down on
me an' shakes his head an' says: 'The *gentleman*,
Gosling?' An' 'e makes the others all smile. But I didn'
mind. To me it meant everything was okay, the solo
school back on the road like.

'Why?' Percy was sayin'. He filled me in. He switched
the envelopes like we plotted an' then went to the river
an' threw the real envelopes with the money over the
bridge. An' then 'e walked back to his old man's house
an' waited till his old man an' 'is mate Frankie

whatsisname arrived back from the pub. An' all they want to know is why he done it. Just that. Why. So I said to Percy: 'What you tell 'em then, Percy?' Percy's grippin' his whiskey an' starin' into the glass but he looks up at me an' asks me what I'd a told 'em. I 'ad to think. I'd nearly forgotten. I said did 'e mean the truth? He sort of smiles at me an' nods. 'Well,' I said, 'I'd a told 'em it was done against Christmas.' Percy tells me then that that's what he told 'em too. Only they didn't understand. They were sittin' by the fire in the 'ouse an' Percy's father hadn't said nothin', it was the Frankie bloke that asked why. Percy explained to them that it was a gesture, that it was for lonely blokes an' all the people that hasn't much an' people that are thought to be cracked in the head. An' finally Percy come to it that he did it for himself 'an all, for when he has to sit in his room with the 'lectric heater on an' a bottle of whiskey to keep him goin'. Somethin' along those lines, Percy put it different but that was it more or less. Then Percy's father spoke up for the first time. The old boy said: 'You have a room? An electric fire? Whiskey? The baby Jesus was in a stable, the only thing keeping *him* warm was a cow breathing on top of him.' Percy told me all this. He lost his temper, he said: 'I can't drink wine. I'm not composed. My hands shake, if I try to eat soup in a restaurant my hands shake and it spills.' His father got angry then. 'I never drank wine in my life,' the old boy said. '*My* hands shake if I never ate soup. But I don't rob money, do I? I never *robbed*. I wasn't brought up to *rob*.' And then he roared at Percy: 'You weren't brought up to rob, were you? Were you brought up to rob?'

Percy told me it was just then it happened – that he didn't see his father old no more, he saw the old boy as if it was back when Percy was a youngster an' he was lookin' up at a big strong man layin' down the law. The same as before they fell out over that rugby business. Percy says that there on the spot he was turned into a boy who wanted to be good an' wanted to please his old man just like normal boys, 'e didn't want fingers pointed at 'im, people sayin' he wasn't good. Everything collapsed, Percy claims, it was like a cripple suddenly has his crutches pulled out from under him. All the things that had kept Percy goin' down through the years weren't there no more. What happened, he said, was that he lost his nerve. The things he used to think about an' think they were right, they weren't right any more. Percy saw it all happenin' in his father's angry face. He said he felt himself blushin' because he used to feel better than specialists in America and Switzerland. I was blinkin' away listenin' but I didn't interrupt him to ask what he meant by that. He said they all came together from all over the world into the kitchen, all strong people, even the president of the United States an' the Queen herself, an' rabbis an' people like that, an' even ordinary-men-in-the-street people wearin' their good suits and it wasn't that they were givin' 'im a bad time or anythin', they were all lookin' at 'im concerned like. An' he was lookin' around for people like me an' Arthur with his roll of lino under his arm an' we weren't there or he couldn't see us clearly. That's if I can remember it right. It all happened in a flash, Percy said. Next thing he was cryin' like a little kid, whimperin'. And at the same time he was mad like a kid gets mad an' he hissed out at his father: 'What *was* I brought up to?' His father knew now he was the boss and shot back at Percy: 'You weren't brought up to rob.' Then Percy shouted: 'What *was* I brought up to? You don't know,' he gave out to the old boy. 'You don't know but I'll tell you.' Percy said the tears was runnin' down his face and he had his knuckles up to his eyes just like a kid an' he was sayin': 'I was brought up to stand on that table there in a basin with Mam washin' me an' you sittin' by the fire asking me to sing "Beautiful, Beautiful, Thomond". And I was brought up to be twiddled in the air like an aeroplane . . .'

Percy got the feelin' then that any lad gets when 'e's been caught out at somethin', he wanted his father to put his arm around him an' pull his head against 'im and say It's all right, dry your tears, you didn't realise, the next time you'll know better, just don't let it happen again. He was standin' there broken up and the two old boys were lookin' at him. But there was no understandin' there, he finally saw that. The way fathers and sons put arms around each other when they're young can't be done when they're adults. They just kept lookin' at him an' slowly like he began to pull himself together an' got out his hankie an' dabbed his face. He heard what he had just said comin' back to him like an echo an' he was embarrassed at havin' let out that he liked standin' in the basin on the table singin' 'Beautiful, Beautiful, Thomond'. He was comin' out of bein' a boy and returnin' to himself again. He felt empty and helpless then. His life was meaningless, all the time dodgin' this way an' dodgin' that way and now ended up standin' there in the kitchen an' not even been allowed somethin' innocent like standin' in a basin on a table singin'. 'E couldn't even 'ave that. An' he was entitled to it, he knew in his heart he must be, it was so little. To have his brain crowded not lettin' him have that made him want to give up altogether. But what the world didn't know cos he only realised himself just then, was that he was brought up not to give up. Everybody in the world, Percy told me, was brought up not to give up something, big or small, an' it didn't matter the size however little or big it was as long as you didn't give it up. An' when he knew that he did a hard thing. He walked slowly down the kitchen to the door. An' then he did a harder thing. He looked back at the two old boys who'd turned their heads round too. He could see how hurt they were and how there'd be no throwin' arms around anyone. An' that was how he left 'em, their faces starin' after him. Percy told it all to me on the boat while he looked into his whiskey.

All Fourth Estate books are available at your local bookshop or newsagent, or can be ordered direct from the publisher.

Indicate the number of copies required and quote the author and title.

Send cheque/eurocheque/postal order (Sterling only), made payable to Book Service by Post, to:

Fourth Estate Books,
Book Service By Post,
PO Box 29, Douglas
I-O-M, IM99 1BQ

Or phone: 01624 675137

Or fax: 01624 670923

Or e-mail: bookshop@enterprise.net

Alternatively pay by Access, Visa or Mastercard

Card number

Expiry date ....

Signature ....

Post and packing is free in the UK. Overseas customers please allow £1.00 per book for post and packing.

Name   ....
Address   ....
          ....
          ....

Please allow 28 days for delivery. Please tick the box if you do not wish to receive any additional information. ❏

Prices and availability subject to change without notice.